HAND IN HAND

A MISSIONARY FAMILY STRUGGLES TO DEVELOP SCHOOLS FOR AMERICAN INDIANS

Kathryn A. Cook

Note for Librarians: a cataloguing record for this book that includes Dewey Classification and US Library of Congress numbers is available from the National Library of Canada. The complete cataloguing record can be obtained from the National Library's online database at: www.nlc-bnc.ca/amicus/index-e.html
ISBN 1-4120-2142-1

TRAFFORD

This book was published   on-demand   in cooperation with Trafford Publishing. On-demand publishing is a unique process and service of making a book available for retail sale to the public taking advantage of on-demand manufacturing and Internet marketing. On-demand publishing   includes promotions, retail sales, manufacturing, order fulfilment, accounting and collecting royalties on behalf of the author.

Suite 6E, 2333 Government St., Victoria, B.C. V8T 4P4, CANADA

Phone	250-383-6864	Toll-free 1-888-232-4444 (Canada & US)
Fax	250-383-6804	E-mail sales@trafford.com
Web site	www.trafford.com	TRAFFORD PUBLISHING IS A DIVISION OF TRAFFORD

HOLDINGS LTD.

Trafford Catalogue #03-2691   www.trafford.com/robots/03-2691.html

10   9   8   7   6   5   4   3   2

HAND IN HAND
A MISSIONARY FAMILY STRUGGLES TO DEVELOP SCHOOLS FOR AMERICAN INDIANS

TRAFFORD PUBLISHING
Suite 6E, 2333 Government Street
Victoria, BC, Canada V8T 4P4
www.trafford.com

This book is a work of historical fiction based on real people and real events. Some details, relationships and conversations are products of the author's imagination.

To Jim, without whose help and encouragement
this work would not have been accomplished.

PROLOGUE

Isaac McCoy was born June 13, 1784 in Pennsylvania. His family migrated to Kentucky in 1790. Christiana Polke McCoy was born November 18, 1787 in Nelson County, Kentucky. Christiana's father Charles was a Captain in the Revolutionary Army. Prior to Christiana's birth, her mother, brother and sisters were taken hostage during an Indian raid on the Fort Kindley Station where they lived. Time and again Christiana heard the story of her family's earlier ordeals. Her mother was taken to Detroit and ransomed by British officers. She took in sewing to support herself and a newborn child for three years until her husband learned of her survival and they were reunited. Their other three children had been taken by Potawatomi Indians to the St. Joseph River region in the wilderness Michigan Territory. Captain Polke went 300 miles alone to search the forest for them. Eventually he found them and persuaded their foster families to give them up.

In 1803 at age 16, Christiana met and married 19-year old Isaac McCoy. They set out from Shelby County, Kentucky for Indiana. They shared a zeal for helping others and began a ministry. Isaac was licensed to preach in 1804, and was ordained in the Baptist Church in 1810. In 1817 he accepted an appointment as missionary to the Indians of Indiana and Illinois. They opened a school in Indiana to teach survival skills to needy settlers and Indians, having learned that just taking them in and helping for a night wasn't the answer. Isaac was an itinerant preacher and made requests for school assistance as he traveled. Generous as they were, with only meager salary, Christiana and Isaac never lived much above the poverty level. Isaac occasionally supplemented their income by making spinning wheels, a craft he'd learned from his father.

By mid-1820 the McCoys had opened a school in Fort Wayne, Indiana. They were encouraged by Indians in the Michigan Territory to re-locate. After many trips and conferences with the American Baptist Mission Board and Governor Cass of the Michigan Territory, a location was selected. By terms of the Chicago Treaty of 1821, the establishment of the new school was sanctioned by the United States War Department. An annual fund of $1,000 was created for support of a teacher and blacksmith. A tract of land one mile square located west of the Saint Joseph River was designated as residence for the teacher and blacksmith.

By ironic fate Christiana had found a way to repay the Potawatomi Indians for their earlier kindness to her brother and sisters. Her brother William, one of those early captives, eventually joined the McCoys at their Carey Mission Station on the Saint Joseph River near present day Niles, Michigan. Isaac also founded Thomas Mission Station in 1824 near present day Grand Rapids, Michigan.

The dedication of these early missionaries is revealed in rules they adopted for themselves in Fort Wayne before they departed for the Michigan Territory: [1]

> "We, whose names follow, being appointed missionaries to the Indians by the General Convention of the Baptist denomination for missions, deem it expedient for our comfort and usefulness to adopt, in the fear of the Lord, the following general rules for the regulation of the mission family, viz:

"1st. We agree that our object in becoming missionaries is to meliorate the condition of the Indians, and not to serve ourselves. Therefore,

"2d. We agree that our whole time, talents, and labours, shall be dedicated to the obtaining of this object, and shall all be bestowed gratis, so that the mission cannot become indebted to any missionary for his or her services.

"3d. We agree that all remittances from the board of missions, and all money and property accruing to any of us, by salaries from Government, by smith shops, by schools, by domestics, or from whatever quarter it may arise, shall be thrown into the common missionary fund, and be sacredly applied to the cause of this mission; and that no part of the property held by us at our stations is ours, or belongs to any of us, but it belongs to the General Convention which we serve, and is held in trust by us, so long as said society shall continue us in their employment: Provided that nothing herein contained shall affect the right of any to private inheritance, etc.

"4th. We agree to obey the instructions of our patrons, and that the superintendent shall render to them, from time to time, accounts of our plans, proceedings, prospects, receipts, and expenditures; and that the accounts of the mission, together with the mission records, shall at all times be open for the inspection of any of the missionaries.

"5th. We agree that all members of the mission family have equal claims upon the mission for equal support in similar circumstances; the claims of widows and orphans not to be in the least affected by the death of the head of the family.

"6th. We agree that when any missionary shall not find employment in his particular branch of business, it shall be his duty to engage in some

other branch of business, as circumstances shall
dictate.

"7th. We agree that, agreeably to their
strength and ability, all the female missionaries
should bear an equal part of the burdens of
domestic labours and cares, lest some should sink
under the weight of severe and unremitted
exertions; making the necessary allowances for the
school mistress.

"8th. We agree to be industrious, frugal,
and economical, at all times, to the utmost extent of
our abilities.

"9th. We agree that missionaries labouring
at the different stations belonging to this mission
are under the same obligations to each other, as
though resident in the same establishment.

"10th. We agree that it is the duty of
missionaries to meet statedly at their respective
stations, for the purposes of preserving peace and
harmony among themselves, of cherishing kindness
and love for each other, love to God, and zeal in the
cause of missions.

"11th. We agree to feel one general concern
for the success of every department of the mission,
for the happiness of every member of the mission
family, and to feed at one common table, except in
cases of bad health, etc., in which cases the persons
thus indisposed shall receive special attention, and
shall be made as comfortable as our situation will
admit.

"12th. We agree to cherish a spirit of
kindness and forbearance for each other, and, as the
success of our labours depends on the good
providence of God, it is our duty to live near to him
in public and private devotion, and to walk before
him with fear, and in the integrity of our hearts,
conscious that he ever sees us, and that by him
actions are weighed; realizing that we are, at best,

only instruments in his hand, and hoping that when we shall have finished the work given us to do, we shall dwell together in heaven, in company with fellow-labourers from other parts of the vineyard, and with those for whom we are now strangers and sufferers in this wilderness, and, to crown our happiness, shall gaze eternally on Him whose religion we are now endeavouring to propagate, to whom shall be ascribed all the glory of the accomplishment of our present undertaking.

"Isaac McCoy,
  Christiana McCoy,
       Johnston Lykins,
       Daniel Dusenbury."
"February 15, 1822."

[1]McCoy, Isaac, History of Baptist Indian Missions. Washington, D.C.: P. Force, 1843.

With these commitments in mind, these missionaries began the preparations for the relocation to the Michigan Territory. Men were hired who were willing to work for a meager stipend and room and board. They were sent into the wilderness where few white men had gone before to fell trees and build the first cabins for the new mission station. The actual relocation began in December of 1822.

This is the story which follows. Special attention is focused upon Christiana McCoy whose dedication and energy was called upon time and again to aid her husband and keep the mission operating.

Locations, dates, names and events in the story are factual. Information was gathered through extensive research from museums and library collections found in Benton Harbor,

Niles, Battle Creek and Lansing, Michigan and the collection of McCoy Papers in the Kansas State Historical Society, Topeka. The person of Singing Bird and dialogue of the characters were fictionalized.

1

Christiana pushed open the cabin door and swept crumbs and sand outside. "Such a nice fall morning" she said, gazing at colored leaves on the trees and the blue sky. In a clearing beyond their cabin she saw her children. Rice, her 15 year old son, had been chopping wood but stopped to allow his younger brothers and sisters a chance to stack the pieces.

"Mama, someone's coming!" Rice called, pointing at a distant horse and rider.

Christiana wiped her hands on her long apron and sighed, hoping no new problem was being brought to her.

"It look's like Papa! I think I recognize his horse," Rice announced.

A few minutes later her husband rode in. Stiff and sore from miles of traveling, he slid from the saddle and staggered toward his wife.

"What's wrong, Isaac? Surely you can't have made the distance there and back so soon."

"That is exactly what I've done," he said. Smiling, he stooped to pick up Eleanor, their youngest daughter, who had crawled to his side. She snuggled into his shoulder as he embraced Christiana. Their eight other children, some of them Indian, surrounded them as they walked into the cabin.

Christiana took Eleanor from Isaac's arm. "Did you travel back alone?' she asked. Seeing how tired and dirty he was she knew he must also be hungry. "Get your Papa a bowl of soup, Nancy." Looking sternly at the others she said, " The rest of you sit quietly."

"Two young men returned with me. They are driving oxen and pulling a supply wagon. I was more eager than they to get home and rode on ahead. They'll arrive tomorrow," Isaac said as he drew a bench to the long plank table. "It is so good to be home with you all," he said smiling. When a bowl of venison stew was set before him he bowed his head in prayer. All eyes were on him as he ate. When he finished and looked more carefully at his family, he realized several of the children looked ill.

Christiana, seeing his concern, shared the recent happenings. "There has been a spread of typhoid, Isaac. Many of our neighbors are still weak from the fever." She lowered her eyes and continued sadly. "Several have died." Swallowing hard to keep from crying she recalled, "It brings back the sad memory of losing our sweet daughter Elizabeth and Benjamin Sears, our dear missionary friend."

Pain crossed Isaac's face. "They are sorely missed. Our own family has been spared this time?"

Christiana nodded replying, "Our children have been poorly but are recovering, thank the Lord. Fortunately, we have neighbors, in and around the fort, strong enough to hunt and provide soup meat." She smiled as she looked at her husband. "It is good you are home. Everyone will want to hear about your journey to the Michigan Territory."

"We had a few problems but once there we got the clearing done quickly. The building was underway before I left. I've come back to help get everyone packed and moved before severe winter hits. By the time we get to Michigan the buildings should be completed."

Shouts of excitement echoed through the barren cabin as the children circled their minister father. "We are going to the banks of the St. Joseph River!" they sang skipping around the table. Isaac and Christiana smiled at their glee.

Late the next afternoon the supply wagon rumbled into McCoys yard. The weary travelers were happy to greet Christiana and follow her into the cabin. They nearly fell asleep while eating rabbit stew and were sent to the loft to rest.

"Rice and Josephus, I'd like you to go invite all our missionary brethren to our cabin this evening," their father said. "It is time to make our plans."

As folks arrived they soon filled the chairs and benches. Children sat on the floor and men leaned on the walls to listen to Isaac's message. "Everything I told you earlier is true. It is a beautiful section of fertile land bordered by the St. Joseph River!" He closed his eyes in delight as he recalled the area. "Large yellow poplar trees were being cut when I left. They will make sturdy buildings for us. Much of the brush is cleared but there is much work ahead for us. I've blazed the trail. It is time now to load supplies and belongings so we can move."

Isaac was rested and eager to get started but as he looked around he was shocked to see no enthusiasm. "We need to pack quickly and make the journey before winter weather worsens," he said, hoping to motivate them.

"Reverend McCoy, we know all these things," stated Brother Jackson in his slow southern drawl. "We have no energy since our sickness. My wife is worried about starting out in winter lest we get sick again."

Isaac saw despair on his friend's face. He was the man designated to become the mission blacksmith. What had happened to his commitment?

One of the women spoke her concern. "Some of your own children are sick. You shouldn't take them anywhere in their sorry conditions." Others nodded in agreement.

"I am counting on God's healing grace to get us ready for our move. I hope you will do the same!" Isaac's stern look halted further conversation. "Once we're there, meat supply will be greater, living conditions will be less crowded. We will stay healthier. I know packing will take great effort. We can help each other."

Christiana watched her husband pace the floor. "I've already set the girls to stowing seed packs in barrels. School books and other things we use everyday can't be packed ahead of time," she said.

Isaac knew she was trying to soothe and please him but felt irritated at the attitude of the others. They had promised to go with him. He wanted to be on the trail or better yet to be at the new mission.

Two weeks later as Isaac and Christiana walked toward the schoolroom in the fort, they again discussed the anticipated move. "The wagons are finally built and lined up. Each day I keep hoping the Baptist missionary fund will arrive in the mail," Isaac said sadly.

"I wish it would come too. Once our supplies are purchased we can get underway. One good thing though, our health is improving during the wait and folks are packing all but the bare essentials," Christiana said. She knew how frustrated Isaac had become. Once plans were made he was impatient until they were underway. The day before she had told him it was a good thing they didn't have fancy carpets on the floor or he would have worn a path right through them. Even her teasing didn't make him smile.

At the school, before the pupils arrived, Isaac went to his corner desk and searched through a stack of papers. "I can't find anything anymore," he said tossing the pages aside. "I guess I'll pack books this afternoon. Why don't you pack blankets or your cooking utensils?"

Christiana looked at him in amazement. Surely he knew they would be using those items right up to the last minute. Shaking her head she walked toward the door to ring the school bell.

Every bench in the tiny room was soon filled. Besides the McCoy children there were six French, one Negro and eight Indian pupils. All morning the McCoys and Johnston Lykins, their young assistant, took turns teaching writing and arithmetic, listening to young voices read from shared books. Coughing and sneezes interrupted lessons. Christiana sent two boys to get medicine from Singing Bird, her Indian friend.

Girls spent afternoons knitting and practicing domestic duties. Sometimes Fawn, a young Indian mother, taught them basket weaving. Before she had disassembled and packed the loom, Christiana instructed weaving, sewing and spinning in her cabin.

Boys fed and took care of the animals, chopped wood or helped pack and carry boxes to the wagons. Johnston Lykins taught them to play musical instruments so they could accompany hymn singing.

One afternoon Christiana, weary of routine, told her daughters to manage without her. "I'm going to help Sister Jackson with her sick baby. Delilah, you and Sarah look after the young ones. Singing Bird is here and will help with the knitting." She tied her warm shawl around her shoulders and walked briskly to her friend's cabin, well aware of the colder weather December had brought.

An hour later Isaac was startled when his wife rushed into the schoolroom where he was writing letters. Her worried look frightened him. "Has something bad happened?"

"Oh Isaac," she sobbed. "The Jacksons have decided not to go with us to the new mission. Nothing I said could change their minds. They kept saying their babies were sick, the winter weather is going to be too bad and being a missionary is just too hard. They are just giving up!"

Isaac gathered Christiana into his arms, trying to comfort her. After a few minutes he managed to say, "I feel as shocked as you. I'm disappointed too. Brother Jackson agreed to be the blacksmith at the mission. Part of the treaty agreement which allows the mission to be established requires supplying a smithery."

11

"What can we do?" Christiana asked as she wiped her eyes. "No one else has tools or training, do they? It almost feels like no one wants to go with us." She removed her shawl, hung it on a peg near the door and motioned for Isaac to join her on the bench.

"That's not quite true my dear," he said. "We have willing workers there already. We know other missionaries eager to do the Lord's work with Indians."

"Yes, Isaac, but the Jacksons promised! We were counting on them." She sighed and walked to the tiny window. "I know you are right. Like it says in the Bible, 'where one or more are gathered, God will be there.' Our family will be there!"

"I have no doubt that when we get our mission school started others will join in our work," Isaac said. "I will go to the Jacksons but I fear no one can change their plan to quit the ministry."

Christiana took her shawl and headed home. Isaac was staring into space and didn't realize she left. It occurred to him suddenly that if the Jacksons were not going, Christiana would be the only white woman making the move to the new mission. That was something he could not allow. Then, head in hands, he sat wondering how he could stand to leave her and their children until other families felt safe enough to relocate

Although he worried about his wife's reaction to his decision he left the schoolroom and walked slowly home. He found Christiana stirring a large kettle over an outdoor fire.

"I decided I'd better practice now that we will be cooking outside during our journey," she said, smiling as she pointed to the bubbling stew. "It would certainly be good if the weather doesn't get worse than this, wouldn't it?"

"We need to talk seriously. Can we be here without interruption?" he asked, looking around to see if any children were near.

He looked so distraught Christiana called their oldest daughter, Delilah, to come take over the pot stirring. "Let's go for a walk toward the stream. There are fallen trees to sit on there. I go there sometimes when I need to be alone."

When they reached the quiet area he sat facing her. Taking her hand, he looked her straight in the eye. "I am about to ask you to do something that breaks my heart," he said, tears gathering in his eyes. "You and the youngest children must remain here, at least until spring. Rice and Josephus and maybe Calvin can go with me but the girls and you cannot go, without other women, into the wilderness. "

Christiana swallowed hard, she withdrew her hand from Isaac's. Closing her eyes she silently prayed for the right rebuttal. Calmer, but angry, she glared at her husband. "Before our marriage we agreed to work together, Isaac. That cannot happen if we are living in different places. The children and I will indeed make the journey with you to the new territory! I am not afraid. My children will not be afraid!" She stood up. Placing hands on hips, she stubbornly glared at Isaac.

Isaac had never seen his wife so determined. Although he was impressed he still did not feel it was sensible. "You can come later when other missionaries are sent. I hope by spring additional teachers and workers will arrive. Certainly weather conditions will be more favorable then."

"If teachers and workers are not forth coming what should I do? Am I to stay here with nothing to do and no finances?" When he didn't answer she continued. "Do you plan to build buildings, farm the land and teach all alone? What will happen when you have to be away from the mission? I've learned to take over for you before. Why is it that you think I can't do it in the new territory?"

"My concern is for you," Isaac quietly replied. "Civilization will be left behind when we embark on the journey into Indian territory. You and the children may be deprived by our residence in that area, especially since the way things stand right now, you will be the only woman. There are things you won't have."

Christian's eyes flashed as she answered. "So might the children become worthless when brought up in a different society, but the additional risk will be more than balanced by the mercy of our Lord who has called us to labor there! We are going with you, Isaac McCoy! As for being the only woman, you seem to have forgotten there will be two Indian women traveling on this journey. I rely on Singing Bird and Fawn's friendship now and will continue to do so when we arrive in the new land. I also rely on you and want you to trust me."

Isaac knew, beyond a doubt, that he had lost his argument. "I do trust you my dear." He rubbed his forehead as if trying to erase his blunder. "I want you and our family with me. I am afraid for your safety and health but I understand now those things are in jeopardy here as well." He moved to embrace her. "Forgive me if I made you feel unnecessary. I want us to always labor side by side!"

In spite of their earlier disagreeable discussion they held hands as they walked back to their tiny cabin. Christiana smiled and said, "Tomorrow we will begin packing in earnest."

There was no smile on Isaac's face as he told her, "There is one more pressing problem I must share. You are forgetting that no money has arrived for purchasing supplies. No salary has been issued for Brother Lykins or I. In other words we are near destitute. I don't know how to change that."

2

Before every meal in the McCoy household there was a time of Bible reading and prayer. Day after day money concerns were pronounced and then prayed over until Christiana almost hated to listen.

Isaac hated the topic too. "It is not appropriate to spend so much time and thought on money!" Isaac often told the family. "It shows lack of faith. I am unhappy about it. Surely there will be a letter today."

The situation finally changed with the arrival of a letter from the mission board in mid-December. Isaac read it to Christiana in faltering disbelief. "Purchase needed items, then send a bill to the board. The necessity of items will then be considered and payment will be submitted accordingly." Isaac was heartsick. They had no cash. There was no way to pay for supplies, yet he felt they could no longer delay their move.

Desperate, he decided to go to the financial leaders of Fort Wayne. He would beg, if necessary, for some financial assistance. A group meeting was arranged and he explained his dilemma. "As you know I have been assigned to build a new mission school in the Michigan Territory. There are men there now waiting for supplies and food which I need to deliver to them. My family, Indian students and their families who will be going with me, have waited weeks for money to arrive from the government and church." He swallowed hard, then continued. "I just received a letter from the mission board informing me no money will be sent until purchases are made and a bill is mailed to them." He paused to study their faces.

"I have been promised a salary of $400 which I will relinquish to you gentlemen if you will allow me that amount of supplies." He swallowed hard again, waiting for their reaction.

"I know you as a man of honor and hard work," said the French owner of the trading post. "I'd like to help but when can you pay?"

"I will give you my salary as soon as I get it!" Isaac replied. "It should be here any day."

"What will you do the rest of the year without your salary to spend?" asked a prominent trader.

"I hope to convince the mission board that my purchases, now and in the future, are indeed necessary so they will pay immediately." He sighed and continued, "I have to believe that God will provide for us. Beyond that, I have no answer."

The men asked more questions. After nearly an hour the trader stood. He walked over to Isaac with hand outstretched. "I trust you Isaac McCoy! Pay me when you can. Use the $400 wisely as you purchase what you need." They shook hands to confirm their promise.

Isaac felt weak with relief. Others pushed back their chairs and started to leave. "When you come to the mill for grain or flour, I will make a good deal for you. I like you too!" said the miller.

Isaac, happy for the first time in many days, hurried home to tell Christiana what he had accomplished. She was equally pleased but later they both realized what a burdensome commitment had been made.

Isaac wasted no time in purchasing supplies. As word got out that the McCoys would soon be leaving, neighbors and friends stopped by the cabin with gifts of clothing, food and blankets. Christiana's faith in God and people were restored.

Bitterly cold winds whipped snow under the cabin door the morning they were ready to depart. Christiana bundled the children in their warmest clothing before sending them out to the wagons. "Delilah, you take these quilts and wrap them around the young ones. I have a few more things to do, then I'll join you."

Smoke filled the cabin as she poured water on the glowing embers in the fireplace. Taking one last look around she walked to the door. In her arms she carried a wooden box Isaac had made for her most treasured items. Wagon space was limited. Most furniture could be replaced. Only Isaac's desk, Christiana's rocker, the cradle, loom and spinning wheels were packed.

Christiana had insisted they leave the rope bed in the corner and table and benches so the next people who moved into the cabin would find comfort. Other furnishings had been distributed to needy families.

Packed among boxes of books and tools, was a trunk of woven wool material and quilts and a barrel of dishes. Barrels of flour, cornmeal, sugar, salt and dried fruit and seeds were stowed in the four wagons. Three wagons were pulled by oxen, one by horses. A few men rode on horseback, most of the rest squeezed into the wagons. Daniel Dusenbury took Jackson's place as blacksmith, but left his family in Fort Wayne. Thirty-two people made the journey. Five cows were tied to the wagons. Fifty hogs were herded by several Indian boys, who thought it to be a great adventure.

As the wagons began to move, heavy snow started falling. As they passed the fort, people came out to bid farewell. A few handed Christiana small packets of food to be eaten on the journey. One woman gave newly knitted mittens to several children. Christiana looked around to see if the Jacksons were in the crowd but couldn't see them.

The oxen slowly plodded down the roadway. Visibility was poor because of the blowing snow but Christiana had no problem recognizing the small cemetery where their daughter Elizabeth had been buried in August. She sighed deeply but then fixed her eyes straight ahead. Since several of the children were still not healthy, she and her older daughters were kept busy wiping noses and forcing spoonfuls of medicine into unwilling mouths.

It was uncomfortable and confining to ride. The trail had narrowed to a path at the edge of a woods. Sometimes the wagons brushed against the trees. Scraping noises frightened the children. Drivers had trouble controlling animals. Things and people were jerked around in the wagons. Cows bellowed in protest.

Christiana tried walking awhile to stretch her legs but her feet got so cold she climbed back into the wagon. Stepping over fallen branches and the bumpy trail made walking difficult, but the children didn't care.

"I'm going to walk awhile, Mama," Delilah said, preparing to jump.

"Me, too," seven year old Sarah said, reaching for her sister's hand.

Fourteen year old Josephus, their older brother, caught up with them. He had hoped to drive one of the wagons but so far had had to herd hogs. "Have you seen Papa?" he asked. "We seem to be moving so slow. I know I could make the oxen walk faster if he'd let me."

"Maybe you could, but I doubt the cows and pigs could keep up." Delilah remarked. Although she was only thirteen her ability to see things logically was very adult. "I think we will get quite far today."

Snow continued to fall and the wind whipped it into drifts. They did not stop for any meal but Christiana handed out strips of dried meat to chew on. Mid afternoon Isaac rode up on his horse to tell her they were stopping for the night under the next pine grove. She was very relieved.

High branches of the white pine provided a slight shelter and wind break for the animals. Tarps which covered the wagons were taken down so the accumulated snow could be brushed off. The pigs roamed the woods in search of acorns and nuts. Other animals were tied to trees, brushed and fed their ration of oats and hay.

The children were sent to gather firewood. They returned carrying wet branches. All attempts to make them burn failed. The meal consisted of cold cornbread and dried meat.

Under low hanging pine limbs the ground was bare. Some of the boys and men crawled underneath trees to sleep, wrapped in their quilts. Younger children and the women snuggled together in the wagons.

Christiana overheard Isaac talking to the men. "I sure wish this storm had held off! If only we had gotten underway last week while the weather was still mild."

"We didn't get very far today," Johnston replied.

"No," agreed Isaac. "With the snow sticking to tree trunks, I couldn't spot the earlier trail marks I made. It is really slow when we have to stop and pull fallen limbs out of the way."

"It must be a really bumpy ride in the wagons. Ruts made by the first wagons go deep making it rougher for the next ones," commented Daniel Dusenbury. "How far did we come? Ten miles?"

"More likely three," Isaac replied.

Christiana recognized the sadness in his voice and shuddered. She remembered hearing Isaac say the distance to the new mission was about one hundred miles. When he joined her in the wagon she held his hand whispering, "Let's pray for more favorable conditions for the rest of the journey."

During the night northern winds increased but the snow stopped falling. In spite of the fact no meal was prepared, everyone was eager to get underway before daylight. As the morning progressed trail signs became more clearly visible. By noon a faint sun appeared and lifted their spirits. An occasional deer bounded across their path. Boys threw snowballs at the frightened animals, making everyone laugh.

They managed to cover ten miles before their evening stop and best of all managed to build a cooking fire.

The next morning Christiana held tiny Eleanor in her lap as she tried to spoon medicine down her throat. Her coughing had kept them awake most of the night. Delilah brought her mother a cup of hot coffee. "Ah, thank you! Even the smell is a welcome treat!"

The weather continued to hold for three more days. Spirits were high until they came to icy streams. Forcing the animals, especially the clumsy hogs, to cross in frigid water, sliding and slipping, was a terrible ordeal. Sometimes the children and hogs could cross before the ice cracked under their weight. Larger animals got cuts and scratches on their shins from sharp ice.

Wet clothing and chilled feet were common complaints. There were no dry shoes, stockings or mittens. Blankets were soggy and provided little warmth at night.

"How many of these crossings do we have to make?" asked the boys who were helping to lead the oxen across.

"We have about done them all," Isaac told them. "They were just practice. Next we will encounter rivers. They won't be so easy." He looked at the boys with concern, wishing again that they had been able to make the journey in warm weather. "We will take turns fording the rivers. All of us have to work together. We'll reach the final creek shortly and spend the night there."

Upon arrival later that afternoon, Christiana joined the girls as they went to the creek for water. By now everyone knew the routine and went about making preparations for the evening meal.

"I've looked at dirty faces long enough," Christiana said. "This water isn't frozen out in the middle. I'm just going to step out aways and get a bucket full. We can all wash hands and faces at least."

Stepping carefully, on what looked like solid ice, her foot suddenly broke through. Losing her balance she fell into chilling water up to her waist. The weight of her wet heavy wool skirt held her motionless. She screamed. She was angry at her clumsiness and the cold water was a shock.

The girls tried to reach her by joining hands and stretching but they also fell and screamed. Two men grabbed guns and came running, not knowing what they'd find. Isaac arrived to find everyone scurrying to climb on shore.

"Mama wanted us to get cleaned up, Papa," said Delilah laughing. "She showed us how." At that everyone, including Christiana, joined in the laughter. They hobbled miserably back to the wagons. After removing their soaked clothes they wrapped up in quilts. Garments were wrung out and hung by the fire the boys had built. Everyone huddled around the warming campfire until bedtime.

The following morning, Isaac led them on the trail. They were very surprised when he stopped at the creek, and got off his horse. Looking very solemn, he asked his wife to step to his side. "I wish you all to know we are hereby naming this noble creek 'Christiana'. It will be noted as that from now on." Smiling at her he continued. "If anyone asks how it came to be named, you will be able to tell them." Christiana blushed. In spite of her damp clothes she smiled and returned to her wagon.

The thin ice broke as the wagons carefully rolled across. Wheels sank into mud but their animal teams managed to keep moving. Children and adults who were walking crossed down stream where the ice was more solid, leading hogs, cows and horses.

As they traveled that day the sun came out, warming their faces. Isaac rode along the line and told them to stop at the next blazed tree. When everyone was assembled, he told them, "I know you are enjoying this beautiful day. This afternoon we will reach the Elkhart River. Stop at its bank! Do not enter the water! You must wait there until even the last pig arrives! I am going on ahead to choose the best fording place."

"Mama, I don't like it when Papa looks and sounds so cross," said eleven year old John Calvin, who was helping Christiana guide the horse-drawn wagon.

"When he does that you know it is serious," replied his sister Sarah. Anna, short for Christiana, another sister, nodded in agreement.

Their mother smiled as she listened but told them, "We all depend on your father's leadership. He has made this journey before and knows its hazards." Silently she was thinking that the river crossings must indeed be serious obstacles to make Isaac warn them so sternly.

The animals plodded on and before noon they reached the river. Happy to get down from the wagon, Christiana and her children walked along the bank. They peered down at the turbulent river. Ice flows bumped along in the rolling water.

"Are we going to be able to make it across that, Mr. Lykins?" Delilah asked the young man as he just joined them.

"Your father and Mr. Dusenbury just went to scout the river beyond the bend there," he said, pointing downstream. "It may be that it runs quieter there. Maybe it isn't so deep."

Just then they saw the men approaching with big smiles on their faces. "We can cross at the narrows. Ice clumps have forced some fallen trees into making a dam which blocked off the flow," Daniel Dusenbury told them in excited tones.

"As soon as all people and animals are accounted for we'll begin to cross," Isaac told the group. "Start moving these wagons toward the crossing area."

3

By the time the boys came whooping and hollering down the trail, chasing the hogs with long sticks, the line up of wagons was completed. Isaac calmed their antics. "Use those sticks to guide the cows across the river. A couple of you stay there to keep them from wandering. The rest of you come back for the hogs."

Singing Bird, Fawn and Christiana took the smallest children on horseback. Men and oldest boys drove the wagons. Other children rode inside. Isaac and Johnston completed the move on their horses.

"Come form a circle everyone!" Isaac called. "Hold hands as we pray in thankfulness for our safe crossing." When his lengthy prayer ended the sun was setting. Preparations for the night began.

"We are a little over two days away from our new mission home," Isaac said as they sat around the campfire eating. The looks of relief quickly changed when he added, "Tomorrow we must cross the final river, the Saint Joseph. It will be more difficult."

Josephus carried his father's watch during the journey. It was his duty to blow the bugle by 5 A.M. making sure everyone was awake. Cold snowy weather greeted the group on this next to last day.

"Only the thought of finally reaching our destination makes me want to reach the river," Christiana confided to Singing Bird and Fawn as they followed rutted wheel tracks behind a wagon.

"Long ago, when I was very small, I lived in a village near the Saint Joe river. I remember the wide water," Fawn said. She looked frightened. Her dark eyes teared. "It was deep with strong currents."

"Maybe there will be a tree dam in it, like the one yesterday," Singing Bird commented. "We could make one if there is not."

Children, energetic as ever, ran back and forth between wagons throwing snowballs and enjoying the day. Christiana took Eleanor from Singing Bird's arms. The fretting child still kept them awake each night with her coughing. "Oh, how I long to undress and lie in a bed with a roof overhead," Christiana confessed. "When we get to the mission with its proper buildings and food we will all feel better. I just know it!"

"Maybe then we can all have warm dry feet," said Fawn.

The morning passed quickly. Before noon, Isaac, who had ridden ahead, came back to tell them that within the half-hour they would reach the river. The trail curved. They heard the sound of rushing water just before they saw the shoreline.

Wagons stopped and men hurried to determine the best crossing conditions. "The river looks to be about forty feet across at the narrowest," they agreed.

"That's bad enough but what about these steep banks? How are we getting down those to the water's edge?" Daniel Dusenbury asked..

"North of here a short way it isn't as steep. That's where we crossed in November," Isaac told them. "I'll ride ahead and look for a better incline. Start gathering all the rope you can find. We'll want to string a line from one side to the other for a safety hold." He patiently explained the whole procedure to the men, then started to mount his horse but changed his mind and located his wife.

"You will need to repack perishable goods so it is stacked tall in the wagons. The water is high today. We may have to unload things and even leave them if it is too difficult a pull for the oxen." He saw the concern on the women's faces but didn't know any way to make things easy. "The men will need help tying rope pieces for a safety line. Get the older children to help. I'll be back shortly," he said as he returned to his horse.

"While we're unpacking, keep out the kettles. I'll ask Calvin and Josephus to start a fire so we can boil up some cornmeal. We need sustenance before we plunge into that cold river," Christiana told Fawn and Delilah.

As they removed supplies they untied bundles and tossed ropes in a pile. While the meal was cooking Johnston supervised the rope tying process. "We need two very long lengths. Double would be better yet," he told them. "The plan is to tie it to trees on each side, eight to ten feet apart. They'll be guidelines. We will keep our wagons between them. The ropes can be something to grab onto if we're walking or swimming."

Isaac was pleased to find everyone busy when he returned. As he ate a bowl of mush he spoke to the group. "We will be crossing south of here instead of north. The river conditions have changed. As soon as you men have eaten we'll locate trees sturdy enough to support our ropes." Several Indian men coiled rope, ready to follow him. "The rest of you men and boys ready the wagons. Move them south." He smiled at Christiana as he handed her the bowl, then mounted his horse.

The children followed Isaac and the men, prodding hogs into a squealing group. When they reached the designated crossing area, two perfectly situated oak trees were found. A heavily wooded area directly across the river offered several possibilities for securing the other rope ends. As the men wrapped rope around the tree trunks the wagons arrived.

"Who is carrying rope over?" asked Daniel Dusenbury as he jumped from his oxen pulled wagon. A couple of teenage Indian boys offered to go but Isaac wanted larger men to carry and tie the heavy ropes. Rice and Josephus volunteered but again Isaac refused the offer, deciding to go himself. Johnston

Lykins agreed to accompany him. Everyone stood silently on the bank watching as the two men on horseback plunged into the chilling water. Rope hanks were looped over the saddle horns. Fighting strong currents, the horses swam toward the distant shoreline.

The rope unwound as they went. Cheers of encouragement followed them as they safely climbed the distant bank. Cold as they were, they managed to wrap and tie rope ends around trees, completing their task. After much prompting Isaac and Johnston forced their horses back to the starting point. The men quickly dismounted and grabbed the quilts offered to them before rushing to the campfire. Boys calmed the horses as they gently rubbed them dry with blankets.

When Isaac's shaking subsided he gathered everyone in a circle. "Let us pray. Lord, we need courage to get ourselves and our animals ready for our icy venture. We entrust ourselves to your guidance and protections. Amen." No one grumbled or complained although the prospect of the crossing was very frightening.

"We will send a wagon, then some horses with riders, then another wagon until we are all safely across," Isaac instructed. "Two children will ride with each adult on each horse. Grab onto a rope for support if you need it. Adults, you'll need to return for more children until they are all across."

The first wagon bounced its way down the embankment, then slid into the water to begin crossing. "It didn't look that deep," said Christiana, watching from above. "Look, water is way up on the sides. I hope the barrels are waterproof." She saw her loom sway and thought surely it would fall out. When it righted itself, just before the oxen plodded up the opposite bank, she breathed a sigh of relief.

Singing Bird rode the first horse across, Sarah McCoy held in front and Anna behind her. Delilah followed with her sister Nancy and a small Indian sister. The water was shockingly cold but knowing they were setting the example the girls bravely endured.

Each wagon churned up mud, making ruts more difficult for the next one. Horses swam outside the ropes. As they bucked the waves made by the wagons, clumps of ice bumped them. Frantically tossing their heads, ears upright, eyes wildly staring, they fought the surging water, swimming, sometimes stumbling as their feet touched bottom.

Oxen, horses and even cows managed to cross in spite of their fear and discomfort. By the time a couple of wagons and teenage boys were safely across large fires were built. Soggy items were pulled from wagons and hung on branches. Men waded in to grab the reins and lead horses or oxen up the bank. Shivering children huddled together wrapped in quilts.

The pigs created another problem. Two boys and two Indian men used long poles to control and guide the squealing mass, as the pigs swam or floated in the waves. Christiana stood on the far bank watching their floundering. Three drowned and she watched with deep regret as their bodies were swept downstream.

Josephus and Delilah were busily tying cows to nearby trees when screams and shouts rose from the river. They dropped the ropes and ran. Christiana picked up baby Eleanor and also ran. When they reached the bank they were shocked to see the last wagon had tipped. The driver and all its barrels had fallen into the rushing water. The driver jumped, staggered and somehow managed to reach shore. The wagon and its cargo broke into pieces, swiftly disappearing into the churning water.

Christiana felt sick to her stomach. Josephus heard her moan and gathered her into his arms, holding her tightly until she regained her strength. Bravely she remained on watch until she saw Isaac.

He was the final person to cross. Before he did, he untied the guide ropes and let them fall into the water. Rice pulled them to shore, and wound them up loosely as his father crossed to his side. Josephus and Calvin rushed to halt the frantic horse.

"Papa, can you get your leg over the saddle so we can help you down?" asked Rice as he joined them.

"He is nearly frozen, we must act quickly. Bring dry blankets," Josephus shouted. Isaac was unable to speak through his chattering teeth but somehow managed to dismount and stand with his son's support. Carrying all the blankets she could find, Christiana rushed to wrap his shaking body. The family helped steady him during Brother Dusenbury's lengthy prayer of thanksgiving for safe passage.

Christiana hugged the children gathered around her and whispered, "We are almost to our new home. We've crossed the last river."

Still chilled to their bones, everyone formed groups around campfires but there wasn't enough heat to dry their soaked garments. "Christiana!" Isaac called hoarsely, "You must help me get these people and animals moving. Anything that stands still will freeze. We should journey until sunset at least. That will shorten tomorrow's trek anyway."

"No one will want to leave these fires," she replied.

"Tell Rice and his brothers to smother the fires. That will get their attention. I want everyone and everything walking in ten minutes!"

Christiana knew when her usually mild mannered husband spoke like that conditions were serious. She did what she was told to do. As she began walking she felt tingling in her toes and fingers. Stiff muscles relaxed. Lethargy was replaced by healthy and familiar grumbling and she knew Isaac had been right to insist they move on.

Three hours later Isaac rode alongside wagons telling everyone the stop for the night was just ahead. They halted under a stand of oak trees. As soon as the pigs arrived they hungrily rooted acorns. As the children rode in wagons they had untied the crossing ropes. Now the men used the pieces to secure the animals to trees before feeding them. No one wanted to search for strays in the morning.

Fires were built as soon as fallen branches were gathered. Cold cornbread and meat jerky was shared while they waited for snow filled coffeepots to heat. Eventually water boiled and dried chicory was added. Even the youngest had a cupful before they slept.

Men dragged in large limbs so fires could burn all night. Even before Josephus blew the morning bugle, Christiana had prepared kettles of hot mush. Reliving the river crossing, she had been unable to sleep. As she stirred the meal her thinking switched to thoughts of their new mission. Isaac had told them they had very few miles to go. She especially was looking forward to meeting the Bertrands, the only close neighbors.

Suddenly she felt faint and sat down. Her head ached. Isaac, also restless, found her lying in the snow. With his help she managed to stand. With his support she staggered back to the wagons.

Delilah made her comfortable, then went to finish preparing breakfast. By sunup everyone was fed, wagons and animals were in line. Isaac drove the family's wagon. Christiana remained hovering in her quilt, oblivious to everything including the bouncy three-hour ride.

Long before they reached the trading post the rumbling noise of the wagons alerted Bertrand's dogs. At their persistent barking, he grabbed his rifle and rushed outside.

"Hey, Hey!" he shouted as he saw visitors approaching. "Wife, come out here! I never seen anything like this."

Madeline, his Indian wife, crept from a tepee situated behind the log trading post building.

A young boy jumped from the second wagon and raced to Bertrand's open arms. "Abraham Burnett, you rascal. Your Papa was here last week wondering when the McCoys would be bringing you. These wagons are McCoys?" Abraham nodded and raced back to walk beside Isaac.

"Welcome, Welcome! Come inside! All of you, come inside!" Bertrand bellowed. Madeline stood quietly behind her husband, smiling shyly.

A few Indians, lingering on the porch of the trading post, watched the wagons and animals pull into the clearing. They eyed the strangers and listened to the new language. Confused, they quietly disappeared into the surrounding woods to observe unseen.

"Come inside!" Bertrand repeated in his booming French accent. He flung open the door and motioned for Isaac and Abraham to follow. "Where is Mrs. McCoy? I want to meet her."

Isaac told him she was feeling poorly. Bertrand hugged Abraham. "She took good care of you while you in Ft. Wayne, huh? Now we take care of her. My wife, she make medicine. She knows Indian cures. Bring your Mrs. by the fire. You all come spend the night. We will feed you!"

"There are thirty-two of us. You can't feed and bed all of us," Isaac said, smiling.

"We have barn and this building. Everybody can sleep under roof. Food we always share," he stated emphatically.

Everyone wandered around the trading post, happy to stretch their legs and to be greeted so warmly. Delilah and Singing Bird helped Christiana from the wagon and led her toward the buildings. Fawn carried Eleanor and kept the other little girls close to her side. When they reached the porch Madeline smiled as she motioned them inside. She felt

Christiana's forehead and spoke to Fawn in their Pottawatomi language, asking her to describe the illness.

Bertrand greeted the women and pointed to a large rocking chair beside the fireplace. Madeline disappeared for awhile, then returned with a wooden bowl of herb tea. Placing it in Christiana's shaking hands, she motioned her to drink. When the bowl was empty she covered Christiana with a bearskin. Within minutes she slept.

Bertrand asked if they had bowls for soup. Delilah and her sisters ran to a wagon and unpacked some. Bertrand's children carefully ladled them full of hot venison stew.

Rather than wake her mother or interrupt her father's discussion with Joseph Bertrand, Johnston asked Delilah for help. "It looks like we will be spending the night here. Would you help me carry in blankets and quilts?"

Delilah blushed and quickly found her brother Calvin to walk back to the wagons with them. Two of her sisters joined them. It was growing dark and a cold wind whipped the snow into drifts. "I'm very glad we can sleep inside tonight," Delilah confessed. "Mama and I are tired of this journey and will appreciate moving into a cabin again."

"I think that holds true for everyone, Delilah. It has not been easy but we are almost there. Keep up your spirit, your new home is nearby," Johnston said.

After they distributed the bedding everyone searched for an empty spot to sleep. Some slept by the fireplace, others crawled under tables stacked with sale merchandise. A few of the older boys and men took quilts to the barn and slept on hay. Bertrand and his children joined Madeline in her tepee.

Christiana awoke feeling much better and joined the group as they ate more venison stew for breakfast. "You must stay longer," said Bertrand. "Madeline will cure you."

"We must get to the Mission and prepare the school for our pupils," Christiana replied. "I'm feeling well enough to travel and eager to see our home." Isaac looked at her with concern but knew he couldn't change her mind.

Bertrand sat on a bench opposite the McCoys. "You are stubborn, like me," he said laughing loudly. "But I know you wish to be situated and ready to begin the new year. We are happy to have you for neighbors!"

While the boys started to fold and repack bedding, Delilah and her sisters cleaned the bowls and took them to the wagons.

The children were fascinated to be able to see and touch the many items in the trading post. Never had they seen so much food, colorful new blankets or strange clothing and interesting gadgets all in one place.

"You spoke of the new year, Bertrand," said Isaac. "It is our custom to invite neighbors and friends for a party on the first day of the year. We would like you and your family to come to the mission on that day."

"You want Indians too? Madeline's family has many chiefs."

"Yes, of course! That is why we came to the Michigan territory. We must meet those Indian leaders and tell them of our school and our need for students," Isaac and Christiana told him.

"We will spread the word," said Bertrand. Within a few minutes they were packed. Two of Bertrand's sons were preparing to go north to Burnett's trading post with supplies. They invited Abraham to go along and visit his family. Isaac gave his permission and waved farewell.

The morning dawned bright and clear as the McCoy group set out. For the first time since leaving Fort Wayne, Christiana sat beside Isaac as he drove a wagon. Their young daughters rode with them. Christiana felt totally relaxed. She let her mind wander to the end of the journey. Thinking about the fresh new buildings and the opportunities ahead, she sighed. "Have you noticed even the wind seems warmer?" she asked

Isaac?

"Christiana, I hope you are truly feeling better. I know you want to get to our new home but maybe we should have stayed at Bertrands longer."

"I am feeling better. I think I caught the baby's cold. Anyway I have a supply of medicine which Madeline gave me. Please don't worry! God wants us to be happy as we approach our new mission. The sun is out and look, the pigs are even behaving themselves," she said smiling and pointing to them.

Isaac guided the oxen over the snow covered trail following the river northward. Suddenly they could hear the sound of a falling tree. Christiana looked at her husband and saw his huge smile. "Yes, my dear, we are nearly home. We have traveled one hundred miles in eleven days. I brought my diary up to date last night. Today is December 20th in the year of 1822."

"Children," called Christiana over her shoulder, "We are just minutes from our new mission school. Keep watching!" Later she regretted having said that.

"I see smoke!" someone yelled. "I can smell it, too."

"Me too, I see smoke!" Concerned voices of children and adults echoed along the line of wagons.

"There's the mission!" yelled Rice as he rode his horse ahead.

Lifting her skirts, Christiana hopped down from their slow moving wagon and joined others running ahead. Pigs squealed as they scampered out of the way. At the edge of a clearing the group stopped, staring. Log mission buildings stood straight and secure before them. Their eyes were drawn to smoke rising from a chimney.

"There's no danger," called Rice, relieved that no uncontrolled fire confronted them. "It's smoke from cooking fires."

"We're here! Here's our new home!" said Isaac, happily

looking around. Christiana gazed at the buildings. They were not as she expected or hoped. Only two cabins had smoke rising from chimneys. The remaining cabins were unfinished. The building she thought was the school was not much better. Her heart sank with utter disappointment.

She held in her feelings however when she saw men and boys, who had been working on the buildings, rushing to greet the newcomers. Isaac halted the wagons and jumped down, eager to unite with the workers.

"Welcome! Welcome! We were getting mighty worried about you, wondering when you would get here," the men said, smiling happily.

"We've had lots of sickness here, made it hard to work," one of the men told Isaac as he pulled him aside. "Our supplies are really meager. Sure hope you brought flour. We've got meat from hunting, but nothing to put with it."

Isaac told him of the loss of barrels as the crossed the Saint Joe River. "We have some flour and meal with us, but we also brought more people to feed. After we get settled in and the oxen rest a few days I'll send someone back for more supplies," he promised.

Leaving him to talk to the men, Christiana strolled toward the largest building. She looked at it with tears in her eyes. The logs weren't chinked. There was no door or windows. Stepping inside, she discovered it had no fireplace or floor and no furnishings. Tears of frustration streamed down her face. They'd made the whole trip so they could start teaching in better conditions and the school wasn't ready. She heard someone coming and quickly lifted her skirt to wipe her face, but not before Johnston saw her.

4

Putting his arm around her, Johnston confided, "I know how you feel. As a teacher I know how I feel. Mrs. McCoy, we're just tired. We will get it finished up quickly and be ready for pupils in a few days. You'll see."

Christiana wished she had his youthful outlook. She patted his arm. "You are right. Our hardest job right now will be to put on a cheerful face," she replied. "We can't let the young ones catch us acting discouraged or frightened."

"You will do just fine! Let's get out of this dreary place and help unpack the wagons."

"Carry the bedding into the finished cabins, the others will be too cold and damp," Christiana instructed the children. With a deep sigh, she struggled to adjust.

The girls and boys soon had a muddy path trampled, from the wagons to the buildings as they moved the boxes and crates indoors. Christiana and Singing Bird sorted through cooking supplies locating kettles and tripods and setting them up outdoors, so a hot meal could be prepared before evening. Children gathered wood for fires, just as they had on their journey.

Men and older boys took care of the horses and oxen before they approached Christiana to inquire as to what she wanted unpacked and moved. Working with her oldest daughters, she busily stirred cornmeal into a pot of boiling water. They were fixing a combination of deer meat and turnips, adding them to kettles over the fires.

"We'll be needing some tables and benches," she told the men. "Maybe there are boards around, if not use the wagon seats or the sides of the wagon beds." Her tone of voice revealed her displeasure. Confused, they shrugged their shoulders, looked at each other and started back toward the buildings. She heard them grumbling and wasn't surprised to see her husband coming toward her after talking to them.

"Christiana, I'm afraid you were expecting too much. We are just going to have to adjust and accept bare essentials for awhile."

"I'm sorry. I am trying," she replied. "I expected the living quarters and the school to be finished. I know the boys and men can build furniture later but I certainly thought the basic structures would be ready for us!"

"The men have been ill. Although the snow is not deep now, the weather has been severe." Isaac explained. " With more of us here now, work will get done more quickly."

Christiana glared at him and turned back to stir her cooking. "Well at least we are not going to have to sleep on cold muddy ground!   I'm certainly tired of all the coughing and sneezing!"

Just as she said that she heard him gasp. She spun around to see him bent over holding his stomach in pain. "Isaac, what's wrong? Let me help you into the cabin so you can get warm and dry by the fireplace!"

He leaned on her as they struggled down the path. Once inside, he began coughing. Christiana searched through boxes trying to locate the medicine Madeline had made. He drank from the jar when she found it. His coughing stopped but his face became bright red. He sat on a packing crate by the fireplace staring into space.

Tears came to Christiana's eyes as she was confronted with one more responsibility. She made Isaac a bed of sorts on the top of two crates of dishes, covering him with a quilt from the stack in a corner. He was shaking with chills but burning up with fever.

Although she didn't want to leave him she had to get back to the girls and food preparation in the cabin they had chosen for food preparation. Delilah, capable as always, had taken charge of the cooking. When her mother returned she offered to go to look in on her father.

In spite of her problems, the sound of pounding hammers made Christiana smile and calm down. Others were working to fill her basic needs. The hired men had set aside rough boards so basic furniture could be constructed. Four of the older boys carried in tables they had made and set them close to the kettles. Calvin and the younger boys brought long boards and laid them on sawed off stumps to form benches. Christiana sent her daughters to locate bowls and spoons.

Everyone but Isaac gathered for the meal. Christiana offered the prayer. "I want to apologize, Lord," she said, "for being unkind and unreasonable. We are gathered here to begin a new life at a new mission. I started out wrong and I need forgiveness." She heard a murmur of surprise from the group and she continued. "There are many things that need building, people to befriend, boys and girls to teach and Christian work to be done. Help us all work together peacefully and lovingly and bless Isaac with a rapid recovery." 'Amen' echoed from all present.

Sighing and smiling, she took her turn eating the first meal at their new mission. Later she took bowls of stew to Isaac and Delilah and told them what she had prayed. Isaac smiled and patted her hand affectionately before he took a few bites. He fell asleep holding his spoon.

Tired of sleeping in wagons and on the ground Christiana and the girls, with Fawn and Singing Bird's help, cleared sleep space in cabins. By crowding close together they managed to find sleeping space in lofts and on the newly laid puncheon floor of two finished cabins. Rice and Josephus moved their father into their mother's rocker close to the fireplace where they could watch him.

The next morning Singing Bird and Delilah prepared cornmeal mush over outdoor fires that had burned all night. Snow began falling before they ate. Christiana said "We have to move kettles into fireplaces before another meal. At least one table will fit indoors, but we will have to eat in shifts". The men agreed to carry things.

The men made a wooden platform which Delilah covered with quilts for her father. He slept fitfully the rest of the day. Toward nightfall Christiana became alarmed when she touched his forehead. "He's burning up with fever again," she called to Delilah. "Bring me a bowl of cold water and a rag." She motioned for the children to come to the bed. She showed them how to cool his skin by sponging the wet cloth over his face and arms and especially his chest.

They kept doing it while their mother prepared and helped serve the evening meal. After evening prayers when everyone else in the cabin was bedded down, Christiana pulled her little rocker close to Isaac's bed. She had just dozed off when suddenly he sat up shouting wildly in delirium as he relived their recent river crossings.

He woke everyone with his ranting. Rice and Calvin rushed to help their mother. They managed to quiet him but the restless tossing continued. At daybreak his fever finally broke. Afterwards he slept peacefully, barely moving for two days.

The third day, while breakfast was being served, Isaac tried to get out of his quilt but was too weak to even sit up. Christiana leaned close to his mouth straining to hear his whispered "What day is it? I must get up and write my sermon."

"You've been sick abed four days," she told him. "You need to eat and rest to get your strength back. Your sermon can wait!"

"Help me," he begged, but when she tried to assist him in sitting he became dizzy and started shaking violently. Christiana kept busy spooning medicine into Isaac and any others who were ill. At the same time she supervised as Josephus hung shelves in the cabin. She and the girls folded blankets and unpacked dishes and books. Isaac's health began to improve.

Mornings, Christiana went often to her small window, watching the building activity at the school. The children had learned quickly how to mix mud, dried grass and sawdust and now used it to fill chinks on log walls. The floor in the building remained hard-packed dirt. She insisted it would be covered eventually with the same puncheon floors they put in the cabins. Before the McCoys had arrived a well had been dug. She greatly admired the four foot stone wall they had just built around the well.

Suddenly, as she gazed outside, she caught a glimpse of a man leading his horse into the yard. He was a white man but she did not recognize him. Pulling her shawl around her shoulders she left the cabin and went to meet him.

"Morning, Mrs." he said. "I'm Squire Thompson. I'm from Union County in Indiana looking for land to buy."

"My soul, you're a long way from home. You look near frozen, come inside."

Isaac was sitting in the rocker, giving instructions to Rice and Josephus as they constructed two new rope beds in the corners. After Squire was introduced, Christiana handed him a bowl of hot broth. "Are you the folks who blazed trees all the way from Indiana?" Isaac smiled. "Yes, those are my markings. Glad they helped you keep on the trail." Squire nodded. "I will be remaining a few days. If I find suitable land I'll go fetch my family and our belongings. Might be spring before we return though."

Isaac moved to their new rope bed, still too week to do much. "Bring your sleeping gear and belongings in, Mr. Thompson. You can take your meals and sleep here. It's not fit weather to camp out."

"I sure appreciate your hospitality. It is getting cold and snowy looking. Truth be told, I get kinda uneasy alone in the woods at night," admitted Squire.

He left every morning to look at different areas, talking to the McCoys about his observations each evening. "My, it seems good to sit and chat of an evening" Christiana said. "We keep so busy every day we forget to speak" One night Squire returned with a deer he had shot tied to his saddle. Singing Bird and Fawn worked outdoors at a table and expertly skinned and butchered the deer. Later they roasted the meat over the fire. The bones were boiled for soup in outdoor kettles.

Isaac's health continued to improve. "I wish I could help," he said sadly as he watched Christiana work. "I don't know how you can keep all of us fed and cared for plus overseeing the building. I know Brother Lykins keeps the children busy. Have the two of you decided when classes will begin?" Christiana shook her head no.

"I like to keep busy but I will be happier when you are feeling able to be up and around again," she said, glancing at his thin shaking hands. "This ague and pleurisy you have is hard on your body. Seeing you able to sit up is good but you must not overdo." The fever and delirium had disappeared but the deep painful cough and the sudden shaking still racked his body.

"If you will kindly hand me some paper and a pen I'm going to prepare a sermon." He saw her hesitate but she located what he asked for. Their son Calvin moved a table beside the bed. Isaac was determined to show her that he could and would give Sunday's sermon.

"Do you truly think you will be strong enough to preach on Sunday?" she asked, almost like she had read his mind.

As she moved across the cabin Christiana stopped at the window. "Isaac, everyday Indians come unto the mission land or watch from the woods. They are really curious but they don't venture into buildings or talk to anyone that I can see.

Are they afraid of us?"

"More likely they think we will be afraid of them so they are waiting to see white people's reactions to their presence. In a few days we will all be braver," he said smiling.

One evening four days after his arrival, Squire Thompson talked of heading home. "I'd better go before bad weather returns." "Two of our workers are leaving for Fort Wayne. Maybe you'd like their company," Isaac told him " Food supplies at the mission have run extremely low, not just for the people but also for our animals." Two days later Squire rode out with the workers, happy to have company on the trail.

Rice came into the cabin to talk to his parents, looking very worried. "Feed for the oxen and horses has badly dwindled," he told them." "Worse yet, the pigs are nearly starving. Poor things just can't find nuts or food under the snow."

Isaac shook his head. "Maybe we could pen them and be sure they get table scraps."

Christiana couldn't help laughing. "Food scraps from our meals wouldn't feed a chicken."

Isaac ignored her and spoke to his son. "I do believe fences should be constructed around all the animals. It would keep them safer and we'd have an easier time of feeding them." He rubbed his head in despair. "I wish I could get out of this bed and help with building and other chores."

"You will be well soon, Papa," said Rice. "What kind of fence could we make?"

"Split rails or cut down sapling trees would be easiest, but this isn't a good time of year for them. I wonder if just stacking tree tops or large branches cut from the building logs and placed in a large circle would hold in the pigs?"

"The boys and I could sure do that." Rice laughed, "The hard thing will be catching and moving the pigs. I can just imagine the younger boys chasing them around. Cows and horses are easier to control." A few minutes later he left smiling, to get help capturing pigs.

Rice got the older boys involved in harnessing the oxen to the largest wagon. They headed for the woods. He had younger boys cut small trees. They broke sturdy branches to make prods to force the pigs into groups. Josephus made a ramp of rough sawn boards which he set up into the wagon. The pigs ran and squealed in panic. They fought the procedure of getting them up into the wagon. They tried jumping and had to be knocked back inside as the wagon moved slowly back to the branch pen the children made. It took half a day to locate and confine twenty-five pigs, half of the herd brought from Fort Wayne. Some had drown, some wandered off or starved and some had fallen prey to wolves.

Late in the afternoon, Christiana, tired of being cabin bound, dressed her young daughters and other girls warmly. She took them outside to watch the frantic hogs run around in their brush enclosure. The children laughed. Christiana was shocked to see how poorly the animals looked.

"I can't understand how they have so much energy, skinny as they are. Look, you can actually see their ribs!" she said shaking her head. "Your papa is right. From now on, you girls will bring all food scraps we have and throw them into the pen here. We must try and keep them alive."

Later, Christiana checked on the pigs and found the meager food scraps they were fed had only caused fighting. "We don't have enough corn meal for ourselves. We certainly can't spare any for animals," she told anyone who happened by.

More Indians began to appear around mission buildings. Several times Christiana noticed women watching the pigs, chuckling with amusement as they stood by the enclosure. She joined them, taking Fawn to interpret conversations. "Tell them about our school. Encourage them to bring their children," she repeated at each opportunity.

She was very pleased when women followed her to the

cabin. They had shyly peered inside the door but wouldn't enter the building. When the women heard Isaac's deep cough they hurriedly left.

The next morning when Christiana opened the cabin door she was surprised to find a basket of herbs and a gourd cup of medicinal looking liquid. Thinking back to the previous day's episode she knew the Indian women had brought a cure for Isaac. Fawn dipped her finger into the liquid and carefully tasted. "Oh, I know what this is," she said licking her lips. "It is medicine made of choke cherry bark, boiled to a syrup. We need to give to Brother McCoy.. It help his cough." She studied the dried grasses. "This is dried goldenrod flowers, hyssop leaves and catnip. I will pound these into powder to be stirred into curing drink. I'll mix these right now."

Christiana said "My grandmother kept bags of herbs and bark to use for medicine. I wish I had paid more attention to things like that! The women were being very friendly to bring this medicine. Now, we need to do something in return," Christiana commented.

Fawn smiled, "They are very shy. I'm surprised there are people around in the winter. I thought they went north to help with the trapping."

Fawn and Singing Bird mixed the cough remedy. Christiana gave her husband a large dose. He looked a little doubtful when she told him what it was but swallowed it quickly, eager to try any cure. As the day progressed and his cough lessened they both rejoiced.

Later, under the warmth of an afternoon sun, Isaac leaned heavily on Christiana's arm and they strolled the mission grounds. "Those pigs are in terrible condition!" he said, pointing. "Are all our animals in such poor shape?"

Christiana nodded. "Brother Dusenbury told me last night that our supplies are not going to last until the men return."

Isaac sighed. "I never should have brought you here."

Christiana stopped walking and pointed to a tree stump. "Sit down Isaac! Listen to me! We are here now. We can't go back. I am amazed at your lack of faith! You always remind others to 'trust in the Lord'. You are setting a bad example!"

Isaac sat up, shocked at her sharp tone. "It's not just a matter of faith! It is many problems, like health and lack of food. Sick abed as I've been, I've been doing lots of thinking. As you realize, the new year will be in two days.. Since we have been married we have always managed to celebrate that day with an open house for neighbors. We've invited the Bertrands. Our neighbors here are Indian families. I'd hoped to put on a friendly feast for some of the leaders. It was to be a chance to tell them about our mission school. With no food, how can we do that?"

Christiana's blue eyes sparkled with tears as she listened to his words.

"If we are not keeping our traditions and we are not meeting Indians and we are not getting more students or feeding the ones we have, what are we doing here?" Isaac asked.

"I know we came to do those things, Isaac. I feel as guilty as you. The Lord must be disappointed in us! Oh my, I remember Bertrand saying he'd pass along the new year's invitation to the Indians. I think we have to have our open house."

"What is it we are going to feed them? Haven't you been listening?"

"Isaac McCoy, I'm truly shocked! You know the Lord always provides!" She pulled her shawl tightly around her shoulders and stomped off down the path, needing some time to control her feelings and her tears.

Her wandering led her to the pig's enclosure. She stood there recalling what Isaac had said. They really are starving she thought, watching them as they fought over scraps of food and dug holes searching for more.

Johnston Lykins saw her standing there and quietly joined her. He listened patiently as she spoke. "Our children drove these pigs all the way from Fort Wayne so we'd have animals to breed and share with Indians. After making it through all the obstacles they are going to die here where it is safe." She wiped tears from her eyes. "What can we do? Are we all going to starve?"

Johnston shook his head. "I don't know the answer. Perhaps we should have waited until spring to come."

"No! " she replied stubbornly. "We were not sent to this place just to starve. It is up to us to build the mission school here. If this lack of food is a test of our determination and ability to carry out God's plan then we will just have to overcome it!" She squared her shoulders and headed back toward their cabin.

5

"Mother, wait! I have to tell you something," called Rice as he hurried to her side. "I just talked to Papa. I thought I'd better tell you he wants me to saddle his horse. Do you think he is strong enough to ride to the neighboring villages like he wants to do?"

"Is he planning to go alone? I certainly do not think he is well enough to do that!" she said.

"Our Indian brother Luther is going along to interpret for him. Do you want me to go too?"

Christiana nodded in agreement. "Yes, stay with him!"

"Papa says we're going to have a New Year's open house. He has been so sickly and looking so sad, I didn't think we'd be celebrating this year."

"He isn't completely well but mostly he is discouraged about our low supply of food. That is why he doesn't smile," she replied.

"Why and how are we having a party when we can barely feed the mission?"

"We need to meet our neighbors, son, and we always share whatever we have. We can exist on broth but our biggest concern is how to feed the animals while we wait for the supply wagon."

"Why feed the animals? Why not eat them?" he asked, smiling at the thought. "We were going to do that anyway, why not now?"

"Oh, Rice," laughed Christiana, "You always make things so simple. That could very well be the solution!   Let's find your father and see what he says." She pulled her arm through her son's as they followed the frozen path.

Isaac was standing by the horses and turned to greet them. "I'm sorry Christiana. You are right. We need to go ahead with our plans."

She smiled at him, then shared Rice's suggestion. His first reaction was a scowl but as he thought about it he begin laughing. The three of them joined in a hug. "We can replace those pigs in the spring. Right now I think we can plan a feast," he said happily.

Johnston Lykins spent his days trying to get the school building completed. "If only we could get benches and desks built it would please me," he told Christiana. "The boys and I could make them but they are constantly having to work on other things."

"I'm sorry for that, Johnston.   I want the school ready as much as you, but it just seems more important right now to have our cabins finished."

"I know," he agreed with a sigh. "With all the sickness and

such cold weather, we need warm places to sleep and eat."

"I wish we could get more fireplaces built! We only have one kitchen fire for the benefit of fifty people." Christiana shook her head in despair. "The cabin fireplaces are not adequate and its too cold to cook outdoors."

"When we have a fireplace in the school we can keep a warm fire burning constantly. It may never completely dry out in here but at least it will be warm enough to conduct classes."

Even though the teachers wanted classes to begin in January a delay seemed likely. Johnston hoped that when neighbors came for the New Year party they would bring their children to take classes at the mission. Meanwhile, he kept busy building tables and benches.

Hired men were busily constructing two more cabins. One would serve as a eating room during the day but its large loft would be the sleeping area for girls. Fawn and Singing Bird would move from McCoy's cabin and sleep there also, taking care of the fires and supervising meal preparations.

The other cabin was built for the Dusenbury family. The blacksmith shop would be built behind it. As soon as his bed was assembled, Daniel moved from McCoy's. As Mrs. Dusenbury had not arrived yet, the mission boys slept in their loft. Having just given birth to a baby boy, she had not been strong enough to travel from Fort Wayne. Delilah helped by unpacking the barrel of dishes and boxes of bedding and books Daniel had brought. Everything was neat and ready. Everyday he hoped to see the supply wagon arrive with blacksmith materials and his wife and children onboard. He missed them.

Christiana had relied on Daniel's assistance during Isaac's illness. "I don't know what I would have done without you and Johnston," she told him the thirty-first of December, when she met him on the path to the school building. "You have managed to keep all the boys busy and under control. The furniture is very nicely made and in place. Perhaps school can start just when we said it should. I don't know how to thank you, Brother Dusenbury!"

"I'm glad to help," he replied. "I have to admit though, that I am glad to hear I don't have to go out hunting deer for our open house." They both smiled as they discussed preparations for the event.

In spite of blustery weather, chores were assigned to every member of the mission. Men kept busy butchering pigs. Christiana covered her ears to buffer the first loud squeals. Bracing herself against sad feelings she went about her work. Singing Bird and Fawn helped Delilah slice wide strips of skin from the stomach area of each pig. Although the hogs were lean they were able to separate a layer of fat from the skin. This fat would be melted down and clarified for cooking lard. Children gathered wood for roasting fires. Older boys dug pit trenches for the fires. Older girls put dried beans in pots of water, ready to be hung in fireplaces to cook all night. Christiana stayed in the cabin making cornmeal bread, feeling uneasy about using most of their supply.

"Do you really think Indians will come?" Delilah asked her mother when she carried in a pail of water.

"Everyday now there are Indians around here. They are probably as hungry as we are. They will enjoy this feast. Also, I think they are curious about us so they will welcome the chance to come find out why we are here."

Toward evening, on that last day of December, the pigs were skewered on long roasting spits. Daniel Dusenbury had made them as he practiced with his meager supply of blacksmith equipment. "I'm no expert at this job but someone needed to get the smithery started. Farm tools need to be made. You boys can be taught the trade," he told the four teenage boys who were doing the cooking.

"That was part of the requirement Papa had to agree to when he first talked to the government leaders," Rice told the other three cooks.

"Oh, I remember," said Luther, "Mr. Jackson, the blacksmith, was supposed to come with us but then his family got sick."

"Watch now, I'll show you how to turn the meat. Careful you don't get burned, working over these hot trench fires. Are you going to keep each other awake all night to do this?" asked Daniel with a jolly laugh.

Fawn quietly helped the boys arrange the meat. "When the smell of this meat carries on the cold night breezes, you will have to fight off the wolves," she teased.

As darkness fell only the boys remained outdoors. As fat dripped onto the log fires flames would leap toward the meat. Black smoke puffed around them as they jumped into action. Sometimes a small hunk of meat fell. They stabbed it with a sharpened stick, sharing it with delight. Wolves did howl, making them laugh as they remembered Fawn's warning. Later when they actually saw animals approaching they weren't so brave. Fortunately, none came close to the fire.

The boys were cold and tired as the early light of dawn stretched across the eastern sky. "Look!" whispered Luther, "Over there in the trees. Do you see all those Indians watching us?"

"I think the first of the visitors are about to arrive," said Rice. "I'll go tell my parents." He made his way across the snow covered yard. Inside the cabin he found everyone standing in prayer. He stood silently until his father dismissed them with a loud "Amen."

"Indian neighbors are arriving," Rice told them. Christiana made sure every child had clean hands and faces and combed hair. After her inspection, everyone pulled on warm coats or shawls and followed Rice outdoors.

Split logs with the smooth flat side up, designated to be used as flooring later, were arranged to make dish shelves. A large bonfire had been laid the day before and was now set on fire. Woven mats were placed around the fire so guests could sit in a warm circle. Two strong hired men carried the kettles of cooked beans from the kitchen fire to a small fire outdoors. Girls brought all the bowls, wooden trenchers and spoons, then lined them up on the shelves.

As the sun rose into the sky a steady stream of visitors arrived. Indian chiefs were dressed in their finest regalia. Twelve year old Abraham Burnett came with his parents from their northern trading post. Happy to see him again, the McCoys asked his assistance as interpreter. Not only was he able to do that but also guided the seating protocol.

Abraham's mother, Kawkeemee, being a sister of Chief Topinabee, was given a seat of honor behind the aged principal chief. Sub-chief Leopold Pokagon, adopted son of Topinabee, was seated beside him acting as spokesman. Both wore warm woven blankets over beaded deer skin leggings and shirts.

Recognizing his hearty laugh, everyone at the mission waved a friendly greeting to their neighbor, Joseph Bertrand. His wife Madeline and their children walked slowly behind as they approached the McCoys.

Suddenly, all eyes turned to watch in wonderment as war Chief Weesaw, tall and straight as an arrow, entered the circle. He wore a snow-white blanket fastened with a large silver brooch over a blue shirt. His deerskin leggings and moccasins were trimmed with colored porcupine quills. Bells decreasing in size, from thigh to ankle, jangled as he walked. Silver bands were fastened around his wrists and arms and large silver rings dropped from his ears. His headdress had a band of white otter centered with a large silver crest which held eagle feathers in place. Following close behind were his three wives. First was his favorite, a daughter of Topinabee, who wore the choicest of tawdry finery. She sat next to her aunt, Kawkeemee.

Chebass, another chief of high rank, slid from his fancily

decorated horse, adjusted his headdress and took his place in the circle.

The curious Indian visitors wandered around the mission. Most were seeing log buildings for the first time. Walking many times around them, peering inside, they eventually entered them to stare at the strange furnishings. They entered McCoy's cabin. Fascinated, they sat on the bed, stamped their feet on the wood floor, pulled out the trundle bed and sat on it. chattering in language too new for Christiana to understand.

One elderly woman sat primly on Christiana's chair. When she started to stand up, the chair rocked. Her startled look made all the others laugh. Soon there was a line of women waiting to take a turn rocking.

The delicious smell of roasting meat filled the air. As morning progressed people wandered toward the cooking area. "Look at that," said Josephus as he saw someone pull a piece of hot flesh from a spit. "They don't even wait for it to finish roasting."

"Remember Mama saying they would come because they are as hungry as we are?" asked Rice.

"Even so, they should wait until they are served!"

"Maybe that is the way these Indians eat all the time," commented Delilah who was standing beside her brothers. "Using proper manners is probably one of the things we're here to teach to them."

Christiana, busily stirring kettles, smiled as she overheard her children's discussion. "Today we'll begin showing our eating ways. Remember though, they may not change their habits, so we must just smile friendly and be patient. Run to get more spoons and bowls. We will begin dishing up."

Daniel Dusenbury and two hired men began slicing the pork, laying pieces on wooden platters. The girls helped Singing Bird and Fawn ladle beans into bowls and then placed a piece of bread and slice of meat on top.

Christiana, followed by her oldest daughters, politely carried the food to the chiefs and then their wives. Some tried eating with spoons but found it awkward. Most used their fingers or tipped the bowls to nosily suck the food into their mouths, handing back the empty dish for refills.

"Are we going to have enough food?' whispered Delilah, as she passed her mother. "It seems to be disappearing at a very fast rate."

"Yes it does, but can you imagine how very, very frugal our offering would have been without the pork?" Christiana shook her head as she thought of how embarrassing it would have been to celebrate New Year's Day without food. "Tell Fawn to brew more chickory coffee. That seems to be popular too."

As the noon sun warmed the January day, the well-fed crowd began to look and feel drowsy. Filled with curiosity, they sat around the bonfire watching Isaac McCoy. He carefully placed his large Bible on the podium the boys had moved outdoors. They sat respectfully, having heard about white man's religion and holidays from earlier French Canadian priests.

Children wandered off to play. Babies dozed in their cradleboards. Elderly Chief Topinabee nodded sleepily. Christiana, followed by her family and all the other members of the mission, joined their Indian guests sitting on mats.

When Isaac began speaking all chatting respectfully ceased. "I have not met all of you. I will begin by telling you my name. I am Reverend Isaac McCoy. This is my wife Christiana," he said bowing and pointing to her. "We welcome you all to our Mission Station on this first day of January, in the year of 1823. My family and all the people who work with us are pleased you came to partake of our frugal meal."

He opened his Bible and read several passages. The group grew restless. He decided to forego any more religious messages. "We have come to your land, occupied by the Potawatomi from time immemorial. Your tribe resided here in one extensive settlement. Many of your ancestors are buried on the shores of the Saint Joseph River."

"We wish to live in peaceful harmony with you. The government of the United States has set aside land for this Indian school. Soon this school will be ready for your children."

Abraham Burnett translated Isaac's message, adding many gestures. Isaac had learned several Potawatomi words and phrases and used them when he could.

"At our mission your children will learn to read and write and speak in the white man's language," Isaac continued. "They will also learn new ways to grow crops and use tools to build cabins and furniture and fences. They will use the ways you have taught and white man's ways."

Occasionally Isaac heard murmurs drift through the crowd. Unsure if his words were met with approval or rejection, he waited for Abraham to inform him.

Encouraged by a positive response he told the adults, "You will also be welcome to come to the mission to attend church services or to get assistance with farming or building."

"We want boys and girls to come to our school. Girls will learn to make clothing and cook and preserve food for long winter months." He saw many nods of approval until he mentioned that they, too, would learn to read and write. Quickly, he changed the subject by telling them when the school was ready he would send someone to their villages to let them know.

"We would like the boys and girls to live in our mission buildings. They will receive clothing and food here. They will be well taken care of, with safe places to sleep and work. We will give them permission to visit in your villages. You are always welcome to come to the mission to visit them."

Suddenly, Chief Topinabee rose and stretched. Everyone else followed his lead. "We will think on what you said," he stated, shaking Isaac's hand. "We did not think there were any more good people among the whites." He leaned heavily on Pokagon's shoulder as he made his way toward the horses. One by one they all departed.

Isaac, worn out from the day's event relied on Christiana's assistance as they trudged toward their cabin. They stopped near the group of mission workers and children who were picking up bowls and cups. "Thanks to my beloved wife and the work of all of you, this is a day to be remembered!" he said contentedly.

A light snow began falling. The fires diminished. "It is so quiet," said Delilah as she and Johnston Lykins finished the final cleanup.

"Yes, very peaceful," he agreed. "The first day of 1823 was very special. When we get our buildings finished and receive new students I know more good days will occur. I'm anxious to have school start, aren't you?"

Delilah nodded, secretly wishing she could be in some of his classes. Rice hurried to catch up with them, amused to see his sister glaring at him as they headed to the cabins.

The McCoy cabin was still unfinished and uncomfortably cold, but as the snowfall increased in the night the inhabitants were thankful to be out of the weather.

Ten days passed and still no supply wagons arrived. Johnston and Rice bravely volunteered to go to Fort Wayne for supplies. "We can't just remain here and watch everyone starve. Most likely we will meet up with the wagons returning from the Fort. We will return with them," Johnston stated.

6

Blowing snow formed three foot drifts along the back of buildings. Four buildings were enclosed but only three had usable fireplaces. The fire in the newly completed cooking cabin had to supply meals for fifty people.

"Religious services appear to be attended by cold hearts as well as cold feet," Isaac commented to his wife as they left evening prayer services.

"This nasty weather and our constant hunger gives everyone a sour face," Christiana replied.

"The best way to keep warm is to keep busy," the adults repeatedly told each other and any child who stood idle. In spite of discomfort everyone continued to prepare for the school's opening. Now that the cabins were finished the men and boys built long benches and trestle tables for eating and smaller benches for school and worship.

When Isaac felt strong enough, he worked on re-assembling the loom they had moved from Fort Wayne. Christiana was eager to teach girls to weave. Calvin moved the spinning wheel from the loft and Delilah started spinning wool they had brought into yarn. Christiana taught her young daughters to knit so they, in turn could teach others. The cabin, already crowded with people, now became congested with spinning wheels and the loom. "I'm always bumping into something!" complained Christiana as she tried to step around things.

To add to her frustration, poorly dressed Indian children appeared daily, sent by their families to attend the new school. "Put another kettle of water to heat," Christiana told Delilah, as she saw new faces at the door. "Then go find Fawn so she can help with the bathing." It required at least three strong adults to control the kicking and wiggling as the children fought their cleanup. Once the bath was over and their hair rid of lice they were dressed as properly as could be, using clothing from the limited supply. Their old filthy clothing was tossed on an outdoor bonfire.

On the thirteenth of January, four men leading two horses staggered into the yard. They were exhausted and nearly frozen. Josephus dropped the armload of firewood he'd been carrying and rushed to help them. "Mama, Papa! Open the door!" When Isaac saw the men he ran outside. Christiana pulled on her shawl and started after him, but stopped, shocked, when she recognized Rice. Stifling a cry, she slowly moved toward the snow-covered men. "Oh! please God, let them be all right!" Together they managed to get the men indoors and removed their icy garments.

Later, situated by the fireplace, Johnston was the first to recover and spoke through chattering teeth. "We found these men two days ago. They were on the way here but the oxen strayed one night. They'd searched two days but couldn't find them." He shook his head sadly. "We'll have to get the wagon later. The men tried carrying sacks of meal on their backs but got so weak they had to drop them. Probably the other things on the wagon will be ruined."

Christiana heard Isaac gasp as the full realization hit. "No supplies and no oxen," he said with tears in his eyes. "No money to buy more." He stood up slowly then sagged to the floor. With help from Josephus, Christiana managed to get him onto the bed. She sat by his side, rubbing his hands and face, relieved when color returned. Johnston moved stiffly to her side, then led her to a chair by the fire.

"I don't know how but somehow we will manage, sister McCoy," he said gently.

"We've got to be more sparing in our food allowance." Christiana said.

"Mama, how can we eat less?" asked Delilah as she looked

at all the thin pinched faces in the cabin.

Christiana shrugged and turned to hide her tears. She didn't want anyone to know how worried she was. "The children need nourishing food. The adults are stronger. We still have some flour. We will just have to stretch what we have!" She turned back to the group gathered in front of the fireplace. "Someone will have to recover our lost wagon and bring back those supplies. We don't have money to buy more." She straightened her shoulders. "God will supply our needs!"

Snow continued to fall. Packed down snow made the paths slippery and difficult to walk. Still, children continued to appear. Near the end of the month there were thirty children at the mission. Food supplies were nearly depleted. Difficult as it was, everyone continued working and preparing for school to open.

"Working makes me feel warmer," one of the hired men claimed.

"Makes time pass faster," said another. "Helps me ignore my rumbling stomach too." All their hard and faithful work impressed the McCoys.

On January 29th, after morning devotions, Christiana bundled up her children, gathered all other children in Singing Bird's care, and marched them all to the school. Isaac followed, calling everyone they saw along the way to come along. All of the benches were filled when he took his place at the teacher's desk. Talking stopped as he stood before them and presented a brief dedication ceremony he had prepared for the first day of school.

The log building was still without a floor, had no shutters over the windows, no door and no chimney. Animal pelts hung temporarily over the openings.

Before breakfast Christiana had had Johnston go over and build a fire in the center of the large room. "I don't care if the building isn't finished," she said determinedly, "We promised to begin classes in January and this is the day!"

At first he had objected although he was as anxious as she to start teaching. "I don't think we will be warm enough there but maybe if I pull the benches around the fire we will be all right," he had said meekly.

Neither one of them anticipated the smoke problems. It swirled around them, causing their eyes to sting and made them cough. In spite of discomfort, lessons were taught all morning. After a skimpy lunch the girls remained in the kitchen cabin. They cleaned up the dishes and began classes in sewing and knitting. The boys chopped wood and carried armfuls to all the cabins. Men ignored other jobs and built a schoolhouse door and shutters. Much to Christian's satisfaction a routine had been established.

Days began at six o'clock when McCoy's son Calvin, an early riser, agreed to blow his trumpet. Everyone attended morning prayers before the six thirty trumpet called them to breakfast. They waited in line until Christiana rang a small hand bell. Oldest students ate first. When they were dismissed for chores the younger children were fed.

At eight-thirty all pupils and teachers went to school. They were dismissed at noon and at twelve-thirty meals began. At two the students were called to afternoon training and dismissed at six. Supper began at six-thirty. Between sunset and dark the whole mission family gathered for evening prayers, singing and scripture readings. Rev. Isaac usually expounded on Bible passages. Bedtime came early. There was total silence after nine o'clock.

School was suspended on Saturdays. Boys did chores in the morning but were given a half day for recreation. Girls had kitchen duty every afternoon. On the Sabbath only two meals were eaten. The trumpet was used at ten-thirty and four-thirty to announce worship time for the mission and its neighbors.

By February, even with much scraping, Christiana was not

able to come up with enough flour to make bread. She wrapped her warm shawl around her shoulders. Praying for help, she headed for the school. Slowly a plan formulated in her mind as she trudged through new snow. She smiled to herself. When she reached the class where Johnston was teaching arithmetic to teenage boys, she motioned for him to join her.

"I used the last of the flour this morning," she whispered.

Johnston looked startled. "What will we eat?"

"I think if we send a couple of these boys to Bertrand's trading post they might be able to get us some."

"How can that be, since we have no money?" Johnston asked, amazed that she had forgotten that fact.

"They can tell him when our supply comes from Fort Wayne we will replenish his supply. I think he will agree."

Although Johnston was skeptical, he chose two students to make the trip. Happy to be out of school for a day, they listened to Christiana's instructions as they walked to the horse corral with her. She watched as they rode off the mission property, then closed her eyes in silent prayer.

Just before dusk the nearly frozen but smiling boys rode in with a large sack tied to each horse. Johnston saw them coming and greeted them with pride and happiness. Only he and Christiana knew the details of the event and never told anyone else except Isaac.

Every morning Isaac studied the sky, wishing the dark snow filled clouds would move away. "All the deer have moved deeper into the woods to search for food. Sending someone out to hunt is fruitless," he commented at breakfast.

Christiana shook her head in despair. "I wish the wolves would move back into the woods. Their nightly howls are sounding closer. Everything is hungry, just like us. I hate to tell you but our flour is nearly used up again."

"We must ration our remaining food," Isaac said sadly.

"You have done a remarkable job of keeping us nourished. We must feed the children. The adults will have to endure with less. Two meals a day will have to be enough."

Looking around the table at thin sad faces and hearing unhealthy coughs made mealtimes even more depressing to the McCoys. "Sometimes it's really difficult to be thankful," admitted Christiana. "Again, I wonder why we were sent here. Yet I trust in the Lord, so I just keep hoping tomorrow will be better. There is too much sickness here, not enough food, no mail gets through, no supplies come and I am very weary!"

"You have every right to be tired and discouraged but I, too, trust in God and know He will see us through this dark time." His voice broke as he swallowed hard to suppress tears. Hoping to leave the cabin before his wife saw just how upset he was, he pulled on his warmest coat and moved toward the door. "I'm going to help the men build."

The men watched him approach. One of them stepped out to talk. "We know it isn't your fault but it is not good to always be hungry. We are not able to lift logs or saw boards when we are so weak." Isaac nodded his head in understanding. "Joe has volunteered to ride to Fort Wayne for supplies."

Isaac's face brightened. He would never have asked one of these hard working hired men to take on this difficult assignment but if it could be done, then Joe, the youngest and healthiest, could manage. "We will all be eternally grateful if he will. I will write some letters for him to take to store owners and Baptist officials."

Isaac rubbed his chin as he thought about the venture. "I think he needs companions for the trip. Let me think about who to send with him." He smiled as he looked at the men. "Thank you all for your support and work! You have made me very happy this morning. My day started out all bad. Now things seem much better!"

As he walked briskly back to the cabin Johnston joined him.

"I overheard the offer to go to Fort Wayne. I want to volunteer also," he said. Isaac started to object but Johnston continued, "There are so few students right now that I won't be missed. My presence on the trail and at the Fort would no doubt be more valuable. I am healthy and willing to go. Please, consider it!"

Isaac and Christiana sat by the fireplace for an hour discussing the men's offer. The more they talked the more reasonable the plan seemed. They agreed Johnston could also go.

They were pleased when their son Rice came from Dusenbury's cabin where he'd been staying. "I would like to go back to Fort Wayne," he said. "Please, will you allow me to do it?"

"Not this time son. You tried if before. You are only fifteen and that's too young for so much responsibility," said his father.

"I knew you would say that," he replied. "You have been so busy you forgot my birthday. Tomorrow is January twenty-sixth, my sixteenth birthday. I am almost an adult!"

His parents smiled at his remarks but didn't change their minds. Unhappily, Rice stormed out slamming the door.

The following morning everyone bid farewell to Johnston, hired man Joe and Samuel, an eighteen year old Indian student with family in Ft. Wayne whom he longed to visit. They were given as much food and blankets as could be spared. The February sky looked amazingly clear. Singing Bird said it was a good omen.

A few days later Isaac decided he'd go to Bertrands'. Bundling up into extra trousers and stockings, he threw a blanket over his head and shoulders and mounted his trustworthy horse. The snow was over two feet deep with drifts several feet deeper. The horse often stumbled. Even though a trail had been recently broken no footprints were visible. His frosty breath filled the air. The sun sparkled on new fallen snow. The cloudless sky was blue. Watching the sun for direction, Isaac was still unsure if he was headed correctly. He felt concern for Joe, Johnston and Samuel, wondering how far they had gotten.

Suddenly he caught a glimpse of a building beyond the trees. A whiff of smoke filled the air. Relieved, he knew he was nearing the trading post. Dogs began to bark as he approached. Bertrand rushed out to quiet them. "McCoy! Look at you, get in by the fire. You're all frosty and cold. What you doing here?"

Isaac dismounted and led his horse to the porch rail, where he tied and blanketed him. Bertrand was horrified when he saw how emaciated Isaac had become in a month's time. "Friend McCoy," he said in his broken English, "you look hungry. Madeline feed you," he said, then yelled for his wife to come. "Tell me why you here? No one come for many days. Too much snow."

Isaac was surprised to learn that Johnson and the others had not stopped at the post but wasted no time in telling his friend about the mission's need for food. Madeline brought in a large wood bowl of rabbit stew. He felt so guilty eating it, thinking of his starving family, that he didn't really enjoy it.

Bertrand sadly shook his head. "I not receive supplies," he said. "I not able to help all you need."

Isaac sat in front of the fireplace shivering. "I understand, but now that makes two problems. We desperately need food and I have only a small amount of cash. I was praying that you would allow me to pay what I can and I promise to give you more when the mail comes through with my check. Maybe I can find Indian villages where they might have corn or grain stored."

"NO!" thundered Bertrand. "You not understand! You not find huts this weather. Snow too deep. Most Indians not winter here. Go north to trap furs. You get lost in whiteness. You follow path back to your mission."

"I can't face those hungry children, Bertrand," Isaac said, tears running down his cheeks.   "This week three men from our mission left for Ft. Wayne to get supplies but I'm not sure we can survive until they return."

"Well now," he rubbed his chin. "If that bad, friend, I give you half of all I've got. If you starve, I starve!" He looked Isaac squarely in the eye. "I'll give you now. When you get supplies, you give me back. I load your horse and one of mine. You get warm."

"I can't take half of all you have," objected Isaac.

"You got lots of mouths to feed. I hate myself I not help a friend."

"You are a good man Bertrand! God will bless you for this!" said Isaac as he sat by the fire drying his clothes.

When he joined his friend outside he found bags of meal and other supplies tied to the horses. Just before he mounted his horse one of Bertrand's sons appeared, handing him six rabbits he'd taken from traps that morning. "Makes good soup," said Bertrand with a loud laugh.   "Little meat, lots of water."

The sun had disappeared. Gray sky suggested snow would soon be falling again. Isaac followed the snowy trail he'd made earlier in the day. Nevertheless, he grew extremely tired and cold.

Big flakes of snow began falling. Just at dusk, his snow covered body hunched over, he rode onto the mission property. Rice and Josephus had been chopping wood. When they saw their father they hurriedly lifted him from his horse. "Papa, can you walk?' they asked. "Your clothes are soaked through. Lean on us. We'll get you inside, then we'll take care of these sacks and the horses."

Christiana was so relieved to see him she didn't even scold.

She helped get him into warm dry clothes. He sat by the fireplace and was able to tell his family where he'd been and what Bertrand had said and done for them. The boys dragged the meal sacks and frozen rabbits into the cabin. The family was overwhelmed by Bertrand's generosity. Beans, dried apples and squash plus dried fish, a quarter of venison and a bag of cornmeal lay before them.

"Oh, look at this," Christiana said pulling a small deerskin bag of herbs from a larger sack of dried chicory roots. "Madeline sent me more medicine. Bless her!"

"We haven't seen food like this for months," said Isaac.

Christiana tearfully gathered the children around and offered a prayer of thanksgiving to God and the Bertrands.

In a matter of minutes cornmeal was added to a pot of boiling water so the family could enjoy a taste of hot mush before going to bed. After the children and Isaac were asleep Christiana pulled on her shawl and carried the rabbits to the kitchen cabin. Fawn and Singing Bird were getting ready to climb into the loft but instead joined her in skinning the animals. After they started kettles of rabbit stew cooking for the next day, Fawn carefully cleaned the rabbit fur for stuffing moccasins.

Christiana did a great deal of thinking as she walked back to her cabin. She realized how foolish Isaac had been to go out by himself. She knew how embarrassing it was to ask for help. Thanks to a good God there were people willing to help each other, she thought. If only she wasn't so tired and Isaac was healthier and the winter would end soon and the food supply didn't run out, then maybe they could make it. Back inside the cabin, she banked the fire for the night and crawled into bed still fully clothed.

Three days later supplies were again running low. Christiana tried not to think about it as she had Fawn add more and more water to dried fish broth.

Walking to school one morning, Christiana was startled to see an elderly Indian squaw riding in on a pony. A basket heaped with dried corn was tied to its side. Abraham was walking near by and came to interpret. "This woman wishes to donate food to us."

That afternoon two young women arrived, pulling a sled loaded with baskets of corn, nuts and dried squash and a bark dish of maple sugar. They set their gifts by the school door. Too shy to say anything, they were curious enough to peek through the window before they left.

Christiana was grateful but concerned. Surely this harsh winter was difficult for them too. Yet they were willing to share. She wondered how they knew of the mission and it's needs.

Shortly that question was answered when one of Bertrand's sons arrived with more rabbits and to take their horse back home. "My Papa spread word to everyone who comes to trading post," he told the McCoys. He stayed for lunch, then spent the afternoon teaching the young boys how to make and set traps for squirrels and rabbits. "Make good soup," he said, sounding just like his father.

Several days of clear weather followed, making everyone's jobs easier. With one hired man still gone, building construction went slower but Christiana was pleased to see them split logs for the school's puncheon floor. "With the spring thaw coming, mud will certainly be everywhere. A wood floor will be healthier and cleaner," she told Fawn and Singing Bird as they prepared more rabbit for the evening meal.

The smoky fires in the school and unfinished cabins continued to inflict everyone with coughs and sore red eyes. "Once the snow melts we will locate rocks for building chimneys," the men promised.

Christiana was startled one morning as she stepped outside

to get a breath of fresh air. Three Indian women were peeking into her cabin. She went back into the classroom to call Abraham to be interpreter, then walked with him to greet them. "Have them come inside to get warm," she told him. Shyly they entered. They had never been inside a white man's home and were fascinated. "They want to know if they can touch your things," said Abraham.

"Tell them they are welcome guests and I would like them to sit down in the chairs by the fire."

They tried the chairs and giggled at their dangling feet. Christiana's rocking chair amazed them.   They carefully stroked the soft quilt on the bed. They laughed with delight when the trundle bed was pulled out. Abraham explained to them that it was for children. They climbed into the loft and admired the rocking cradle stored there. "If it is for a baby, where is baby?"   Abraham kept busy answering all their questions.

Christiana learned their names were Moonbeam and White Feather.   The third girl was Theresa, one of Bertrand's daughters. They pronounced hers, 'Christian'. They so enjoyed repeating it she didn't correct them.

At the end of their visit, each one pulled a deerskin bag from under her blanket shawls and presented them to Christiana. One was filled with ground cornmeal, one was dried cranberries and Theresa gave herbs for tea. She explained with Abraham's help that, "It is woman's work to grow corn and food and try to produce surplus for giving. Giving brings prestige. We share."

Christiana thanked them for their gifts. "I am honored that you came and brought them."

"It is appropriate to return a gift," Abraham whispered.

She looked around, embarrased at her meager possessions, wondering what to offer them. Noticing their cold red hands, she went to a storage chest used for sitting beside the fireplace.

Opening it she pulled out three pairs of mittens students had made back in Ft. Wayne. She presented them with great dignity. First she helped Moonbeam pull hers on, then moved to White Feather and Theresa and did the same.

Keeping them on, they smiled and went around the cabin touching things again. Christiana smiled as they stroked her light brown hair and stared into her blue eyes. She was used to Indian children doing these things. They had only seen dark eyes and black hair. The women suddenly grew tired of the investigation and departed without a word. Christiana had Abraham run after them. "Tell them I'd like to have them visit again."

7

On the morning of February thirteenth, Christiana headed toward the school. She walked briskly, holding little Eleanor. The frozen ruts of the path hurt her feet, right through the soles of her hightop shoes. The child whimpered as they turned into the wind. "I know you're cold, baby," she said lovingly, as she drew her closer under the woolen shawl. "We'll go inside as soon as we find Papa. I have to tell him something." She stopped. "Listen! It sounds like a wagon coming."

Lifting her heavy skirt with her free hand, she ran toward the trail as fast as she could. Two men stopped their work to watch her. "Someone is coming!" she shouted.

"It's our supply wagon!" called Josephus, who was running toward them. Chopping wood close to the trail, he had seen the wagon approaching and was now running to alert the others.

Out of breath, he stopped by his mother, hugging her and

his tiny sister. Christiana fell to her knees in gratitude. The long hungry wait was over. "Thank you, God, for saving us from another day of want," she prayed. Josephus took Eleanor from his mother and helped her to her feet. Joe, their hired man, guided a team of horses into the yard. They pulled the wagon to a halt right beside them.

"Joe and Samuel, you have no idea how glad we are to see you!" she called to them. "You not only managed to reach Fort Wayne, you found our wagon and got back safely. What a blessing! I guess the oxen are lost?"

Joe nodded, "Couldn't find them Mrs. McCoy. I'm sorry." He climbed stiffly down and reached into the wagon to uncover two small girls. Young Samuel jumped to the ground and looked shyly at Christiana. "I know you don't need more mouths to feed but I have been praying you will let my sisters come to your school." Without a minute's hesitation, Christiana reached up to help the girls down from an assortment of sacks and boxes.

Isaac came running from the school, followed by all the students and their teachers. "This is a day to remember!" Isaac shouted. "Thank the Lord! Thank the Lord!" Suddenly, after looking around, Isaac realized Johnston was missing.

"Why isn't Johnston with you?" he asked. Delilah pressed close to listen to the answer.

"He stayed in Fort Wayne to talk to Baptist leaders. He will be returning in a few days."

The McCoys sighed in unison. Delilah's face turned pink as she smiled. Christiana felt a great sense of relief. She truly admired Johnston, plus his ability to teach allowed her more time to carry out her motherly duties.

As they walked from the wagon Daniel got close to talk to Joe, "Did you see my wife and children? Are they all right? Will they be coming soon?"

When Joe smiled and answered 'yes' to all his questions

Daniel brushed a tear from his face and turned to help unpack.

Isaac and Rice lifted the tarp, uncovering three barrels of flour and sacks of meal. Men and boys began to carry supplies to the cooking cabin. Several boxes and crates were taken to the school. Children skipped along behind, eager to see what they contained.

Isaac and Daniel carried the largest crate. They pried open the lid so the curious children could peer inside. "We'll open just this one now, but no unpacking until lessons are completed," Daniel said. The children happily recognized clothes and shoes and their excitement was hard to control. The teachers couldn't help smiling as they watched frequent quick glances toward the boxes. Just before lunch all crates were opened and everyone crowded around.

Families back at Ft. Wayne had donated used clothing. Christiana was pleased. "We can alter these garments and put them to good use," she said, as the girls and boys pulled things from the crate. "We'll have a 'trying on' party later."

Christiana spent the early afternoon in the kitchen, humming happily as she scooped cups of flour from a barrel and began making bread. "We have to divide up this flour and take some to the Bertrands, but today I want to see the whole amount," she told Fawn. "No cornmeal tonight!" she promised.

The girls put dried apple slices into a crock to soak in water while they began preparations for making cobbler. "Tonight we will have real stew," said Delilah who was adding dried vegetables to pieces of rabbit already boiling in the kettles.

Samuel's sisters spent the afternoon in the McCoy cabin. First, Singing Bird tossed their filthy clothes into the fireplace. They watched the flare of fire while being scrubbed in a tub of soapy water. When they were clean and dried, Singing Bird searched through the supply of clothing until she found some to fit them. She brushed their hair, then gave them bowls of broth to eat. Samuel came to the cabin to see them, and told

Singing Bird how relieved he was that they were now a part of the mission. He helped Singing Bird convince them to sleep in the corner bed, another new experience for them.

Singing Bird returned to the kitchen cabin. "The girls were too tired from their long cold journey to even miss their mother," she told Delilah. "They are clean, fed, and asleep in your bed."

While the kettles of food bubbled over the fires, the women and girls returned to the school and spent the afternoon sorting clothing. Large flower bedecked bonnets were drawn from the depths of the crate. The girls took turns wearing them as they paraded around benches laughing.

Christiana groaned inwardly as the impracticality of items became apparent. Along with the hats were high heeled, pointed-toe shoes, lace trimmed shirts, frilly underclothes and summer garments. "The previous owners no longer wanted these items and evidently thought them good enough for charity gifts."

"Look, Mama," whispered Delilah. "These things are not even clean."

On close examination Christiana found torn seams and buttons missing. Saddest of all was the fact that there were very few children's things and nothing for boys and men. Brushing aside tears of disappointment, she allowed the girls to continue playing.

"These fancy things are cheering the children," she said to the women, "But, most of these things have to repaired and stored for summer or discarded."

While the women and children kept busy. the men and older boys gathered in the Dusenbury cabin. Joe and Samuel recalled their difficult journey to and from Ft. Wayne.

"Crossing frozen rivers and streams was the easiest part. It was the deep snow drifts and unbroken trails that were hardest," said Joe.

"When we found the wagon the wheels were frozen fast to the ground. We had a hard time digging them loose and getting our horses yoked to it," Samuel admitted.

"Fortunately, where we found it was only a short day away from the fort, 'cause we didn't have very sturdy hitching," Joe added. "The oxen were never found according to people we questioned at Fort Wayne."

Isaac shook his head in despair. "Did you have problems getting supplies?" he asked. "How did we pay for them?"

"Well sir, we gave the letters you sent along to the Church leaders and they issued a money check for purchasing items at the trading post," replied Joe. "I guess we spent it all because we didn't get any money back."

"Some of the people living in Fort Wayne gave clothing and blankets. My mother's people sent vegetable seeds and dried squash. They also gave food for us to eat in our travel," said Samuel. He looked shyly at Christiana. "My mother is not well. She gave my sisters to me to care for. I thought it best to come back here." Christiana patted his arm and smiled. "You did the right thing."

"Was there any mail there for us?" asked Isaac.

"Only these reply letters from the people at the Baptist Church and the trading post. There is a note from Mr. Johnston too." Joe said. Pulling three grubby letters from his pocket, he handed them to Isaac.

"Thank you, Samuel and Joe, we all thank you! You deserve our deepest gratitude and a long rest. Tomorrow we can unpack the building supplies you brought. You go get some sleep," Isaac told them, patting them on their backs as he guided them toward the door. "There will be food waiting when you wake."

Clutching the precious letters in his hand, Isaac hurried back to his cabin. Christiana found him later, seated at his corner desk. He started to hand her the pages but she shook her head. "Just tell me what they say."

"They are concerned for our health and well being and say they hope we now have enough supplies to last the winter. I can't believe they are so naive! Surely they must know we have many mouths to feed, plus clothing needs and medicines and books and other school supplies and tools and--."

Christiana put her arm around his shoulder, "Hush! Don't get all upset like this. Of course they know." She sighed, "I'm just wondering if they think we are not good stewards. It doesn't seem as if they think we are using things wisely."

"That is not the worst problem, my dear. They did not send money for my salary. We still owe people in Fort Wayne. I promised Bertrand some money. Now, I don't have any," Isaac's eyes watered and he brushed a hand across his face.

"What is the delay, Isaac? The payment will come, won't it?"

He shrugged his shoulders. "I'm afraid if Johnston can't convince them of the urgency I'll have to make the trip back myself to get this straightened out." He caught her look of despair. "Don't worry, I'm not planning to go just yet. I do need to go to Bertrand's however."

"Remember, Bertrand said he would accept some of our flour and meal as payment. He needs the supplies so he can trade with the Indians. I don't think paper money is too useful to him. As for our other problems, we will continue on sparse rations. We are going to manage!" said Christiana.

Once again, Isaac marveled at his wife's determination and faith. "We can't help but succeed with you as an example!" he said rising to hug her before they walked to the kitchen cabin where Christiana helped ladle food into bowls. The first hearty meal in many days temporarily erased unpleasant memories.

After all had been fed, the McCoys led everyone back to the school. They joined hands sharing in evening prayer which ended: "We thank you Lord, for the arrival of our supply wagon. We give thanks that for the first time in a long time we have all been well fed. Help us to remember this celebration as we return to our more frugal meals and daily routines."

Late afternoon toward the end of February, just as the girls were setting the tables for supper, Johnston Lykins rode in. A heavily loaded packhorse was tied to his own. Mealtime was forgotten in the excitement of greeting him and watching him unpack.

Besides his personal belongings, he had collected several textbooks, slates for the students, paper, pens and ink. Everyone watched as he opened packages containing hammers, nails and other small tools. The girls were fascinated to see needles and thread and several yards of flowered material he'd brought for them. Delilah seemed especially excited.

Christiana noticed her oldest daughter openly staring at Johnston. Delilah blushed as she realized her mother was watching her. Christiana shook her head as she glanced from Johnston back to thirteen-year-old Delilah. Returning to the table, she called Delilah to help slice bread.

Isaac pulled Johnston aside to talk. "It is very good to have you back safely. I can't help but notice all the things you bought. Does that mean you received your salary?"

Johnston's face beamed. "I am pleased to inform you that you are correct! I have your check right here, plus some letters," he said, handing them to Isaac.

Tears welled in Isaac's eyes. "Thank you for staying in Fort Wayne long enough to accomplish what I was beginning to think was impossible." He sighed "Now I can pay some of our bills. What a burden you have lifted tonight!" he said through his tears of gratitude.

After the children were asleep, Christiana pulled the rocking chair next to her husband's desk. "We need to have a serious conversation," she said, taking his hand. "Our children are growing up, Isaac. Today I saw Delilah showing interest in a young man. It frightened me. She has been on my mind often recently. Much as I hate the idea, I'm thinking it might be time to send her to a boarding school so she can receive opportunities she can't get living here."

Getting no response from her husband, she continued. "Our boys need more experienced teachers and advanced courses than we can offer. I'm not just talking about our sons, I mean all the boys as they get above sixteen."

Isaac reached over to pat her knee and smiled. "I've had these same thoughts, my dear. It is my greatest hope that when the boys have learned everything they can here at our school we will be able to get them into a college."

Worried that Isaac might be thinking it was only important for boys to get advanced training, Christiana made a new point. "Girls deserve instruction in music and art and social niceties before settling down to be wives and mothers. Some might like training to be teachers."

Isaac looked at her in astonishment. "Of course! I realize education is important for all children. My concern is how to finance any child's schooling. It's hard to believe I received the check from the mission board tonight and already I don't have enough money to do what needs doing."

He shook his head in despair. "Money isn't our only concern. I know how hard you work and what a good teacher you are. You have been overburdened, caring for all the students and our own family, plus a sickly husband. We have Johnston back now to help and I am feeling much improved. We must all concentrate on teaching to our best ability."

Christiana interrupted. "We can only teach what we know. What worries me is whether we can teach them enough. Some of these children may want to become doctors or lawyers or ministers."

"Believe me, I understand. I have been thinking about

sending letters to schools and possible donors so when we have students ready to advance, they will have the place and means to go," Isaac assured her.

Christiana suffered pangs of regret for having mentioned the subject. She wanted the children to have opportunities and, of course, to live good productive lives but she did not want to be separated from them.

"Oh, Isaac, I feel sad at the thought of sending them away to school. What if they don't come back to us after they sample town life?"

"Christiana, where is your faith? First you worry about keeping them isolated here. Now you worry about their going. I think we had best pray about the whole situation!"

When they went to bed, although she seldom cried, Christiana could not hide her tears. Isaac gently held and comforted her during the night.

Eventually warm March winds melted most of the February snow. After chores, the children played outside, having snowball fights and making snow forts. Sometimes they walked along the riverbank to watch as thick slabs of ice floated down the St. Joe.

Just when they were convinced winter was ending, more snow fell. Huge thick flakes covered pine trees in the surrounding forest. Christiana and her daughters were walking toward school one morning when the sky darkened and the wind blew in a freezing rain. "Run! To the building," she called to everyone in the yard.

Shortly, everything was coated with glistening ice. Trees bent over with the weight. Branches snapped off pine trees.

The teachers tried to carry on their lessons as usual. Occasionally someone would go to the window and exclaim about the storm's activities. When they tried to open the door and found it was frozen shut, they panicked. Fortunately Joe and other hired men were close enough to hear their cries and pried it open.

Walking became nearly impossible. The total yard was covered in ice and very slippery. At first the children thought it was fun to slide and even fall but after a few were seriously hurt changed their minds.

Drawing water from the well and carrying it to the buildings was very time consuming. The boys laughed as they tried sliding buckets along the path but when water sloshed over the sides the path became even more treacherous.

Chipping ice coating to loosen the woodpiles before they could carry in firewood made even that chore difficult. When cold logs were added to the fires, they sputtered and smoked as the sap inside thawed. The wood gave out less heat so meals took longer to cook.

"Good thing we got a shelter of sorts built for the animals," the hired men said as they fed and watered the few remaining cows and horses.

"The oxen don't seem to mind standing out in it. Guess it's because of their thick coats," said Joe.

"I don't know what would have happened to them if you hadn't gotten oats in Fort Wayne. There's no way they could get anything to graze."

"You think they'll be strong enough to plow, come spring?"

"We're in bad trouble if they can't be worked," said Joe as they finished chores. "What we need most of all before spring is a real blacksmith. Reverend McCoy says we have to have one according to the Indian treaty to start this mission. I haven't heard about us getting one. Daniel tries but he doesn't know all the tricks of the trade."

"I guess he will be going back to Fort Wayne come spring if his wife doesn't come. Maybe he'll find someone to replace him. Or else maybe he can buy rakes and hoes and shovels."

"What about plows? It sure would be better to make them here. I think Daniel Dusenbury is getting good at it. I would kinda like to learn how myself, wouldn't you?"

"What I'd like is for spring to come! Can't wait to smell that earth all worked up."

"Or, to taste some fresh greens?" replied Joe.

"Ah, spring will bring lots of good things!" they all agreed.

Snow, usually ten to fifteen inches deep, lasted until mid-March.

8

During the third week of March, cold blasts of winter finally ceased. Daylight lasted longer. Nights were cold but the sun felt warm. Snow melted and turned the ground into soft, sticky mud.

"You can almost smell spring in the air," said Isaac, coming in from an early morning walk. "Time to ready the plows!"

As adults stood around waiting for the children to finish their breakfast, Isaac told them he was planning to return to Fort Wayne. "I'm hoping to bring back a cow or two and maybe some pigs. I'll buy seeds too. Mostly it is extremely important that I locate some one willing to be our blacksmith"

"We're going to need more hired men to help with the plowing and farm work," Joe reminded him.

"I'll be looking for additional workers. What we really need is a smithy to make and repair tools. He could teach our older boys some manual skills. The original routine for the mission was one that mixes school work with outdoor work. After a long hard winter indoors we all need to tighten our muscles."

"It sure has been a hard winter," they all agreed.

"God willing, we'll be able to grow and store enough food this summer so we won't run short next winter," Johnston added.

"Part of the treaty agreement was to teach Indians to farm and build better housing, so we have lots of work ahead," said Isaac.

"Speaking of Indians, have you noticed more of them around the last few days?" asked Daniel.

"Yes, Singing Bird says they are returning from their northern trap lines," Johnston said. He looked at the other teachers and smiled.

The following Saturday afternoon a group of children were playing along the river bank and spotted several canoes approaching. Sarah and Anna McCoy ran back to the mission yelling, "Indian canoes are filling the river!"

Rice and Josephus, followed by Daniel and Johnston, ran to the shoreline, fearful that the Indians might be hostile. What they saw, as the boats glided past, were mostly women, children and elderly men. Curious Indians stared at the white settlers and strange log buildings, none of which were there when they left the area in the fall.

The mission group stood silently watching until they saw the canoes round the bend. A short distance beyond the Indians paddled the canoes to shore, climbed out, and disappeared into the woods.

The next few days Indians were seen moving leisurely among the trees, sometimes with hatchets in hand. One of the hired men secretly followed two of them and reported back.

"They stopped by a large tree, I think it was a maple, and struck it a hard blow. Sap came leaking out. Then they pushed a curved piece of bark into the wound and set bark pails underneath to catch the drips."

Gray Rabbit, a shy teenage Indian student, explained the activity. "They are collecting maple sap. The women boil it into syrup. When syrup hardens, it is used as sugar or sweetener. They trade sugar for supplies."

Singing Bird added to Gray Rabbit's statement. "Sap is also collected from birch and ash trees. We make it into medicine."

"Is it only done in the spring?" asked Christiana.

Gray Rabbit nodded her head. "Warm days after cold nights makes the sap run."

A few days later the sound of trees being chopped down caused new alarm. The men went to find out what was happening and found huge piles of firewood stacked in a clearing. Whenever they had the chance, the mission children raced into the woods. They hid behind trees to watch Indian women and girls collect sap buckets, then carry them down a dark path. Plans where made to investigate further on their next free Saturday.

With Delilah and John Calvin accompaning them, they quietly followed the path deeper and deeper into the woods. When they came upon the clearing, they hid and watched. A line of pails sat on the ground. Women came, picked them up and carried them to a large hollow tree which was laid upon big rocks. The women poured sap into it.

"It looks like an upside down canoe," whispered Sarah.

"Do they just leave the sap sitting there?" asked John Calvin. "Won't it spoil?"

"I'm not sure but it is getting dark. We'll have to come back another time."

Later that night, the smell of smoke awoke people at the mission. Isaac and Johnston had both left their beds to walk around buildings, trying to locate it's source. "It's coming from the woods," Johnston decided. "Let's get warm clothes on and a few more men and go scouting."

Eventually the burning wood smell led them to the clearing the Indians had made in the woods. They were amazed to see old men stirring hot liquid in large troughs over cooking fires. Large hot stones were removed from bonfires with wooden paddles and dropped carefully into the troughs.

"They're boiling sap," said Isaac softly. "Remember Gray Rabbit telling us about it? Let's not disturb them." Relieved that it was campfires, not a forest fire, they returned quietly to their cabins.

Between church services the next day the children returned to the woods. They had heard the men talking about the syrup cooking and wanted to watch. In the daylight they saw Indian children using pointed green branches to scoop hot rocks out of fires. They carried them to troughs and carefully slid them into the bubbling sap. Older girls removed cool stones the same way, then dropped them in buckets so they could be rinsed in the creek and then reheated. Women stirred with long paddles. When they lifted the paddles syrup dripped in long strings. The children sniffed the sweet aroma as they watched the process.

Occasionally, a paddle was lifted out over a pile of snow sheltered under a pine tree. The syrup dripping from the paddle would harden and form a candy. Laughing Indian children would grab handfuls and run into the brush to eat.

Although the mission children remained silent and hidden they did not go unnoticed. Two Indian women walked toward them smiling and motioned them to come join the tasting party. Knowing they must return for evening vespers, they grabbed pieces of the sticky syrup strings, said a quick "thank you", and ran back to the mission.

Christiana had been looking for her daughters and the other girls. She was surprised to see them running from the woods. She was even more puzzled when she noticed them licking their fingers.

Several evenings later men's loud shrill shouts and beating drums echoed from the woods. The noise frightened children at the mission and bothered the rest of the listeners.

After a couple of hours Isaac decided he had to take action. "Daniel, come with me. You too, Abraham. I may need an interpreter. We'll go investigate the trouble."

The three pulled on heavy coats and stepped out into the windy night. Clouds were blowing across the moon but it was bright enough to see the trail. They walked swiftly toward the noises and soon reached the sugar camp. From behind a clump of trees they watched an Indian celebration dance.

Obviously, the making of the maple sugar was finished. Birch boxes, wooden bowls, gourds, duck bills, anything hollow, were now full of syrup or hardened sugar.

Isaac and his companions were spotted and invited into the clearing. Abraham spoke to the son of one of the chiefs, then smiled and translated, "We are all invited to join them."

"We are already here," said Daniel.

"No, No," said Abraham. "Everyone at the mission is invited. We can watch the dances and eat," he said, jumping with excitement. "Can I go tell the others to come?"

Isaac started to reject the invitation but didn't wish to offend the Indians or keep his mission family from attending a party-like ritual. When he nodded 'yes', Abraham took off running. Isaac and Daniel moved into the clearing and sat on the ground near a fire.

Christiana bundled up all of the children in coats or blankets. Abraham led the way, more slowly this time. The men carried the youngest. Everyone else followed. Women carried loaves of bread to share in the festivities.

What they saw when they entered the clearing surprised them. Indian women and children were dressed in their finest embroidered and beaded deerskin outfits. Lifting first one foot and then the other, they swayed and shuffled in a slow moving circle around a blazing bonfire. Some of the Indian children from the mission joined the circle.

As the beating drum grew faster, women and children left the circle. Men began to dance. They had just returned from their winter trapping and hunting, and now enacted their experiences, chanting and shouting above loud drums.

Christiana hugged the youngest children close to her as the noise resounded. Fire bursts blazed from pine knots. Sparks shot high into the sky. Although the night was cold and damp, no one was aware of it.

During a time of rest, bowls of cooked rice mixed with syrup were passed around. Most of the hardened sugar was stored for later, but small pieces were offered to everyone, along with sweetened meat and corn cakes. Christiana added their bread to the shared food. It was torn off in hunks, which were then dipped in syrup.

The drums called dancers back into action but the repetition of the sounds and movements, added to full stomachs and late hour, caused the children to grow sleepy. Indian babies slept in their cradleboards, swaying from nearby tree branches. When the ceremony ended the McCoys gathered their mission family.

Teenage boys lit branch torches in the fire and led the way back to the cabins. "Being included in their celebration is a good sign, isn't it Isaac?" asked Christiana, as they walked hand in hand. "It is important to know the Potawatomi ways. I fear that our pupils may get homesick for their customs and language. We need to teach them new and useful ways of living but they should not forget their old ways."

"Much of their sugar is for trading. If we can improve their farming habits so they can eat all year, it will make life better for them," explained Isaac. "It will be good when they learn to speak white man's language. That way they won't get cheated. Our mission has many purposes."

"Not to change them completely, Isaac. That would not be right! We need to learn their language too, don't we?"

The temperature remained warm night and day. With the coming of the leaf buds, the sap stopped running from the trees. Snow completely disappeared. Chirping birds returned to the woods. April arrived. Isaac made plans to go to Fort Wayne. Daniel approached him with a letter to be taken to his wife.

"Brother Isaac, I think you know how very discouraged I am about life here at the station," he said sadly. "I'm very lonely for my family."

"I know you are, Daniel. It has been a very difficult winter for all of us."

"I'm afraid I'm not as dedicated as you, Isaac. I am thinking that I should go back to Indiana and get other work. I wrote to Grace. If she won't come here, then I feel I must leave."

Isaac shook Daniel's hand. "I understand. I will deliver the letter. I pray she will return with me!"

A few days later Isaac left the station with Rice riding beside him. The weather was fair but on occasion they saw areas of unmelted snow. Thin ice covered some of the rivers and broke under foot as they tried to cross. Evenings were spent drying their boots and stockings as they sat before their campfires.

One of the topics they discussed as they rode was, of course, the mission school. "While I am meeting with the Baptist leaders in Fort Wayne I plan to make some inquiries about advanced education for the mission students," said Isaac.

Rice surprised his father by saying, "Papa, I want to become a doctor. Josephus thinks he will be a doctor or teacher. Will we be able to do that?"

"Your mother and I have discussed the necessity of sending you children off to schools. Since we have no funds, I will have to investigate other means. We will be proud to have you children trained to serve others."

When they reached Fort Wayne, Isaac met with several Baptist officials. He was questioned at length about the school and its conditions. "How is your family and our other missionary brothers?" they asked.

"We suffered severely through the winter. Our unfinished

buildings didn't protect us much from the weather." He sighed. "The worst thing was times when our food supply ran out. If it hadn't been for our Potawatomi neighbors and trader Bertrand we would have starved," Isaac told them.

Sam Clark, the Board director looked at him sternly. "What do you mean? You left here in December with more than adequate supplies."

"Isn't wild game plentiful in your forest?"

Several of the men chuckled. Isaac glared at them. "Animals aren't easy to track or shoot in deep snow! Anyway, much of our supplies was lost in transit."

"Sounds like carelessness to me," scoffed a man Isaac hadn't met.

"The rivers were treacherous to cross. Mishaps couldn't be prevented," Isaac said sadly.

"Why didn't you come back here for more food?" asked Sam.

"We sent men back three times but wagons got stuck or broke down or oxen wandered."

"Well," Sam Clark interrupted, "let's not prolong this. You are here now. What is it you need to run your school, Reverend McCoy?"

Isaac reached into his pocket and pulled out his list. Scooting his chair closer to the oval table he studied his requests. "First of all I'd like to tell you that our school opened in January. Our missionary staff is nearing exhaustion what with teaching classes mornings and readying the buildings, building furniture, making clothing and cooking and caring for nearly eighty people."

"Really? It's grown that much?" asked the director, eyebrows raised in surprise.

"New students arrive almost daily."

"Well then, Reverend McCoy, you will be happy to know we have two teachers ready to return with you. James and

Martha Wright, a father and daughter missionary couple, have been assigned to your mission station."

Isaac was elated to hear this. He thanked the Board but continued making his requests. "I guess what we need most, gentlemen, is cash. I'd like to hire five or six men to help with building and farming. We desperately need a blacksmith. I'd like to purchase some cattle, four oxen and two wagons." He handed a piece to paper to the director. "These are the food supplies and tools we need to carry us over until crops can be grown."

"Seems like a lot of things, but knowing you, Reverend McCoy, I'm sure you are only asking for the basics. Most of these things we can get from our warehouse. I know there are boxes of donated clothing available. I imagine you can put it to good use."

"As missionaries we vowed to serve our Indian brothers and sisters, young and old. Every item we receive will be used toward keeping us healthy and active so we can teach and share with others," Isaac told the group before they adjourned. The group of men seemed very subdued after Isaac's humble statement.

As soon as she heard the McCoys were at the fort, Grace Dusenbury came with her children to visit them. Isaac gave her the letter from her husband. She read it eagerly. Brushing her tears away she told him she would be packed and ready to return with them. "I've been praying you would," Isaac said, putting his arm around her.

Each day Isaac asked the people he met for advice about getting his children into boarding schools and the mission students entered into colleges. He compiled a list and spent several evenings writing letters, which he then left at the fort to be mailed.

He and Rice visited nearby farmers. Eventually they were able to purchase twelve head of cattle and a few chickens with money a friend contributed.

Isaac met again with the Baptist Board members and discussed finances. He also pleaded with longtime church friends he met. However the only other money he received was a check from the Michigan Territory, his salary for teaching.

Baptist church leaders located some items on Isaac's list from the warehouse. They also arranged limited purchasing credit at the trading post. Many items weren't available and had to be forgotten.

"Reverend McCoy, every expenditure you ever make must be documented. Send the receipts for things purchased. Our Board will keep an account for the mission station," the Board chairman reminded.

Isaac grew weary of all the meetings and negotiations. "Son," he told Rice, "I'm anxious to leave but I hate to go without getting all the necessities. Your mother is going to be mighty disappointed in the selection of sewing materials."

"She also wanted large kettles. These are much too small," Rice said as he looked at the store shelves.

"Well, we did manage to get flour, seed corn and vegetable seeds. I talked the storekeeper into letting us take some nails, shovels and rakes, even though they weren't approved items. I haven't been able to get but one wagon and two oxen. I'll have to hire two men and their wagons with oxen to pull them."

"What are we using as money?" asked Rice.

"My teaching salary check. All my earnings go back into running the mission. We all agreed no one would profit from the work there."

Rice looked at his father in surprise. He felt pride in the fact that his father considered him old enough to know this information and was impressed at the commitment the adults had made. "In other words, you and Mama are working for no pay?"

"As are the others. At least for now."

He was able to purchase a used wagon and selected a strong team of oxen. Locating men with wagons and oxen willing to make the journey took several days. Once it was completed, they began to load supplies. The Wrights appeared one morning with a trunk and some crates which they were forced to repack.

"We sold most of our belongings. All we own is right here," said Martha, smiling at Rice who was about her age.

"You won't need many things," he said. "First of all there isn't much space for storing things and nothing we do there is very fancy."

"I don't expect to live fancy!" she replied with a haughty look. "We have been missionaries long enough to know that!"

"Well, you better dress warmer for traveling. You will freeze in that outfit. You'll be getting dirty too. Getting to the Michigan territory is a hard journey!"

Martha glared at Rice, turned and marched off toward the trading post.

9

By the fifteenth of April wagons were packed and the oxen were yoked. Isaac was busily tying three cows to the back of a wagon when a young boy rode up on his pony. His very pretty Indian mother walked behind him.

She spoke to Isaac in English. "I want my son to leave this place and go to your school. There is no future for him here. His name is 'Red Squirrel', you give him a Bible name and take him!"

"I will take him if he wants to go," Isaac told her. "If he doesn't want to go with us then I am afraid he will run away and bad things could happen to him."

She spoke to the boy. He slid from the pony and walked to Isaac's side. "I go," he said.

Isaac touched his shoulder. "I will call you Mark, your Bible name. We will be leaving tomorrow at daybreak."

"I will pack his belongings," the mother said and they headed back to the fort.

A few minutes later another interruption occurred. From out of nowhere, what seemed like a hundred sheep suddenly approached the wagons making a huge cloud of dust.

Isaac ran to steady the oxen and was surprised to see Rice and one of their church friends on horseback, using long cane-like poles to herd the charging animals.

"These sheep are for us!" yelled Rice, over the din of bleating. He jumped down and rushed to his father. "The church couldn't give us money but some of the members donated a few sheep each and now we have a hundred and ten."

The sheep ran until they found a meadow of grass and stopped to graze. Isaac was dumbfounded. He had no idea how to get them to the mission and even less of an idea what to do with them if he did get them there. Sheep were not something he wanted!

"What is going to keep them from wandering away tonight?" asked Isaac. "Someone needs to tell me how to herd them or raise them! I don't know anything about sheep habits or food!"

"We thought you'd be pleased," said several men who joined the McCoys. "These are good stock. They eat weeds out of any old field and make it fertile."

"Haven't you ever eaten mutton?"

"Shear their coats in the spring and you have wool. Your misses can spin it into yarn for mittens and stockings and hats. Can't believe you don't know these things already!"

Isaac stared at the scrawny looking, newly-sheared sheep.

They were all sizes and ages from new lambs to a large horned ram. "I 'm sorry if I seem ungrateful, but I really don't know a thing about sheep."

"We'll get them corralled in a fenced area tonight. Don't think you'll have problems keeping in line on the trail. They'll mainly follow the leader's bell."

"Can you spend some time tonight giving us more detailed instructions?" Isaac asked again.

"Sure," said William Bell, his Baptist friend. "Better than that, I can ride aways with you, tell you as we go." He laughed. "I've got a book I can give you. Seeing as how you are a teacher you'd probably like that."

Isaac shook his head. "I wish we had gotten an earlier start and avoided this last gift," he said to Rice as he sent him to locate the men who would be going with them. "Tell them we are leaving at sunrise but I need their help tonight. Better remind the Wrights too."

He smiled as he saw Rice blush. "When the men come to watch the animals we'll go help Grace Dusenbury pack her belongings. Maybe you should sleep in her wagon tonight. In the morning go over to where the Wrights are staying and get them aboard. We'll line up here."

Everything worked as planned. They were able to leave Ft. Wayne on the tenth of April. The men kept the sheep moving at a steady pace. As they rode, Isaac listened carefully to William's instructions about sheep raising. He was sorry to have him return to the fort after their noon meal.

"Crossing creeks could be exceedingly troublesome," Isaac told the men as they rode along. "All the snow melt has probably made the water very deep and running fast."

"One good thing," said Rice. "Mr. Bell said sheep don't seem to like moving water so they won't be wandering off. Actually, they are staying close to the trees."

"One bad thing," replied Grace Dusenbury who was

bouncing beside Martha on the wagon seat, "The trail is certainly bumpy and muddy!" The crates and trunks shifted, causing the sacks and barrels of food to tip. Grace constantly watched to make sure her children were safe. They teased to hop out and stretch their legs but their mother refused.

When they stopped the first night everything had to be repacked. Several men complained. "You didn't mention we'd have so much work on the trail."

"Plus the mud and damp ground to sleep on."

"The food isn't so good either!"

"Sheep are sure smelly!!"

The second day, closer to the waterways, the ground became more spongy. Several times each day everyone had to get behind the wagons to push them out of ruts. Fatigue made them all irritable.

Isaac's warnings about the deep water came true all too soon. At some crossings the sheep had to be actually dragged across. Grace's children held the squirming lambs in their arms as they huddled in the wagon. The stubborn oxen were unwilling to swim. The men wrapped ropes around their horns and pulled them with the horses. Tempers rose. One yoke of oxen grew too weak to continue. Their owner emptied his wagon and returned to Ft. Wayne. After several attempts at repacking, Isaac and Rice managed to stow the items in the remaining wagons. Two other men discussed going back to Ft. Wayne but then decided the return trip might be worse.

"We can certainly use your assistance in getting us to our destination," Isaac told them and was pleased when they continued with the group.

At the Elkhart River things grew worse. The dark rushing water frightened them all. They set up camp close to the shoreline. After scouting the area for a safe crossing the hired drivers decided not to risk it. They unloaded barrels of food from their wagon. Isaac tried to change their minds but in the morning they returned to Ft. Wayne. Isaac was disgusted and angry.

Isaac sent all but three men with the women and children. Mark rode his Indian pony in front of the wagons, trying to point out the driest path. They were to go downstream, hoping to find a more shallow and narrow crossing and wait.

After much discussion Isaac and the rest of the men came up with a plan for the unloaded supplies. They decided to take advantage of a tall hollow tree which had fallen near the shore. With a little work with an ax they made a large pirogue canoe, intending to transport some of the load down river. Two men sat amidst boxes and barrels, being careful to keep things well balanced.   As soon as they left shore it quickly became impossible to steer and control the canoe. The current was swift as a mill race. The canoe became entangled in a tree root extending from shore.

The men struggled desperately, until they worked the canoe free. The force of the river pushed them into another large root. They capsized. Floundering, gasping and grabbing each other, they managed to make their way to shore. Isaac and Rice stood, arms around each other, crying in frustration. Beans, potatoes and barrels of flour and salt were all lost.

Too exhausted to continue, the cold soaked men huddled together until morning. Chilled as they were, the next morning they followed the river downstream knowing they would be needed to help get the wagons and animals across.   They watched the water angrily as they walked. Isaac tried to ignore the men's whining voices. It startled him to hear someone happily shouting, "Hurry! Hurry! Come see!"

Running as fast as their stiff legs could go, they reached a bend in the river and saw some of their missing barrels caught in tree roots, others floating along the river. The wagons were already on the opposite shore. The current in this area was much calmer. The barrels had slowed enough to allow the men to wade into the water and grab them. Tired as they were, they rolled them up the bank onto dry ground.

After several hours of hard work, they had saved what they could. They were able to count eight and a half barrels of flour, two of cornmeal, and a little seed corn. That, with the boxes of dried fruit and articles of clothing still in the wagon, plus the animals, had been saved after all.

Isaac called to the group waiting across the river. "Wait there until morning. We are too tired to ford the river today!" he yelled. "At dawn tomorrow we will cross over!"

Maneuvering wagons and animals across took until noon. Grace and Martha had cooked coffee and mush for them. Wagons were again repacked with the remaining barrels. By evening they had advanced only a few miles. In spite of the hardships their mood improved.

The following two days travel went quite well. The second night as they set up camp, it began to rain. Next day a severe storm prevailed. High winds broke branches which crashed to the ground, frightening people and animals.

"It is safer under the wagons than in them," Isaac told his companions. "Grab some blankets and crawl underneath."

Soaking wet and cold, they huddled together through the dark unpleasant night. The storm lessened by morning and Isaac ventured out to check on conditions. Horrified, he found about seventy sheep had wandered away. Rice and Martha rode horses to search, others walked. In spite of rain and mud, Martha did not complain. Rice began to rethink his opinion of her. Discovering twenty sheep standing under some pine trees brightened their day. By nightfall all the searchers returned leading sheep. They had recovered all but one.

A temporary corral was made from fallen limbs. A second night was spent under the wagons. "Remember the Bible story, Papa, about the sheep getting lost?" asked Rice trying to give the group something to think about.

His father looked at him unhappily. "Yes, only in the story Jesus kept searching until he located the last missing lamb." He shook his head sadly. "I didn't do that well. Somewhere out there one sheep is still lost," he sighed. "We'll keep a watch as we travel but we must get back to the mission. Tomorrow we should reach Bertrands, then another day and we'll be home."

When they did arrive at Bertrand's trading post they enjoyed a warm fire and plenty to eat. "Seems like I always come here in miserable condition," Isaac said, apologizing to his friend.

Bertrand's hearty laugh, as usual, made everyone feel comfortable. They sat up half the night talking. Isaac had insisted on replacing supplies they borrowed over the winter. Early the next morning they reached the mission, surprising everyone at breakfast.

Daniel shouted with joy as he recognized the woman and children jumping from the wagon. "Oh, my dear ones!" he said, ignoring their muddy clothes and hugging them. "I was afraid you wouldn't come. I didn't really want to leave here but I was afraid you wouldn't come." Tears of happiness streamed down his face.

Christiana hugged the two women, happy to have more female companions. "Come inside, there is hot food enough for everyone," she happily announced. As places were cleared for them, Isaac began telling of their difficult journey and thankfulness for a safe return.

Christiana motioned for him to join her near the fireplace. "I thought I should remind you that on the thirteenth Josephus and Sarah had their birthdays."

"I remembered it when I was at Fort Wayne, but then it slipped my mind. I'll speak to them about it." He smiled as he suddenly thought of gifts for them. "Do you think a lamb would be a suitable gift for a nine year old girl? I could give the ram to Josephus.   It will need special attention and a separate pen, seems like a fifteen year old could manage that."

Christiana nodded in approval. She was overwhelmed with the addition of the sheep and cattle. Isaac explained to the mission workers how he had acquired the animals and told them how to care for sheep.

"How fortunate we will be to spin our own wool. We can knit plenty of warm winter things.   I'm so thankful!" Christiana said over and over.

Two of the hired men who had helped Isaac with the pirogue's disaster became very ill. "We hardly spent a day without wet clothes, what with rain and creek and river crossings," Isaac explained to Fawn, who was doctoring them. Fawn busily made herbal teas and mixed medicinal powders, forcing large doses into the men. She also made sure Isaac and the other travelers swallowed some remedies, just in case they might have picked up a sickness. "This stuff tastes so bad we'll get well just so we can stop taking it!" everyone agreed. In just a few days they were feeling fine.

With the addition of the Wrights, Christiana was allowed more time to organize afternoon sewing classes for the girls. Fawn taught them to make baskets from pine needles and from wood strips peeled from fallen ash trees.

Kitchen work became Singing Bird's full time work. Some of the girls enjoyed helping her prepare food but Christiana often had to step in and insist they also wash dishes and clean the floor.   Cooking and sewing were done not so much by choice but of necessity.

When the soil grew warm in the April sun farm work began. The men and boys made good use of the oxen. Fields were plowed as the soil dried. Hired men not only worked, they instructed and helped the boys. Vegetable seeds were planted in long rows, which was a new experience for the Indian boys. Some neighboring Indian men stood at the edge of the woods and watched with interest as split rail fences were erected and sheep and cattle were confined.

Indian women wandered uninvited into mission buildings day or night, observing the mission activities. Indian custom taught the sharing of food. Whenever Indians were hungry they helped themselves. Christiana was no longer startled to see them standing in the kitchen doorway watching her make bread, but when they grabbed a loaf cooling on the table and started eating she was annoyed.

"I know they gave us food this winter, but I wish they'd wait until I sliced them a piece," she commented to Singing Bird.

"They haven't learned your ways yet. They will in time."

"I know. I must be more patient. Well, at least we have taught the children to eat with spoons and from bowls."

"It is amazing to me how much you have taught them," said Martha as she helped in the kitchen. "I have seen how wretched and ignorant some of them are when they turn up on your doorstep or at the school."

"Yes," agreed Christiana. "However, we refuse no one!"

"I find it amazing there are now thirty-nine Indian scholars in our family. All of them are pursuing their studies and labors promisingly," Isaac commented. "Preparations for new crops are advancing well too. Tomorrow, May fourth, I will have the privilege of preaching at home! You can be certain I will be mentioning all the good things the Lord has allowed us!"

May brought drying winds. With the trail less muddy it became increasingly common to have white visitors appear at the mission. Most of them were searching for homestead land. They remained a few days, observing the routine, sharing whatever food was available and sleeping in their blankets before fireplaces in one of the cabins.

The McCoys were happy to have Squire Thompson return. After a few days of surveying with Isaac's help, he made his final choice of a location. Two of the pupils from the mission were chosen to help him build a cabin nearby along the river. He hired the use of a team of oxen and cleared and planted several acres of land. The boys agreed to keep an eye on things when he left to get his family in Indiana.

Unfortunately, not all visitors were so likable. Scruffy looking men wandered in hoping to trade liquor for food or horses. They were never refused a meal and usually moved on but Isaac worried that they might be heading for Indian villages. He feared they would take advantage of the Indians.

Whenever he got a chance, Isaac would spend afternoons riding to nearby villages. He tried to purchase potatoes and corn but it was impossible to obtain large quantities. He encouraged Indian adults to visit the mission and especially to send their children to school. He was heartbroken when he saw empty whiskey bottles or drunkenness.

Warmer weather and outdoor activities improved the health of the missionaries and children. Green edible plants sprouted in the meadows. Men and children caught fish in the river and streams. Garden vegetables grew in the planted rows. Corn seemed to grow over night.

Walking to school one morning Christiana felt the early stirrings of her eleventh child. "Things will be easier for you this time! You'll have better food and less work strain," Isaac said when she told him about the baby.

Mid-May a traveler arrived bringing a small bundle of mail. As he handed letters to Isaac he introduced himself. "My name is William Sears. I have been employed by the governor of the Michigan Territory. After you read his letter you'll understand why I am here."

Isaac read it twice. It instructed him to go to the Ottawa territory on the Black River. According to the 1821 treaty, a mission school was to be established there under his direction. He already knew this but had been postponing action until things were more established at home.

Isaac felt very unhappy about leaving his family. Christiana tried to hide the overwhelming sadness which occurred each time he traveled. Hearing her deep sighs, he tried to reassure her. "I'll return as quickly as possible. At least this time I leave you with adequate help."

Although the weather was suitable for the journey, he didn't relish the canoe and portage up the several rivers necessary to reach the Grand River. He had met Chief Noonday in Ft. Wayne and had been given a map, carved on birch bark, which directed him to the Ottawa village.

Isaac hired a Potawatomi Indian as guide. Young Abraham Burnet acted as interpreter and accompanied William Sears and him. They camped each night by a waterway. During the days they often met Indians in the woods. Isaac had packed a tote bag with fancy charity garments and trinkets to use for gifts and bartering. Occasionally, they stopped at a village and were able to trade items for corn or other food.

One evening they watched a group of women carrying kettles of food to a burial site. The grave appeared to be several weeks old but the offerings continued. "That is for the journey into eternal life," Abraham explained.

When they finally reached the village of Chief Noonday, they were greeted with several ceremonial gatherings. During their talks Isaac drew sketches and discussed the need to cut down trees to be used for buildings. He was pleased that William understood the process and was willing to remain and work with the Indians.

"When the school building and some cabins are completed send a messenger to me. I will return with teachers and books," he told the chief. "Your children will soon be learning white man's ways."

The return trip took only four days, due partly to the fact he now knew the trail and partly because of agreeable weather.

As always everyone at the mission was pleased to welcome him home. Christiana especially felt more secure. She immediately led him to the animal pens. "I have something to show you," she said.

During Isaac's absence 100 pigs and a herd of 150 cattle had arrived. "Where did they come from?" he asked, as he strolled around the grounds with Johnston and Christiana.

"We aren't exactly sure," Johnston replied. "Right after you left a group of four explorers came through. They were on their way to the source of the Mississippi River. They told us a large amassment of animals was being driven this direction. Their guides told them about our mission and they came out of their way to see the school."

"Anyway, a few days after the explorers came, six men on horseback herded in all these animals," Christiana added. "We were told they were donated from as far away as Tennessee, Kentucky and Ohio. They claimed to have lost about fifty along the way. We don't know who to thank except the Lord, and we have indeed thanked him!"

By July crops began to produce much needed food. More fences had to be built to control and confine animals. They adjusted well to the large grazing areas.

Squire Thompson returned once more, bringing his wife and four children to visit. He was disappointed and angry to learn the mission school was only for Indian pupils. "Why can't my young ones attend? Will you take them in if I pay you something?"

"It will have to be discussed with the other missionaries," Christiana told him in Isaac's absence. "It is written in the treaty, but I would hate refusing any child an education."

Later that evening the McCoys discussed the situation with the other teachers. They decided to allow a few white pupils to attend morning classes. "That way, they will not be living at the mission. We will not be feeding or clothing them. If we get any other near neighbors they could do the same."

Joseph Bailley, a French Canadian trading post owner, once fur trader and voyager, rode in one afternoon with Bertrand. "He has a young half breed daughter he wants you to educate," Bertrand told Christiana. "He can bring her in a few days. She will have to live here. Their home is far away on Lake Michigan." He laughed heartily as he thought of something. "She speaks French and Indian, Ha Ha! They want her to talk American."

Christiana was embarrassed as she noticed Bailley staring at their poorly dressed pupils and her own shabby skirt. It was obvious from his clothes that he was a man of wealth. His daughter, no doubt, had fine garments.

Bailley looked at Christiana kindly and said, "It will be good for Rose to come here. She needs to be taught your ways."

"We will be pleased to have your daughter attend our school." When Rose arrived two weeks later, with a large trunk and several boxes, Christiana feared she had made a mistake. The mission children gathered around the fancy horse-pulled cart Joseph Bailley was driving. Rose was dressed in a beautifully embroidered deerskin dress and moccasins but carried a fancy flowered umbrella to keep the sun off her face. The children giggled and stared as Rose twirled her umbrella before closing it. She laughed too as they reached to help her down into their midst.

Within the next few days Rose parceled out all of her belongings to her new friends. She now wore a faded dress and moccasins. Christiana smiled as she saw many children wearing bows and trinkets as well as fancy shirts or shoes that had previously belonged to their newest pupil.

The routine at the school, which had become well established, was greatly altered when the Wrights received a letter reassigning them to a teaching post in Ohio. James had become quite proficient at simple blacksmith work and had been teaching two young men. Martha taught many feminine niceties to the girls, things that Christiana had no time or talent to teach.

"We will surely miss you! You have assumed so many responsibilities and been so helpful," Isaac told them, as they sat beside his desk enjoying cups of chicory coffee.

"Our two months here were very challenging. We had hoped to remain but one must go where they are called. I do wonder at the wisdom of this move however," James said. "I wish we could have done more. Is there anything we can do for the mission before we leave?"

"I hesitate to ask but there is one thing my wife and I need," Isaac said wistfully.

"Name it!"

"Well, it has to do with our own children. We are concerned that their social education is being sacrificed by living here, especially the girls."

James nodded, understanding. Martha, who had overheard the men's conversation, spoke. "Let us take Delilah with us. She is close to my age and I would love to have her live with us awhile. She can attend the school where we will be teaching."

"Oh, I think that would be an imposition. I didn't mean you should do this. I just thought perhaps you might write us if you heard of a school where we could send our daughters."

The Wrights knew he was embarrassed. They smiled kindly. James winked at Martha, then said, "Tell Christiana to pack Delilah's belongings. We'll leave in a few days."

In late July everyone at the mission gathered to bid farewell as the Wrights mounted their horses to leave. Delilah hugged her parents. After glancing around unhappily at all the familiar faces, she climbed upon her horse. Christiana swallowed hard, trying not to cry. A few minutes later they rode out of sight.

10

Since he was now well acquainted with the trail, Rice accompanied them. He and Martha had recently become good friends. As they rode they talked. "I'll only be going as far as Fort Wayne so I won't know where you live. Will you write to me?" Rice asked, blushing. "Maybe I can visit sometime if it isn't too far away."

"I'd like that," Martha replied. "Soon you will be going off to college. It may be close to where we live. We will meet again I'm sure." She smiled, recalling their first meeting. "We started out wrong but I've truly enjoyed our friendship."

Delilah remained very subdued and rode for hours without talking. She already missed her family and Johnston, her favorite teacher.

As long as it was daylight, James Wright constantly read a book as he rode. He only spoke when his horse halted at a stream or they stopped for meals or dismounted for the night. On the final night of their journey, as they camped outside Ft. Wayne, he called Rice aside. "I've learned many things from watching your parents. It has been inspiring to meet them. As much as I wish to, I don't think I can ever serve others like they do." Looking around to make certain Martha wasn't watching, he handed a small pouch to Rice. "Please, take this cash and give it to your father. He will make better use of it than I could."

Rice looked inside the pouch. "But, Sir, this must be your teaching salary. You will need money to get to your new job. Won't you need it to purchase things? I don't think my parents would like me to take this."

"I've saved out a small sum. Martha won't miss it and anyway she has money. That's all we'll need. Please keep it!"

Rice humbly stuck it in his pocket. They walked back to the campfire and joined the girls for supper. The next morning they parted company. Rice smiled at Martha, causing her to blush. He then hugged Delilah. As she bravely tried to hide her tears, he whispered, "I will miss you. Learn all you can and come home." When all the farewells were said, Rice started his lonely return trip.

After four days of constant rain the sun finally reappeared, bringing with it swarms of mosquitoes. He built a smudge fire each night and rode as fast as possible during the days, trying to avoid the pests. "I'll sure be glad to get home," he told his horse over and over.

The seventh day of his journey he entered mission property and heard familiar voices. "Come grab a hoe. There's plenty of rows left for you!" the boys called, when they saw him ride by. "I'll be back! I have to let my family know I'm home."

When he reached home he turned his horse loose, then searched for his father. "Mr. Wright kindly gave me this donation for the mission," he told him and put the pouch on the desk.

Isaac hesitated before picking it up and peeking inside. "Did he have it to spare?"

"I asked him about it. He said you and Mama are doing such fine work he wanted you to have this money and they could manage without it." Isaac smiled and pocketed the pouch.

A few days later on a particularly warm afternoon, Christiana sat on a stump cutting and cleaning dandelion greens for supper. Suddenly, Sarah and Anna rushed into the cooking area shouting, "Mama, Mama! Two boys fishing down by the river got bit by snakes. They are hurt bad! Come quick!"

"Singing Bird! Come help me!" Christiana screamed. "Bring medicine!"

The women ran as fast as they could to the river bank. Singing Bird looked at the smashed head of a snake someone had flung away from the victims. "Massasauga, deadly rattlesnakes. We must work fast! I need something to tie above the bites."

Christiana yanked off her apron, and began tearing it into strips. She quickly tied one around the upper leg of one boy. Singing Bird grabbed a strip and tied the arm of a second boy. Pulling a knife from inside her deerskin boot, she slashed both wounds, then bent to suck and spit poison from the re-swollen gashes.

"Sarah, wet these rags in the river!" Christiana ordered her eight year old, as she handed her pieces of the apron. "Help her wring them out, Anna. Place them on the boy's faces."

Singing Bird ran along the edge of the river, pulling plants and squeezing them in her hands to release their healing juices. "Take my knife and slash some bark from that burr oak over there," she called to Christiana. "Children, go pull some yellow yarrow from the meadow."

When everything was collected the women made poultices and laid them on the wounds. Curved bark pieces were placed over the medicine, then they packed them with cool river mud. Next, Singing Bird slowly released the tourniquets.

"We need to move the boys into the shade or carry them back to the buildings," said Christiana. "It is too hot here in the sunshine." The boys, in their stoic Indian way, did not cry or complain but their dark eyes revealed pain and fright. It took four strong boys to gently lift the injured ones. "Carry them back to my cabin," Christiana supervised.

"The rest of you go back to the meadow to play," she ordered. Several boys had begun killing more snakes and were dancing around the squirming mass of bodies. "We don't need any more casualties! You can't play here by the river without supervision!"

The women led the way back to the mission, stopping along the way to inspect the boys' wounds. "Medicine is working," Singing Bird stated.

Christiana spoke softly, "Let's rest here in the shade. Singing Bird makes powerful medicine but it takes time to heal." Singing Bird, pretending not to hear the compliment, looked at the ground.

"Sarah, you and Anna did the right thing, calling for help. I am proud of you," Christiana told her daughters as they once again began the walk to the cabin. "Now, I need you to go find your brothers to help carry the boys."

Two young boys approached Christiana and asked, "Why did the snakes come out today and not other days when we played there?"

"I have been wondering about that too," she said. "Fawn and I wash clothes in that same area and we have never seen them. It is a very hot day, perhaps the hot sun coaxed them out."

"I think we killed them all. Don't you?" One of the boys asked.

"I hope you are right but you must always be observant when you walk. No matter where you go you must be careful and watch out for danger," Singing Bird told them. "It is the Indian way!"

That evening during prayers the near tragedy became instead a time of thankfulness. "Another lesson in wilderness living," Christiana told Isaac as they walked home together.

Over the summer, Singing Bird and Fawn often took the girls into the woods and meadow to search for herbs and medicinal plants. From them they learned to dry and preserve leaves and roots and to mix the proper portions for cooking or healing medicines.

Each day when classes and work were completed, the children were free to spend time enjoying outdoor activities.

Grace Dusenbury and Christiana showed the girls how to cut and gather the long-stemmed prairie grass. They stuffed the sweet smelling bunches into clean cloth covers replacing old cornshucks they had used for mattresses.

Often they roamed the woods and meadows searching for nuts or berry bushes as they played. One evening, during a game of tag, some of them stopped under a tree. "Listen," said Anna. "This tree seems to be making a humming noise."

"Look!" shouted Mark as he pointed upwards. "Hundreds of bees are up there! Someone needs to go back and tell Mr. Lykins." Eager to escape the bees, several girls ran back to the mission to tell their teachers.

Carrying a fire pot and armed with axes and long limbs wrapped with rags, two hired men cautiously approached the tree. After they sent the children away, they lit the rags and set fire to the swarming bee's nest. When things calmed down the men chopped open the tree trunk. Golden honey dripped down their arms as they scooped it out. "Go get some kettles," they called to boys standing nearby watching.

When they collected all they could carry they returned to the mission. Everyone enjoyed sweet honey on cornbread for many days.

Garden yields were impressive. Along with regular meal preparations came the preserving for the long winter's use. Christiana, Grace Dusenbury and Singing Bird erected drying racks in the kitchen and in cabin lofts. Bunches of herbs, strings of beans and ears of corn hung in abundance. Pumpkins were sliced and threaded on poles and fastened into corners.

"This winter will not be like the last ones," Christiana commented as she worked with Grace.

Johnston and Daniel were putting away books one afternoon when Isaac rose from his desk "I have been trying to figure out a method for grinding corn and maybe even grain," he said. "The other day Calvin showed me some rather flat boulders along the river. I think by laying the largest one on top so it can pivot around it should do the job. Daniel, could you make a box so we can set the stones inside it?"

The next day when it was assembled, all the men stood watching as he tried to demonstrate. It soon became obvious that he could not turn the stone alone. Several came to his aid. After much tugging the dried corn placed between the stones was ground into very coarse meal. "Strong men, by constant labor, are able to make poor quality meal," admitted Isaac, looking discouraged but trying to sound jovial.

Christiana walked by. Bending over she ran some of the meal through her fingers. Seeing how disappointed Isaac looked, she smiled and said, "It is sufficient for making bread for the family."

"We tried to grind wheat flour but the kernels are too small and slip through the stones." He shook his head, chagrined. "Nearest grist mill is 190 miles distant. I wish we could manufacture flour here."

Things looked brighter a few days later when visitors arrived and handed Isaac a pack of letters. Waving some pages in his hand, he entered the school and motioned to his wife and Johnston. "Remember, back in April, when I told you I'd written to arrange for supplies to be brought by schooner from Detroit?" Both of them shook their heads.

"They couldn't navigate around to Lake Michigan because of the ice flows, isn't that right?" asked Johnston.

"Yes, that's right," Isaac replied. "But now they have written to tell me they will unload our order at the mouth of the St. Joe River mid-October. The vessel will be bringing four or five hundred dollars worth of merchandise for us, including iron for the blacksmith we've yet to employ. We are going to get our supplies without having to go back to Fort Wayne," he said happily.

"We'll send some boys and a couple of hired men with our wagon and extra horses up river." He saw Christiana's look of relief. "I won't have to go," he said, patting her arm.

Isaac drew maps of the trails showing the way along the St. Joseph river until it reached the Lake Michigan shore. October tenth, Abraham and the men left the mission with the McCoys' blessings. "This way of transporting supplies will be much easier," he assured his fellow workers. Abraham was happy at the thought of visiting his family at their trading post.

Twelve days later when they returned with only seven barrels of flour, one barrel of salt and two or three other small articles, Isaac wished he hadn't forecast their success.

"What happened?" he asked, feeling like he'd been kicked in the stomach.

"It's a long story. Everyone should gather around, then it won't have to be repeated," the spokesman said. Isaac sent Abraham to find Calvin. "Tell him to bring the trumpet."

Calvin blew three blasts on the trumpet to summon an assembly at the school. Leaning on the teachers' desk, the speaker began his tale. "On October seventeenth, the captain anchored his ship. He came ashore with two men in a small boat. About this time the wind became so severe that their cable parted. The waves were enormous! The ship tossed and turned." He looked around at his audience, then continued, "We stood and watched, shocked as the schooner was driven far out in the lake."

Christiana gasped, thinking of the loss of hundreds of dollars worth of supplies.

"We went to a nearby Indian village to sleep before heading back. The captain went with us but he left his men on the beach. His small boat was pulled up on the sand so it wouldn't float away too. In the middle of the night the men came running into the village shouting. They said the vessel had again come into sight. The captain told us to be at the shore at daylight."   •

"We were there waiting and hoping to receive our goods. The ship was closer to shore and the captain's little boat made it through the rough water and back only once. Unfortunately they were only able to land the few items you saw." He wiped a tear from his cheek and sat down.

"What happened to the rest?" asked Isaac, disappointed and suddenly very weary.

"The captain wouldn't allow the sailors to attempt another trip to shore. The remaining cargo was carried back to Detroit, to our great loss."

"Yes, and to our serious inconvenience in other respects," Isaac concluded, rising to leave. "We thank God for your safe return. We will just have to work and pray harder."

The fall harvest of corn kept everyone at the mission busy, including the hired men and some helpful Indian neighbors. After the stalks were cut the girls pulled off the ears of corn, removed the husks, and tossed them in piles. Small boys then threw the ears into baskets. Shocks were formed from stalks and left to dry for animal bedding. The proceeds amounted to a grand total of 900 bushels.

"Praise the Lord, we will have some corn to sell," Isaac announced one evening after devotions. "You have all been wonderful workers! The profits will go into a fund for higher education for anyone who desires to go to college." Their pupils looked stunned. It was obvious no one had anticipated advanced schooling.

"We want you all to set high goals." He looked pointedly at his own sons. "Some of you will make fine teachers or doctors or lawyers. I have been writing letters to colleges in your behalf, trying to find openings. We will talk more about this later," he concluded as he dismissed them.

When the school had opened, twenty-eight of the pupils could neither speak nor understand English and most of the others had scarce knowledge of the language. Now, just a few months later, all were pursuing their studies and labors promisingly. Some could read, write and speak with ease. The teachers had learned enough Indian words to be able to carry on short conversations. Not being able to converse still disturbed both Isaac and Christiana.

Near the end of October the mission had a surprise official visit from a Michigan Territory inspector. "My name is Charles Noble. Governor Cass sent me to see how things were progressing," he told Isaac. "I don't want to intrude but if I could stay here a few days I'd appreciate it."

"You certainly may, but I'm afraid you will find our living rather primitive."

"I'm not used to fancy trappings. I'll just follow you around and write down what I see."

Johnston had moved into the cabin vacated by the Wrights. He invited the inspector to join him. "I'm very impressed to find fifty acres have been cleared, planted, and harvested," Mr. Noble told Johnston one evening as they sat together. "You'll soon have about sixty acres fenced, looks like."

"With the boys and girls spending half of their days in manual labor we have been able to accomplish a great deal," Johnston explained. "The girls don't work outdoors much but the sewing and weaving they've learned will benefit them forever."

"Yes, I've seen their work. It is very good quality." He laughed and patted his rotund stomach. "I've been enjoying the food here. I know the meal preparations are done by the girls too."

Johnston nodded, smiling as he put another log on the fire. "Have you found some problems here that need attention?"

"Well, quite frankly I have not. Except, of course the early trumpet blast jarring everyone out of bed. I'm not fond of all the worship times either but that is not to say these young ones don't benefit from it. Their singing is certainly music to the ears."

Smoke rose from his pipe as he sat, relaxed and friendly. "Are the Indians who wander in unannounced causing any trouble to you folks?"

"They beg for food or sometimes just help themselves, which annoys Sister McCoy." The men laughed. "Indians think everything is meant to be shared. We have been encouraging them to copy our way of farming and building. We could do a better job of that," Johnston told him. "We have not been able to hire a blacksmith. We need more tools made, like hoes and shovels. If we had tools to give to the Indians they could cultivate their own fields. We plan to give them domestic animals. Then they'll need fences and buildings. The more we can teach them the better off they will be."

"Are more settlers moving into the area?"

"Not yet. Our biggest fear though is the increase of traders with liquor to offer. We hate to see them around!"

"What, pray tell, do these Indians have to trade?"

"Oh, they have animal skins and maple sugar, plus they make dried jerky or dry fish." Johnston listened to the trumpet call. "Speaking of food," he said, "we only have two meals on Sundays. We'd better get in line. After the second meal we have another worship service."

"I'm leaving in the morning. Think I'll just rest after we eat."

The next morning before Mr. Noble left he told the McCoys his report would be a favorable one. "I'm amazed at your dedication to educating these Indians! Governor Cass spoke highly of you before I came. Now I know why."

"Give His Honor our best wishes," said Isaac.

"We will be happy to see you again if you return," added Christiana politely. She was not feeling very well and was happy the added burden of the inspection was over.

November arrived and with it came a young man carrying a bundle of mail. Grace Dusenbury, walking in the woods gathering nuts, was the first person to see him. "Oh, my!" she said, dropping her basket, "I didn't even hear a horse coming. You frightened me!"

"My name's Sam Martin. I have letters for this Mission." He laughed as he helped her pick up spilled nuts. "I'm a harmless person, you don't have to fear me. Actually, I am a teacher looking for a position." They walked together to McCoy's cabin. Christiana welcomed them inside.

The mail was sorted before Isaac arrived. "We have a letter from Delilah," Christiana told him, smiling happily. She moved to her rocker to read it. Grace left with her mail.

Isaac questioned Sam about his teaching qualifications and decided to hire him. After sending him to Johnston's cabin to unpack he told Christiana, "He is a decent young man. He said he will adhere to our rules and routine."

"Is he a Christian?" she asked.

"If not, I believe he would be agreeable to becoming a Christian. His training is more than adequate. He even brought along books and supplies." Isaac sat at the table looking through the stack of letters. "Now, tell me what our daughter wrote."

Christiana looked at him sadly. "She is very homesick. She says she has learned to set a fine table and has been taught proper manners but wishes she was home where those things really aren't important." She shook her head. "Did we do the right thing sending her away?"

"It is too soon to tell, my dear. Didn't she say anything about reading fine literature or learning to play musical instruments? Those are the things we wanted her to learn."

"Perhaps she hasn't been exposed to those subjects yet," her mother replied, still wondering about the wisdom of letting her go so far distant. "She said to give her regards to the family and Johnston."

"I will write and tell her she must adjust to her surroundings. She needs to remain there and take advantage of the things we can not offer or teach here," Isaac insisted.

Christiana's sadness over the letter remained for days. "Let's go for a walk," she said to her youngest daughters one cold crisp morning. "Instead of going to school, I need some fresh air and some fresh thoughts. We must dress warm. It looks like snow might fall today."

The girls were more than willing. Nancy happily chased two year old Eleanor around some large oak trees. Two young fawns watched, then scampered into the brush. Christiana felt at peace as she walked and watched leaves swirling to the ground. Vaguely, she heard what sounded like wagon wheels rumbling in the distance. "Listen, girls!" she called. "Is someone coming?" They stopped their play and came to her side.

"Let's walk toward the trail," she said, taking their hands. Leaving the woods, they walked along the rutted tracks. By straining her eyes, Christiana could see an oxen-drawn wagon and two horses approaching.

As the wagon drew near she suddenly clutched her heart, recognizing her brother William and his family. Picking up her skirt she began running toward them as fast as her legs could go. Eleanor, unable to keep up with her sister and mother, sat on the ground and howled.

William halted the oxen so his family could jump from the wagon. Arms spread wide, they ran to greet her. "William and Mary, I'm so happy to see you!" Christiana repeated, over and over.

The horseback riders dismounted. Christiana recognized one as her nephew John. The pretty red-haired young woman was a stranger. "My name is Fanny Goodrich. I have come from Lexington, Kentucky to be a teacher here." She smiled and hugged Christiana. "I assume you are Mrs. McCoy."

Christiana caught her breath, feeling a sharp grabbing pain in her back. "Sorry," she said, trying to hide her discomfort. "I shouldn't have run. I'm so excited! Two wonderful surprises, my brother and a new assistant. Welcome, welcome to you all!"

William picked up his little nieces and carried them toward the wagon. "Let's all ride to the mission."

"I'm afraid I can't step up that high," said Christiana pointing to her swollen stomach. "I'll follow the path back and you continue on the trail."

"Let me walk with you, I need to stretch after so many hours in the saddle," Fanny said. "I'll tie my horse to the wagon and be right back."

Christiana enjoyed Fanny's good-natured banter as they followed the footpath. Her energy and youth was exciting. "I thought I was going to have to travel alone but then I heard the Polke family was headed to the mission. What a blessing that was! They are such fine people!" Fannie told her. "The Baptist Board sent some church supplies with me. I think your husband will be surprised and pleased."

Before lunch at prayer time, Isaac introduced the Polke family and Miss Goodrich. "Today we have received valuable additions to our mission and our work. Thank the Lord!"

Johnston moved his belongings from the cabin he'd been occupying over to Dusenbury's loft. The Polkes unpacked their clothes and meager furnishings and moved into the cabin. Fanny joined the McCoy girls in their loft until permanent arrangements could be made.

Later Fanny had Rice carry two large crates to his father. As they unpacked the carefully wrapped items Isaac was overwhelmed. "A Communion set! I never expected to have such a beautiful gift," he exclaimed when he saw the shiny silver cup, plate and candle holders. He carefully rubbed the glossy finish and set the items on his desk. "We will need an appropriate table to display them."

"The Board also sent books and materials for teaching Sabbath School classes," Fanny told him as she pointed to the second crate. "Have you been teaching the children?"

"No, but we have Bible readings and discussions most evenings. Their understanding is improving but there are few actual Christians," Isaac commented. "If you wish to begin teaching lessons, I would not object." He unpacked the religious books and stacked them on his desk, glancing at the titles.

"Should I teach on Sunday afternoons?"

"Yes, but now that I look at this material I see it is written for all non-Christians," said Isaac as he thumbed through the books. "I think we have Indian neighbors who don't attend Sunday services and could benefit too, especially women who haven't had the opportunity to hear the message. I'd like to think it over but maybe we should ride to some villages and offer lessons there during the week."

Before noon the next day the wagon had been unpacked and distributed. Besides several barrels of much needed flour, the Polkes had also brought a barrel of salt, a tin of coffee and to the delight of everyone, a trumpet and two violins. "I brought my own violin," said Fanny. "I could teach others to fiddle."

The wooden crates were carefully disassembled. The wood pieces were used for building window frames and shelves.

Mary gave Christiana a bolt of material, thread and needles which so thrilled her she cried. Christiana then helped Mary unpack her dishes, placing them on the table and fireplace mantle. They hung clothes on pegs. William had set Mary's rocker and spinning wheel beside the fireplace. Mary said, "I'm glad to see there is other furniture here already."

Due to the help of William and Fanny, the McCoys felt a great sense of relief from everyday pressures. William, a large burly man, was willing and able to work as carpenter, teacher, or farmer. Although he was a lawyer and judge, he even did small blacksmith repairs. Mary loved everyone. She was friendly, helpful in the kitchen, and took over chores for Christiana. The Polke children adjusted quickly into school and work routines.

Fanny's enthusiasm spread. Her Bible studies added a new spark of joy to teenage girls and area Indian women who helped at the mission. Between morning and evening sermons on Sunday, she held Sabbath school. Indians from the vicinity, hearing the trumpet blast, would often wander in out of curiosity and stay to listen.

Encouraged by their acceptance of her teachings, Isaac and Fanny rode to nearby villages. Although some of the men had learned bits of religion from early Catholic priests, women had not been included. Fascinated by Fanny's red hair, they watched her every move and listened quietly. Fanny couldn't decide if the women were enlightened or just entertained.

Isaac watched and approved her work but he would not allow her to ride alone. "These people will not hurt me," she insisted.

"I agree! You do not have to fear these people, but there are wild animals in the woods." Hesitating, he added, "I must warn you of something else. People do not act the same when they drink too much. Indians who drink alcohol sometimes act savagely."

"If we get our religious messages to them perhaps they will not drink."

"Yes, Fanny, that's our hope also, but until then someone must accompany you!"

Despite some differences of opinion, Fanny and Isaac worked well together preparing church services. On the last Sunday in November 1823, the sacrament of the Lord's Supper was administered by Protestants for the first time in the southwestern Michigan Territory.

11

Hired men, now finished with the harvest, began building two large cabins which would be used as boys and girls dormitories. William worked with the young men as they prepared winter shelters for sheep and cattle. As always, younger boys chopped wood, stacking it in piles close to each building.

For months fat drippings from endless cooking had been saved in containers. "In the spring we can make soap from the grease along with wood ashes saved from the winter fires," said Christiana. "But now we'll set up kettles outdoors and make candles."

Mary and Grace stirred the melting fat, mixing in chunks of beeswax. Girls braided yarn strings and tied them to a stick. By holding one end of the stick they could slowly dip the strings into the kettles until wax formed long tapers and began to harden in the cold November air. Smoke in their eyes and constant fear of someone getting burned made the chore an unpleasant one. After a long day's work, Mary said "We now have a good supply of tapers for dark days and nights ahead. Aren't we glad this chore is done?"

Toward the end of the month snow began to fall in large amounts. The wind blew cold air and snow under doors and around windows, often blowing out nearby candles. "It is very cold and uncomfortable, but nothing like last winter. Remember our journey here?" people were constantly asking each other.

Early the morning of the twenty-ninth Christiana lay in bed thinking about the year and changes they had made. Isaac sat at his corner desk writing in his journal when he heard her call out in pain. "Get Mary or Grace! The baby is coming!" she gasped. "Please, tell Singing Bird I need her."

Isaac alerted the women, then disappeared for a day of teaching. He stayed away all day. As he walked home following evening prayers he heard a faint cry. He walked faster. When he opened the door he saw Christiana propped against pillows, smiling as she held their new baby.

"Come see your new daughter," she said. Singing Bird was busy cleaning and putting kettles back on shelves. The other women had returned to their homes.

Isaac held the baby briefly, then gently placed her in the much-used cradle someone had carried down from the loft. "She looks very healthy," he said. "How are you faring, my dear?"

After she convinced him they were both fine, she told him to bring the other children home. "They can help choose a name for their sister." Within minutes they chose 'Maria Stoughton' as her name, in honor of a family friend in Indiana.

All December was chilly and snow fell almost every day. Wood smoke hung in cabins, once again causing sore eyes and bad coughs. The women spent one afternoon up in the McCoy's loft searching through the charity boxes. They hoped to find warm clothing but found few useable articles. Mary and Grace mended whenever they sat down.

The dried food supply was adequate but mundane. Whenever the boys were able to trap animals to be added to soup broth it was always appreciated.

Singing Bird always saved rabbit skins. She made a cradleboard lined with the soft fur for baby Maria, who slept propped against her mother's desk each morning. Fawn had a bag of mixed furs. She taught girls how to pad moccasins and shoes for extra warmth. They made mittens with the fur side in for the men.

Neighboring Indians entered mission buildings begging for food or just warming themselves by the fireplace. It was not unusual for teachers to find visitors in the school when they arrived in the morning. Unless they were intoxicated there were few problems.

"Our workers are dedicated, capable missionaries," Isaac remarked one afternoon when he and Christiana were alone. "I only wish there were more."

"In one year there has been much progress."

"Much is left to do, Christiana. More pupils, more workers, we'll require more food, more clothing, more buildings." He banked the fire and stood staring into the fireplace.

Christiana watched him, wondering what he was thinking.

"You know my dear," he said. "right now there isn't much going on here. The routine is well established. Most of our Indian neighbors are north for trapping. It isn't likely we'll get more students until spring. The food supply is adequate. There are no unusual health problems--."

"What is it you are trying to say Isaac?" asked Christiana, dreading the answer.

"Well, I'm thinking this might be the right time for me to head east to talk to politicians and mission boards asking for financial aid." He smiled and gently patted her arm as he saw tears sliding down her cheeks.

"I was hoping we could enjoy this winter together," she sobbed.

"We didn't come here just to enjoy an easy life, did we?" he asked, then realized he may have said the wrong thing. "I don't mean to sound cruel but we promised the church board we'd sacrifice our own desires for the good of others."

She turned her head away, searching in her apron pocket for a hanky. Clearing her throat, she asked quietly, "When are you leaving?"

"Whenever a break in the weather occurs. Probably in a day or two," he replied, moving to the desk to gather some papers. "I'll need your help in packing food and clothing."

A week after Isaac left, Christiana was walking between buildings. Suddenly she heard a man scream. Dropping the books she was carrying, she ran into the woods toward the sound. Two small boys followed her.

A second scream led them to one of the hired men lying on the ground holding his bleeding foot. His ax leaned on a newly cut tree trunk. "Help me!" he gasped. "My ax slipped. I think I chopped off my toes!"

Christiana felt sick as she saw the huge amount of blood gushing from the hole in his boot onto the ground. She pulled off her apron and tied it around his leg. "Run get Singing Bird," she ordered the boys.

She tried to help the man but he fainted from the pain. She packed snow around the foot thinking cold would slow the flow of blood. She felt dizzy watching and closed her eyes, praying for help.

When she opened her eyes, Singing Bird was removing her bag of medicine from her belt. As Christiana watched, she managed to pull the boot from his foot. Next she pressed leaves and powdered herbs around his dangling toes. The bleeding stopped. William had followed Singing Bird. He quickly tore a sleeve from his shirt and ripped it into strips. Together they managed to wrap and tie the foot and ankle.

Christiana walked away to control her sick feeling. Her walk ended at the well. She filled a pail of water, took a drink, then returned to the injured man. She managed to assist

Singing Bird clean up and revive the man. He slowly regained consciousness and groaned. They propped him against a tree. "Stay very quiet," Singing Bird told him.

"We must move him and bury these rags before wolves catch the scent of blood," said Singing Bird. William went to find help. When he came back with three teenage boys they lifted him gently. Keeping his foot elevated, they slowly carried him to the McCoy's cabin where the women could better take care of him.

"I don't know what I'd do without your help, Singing Bird," Christiana said. "Your medicine is powerful!" Singing Bird as usual looked at the ground, pretending not to hear. "We need to change clothes after that ordeal," said Christiana. "Look at all the blood and dirt on us." Singing Bird left briefly to clean up.

During the night the women took turns responding to the man's needs. Drinks of herbal tea calmed him enough so they could apply more medicine and change bandages. By noontime the next day he was able to eat, then later hobble to the workers' cabin.

As Christiana cleaned her cabin she suddenly realized the new year was approaching. "We need to send men out to invite our neighbors to come celebrate New Year's Day. Bertrand will spread the word for us, I'm sure," she told Johnston when he stopped in to visit. "Will you be in charge of the welcoming message? I will get the girls involved in food preparations. We only have a few days of 1823 left."

As always, for several days after Isaac left Christiana listened for his familiar laugh. Each time she went outdoors her eyes shifted to the break in the woods where she'd last seen him. Once again the trees stood bare and lonely against the winter sky.

"I don't see how you manage, sister, caring for a new babe plus supervising the school and all the children," Mary commented, shaking her head.

"It is better for me to keep busy," she always replied, but secretly she was unhappy and close to exhaustion. She looked forward each evening to the time she could extinguish the candles and crawl into bed. Most nights her sleep was interrupted by children, who woke crying or coughing or too cold to sleep. The only way to comfort them was to bring them to her bed.

Long before daybreak she replenished the cabin and kitchen fires and hung kettles of water to heat for porridge. Singing Bird and Fawn joined her in breakfast preparations. Then she returned home to dress her small daughters and begin the day's routine.

Logs sputtered and burned in all the mission fireplaces. Rice and Josephus were in charge of keeping wood boxes filled. Younger boys had to help carry logs. Wind drafts down the chimneys caused smoke to fill the buildings. Coughing interrupted many recitations during school hours.

"Well, at least the flies and mosquitoes are gone," Johnston said one morning when the other teachers complained about the miserable conditions.

School was canceled for New Year's Day. The celebration was not the grand pig roast affair of the previous one. At Christiana's insistence, they set up tables of food so any visitors could be fed. Her brother William assisted Johnston in leading a worship service for the mission. Several neighbor chiefs arrived and joined the fire circle. Chebass seemed very disappointed that Reverend McCoy was not present.

Johnston, using Abraham as interpreter, read an important document to all who were gathered. "You have all come to know this place as a mission school. We have recently received written word from official Baptist church leaders giving a name to this school. 'At the Triennial Convention in 1823, the name of Carey Mission Station has been given to this place on the Saint Joseph River in Michigan Territory.' It is named after a famous Baptist missionary, a religious man, who worked in a land far away helping many people live better lives. We are proud to use his name."

Knowing Isaac would have been pleased, Christiana smiled to herself as she overheard Chebass talking to William about farming. Later she saw him admiring the log structures. Once again, neighbors walked through all the buildings, touching and inspecting every nook and cranny. They left many fingerprints and dirty footprints behind.

During January and February, by enforcing the routine as close as possible, things ran smoothly. As wood piles dwindled, the winter also began slipping away. The food supply, supplemented by the boy's and men's ability to trap rabbits and hunt and kill deer, remained sufficient.

Trails were snow covered. Weather remained harsh. Except for the occasional appearances of neighboring Indians there were few winter visitors. One day in early March, just as ice was breaking up on the river, Rice and Josephus were in the woods chopping trees. Suddenly they heard frantic shouts. Running toward the river they saw two men waving their arms on the other side. 'We have mail for the Carey Mission," they called. "How can we get across?"

The boys shrugged their shoulders as they looked at the broken ice. "We'll go get some rope and more men," they shouted, then ran for help.

The impatient young men didn't wait. Instead, they grabbed two large dead limbs to use as poles, threw their knapsacks onto a large cake of floating ice and jumped on.

Alerted by Rice and his brother, many mission pupils and adults had rushed to the river and watched in horror as the churning ice chunks flowed past. Time and again the men tried to push themselves across but the current was too strong. It seemed very possible they would be swept rapidly downstream. At times they were shoved closer to the riverbank, almost in reach of men who ran along the shore. Miraculously, just at a bend in the river, Daniel Dusenbury grabbed the limb the men were holding. Rice also caught hold of the limb. Between them they managed to wedge the ice float into the bank. The men and their sacks were pulled to safety. Much subdued, they spent the rest of the day and night by McCoys' fire.

Christiana welcomed the letters. One was from Isaac, telling of his visits to important officials soliciting help and money for the mission. His descriptions of New York and Washington and the fine homes he visited and slept in were beyond her comprehension. The fancy dishes and meals he enjoyed made her once again realize how different they lived.

A letter from Delilah, revealing her continued homesickness, made her feel sad. After she read the letters to her family, they spent the evening writing letters for the young men to take back to Ft. Wayne.

By noon the next day the river was calmer. The young men borrowed horses and rode across. The horses were to be left at the Jacksons' cabin in Ft. Wayne until someone from the mission reclaimed them.

Eventually warm winds of March melted the last of the snow. Muddy paths dried. Soft green grass grew around the buildings. Balancing Maria on her hip, Christiana strolled through the garden area planning where to plant the seeds they had saved.

The plowing had not been done yet as the men were busy finishing the dormitories and a blacksmith shop in hope that a smithy would soon arrive.

Christiana saw Grace standing in her doorway watching her children play and walked over to talk. "We just came back from visiting the cows," Grace said, laughing. "They certainly look healthy. Two new little calves have been born."

"It will be nice to have milk again, won't it?" Christiana said. "Imagine making butter and having milk for the youngest ones at least."

Grace smiled. "Guess we'll be seeing lambs soon, too. Have you ever sheared sheep? That has to be done in the spring, doesn't it?"

Christiana shook her head. "Still things to learn. I hope the hired men know how to take care of sheep and lambs. I know Isaac told them what he knew last year. I don't think women and children could manage them."

She started to walk away, then turned back. "If the weather holds would you help me get some clothes washed? All winter I've just washed the necessary items but our pupils' clothing and bedding should be scrubbed and aired."

"Get's warm enough we can scrub the children too," Grace replied cheerfully. "Some of their clothes are so raggedy they won't last through a wash. When we get cloth woven we can make some new garments. Won't that be a blessing?"

Shortly after the calves were all born the girls were taught to milk the cows. The cream was rich. They learned to make delicious butter and cheese. "It is a wonderful treat to spread butter on bread and worth all the work," Mary told the girls as they helped her churn.

One April morning following breakfast children began complaining of stomach cramps. Soon after adults became ill. Christiana and Singing Bird, who hadn't eaten breakfast, had no discomforts so kept busy soothing others. They made peppermint tea and insisted everyone drink it.

Baby Maria was flushed with fever. She screamed in pain, drawing her little knees to her chest. "What has happened to make us so sick?" asked Johnston, fighting his own discomfort.

"I don't know," replied Christiana. "If it is food, Maria shouldn't be sick. She didn't eat. She only had a tiny bottle of milk."

"Maybe that's it! It's milk sickness," said Fannie.

"But the adults don't drink milk."

"No, but our butter is made from milk. Maybe the cows are sick," said William, looking very worried.

"This is awful, my mouth tastes like onion, and I haven't eaten any," said Rice.

"My stomach feels like it does after I eat onions," said Calvin.

"Singing Bird, smell the milk and butter," Christiana told her, then did the same. Fannie watched as they wrinkled their noses in disgust. She took a tiny amount on her finger and tasted it. "It is onions. The cows must have eaten wild onions!"

"Is it serious?" Christiana asked.

"No, no," laughed some of the men. "It's just good spring tonic."

"Well," commented Johnston. "One dose is enough! Let's get rid of this butter."

"What about Maria?" asked Sarah, who had been holding her sister trying to make her stop crying.

"I'll take her to our cabin and bathe her, maybe that will help her relax. Bring some tea in a cup, we'll spoon some of that into her," said her mother. "Just when I thought we'd have a healthy springtime --."

"Let's go move those cows to another pasture," William said to the least afflicted boys.

Christiana longed for her husband's return. She was constantly tired. The added worries of sick children, especially baby Maria, were overwhelming. "There is one good thing anyway," she said to anyone who would listen. "The daylight hours are getting longer and our weather is warmer. Sunshine always improves one's outlook."

Early one brisk April morning, Christiana glanced toward the woods and marveled at the tiny leaves showing on the trees. "Oh, my!" she exclaimed, startled to see a group of Indian men on horseback watching her. Then Chief Chebass, dressed in all his finery, rode toward her.

The dogs Bertrand had given her sons started barking wildly as more men rode toward the buildings. Her brother William and Daniel Dusenbury, hearing the noise, joined Christiana and waited. Abraham and Luther ran over to act as interpreters.

Chief Chebass halted his pony. Daniel assisted him to the ground. "We have come to visit. We must talk to Father McCoy," the chief told them.

"Like many older Indians he remembers Catholic priests. He thinks all religious men are called Father," explained Abraham.

Christiana told him, by using many gestures and her interpreters, that Isaac was still on a long trip. She invited the men inside the school where a bright fire had warmed the building.

Chebass strolled around and around the room, followed by ten of his village men. The pupils watched and waited respectfully. Finally he stood still before the fireplace and spoke. "I want a building like this one for myself and my people. No snow and cold winds come in here. No rain falls inside. No hot sun shines in. I came to tell Father McCoy to build me a strong house like this." He sat down on the floor.

Christiana and the teachers formed a group in the corner, discussing the request. "Our mission does plan to help fence farm land for the Indian villages but can we spare men so close to planting time for erecting buildings?" asked Johnston.

"What would Isaac say if he was here?" Daniel asked.

Tired from his early morning ride, Chebass dozed off. His men leaned on the wall and waited. The children worked quietly at the desks along the wall, peeking at the chief from time to time.

When he awoke he stood up and motioned Christiana to come beside him. Luther stepped to her side. "You are teaching good things to our children. They live in strong buildings. They learn to plant food and take care of animals and build fence. I want log buildings to live in and fences around some animals." He sat down again, waiting for her response.

She smiled at the other missionaries. "We came to educate young and old to better ways of survival," she reminded them. "We can't do for some and not for others."

The chief seemed to know his request would require time for an answer and nodded off into another nap.

"Christiana is right," Daniel stated. "It will be good training for the boys to construct log cabins. I know it is planting time but couldn't we spare a few days?"

Children pretended to read but were listening to the adults. The talk about farming and building interested them.

The adults came to an agreement. Johnston walked toward Chebass, clearing his throat loudly enough to wake him. "Abraham, tell him we will come to his village in three days to begin cutting trees for building."

The chief nodded his understanding. He stood up, nodded, and his men filed from the building. They wandered around the mission grounds. A few Indians entered cabins unannounced, helping themselves to food. The women, no longer startled but still displeased, kept silent. Before noon the Indians mounted their horses and departed.

Christiana had order established quickly. As always, she insisted routine be kept. "The only way to teach and learn is to keep repeating things," she told the teachers.

12

April showers and the resulting mud cancelled all hopes for early plowing and planting. The men and oldest boys left the mission grounds every afternoon to help fell trees surrounding Chebass' village. Despite the weather, by the end of the month three log cabins were erected. Young boys went along the final two days. They collected long branches and skinny trees, using them to make rail fencing around two considerable fields. Chebass watched the daily progress but never spoke. When finished, the men told Chebass they would return later on to plow. He nodded in his usual stoic manner.

Ice left the river. Once again Indian canoes floated by as April sunshine warmed the area. Cold nights followed by warm days made the maple sap run. Syrup preparations began in the nearby woods.

Singing Bird placed birch buckets under several medicine trees she had slashed. The concoctions she mixed worked many healing miracles. Maria's wracking cough improved but Christiana shuddered, watching her sickly baby's struggle to breathe.

The end of April the mission family were again invited to the sugaring feast. Despite the language barrier the beat of the drums and shouts of pleasure, mixed with the delicious smell, combined to make a joyful festival of sharing. Even Christiana happily joined the women's shuffle dances with all the girls.

The missionaries encouraged Indians to begin farming their village lands. They gave them seeds, hoes and shovels, and taught them new methods of planting. They welcomed their help at Carey Mission. Christiana rode a horse around the fields one afternoon knowing Isaac would be pleased at the progress of the farm.

After so many months of smoke-filled buildings she enjoyed inhaling big breaths of fresh spring air. When she walked she felt the soft green grass. "It's wonderful to walk on," she said to no one in particular. When chores were over for the day, pupils happily played tag or tossed deerskin balls to each other. Sometimes they joined adults fishing along the shore of the river. The fish they caught were cooked and added delicious variety to meals.

Except for being very tired and missing Isaac and Delilah, Christiana felt at peace and contented with her life. When she stopped to chat with Mary and Grace, they often sat on a log watching children or maybe shelling early peas.

Hearing the sound of an approaching horse one afternoon, all three women stood up. "We've all been praying for brother Isaac's return, Christiana," Grace said. "Maybe our answer is arriving."

Christiana's heart skipped a beat as she saw a tall thin rider getting closer. They all waved but their smiles vanished as they realized it was a younger man. He slid from his horse and bowed with a friendly grin. "Ladies, you have no idea how glad I am to see you!" he exclaimed. "Been riding ten days and only met Indians."

He shook the dust from his hat and brushed his clothes. "I'm headed for Carey Mission. Got some mail to deliver there. Hoping for a place to stay while I look for land to settle. Once I make my claim I'll go back for my family. Samuel Hopkins is my name," he said as he held out his hand.

Christiana shook his hand and introduced the women. "This is Carey Mission Station. Evening meal is at six. I will show you where to tie your horse," she said as she nodded at the women and walked toward the buildings. "We will find a place for you to bed." She smiled, "You can give me the mail."

No letter from Isaac was in the packet. Christiana had mixed feelings. Either something had happened to him or else he must be on the way home. She decided to choose the latter.

A short letter from Delilah was in the mail. It upset her. "Delilah is coming home as soon as she can find someone to travel with. She feels her schooling is a waste of money and time. She only wants to be and work here," Christiana told William and his wife that evening. She had passed on mail for the mission to Johnston.

By the end of May all crops were planted. Amazingly, the garden produced some beans and tiny early potatoes. Flour had long since been used up. Dried corn, used for meal, was of poor quality. Fresh vegetables were their mainstay. Children were outgrowing their clothing and shoes. "Even a missionary box would be welcome," said Grace looking at everyone's outfits. The freshly washed and repaired clothes still looked pitiful.

On June 5th Christiana thought she heard horses in the distance but forced herself to stay calm. She didn't want to get excited at the possibility of Isaac's return and be disappointed. Shifting Maria to her hip for easier carrying and taking three year old Eleanor's hand they slowly walked toward the trail.

It was play time for the children and the woods echoed with their shouts and laughter. A small boy startled Christiana when he jumped in front of her, shouting, "Reverend McCoy is coming! I saw him coming while I was down by the river."

"Run, tell the others," she urged him. "I'm going to meet him. Oh girls, your papa is coming! Look, I see him!" Christiana began walking as fast as she could, still being careful not to stumble on uneven ground. Within minutes the galloping horse met them. Isaac slid from his saddle, hugged his wife and daughters, making Maria whimper, then scream.

He lifted her from her mother's arm. "She isn't used to men. I'm sorry, Isaac."

"No," he groaned. "I'm sorry! I never intended to be away so long. Five and a half months! My own daughter doesn't recognize her father. I am sorry!"

Christiana soothed their weeping daughter. They began walking home, with Isaac holding the horse's reins. "You must be exhausted," she said as she looked at his pale thin face.

"According to my calculations I have traveled over 3,300 miles. Fortunately they weren't all on horseback," he replied laughing. "I have so much to tell you, I don't know where to start. I need to rest awhile first. I hired this horse in Detroit and rode home through the wilderness without many stops."

"Detroit? How did you happen there?"

Isaac smiled, "You aren't going to wait to learn all the details are you? I'll just give you a short version of the journey. You will be happy to know while I was out east, I was able to hire a blacksmith for us."

Christiana's face brightened. " Thank the Lord for that! But where is he?"

" Well, that's why I was in Detroit. We had already crossed Lake Erie." He grew quiet a moment then said, "I'll tell you of that horrible adventure later. We purchased the iron he'll be needing for the smithery and had it put on board a vessel headed for the mouth of the Saint Joe River.   Robert Simmerwell, that's his name, continued with the supplies and I rode home."

Everyone in the mission came out to greet Isaac. Tired as he was he recognized the stress they were under. They appeared thin and close to exhaustion. Looking around he could see all the farming and building that occurred in his absence.

"It is very good to be back with you," he said. "I can see you have been working diligently. I hope I can lift some of the burden now that I am back."

While they were eating, he studied Christiana's face. She seemed to be in poor health and spirit, rarely smiling. "How did the food last over the winter?" he asked. "Have supplies from Fort Wayne been arriving this spring?"

"No, Isaac, there have been no supplies at all. We have had no money to buy things from Bertrand." She sighed deeply.

"On my visits to Boston and Philadelphia I received donations of $1,623. We can purchase what we need. There are several barrels of flour and other foodstuffs coming on the boat."

"We have been without flour for weeks," she replied, showing no reaction to the sum of money Isaac mentioned. "We are harvesting garden vegetables now but we have no more seeds to plant."

Tears began streaming down her cheeks. Isaac watched helplessly until she got herself under control. "Let's go to our cabin. We need time alone to rest and talk."

Entering their home, they found Singing Bird caring for their five young daughters. She glanced shyly at Isaac and said, "It is good you had a safe journey." Seeing how distraught Christiana appeared, she picked up Maria. "All the children will come to the cooking cabin to sleep. You need to rest with no one to disturb you."

"I'm going to the boy's dormitory and talk to our sons first," Isaac said, heading for the door. "I'll tell the other mission workers to expect us in school in the morning. I'll speak of my trip then."

When he was gone, Christiana prepared for bed. Totally exhausted, she fell asleep as soon as she lay down. She didn't hear Isaac return. In the morning she was startled to see him standing by the fireplace. "Did you just get up?"

"Yes, I'm sorry if I woke you. It is time to join the others for eating. Do you feel well enough?"

Out of long habit, she forced herself to prepare for the day's activities. "The house is so very quiet. It doesn't seem like I'm in the right place," she said as she pulled the quilt neatly into place. "I'm sure everyone is eager to hear of your journey. We better go."

Later, at the school, everyone listened as Isaac told about visiting Baptist officials, educators, bankers, the territorial governor and even the President of the United States. "I told each of those men about our mission station school and our needs. I tried to make contacts with colleges so you pupils can be sent there when you are prepared. I asked for financial help and received money from generous Christian men. It was an amazing experience. People everywhere were interested in our mission. Many agreed to help by giving money and food."

The pupils and teachers showed surprise as he described the places and people he had visited. He omitted the hazards and hardships he had suffered, not wanting to frighten them.

"I'll be telling you more about my experiences later but first I want to share some good news. Thanks be to the Lord, I was able to hire a blacksmith!" Isaac saw many smiles and was pleased by the response.

"His name is Robert Simmerwell. He is traveling with our supplies on a large schooner from Detroit. The ship will be coming into the Lake Michigan harbor where it connects to the Saint Joe River. We had an unhappy experience when we tried to unload supplies there before. We'll need to send people from our mission to help unload and bring supplies back." He cleared his throat, then continued. "I'll need to make a map and select the people to go. I will do those things today. Now, let's begin classes."

As the teachers began lessons, Isaac and Christiana walked from bench to bench observing. They smiled at each other in shared pleasure as they listened to young voices reciting Bible verses they had learned.

Later, hand in hand, they stepped outside. They watched Fawn and Singing Bird milk cows. Isaac laughed when

Christiana told him of the onion-flavored milk episode. "It's funny now but not then."

They inspected the garden. "I can't believe how tall the corn is growing! Later I'll saddle a horse and look at other crops."

"I'll go with you. I haven't ridden around the fields in awhile," she told him.

"In the next few days I should visit neighboring villages. Would you like to join me?"

Christiana smiled, happy for once to be included in his plans. A few minutes later she surprised him with a question. "Would you consider sending our three sons to meet the schooner? Men can't really be spared and the boys are restless. Rice, Josephus and Calvin could use a challenge. I know they would be proud to do something important."

Isaac's face lit up. "That is an excellent idea! I'll send Abraham with them. They can visit his family and he can be interpreter if required. When we get back home I'll draw them a map.

That evening he called the boys into the cabin. They were surprised and delighted with the plan. Isaac unrolled a large territorial map and pointed to Detroit. "The first week of June our cargo was shipped from there. The boat will be sailing through the Mackinac Straits, then down Lake Michigan," he said, tracing the route with his finger. "By my calculations the ship should be arriving at the mouth of the river within a few days."

"What all is coming on the schooner?" asked Josephus, wondering what they should expect.

"All the blacksmith's iron, plus tools, books, clothing, seeds, and barrels of food like flour and salt. Everything we need and want is on that boat. Everything!" their father emphasized.

The boys wiggled uneasily, sensing the importance of their assignment. He continued, "Although we all work hard here we truly can't continue to exist without those supplies. Some items were donations to the mission. Others have been purchased using donated money. We can not afford to replace this cargo. Getting this shipment to us is a very important responsibility!" His voice cracked with emotion.

"What exactly will we be required to do?" asked Rice. "Do we have to unload it? How are we going to transport the cargo? Are we taking the wagon?"

Johnston and Christiana, finished with their nightly chores, entered the cabin and sat beside the boys listening to Isaac's plans. "Your first task will be to build several fires along the Lake Michigan shore. These fires will be a beacon for the ship so the captain can see where to drop anchor. The captain suggested this strategy when we loaded cargo. There is no way of knowing when the ship will appear. You could be there for days. When the boat arrives Mr. Simmerwell and the crew will unload, probably into small boats, and come ashore."

"What are we supposed to do then?" asked Rice.

"I want two of you to remain guard over our supplies. Maybe Mr. Simmerwell will stay too. Anyway, the other two will bring a sack or two of flour back here so it can be put to use immediately. When you get here we'll know the supplies are ready for us to pick up. We men will start out as soon as you arrive. While you are gone we will be building river boats to use."

The boys looked at each other and shrugged. "Our main task then is to build nightly fires. So what will we do during the days?" asked Calvin. His brothers both jabbed him in the ribs making him cry out in pain.

"We have to sleep sometime. Also, we have to watch for the boat during the days. We'll have to signal somehow, maybe wave our arms or something," Josephus said, laughing.

Their mother leaned over to give them a stern quieting look. "I've forgotten. How far is it to the river mouth?" asked Christiana.

"Following the Indian trails it will be about thirty miles. It will probably take two or three days on horseback. I have drawn a map for the boys. Abraham, I'm sure you will recall the trail to your family trading post. Your father can direct you from there. Go get some sleep. Tomorrow morning you will leave."

Following morning devotions, Christiana packed food and cooking utensils. Isaac scooped fireplace embers into two small covered firepots. "I hope these pots will ignite wood they find along the way. They will need to keep the embers active and replenish them each morning."

"I will give them flint stones to scrape together," said Singing Bird as she climbed to the kitchen loft.

"The boys have packed hatchets and an ax. They have learned to be resourceful. I'm certain we can depend on them," Isaac said to reassure the others.

Rice led four horses to the door. Calvin showed his mother their jackets and blankets. Shouts of "Have a safe journey" echoed across the field as the boys departed. Christiana said a silent prayer as she watched them disappear into the woods. Although she thought about them often during the next days, she kept her usual daily routine.

Isaac joined her as she helped serve the noon meal. "Everyone will be busily occupied with their chores this afternoon. I'm going to visit Chief Chebass and see his cabins. Come with me. I will saddle three horses and we can take Mark along to interpret. He has acquired considerable knowledge of English."

Christiana, who had not ridden any distance for months, welcomed the chance. Following the trail five miles along the river, they entered Chief Moccasin's village. Women were working at usual occupations. One was pounding corn to make meal, two were sewing deerskin garments, one was cooking over a small campfire. The McCoys and Mark dismounted and walked around the village.

Most of the men were idle. The chief and a few others were off in a circle tossing stones in a gambling game, too absorbed to take much notice of the McCoys. The rest of the Indians received their visitors with expressions of friendship.

"One day soon I would like to talk to you about religion," Isaac told them.

"We would be glad to hear you. Anytime you want to visit we will listen."

Eventually Chief Moccasin put down his game stones and repeated, "No one will be sorry to see you. We will be glad when you come!"

The McCoys left and continued riding south until they came upon a deserted village. They dismounted and walked around empty huts. "Look at these healthy young trees, Isaac. Are these apples?" she asked fingering tiny green fruits. "Who do you suppose planted them?"

"I don't know how they got here, but yes, they are apples. Since this is an abandoned area I am going to claim them. I'll bring a wagon and some boys to dig them out. Yes sir, we will start an apple orchard on our property."

"I wonder what other fruits would grow in this region," Christiana asked, thinking how nice an addition it would be to their diet. "If we could get seeds we could grow many things."

When they reached Chebass' village Mark asked the chief about the apple trees. "Black robe priests planted seeds in many villages," he told them. He motioned the McCoys to walk with him to an area of young trees. Small fuzzy fruit hung from the branches. "These grow sweet and juicy. Not ready to eat yet."

"Those are peaches, Chief Chebass. Very good for eating. We would like to plant some of those trees. Would you save some seeds for us?" asked Isaac.

Chebass nodded in agreement. "Come now, my wives will bring food." They followed him into his cabin. The only furniture beside a shelf-like bed was a low table near the fireplace. They sat crosslegged on the floor by the table and were served a wholesome bowl of cornmeal mixed with dried venison and beaver, about the consistency of mortar. Folllowing Mark's example they dipped their fingers into the thickened paste then licked them, surprised and pleased at the taste.

Chebass was exceedingly cheerful during their visit. His face beamed as he thanked Isaac for his cabins. On the way home Christiana quizzed Isaac about the peaches. "When did you ever eat peaches?"

"On one of my journeys east I was given one. I remember everyone laughed when I bit into it. The juice ran down my chin. It was a real delicacy. Expensive to buy. If we could grow them here we could ship them east at a profit." He smiled at the thought.

"Do you really think we could earn a profit from our farming?" Christiana asked wistfully. "If you didn't have to go begging for funds anymore it would be worth it to work harder."

By the end of the week, Isaac had hired men plowing a large field. After studying his agriculture books he took several boys into the field to practice surveying. In one afternoon they staked out diagonal rows, all in preparation for the new orchard.

Saturday morning, after loading the wagon with boys and shovels, Isaac and Daniel Dusenbury followed the trail along the river. They stopped frequently to dig up fruit trees. "Make sure you don't cut the long tap root," Isaac instructed. "Try to keep the roots covered with wet soil. Can't let them dry out."

Before noon they returned to Carey Mission with over a hundred healthy trees, ready for transplanting. All morning the youngest boys had dug holes, supervised by Johnston and the hired men. Girls had filled buckets of water at the river. As trees were removed from the wagon and carried to the holes, Isaac loaded buckets and returned to the field.

As soon as a tree was placed in a hole, water was poured around it. Girls and boys ran back to the river with empty buckets to fill and Isaac returned with the wagon to pick them up again. Christiana and the youngest children watched the frantic workers. Everyone laughed as water spilled and mud squished between their bare toes.

All afternoon orders were being shouted. "Cover the roots tightly. Keep the trunks straight! Keep the trees in line! Remember orchards run in straight lines! Give those trees a good drink!"

Nearly exhausted, they finished the planting about an hour before the evening meal. Christiana eyed the muddy hands, feet and clothes. She looked at Isaac and smiled. "Seems to me everyone needs to go to the river for a quick clean up," she said. In a matter of minutes everyone was happily jumping into the cool refreshing water.

Isaac rolled up his pant legs and waded in, coaxing his young daughters to join him. Later he joined his wife and baby sitting on a tree trunk. "What a thoughtful idea you had," he said patting her arm. "It has been a wonderful day! By working together, we accomplish so much. Our pupils have learned many lessons today and had fun doing it."

"It should be easy to write your sermon this evening. All seems right with the world!" They sat watching children, then walked hand in hand along the shore to where the newly built river boats were anchored.

Isaac sat in one of the boats. "The men did a fine job of building these. They will be useful to our mission in many ways. Someday, I hope we can ship supplies out on Lake

Michigan. Imagine sending things to sell in Detroit or other ports along the way."

Christiana was lost in her own thoughts. "I wonder each morning when the boys will be returning to tell us our supplies have arrived," Christiana said wistfully as they headed back home.

The tired children had eaten and were preparing for bed by the time the adults filled their plates. As they sat down to eat they heard horses approaching. "Do you think the boys are back already to tell us the ship has arrived?" asked Johnston.

13

Isaac went to the door and watched as a young couple dismounted at the hitching post. Not recognizing them, he started walking in their direction. Suddenly a well dressed woman turned, then began calling, "Papa, Papa, I'm home!"

Isaac blinked, unable to believe his eyes. "Delilah?" He rushed to hug her, then backed off to look her over. Her clothes were of the type he had seen during his eastern travels. "You look so grown up." He heard a laugh and turned to greet Delilah's companion.

"Papa, this is Baldwin Jenkins, from Ohio."

"I'm pleased to meet you, Reverend McCoy!" he said shaking hands. "I'm related to the Wrights. When they heard I was coming to Michigan Territory to purchase farm land they arranged for your daughter to travel with me."

"I've been wanting to come home a long time, Papa, but I couldn't come alone. Where is everyone?"

"You are just in time for evening meal. Come in and surprise your mother." Isaac smiled, wondering how she would react.

Christiana gasped when she saw her fifteen-year old daughter enter the kitchen. She heard another gasp and turned in time to see Johnston blush. They both stepped toward Delilah, then noticed she wasn't alone. "Mama, Mr Lykins," she said, reaching for their hands. "I'd like you to meet Baldwin Jenkins. He accompanied me all the way from Ohio."

"Just the two of you?" asked Christiana, wondering about their relationship.

"Others joined and left us along the journey, but most of the time it was just the two of us. Mrs. McCoy, I took good care of her," Baldwin said smiling. "We were both so eager to get here we rode many miles everyday."

Delilah smiled at everyone in the kitchen. "I'm so happy to be home! I don't ever want to leave here again!" She quickly filled two plates and motioned Baldwin to join her at the table. "We haven't eaten today," she said.

Christiana noticed with pleasure the dainty way Delilah held her fork and how attractive she looked in her store-bought dress. She couldn't help wondering what her daughter had learned in Ohio.

Johnston stared at Baldwin in an unfriendly manner. "How long will you be staying with us, Mr. Jenkins? I think there is room in the loft at the Dusenbury's cabin."

Grace looked startled but offered to show him the way. "I'm sure you must be very tired after so many days of sitting on a horse. I know I would be."

"I'm anxious to get Delilah home so we can hear all about her schooling," Christiana said.

"We are all exhausted after our hard day's work but I must finish my sermon. We can walk back together," Isaac told his wife and daughter.

"Where are my brothers? I didn't see them," Delilah asked. "You haven't sent them away to be schooled have you?"

"They are away on mission work. We'll tell you about it tomorrow. Tonight, after you've greeted your sisters, I want to hear all about your time in Ohio," said Christiana, leading the way into the cabin.

Squeals of joy met Delilah as her four young sisters jumped from their beds into her arms. After things had quieted down she noticed the cradle. She rocked it gently and touched the sleeping baby's face. "Hello, Maria. I'm your big sister," she said softly. "She seems so small. I should have been here to help care for her."

"You should have stayed in school and learned other things besides caring for babies," Christiana commented. "Papa and I wanted you to learn music and manners. We wanted you to meet better educated people. We thought maybe you would study to become a teacher."

"I didn't fit in, Mama. I am more comfortable and happier here. You already taught me needlework and cooking. I love taking care of babies and helping at school. I did not like being away from my family!" Tears began falling. "I know you and Papa think you are not giving your children a good life but you are wrong! This is the right life for me!"

Christiana gathered her in her arms, "Hush now, don't cry. I'm sorry you were so unhappy away from us. Maybe you will change your mind later."

"Please, don't send me away again!"

Isaac had been working at his desk but when he heard Delilah's sobs he came to her. "You do not have to go back! I'm sure you tried to take advantage of the finer life style but if you truly don't want that way of living, we won't insist." He handed her his handkerchief. "Dry your eyes. It was only for your own betterment that we sent you. We all missed you and will be happy to have you back home."

"What about Mr. Jenkins? Have you felt any romantic interest in him or anyone else in your absence?" asked her mother.

Delilah looked shocked. "Of course not. I think I am too young for that!" she replied emphatically.

Christiana and Isaac smiled, content with her answer. "Let's prepare for bed. This has been a very long hard day!"

When Baldwin Jenkins didn't appear at either Sunday service, Christiana was glad Delilah hadn't become involved romantically with him.

Two days later Grace told her Baldwin had located some land about eight miles distant. "He plans to build a lean-to and stay on his property. I don't think he'll be back except to visit." A few days later one of the hired men reported he talked to Baldwin at Bertrand's trading post and learned he was going back to Ohio until spring.

Delilah took over the care of her youngest sisters, making fewer demands on her mother's time. Everyday Christiana prayed for her sons return. Not only did she worry about them but the supply of dried corn, which they ground for meal, was running very low. "Without flour or meal our main sustenance is absent," she complained worriedly.

The very morning she scraped the bottom of the barrel of meal Calvin and Josephus rode in, bags of white flour tied to their horses. "Mama, Papa!" they called. "We're back!"

"I thank the Lord for your safety and for what you brought!" Christiana said, rushing to help them carry a sack of flour into the cooking cabin. "I'm starting right now to prepare bread. One of you boys stay and tell me all about the ship's arrival. Are the other boys and our new blacksmith safe?"

Isaac and Johnston helped Calvin with the horses and items they'd brought. Josephus had remained with his mother. "Did Mr. Simmerwell and all the supplies arrive safely?" asked Isaac.

"Everything is on shore and safe. Rice and Abraham stayed with Mr. Simmerwell to watch things. We really like Mr. Simmerwell." Calvin yawned and sat on a stump. "We truly had adventures, but I'll let Joe tell them. I'm too tired and hungry!"

Johnston laughed. "It is good to have you boys back! Your sister Delilah came home while you were away. You'll be glad to see each other, I'm sure. Go find her. She'll feed you, then get some sleep. I'll help your father."

Isaac told Johnston he'd ride out to the fields. "The hired men need to have the boats ready by morning. Tonight we will all gather to listen as the boys tell their experiences."

That evening, well fortified by sleep and thick slices of white bread, the boys took turns relating some of the difficult days they had spent on the Lake Michigan shore. Isaac had Josephus stand before the mission group and tell about the schooner's arrival. He was nervous. "First of all," he said, clearing his throat, "we had a million tiny problems along the trail called mosquitoes." Everyone laughed, and he relaxed.

"After we left Burnett's trading post, the worn trail along the river through the woods changed into open grassy but sandy soil. It was hard going for our horses, so we walked. The closer we got to the lake the steeper we climbed." Everyone listened quietly as he continued. "Suddenly, on top of a tall sand hill, we caught a glimpse of the most beautiful sparkling water we ever saw."

Calvin smiled in agreement and added, "Big white foaming waves splashed on the shore, rolled back. then pushed ashore again and again. The noise rumbled like thunder."

"Yes," interrupted Josephus, "we wondered how any boat could sail in those waves. Anyway we tied the horses under some trees and carried our belongings down near the water. That's when we realized how difficult a task we had. The sand was so deep, we sank in almost to our knees. We dragged some dry limbs down behind us but every time we got a fire started, the water spray or blowing sand put it out." Josephus looked at his father. "We built sand walls around the fire but they didn't last. Even if a fire had burned, the smoke would have disappeared immediately. No one could have seen it. We gave up and climbed back up by the horses. Calvin, you talk awhile."

"The sun reflected so bright on the blue water you couldn't stand to look at it. We took turns watching for a boat and gathering wood. We decided to make the fire on the hill." Calvin continued talking, much to Josephus' relief. "We learned that the wind usually calmed down at night, so once we got a fire started we took turns sitting beside it and adding limbs. One day Abraham made a spear from a branch and caught some fish by wading out into lake. We roasted them in our fire. They were sure good!"

"Let me tell the rest," said Josephus, thinking his parents wanted their tale to end. "On the fourth night, things changed. Clouds drifted over the moon. We were in total darkness. Suddenly gusts of wind whirled sand into our faces and stung our eyes. Sparks flew and wood pieces rolled off the fire. We couldn't see any glowing embers." He swallowed hard, remembering the night.

"When we felt rain beginning to fall we scooped up every twig that was still warm and filled the fire pot. By morning everything was drenched. We had no fire left. We tried using our flint stones but everything was too wet to ignite. We hung a blanket in a tree as a signal for the schooner, but it blew off."

"What did you do?" interrupted a young boy, anxious to know how they solved their problems.

"We did lots of praying! Finally, God sent us the answer," Calvin responded. "He sent two Indian boys to fish along the shore. When we saw them, Abraham ran down to talk to them. He brought them up the hill, then we went with them to their nearby village. The women in the village filled our fire pot, gave us a meal and some dry wood. It was like a miracle!"

"We started two fires, one on the hill top and one halfway down. We cut down a big pine tree and the dark smoke from its branches rose up really high." Josephus said, taking over again. "We kept a constant watch on the lake. Sometimes we actually thought we saw ships, but then the visions faded."

"One afternoon we saw a beautiful rainbow over the water," Calvin recalled. "I wish you could have seen it!"

Josephus nodded and got back to his tale. "We kept the flame burning each night and made dark smoke in the daylight. Just before sunrise on the seventh day a terrible, ear-splitting blare scared us right out of our blankets. I can't really describe it but it sounded like a dozen cows bellowing."

"Then, two loud toots came and we saw the schooner," interrupted Calvin. "Close to shore, on a sand bar, right in front of us. We saw men in a small boat coming ashore and we ran down to meet them."

"Captain Petersen was the first man to step on the beach. He was dressed in a blue coat with gold braid decorations. He asked if we were from McCoy Mission," said Josephus. "We introduced ourselves and met Mr. Simmerwell, who was with him. The Captain said he thought he was right on course but wasn't sure until he saw our beacon fire. He was rather upset to learn no men were there to help unload, but finally agreed to have his crew haul our supplies on to the beach. He said he had to get his ship back to Detroit. We told Mr. Simmerwell we needed to take flour home and that men with boats would come back for the rest of the items. He rowed a boat back to the ship, got the flour, then stayed to help unload and guard the cargo. I guess that about covers all the details."

"Will everything fit in our boats or should we send the wagon too?" asked Isaac.

"Mr. Simmerwell did say some boxes of clothing and other benevolent gifts were added at two ports," Josephus said. "Actually I think it would be a difficult journey for a wagon, Papa. The trail is narrow and the sandy part would be near impossible."

"Well, men," Isaac said dejectedly, "I'm sorry, but I'm not feeling well enough to make the journey." He managed a half smile and said, "I have every confidence that you will be able to stow everything aboard the keel boats. Let's retire now. We'll send you off at daybreak." He started to walk away, then stopped. "For the first time we will be receiving a complete shipment. Praise the Lord!"

"Ample supplies and a blacksmith! We all praise the Lord!" Johnston said, looking around at all the smiling faces, except for Christiana's.

She was startled to hear Isaac say he was ill. He'd made no mention of it to her. On the way back to their cabin, Isaac insisted he was merely tired. "A few days in bed, I'll be all right."

Christiana and a few others watched the boats' departure the next morning. A crowd quickly gathered on their return ten days later. Robert Simmerwell was welcomed into the mission family. "You are going to be very busy here," Christiana told him as she and Johnston led him to the smithery. Isaac had not regained his strength. The burden of his duties again fell on Christiana and those she could delegate to help her.

"I came to work," Robert replied as he looked around the small building erected for his smithery. "Has anyone tried to make brick here? The river soil probably has enough clay. Mixed with dried grass it should harden. We can build some forms and try a few."

"What will you use brick for?" asked Christiana.

"I'll need a contained fire area so no one gets burned by embers jumping out. It needs to be built waist high so I don't have to constantly bend over. Smithey fires are kept very hot as you'll soon see."

"We can get some young lads to help. We haven't tried brick making before. If it works maybe we could use them to finish building fireplaces." Johnston said. "When can we start?"

Robert smiled. "I think we are going to be good friends. I like the way you get right to solutions. First, we'd best unload the boats. After the iron is carried over we can build some forms."

"Let's get you settled first. That end cabin was built for the blacksmith and his family," Christiana said, nodding her head in the general direction. "Since you are a single man, if you would prefer you could stay in the boy's dormitory. Either way you'd take your meals at the mission kitchen."

"I would prefer the cabin. My hours will be irregular and I want to stay close enough to keep fires burning." He laughed. "I am glad I won't have to eat my own cooking."

Christiana and Johnston walked with Robert around the mission grounds, stopping to introduce him along the way. Fanny blushed as Robert studied her carefully. "I didn't think missionaries were supposed to be so pretty," he said smiling at her.

Leaving the school they headed back toward the river. Christiana was surprised to find Isaac sitting on a stump supervising the unloading. "I wish I felt strong enough to carry off these barrels and crates, but I don't," he confessed. "Did you ever see so many things, Christiana? I am making a list of every article so thank you letters can be sent to donors."

Christiana was very happy to welcome her three sons back into their household. "We are glad to be back Mama, but we need to learn how to manage on our own. Remember, Papa has written letters on our behalf so we can go away to school," Rice reminded her.

"We won't be like Delilah! We want to get training so we can become doctors or ministers. We'll be too busy learning to get homesick."

Christiana wiped a tear before they saw it fall. "I want you to go as much as your father does," she said stubbornly. "I want you to have opportunities we can't offer here, but I will miss you! I hope you won't all go at once"

Although neighboring Indians had planted their fields in May and June, the time until vegetables ripened was the most trying time of the year. Swarms of hungry people appeared at the mission in hopes of getting a few crumbs, bones from their tables or broth from any boiled food.

Isaac and Christiana grieved as they witnessed the growing starvation. Supplies they had so happily received had soon diminished. An Indian woman appeared with moccasins hoping to exchange them for powder and lead. "My nephew could hunt for food if he had the way," she pleaded. "We will die without food."

Begging occurred hourly. One old woman requested a bowl of salt. Christiana cried when the woman told her, "This will season the weeds on which I feed."

A young mother brought a little girl and secretly left her without saying anything to the McCoys. Her brothers had been living at the mission school. The girl was discovered with them at evening prayer time. Christiana stripped the poor wretched child of her rags, cleaned and dressed her like the other children, allowing her to remain.

By mid-July garden vegetables were ready to be eaten, which of course lessened Christiana's worries. "We must begin immediately to preserve some of this bounty," she told Singing Bird. "We cannot give away or eat all we are harvesting or next winter we will be starving again."

Once again Grace and Mary worked with the girls, threading string beans and hanging herbs and squash rings to dry.

Occasionally Singing Bird disappeared from the mission for several days at a time. When questioned about her absence, she annoyed Christiana by looking at the ground and refusing to answer.

"I worry about your safety. I miss your help in the kitchen and with the children," Christiana always said. "If you must be away please tell me before you leave!"

One evening, after prayer time, Singing Bird surprised the McCoys with a visit. She was accompanied by a handsome Potawatomi man from the village of Chebass. "We are mated," she said shyly. "Can Grey Wolf live here?"

"Grey Wolf must work here if he lives here." He nodded his acceptance. "Also, we must speak to Fawn. If she agrees to move, you can have the kitchen loft for your home," Christiana told them.

"Fawn is going to live in Pokagon village with the mate she has chosen."

Isaac glanced at his wife, not knowing what to say. "There are still customs we do not understand. It seems we have no choice but to accept what has happened," Christiana said. "I will miss Fawn. Tell her I wish to talk to her before she leaves. If you and Grey Wolf choose to remain and work we will welcome you."

The next morning Grey Wolf was seen working in the fields with the other men and Singing Bird was busy in the kitchen.

On July fourteenth, five fancifully attired Indian chiefs followed by their village people, numbering about one hundred, assembled outside the Carey Mission. When questioned they said they were gathering in preparation for their yearly journey to Detroit and Canada. "We go to collect money and gifts from British in exchange for past military war duties."

"Even with Abraham or Luther's help, listening to their long speeches day after day has been difficult. My knowledge of their language is improving. Mostly what I am hearing are pleas for travel food," Isaac told Christiana. "Tomorrow I must reply."

"What will you reply?"

"I've thought about it, discussed it with others and prayed about it. What do you think I should say?"

Christiana shook her head. "We don't have food to spare! Anyway I don't think we should give food to anyone who hasn't worked or earned it somehow."

Isaac smiled. "I agree. We cannot grant their request, but Daniel and William suggested we give them some powder and lead. They can use that to procure wild game along the journey. This is an opportunity to teach them a civilized habit of life. That is one of our reasons for being here, so it makes me happy!"

"That will be a good solution. You are right as usual. I have been pleased to observe no whiskey being passed in the group," Christiana commented. "I hope none is given to them along their journey."

Speaking to the Indians exhausted Isaac. His health had been failing since his return from the East. On July twenty-sixth he became confined to his bed. Numerous annual reports and letters needed to be written. He felt compelled to write whenever he was able to sit up and sometimes as he lay in bed.

Christiana tried to keep the children quiet so their father could rest. She became Isaac's caretaker growing more concerned over his illness everyday. The total responsibility of handling school problems and pupils also fell to her. Delilah helped Singing Bird with the cooking and watched her sisters when she could.

On the eleventh of August Isaac was so ill his brother-in-law William saddled a horse and started for Ft. Wayne to locate a physician. On the thirteenth, while Christiana was teaching, Isaac sent little Sarah to the blacksmith shop for Robert Simmerwell.

"I need to express my views of missionary affairs and make proper arrangements for my family and the brethren," he confided. "Would you please write a will for me? I am sinking under my disease. I cannot sustain many more days of this affliction!" Shaking with chills and nearly in tears he whispered his real fear. "I am so very worried about who will comfort Christiana."

"I haven't been here very long, brother McCoy, but you need not fear for your wife and children. Everyone here will provide for them if the need arises! I believe our good Lord still has work for you to do. He will sustain you! William will return soon with medical help. You will be healthy again!" said Robert in a rare serious mood.

August was hay cutting time on the prairie. Since Isaac was ill, it was necessary for Johnston to take charge of superintending the older boys as they labored in the fields. Then he and Daniel became bedridden. William was still absent. Robert Simmerwell was the only male missionary on the premise able to keep the others laboring. "I know very little about farm work or handling young men. We'll have to learn together," he said, stopping at every cabin to offer assistance or ask for advice.

Robert and Christiana were worn out by the time the doctor arrived with William. The week he remained, he was kept very busy dispensing medicine and curing many complaints. Remarkably, Isaac's health improved enough so that he was able to walk with a cane.

"I must return to Fort Wayne. Others will be needing me," the doctor told the McCoys. "Take care, Reverend McCoy!" he called as he rode out, clutching a sack of fresh vegetables as part of his fee.

On the twentieth of August Chief Pokagon, known as a man of great intelligence and respectability, came to inform the McCoys of liquor in the area. "My village people wish to go seize it. The use of spirit water makes people go crazy! Once they drink it they don't want to stop," the chief said sadly.

"I understand your concern. It is our concern also," Isaac told the chief and his accompanying warriors. "I do not believe that seizing it will cure the problem. It could lead to fighting and worse. We will try to keep white traders from selling liquor. You must try to keep your people from drinking it. I don't know any other peaceful way to act." They shook hands in a solemn promise to work together to prevent alcohol sales and use.

14

Long before sunup on a September morning, the McCoys were startled awake by loud shouts followed by screams. Isaac grabbed his gun and rushed to open the cabin door. Christiana, followed by several children, crept behind him. Weird noises echoed from the woods. Straining their eyes, they saw several Indian males chasing another. They quickly disappeared from sight. Quiet was restored and the family went back to bed. Several men from the mission scouted the woods after breakfast but found nothing out of the usual.

That evening Isaac sat outdoors waiting for the girls to get ready for bed. A man staggered toward him. The man tripped and fell in a drunken stupor. Isaac recognized Miami tribal clothing and wondered why the Indian was so far from home.

"Christiana, I'm going to find William and Daniel. I'll be right back. You and the girls stay inside," he called at the doorway.

When the men returned, the Indian had fallen asleep. They half carried, half dragged him a short distance into the woods out of sight of the mission and covered him with a horse blanket from the corral.

The next morning Isaac returned to find the man sober and willing to talk. Isaac was able to interpret his words. "I don't know how I got here. I remember going with others to Fort Wayne for our annuity. We bought many drinks. There were fights." He hung his head, looking both worried and sick. "I think maybe I killed someone. I ran many days."

Isaac talked to the man at great lengths about bad effects of liquor. He walked to the kitchen cabin and came back with a bowl of soup. When the man had eaten he stood up. Looking Isaac in the eye, he said earnestly, "I will try not to drink anymore."

Isaac had his doubts but was thankful he had been able to communicate, at least partially, in the man's language. He had acquired enough ability so that he could write and then read his religious papers in Potawatomi villages in their own language. Indians liked this better than listening to an interpreter.

Fanny Goodrich continued to join Isaac in his village visits. She taught lessons from the Bible to the women. They liked Fanny and were eager to learn. She was able to answer many questions and always invited them to the mission church service. When asked, "When will it be Sunday? When will it be Prayer Day?" both Isaac and Fanny were very gratified.

Attendance at church services increased each Sunday. Two boys now blew their trumpets to announce church. Indian neighbors appeared soon after. Isaac's health improved and his sermons grew longer. Neighbors spent the whole day at Carey Mission.

Christiana still assumed responsibility for much of the mission work, allowing Isaac more time for writing letters and filling out reports. He worked long hours on writing translations and faithfully kept his diary. Christiana was close to exhaustion when she learned that her husband was sending Rice to Ft. Wayne and on to Ohio to attend to some business problems.

"If anyone should go from here, it should be me!" she said. "I've been involved in mission concerns. I should be the one to make decisions!"

Isaac was shocked by her outburst. Until then he had not realized how much stress had been placed on her. "My dear, you must relax. You have been overburdened by my illness and all the chores." He put his arm around her and led her to her rocking chair. "I'm feeling much improved and can take over here. You just rest a few days."

Rice listened with concern. "Why can't Mama go with me? I would like to have her company and we could handle the business calls together."

Christiana welcomed Rice's suggestion. Isaac hesitated. He knew she needed a respite from work. He wasn't sure how he could care for their children and the mission without her. She kept rocking, waiting for his reply.

"It would give you a chance to see old friends," he finally said. "Maybe while you two are visiting you would be able to locate a blacksmith for Thomas Station." He cleared his throat, then added wistfully, "Some of the other women here will no doubt help with the girls."

Christiana smiled for the first time. "If we take the wagon, Maria and Eleanor can go with us. The others will be in school."

"If you think the girls can complete their chores without your supervision, then I guess there is no reason you can't go," Isaac finally agreed.

Tired as she was, preparations for the journey excited Christiana. Delilah searched through clothing boxes and located a pretty skirt, fancy dress collars and undergarments for her mother. Fanny helped cut apart old dresses and they sewed new outfits for the little girls and two shirts for Rice.

Grace helped Christiana wash clothes and pack food and blankets. As a special treat Christiana baked enough fresh bread to leave some for her family. Isaac wrote many reports and letters for her to deliver to people in authority. He gave Rice a long list of things to do and purchases to make. Dusenburys and Polkes each gave them letters to deliver and lists of items they needed as did several others.

On the ninth of September they were on their way. The weather was warm and dry. The little girls slept. As Christiana rode beside her son she basked in the beauty of the fall foliage. "Oh, Rice, I thank you for changing your Papa's mind." She patted his arm. "I needed to get away awhile. I hope he will forgive me for leaving."

"Mama, you don't need forgiveness! You work too hard. You deserve a time away, not that this is going to be an easy journey."

She laughed as the four of them bounced over rough and dusty trails. "This has certainly become a well worn and rutted path. Remember what a horrible time we had traveling from Fort Wayne the first time?"

"Yes, I certainly do. We nearly froze and starved! I remember every time I make this journey."

Rice had no difficulty fording the streams and rivers, shallow after the summer heat. The girls played happily in the wagon each day or gathered colored leaves and nuts as they walked with their mother. At night they all slept in the wagon.

Occasionally they saw Indians fishing along a river. Once two young men traded three fish for a half a loaf of bread

Christiana offered. As they neared Ft. Wayne they met a young man on horseback headed for Carey Mission.

"John Lybrook's the name," he said. "I heard tell that they need hired men there. I'm a cooper by trade and can do some smithy work. If I like it in that territory I might purchase me some land."

Before he departed, they told him all about their mission. Christiana quickly wrote a note for him to take back to Isaac.

Their stay in Ft. Wayne was less than a week. Rice and his mother took care of mail, met with Baptist Board officials and gave them Isaac's reports. Friends happily invited them into their homes so they could share all the latest news. Several families had moved on to other locations, some friends were sick and couldn't have company.

Both Rice and his mother were eager to reach their Ohio destination. Christiana planned to visit friends and family in Troy. Rice had other intentions. He was going to visit Martha Wright, hoping to rekindle their friendship. "I haven't received any letter since Delilah came home. I hope she isn't angry," he said to his mother.

Christiana didn't want to upset him but silently worried that perhaps Martha was ill or had committed to some other young man. In her way of thinking, Rice should be planning for college and not a wife. "I'm sure she must be very busy, son, teaching and caring for her father's needs."

"I've been thinking maybe she moved, but then she should have let me know. The only way I'll know is to go there."

Every time he mentioned Martha, his mother switched the conversation to the importance of education and his training to become a doctor.

After a few days of rainy weather the pleasure of traveling faded. Sitting day after day in soggy clothing and sleeping under damp covers made them all irritable. Their remaining food became moldy. Christiana began wishing she had stayed at Carey Mission.

Before they arrived in Troy, both Maria and Eleanor developed runny noses and were coughing. "Aren't we a sad sight to be moving in with friends?" Christiana said to Rice.

"I think they will be happy to see you, no matter how we look," he said. "It will be good to sleep in a house and have a chance to get cleaned up."

Rice was wrong. The village of Troy had been hit with an epidemic. Every household had sickness. Rice stopped their wagon in front of a general store. He asked for directions to the home of his mother's friend, J.R. John. As they rode along the muddy, bumpy streets they saw many boarded up places. The few people they saw were covering their faces with towels as they hurriedly walked.

"Rice, what have we come into?"

He swallowed hard trying to appear unafraid. "Everyone must be busy inside today. Each family probably is caring for their own. They are not out and about."

When they reached the John's home, Rice halted the horses. Christiana walked to the door. She was greeted with surprise. Her friend, J.R., looked beyond her to the wagon. "Oh, you have brought your children. You must bring them in quickly."

"Are you sure?" she asked, seeing how distraught he appeared. "We can go on to a boarding house or continue on to the old family homestead." She stood on the steps waiting.

"The sickness has left this house," he said sadly. "Two of our children died. The rest of the family is recovering."

"Can I be of help caring for them?" Christiana asked. "How is your wife, Hope? Would she like to have me here?"

"Come in, come in, Christiana." called a weak voice.

Motioning for Rice to bring the girls, they followed J.R. to a small bedroom.. "Make yourself at home," he told them. Rice carried in their belongings and prepared his sisters for bed while his mother began caring for the household.

"Now, Hope and J.R., you just let me take over here. You need to sleep. We can talk later," Christiana said as she began clearing the table. "I'll wash dishes and cook some soup. Rice and I'll look after the children."

She handled her friends beautiful china with care, thinking back to the wooden bowls of the mission. As she dusted upholstered furniture and swept the carpet, she thought of the stark furnishings in her own cabin. With so much to do, she didn't dwell on the differences.

After three days of constant work, Christiana was finally able to rest. "Rice, I appreciate all your help, but I can manage without you now. Go find the Wrights, then get the supplies and go back to Carey."

"What about all the business needing to be done here, Mama?"

"J.R. can help me find the offices I need to visit. I'll just stay here awhile longer. Someone else can come get the girls and I."

A week after Rice left, J.R. accompanied Christiana to the bank and land office so she could make long overdue payments on a small piece of property she and Isaac were buying. Years before they had chosen the area as a place to build and live when their missionary work ended. She mailed letters to Isaac and to Baptist missionary boards, enjoying the convenience of community stores and seeing nice homes.

Four days after their walk through the business district, J.R. collapsed with the typhoid fever which still permeated the community. Christiana and Hope took turns sponging his feverish body and tried to ease his sore throat and cough. No physician was available, even for an important businessman like J.R.

Christiana boiled water and scrubbed everything, hoping that would stop the spread of the dreaded disease. The John's children, pale and weakened from their recent sickness, enjoyed playing with Maria and Eleanor. Days blended into more days. Just as J.R. improved enough to sit up and eat, Maria and Eleanor developed high fevers and rashes on their bodies. Soon their coughing and cries of pain filled the house. Christiana worked full time applying cool cloths to cut the fever. She tried desperately to force liquids down their sore throats. Eleanor responded to treatment but tiny Maria became dehydrated and lapsed into a coma.

The Johns took turns with Christiana, who was now also ill, in caring for her baby. On October eighteenth, eleven month old Maria died. Christiana was too sick to prepare her daughter for burial. The task fell to her friends who had so recently buried two of their own. "Could you make a white dress for her from my fancy petticoat? I don't have anything else to offer," Christiana asked tearfully. Hope wiped her tears and agreed to make the dress the way her friend wanted.

Rice arrived unexpectedly on the twenty-fourth of October to a very forlorn household. Christiana sobbed as he held her thin and shaking body. "Take me home, take me home Rice, I can't stand to stay here any longer!" she begged.

Rice had returned to Carey with a blacksmith and wagonload of supplies and smithery articles in early October. When he told his father of the epidemic in Troy, he had been allowed a two day rest, then was sent to bring back his mother and sisters.

"I came on horseback, Mama. Surely you don't feel up to riding back yet. You are too weak!"

"It won't be any easier a journey on a horse or with a bumpy wagon. It will be faster by horse. I want to go home! Eleanor can ride in your lap. Please!"

The Johns agreed to erect a small tombstone marking Maria's grave. They were sorry to have their friend leave but understood her need to go home, especially with the approach of winter.

After a brief stop at the cemetery, where she placed a bouquet of brightly-colored leaves on the burial site, the three McCoys started their journey home. Only at night, when they sat around their cooking fire, did they talk to each other.

"Martha married a widow man with two children. She is still teaching and running a household. That's why she had not written," Rice confided dejectedly.

"All in all it was an unhappy journey for both of us, son. Indeed, I am very sorry we went!" she said sadly. "I now understand Delilah's longing to return home when she was away at school. I want to get back there too!"

On another evening, Rice was startled to see his mother smiling. "What has made you suddenly happy?"

"You are the first to know, son. I was afraid there was a problem but everything is all right. There will be a new baby in our family in a few months. I just felt it kick."

On November first they arrived at Carey Station. After the initial shock and sadness of Maria's death was shared, they were absorbed comfortably back into the mission family and routine. Christiana was surprised but pleased to find four Indian women helping Singing Bird in the kitchen and with cleaning chores.

"When did these women become part of our mission?" she asked Isaac.

"During harvest some men from Pokagon's village came to join in the work. Their wives followed, of course, and made themselves useful cooking and scrubbing clothes. They asked to remain. Thinking it might make things easier for you, I agreed."

The day after Christiana and Rice returned, John Lieb, appointed by Gov. Cass, arrived from Detroit to make the annual inspection of the mission. He remained three days, writing pages of notes as he walked the property. He looked inside every building and rode the fields.

"The harvest is remarkable!" he said, praising the McCoys' work. "1,600 bushels of corn, 400 bushels of potatoes, 1,000 head of cabbages, besides all the oats and turnips. The governor is going to be very surprised and pleased!"

He talked with many pupils and all the teachers. He sat beside Christiana one noon and told her, "I only found three or four girls who cannot spin or knit. That is amazing! The 294 yards of cloth woven on your looms is very fine quality. I heard you plan to make uniform clothing for the youngsters. That is a big undertaking, but as you say, uniforms will be much superior to castoffs."

One morning he rode with Isaac to nearby Indian villages. "I didn't expect to see so much land planted and with fences around them! Your mission is a good influence on them."

"I only wish we could stop white settlers from selling whiskey! Many Indians claim a dislike for these ardent spirits but they seldom can withstand the temptation to drink. When we talk to settlers they just laugh."

"I'm sorry to hear about that. I guess there is no way to stop a person with bad motives from buying land, is there? I will mention the problem to Governor Cass," said Mr. Lieb.

"By the way, the governor met Mr. Simmerwell, your blacksmith, in Detroit this spring. Looks like he is doing good work. I saw two apprentice boys working in the smithery. More will likely become interested later on. The smithy waiting to go to Thomas Station seems skilled too."

Before Mr. Lieb left, he spoke once more to the McCoys. "You have six hired men who keep busy in the agriculture and improving buildings and five Indian women working as domestics, but don't you think more should be hired? No need to overburden yourselves."

Isaac shook his head in agreement. "We have requested additional monies from the Missionary Board and from the Governor so we can hire help. Letters and money take a long time to arrive. We not only need money to pay our help, we also need winter supplies like flour for bread and salt to preserve meat."

"I will personally deliver any requests you hand me. I will be back in Detroit in a few days. I can take letters you want mailed as well." Isaac sat up all night preparing letters to give Mr. Lieb.

Fanny Goodrich's cheerful influence on the pupils was very positive. Robert Simmerwell admired her shyly from a distance. She approached everyone with a warm smile and a friendly greeting. The girls under her care began to pay more attention to their clothing and hair. More importantly, the quality of their schoolwork improved and they participated in religious discussions.

Although it was November, the weather remained unusually mild. Ezekiel French, a hired man, was baptized in the St. Joseph River on November seventh, although the ground was covered with snow. Everyone huddled around a fire, built on the bank for comfort, as they watched the first Protestant baptism in the river. Isaac and Fanny participated in religious conversations many times each day. On the fifteenth of November, Ezekiel Clark, Charles Potter and Jared Lykins, a cousin of Johnston, were baptized. Of the sixty-six pupils, many watched the ceremony with great interest.

A northern Ottawa Indian chief named Gosa brought the sixty-seventh pupil to Carey Mission. The boy was from the Grand River area. Gosa remained for nearly two weeks, fascinated with the work he observed going on there.

One of the letters in the packet Rice brought from Ft. Wayne held special news for the McCoys. "I've been waiting to tell you something important," Isaac told his family as they relaxed together on a Sunday afternoon.

He held up a letter. "This contains small scholarships for Rice and Josephus so that they might attend Columbian College in Washington City."

Christiana and the boys looked stunned. Rice finally spoke. "Can we really go? How long will be allowed to stay? How can we pay for college training?"

" I wish your mother and I could pay your way," Isaac said wistfully," but there will be ways to earn your room and board. You are healthy, capable young men not afraid to work. The most important thing will be to choose your classes carefully and allow enough time to study. However long it takes is how long you should stay."

Christiana sighed as she quickly brushed away a tear. She knew from looking at their excited faces that they were eager to go but she also knew she would miss them terribly. "When will they leave us?" she asked.

"Before the month is over. The journey will be lengthy. They'll need time to find housing and jobs before classes commence in January."

"Oh my, Delilah, you and I must quickly sew some shirts and other garments. They'll need new brogans made. Ezekiel Clark does cobbler work, doesn't he? You girls can knit socks and caps and scarves for your brothers." By taking charge of the preparations, Christiana overcame the sad feeling of losing her sons.

15

"Mama, may we bring down the charity boxes to look for garments or at least buttons?" the girls teased. Christiana shook her head. She couldn't understand why used clothes were so fascinating but since it made them happy and could prove beneficial she gave permission. Looking through the boxes did indeed prove useful. With a few tucks and seam changes, both boys were outfitted with coats, trousers and fancy shirts.

While they sewed, Delilah talked to her mother. "Rice and Josephus will do well in college. They are not like me, Mama. They will be together. They will not get homesick and disappoint you and Papa."

"We are not disappointed in you, Delilah. We are disappointed for you. We want good training for all of you, so you can find happiness."

"I am very content here at home," Delilah insisted.

A week after the boys left, Isaac did too. He had made an earlier commitment to Chief Noonday that he would supply the new Thomas Mission Station with a blacksmith. Now Sam Stout, the man Rice had located in Ohio, was prepared and eager to move his supplies. Isaac needed to be certain that the buildings were constructed and ready for the blacksmith and teachers to begin working there.

Accompanied by Chief Gosa, Isaac and Sam followed the St. Joseph River to the Grand River. During the journey they often had to swim the horses in icy water. Isaac became ill with dysentery. Unfortunately, he had not remembered to pack medicine. His companions managed to get him safely to Chief Noonday's village. The Chief called together all his curing people. By singing, chanting and using remedies made from forest plants they were able to heal Isaac enough so he was able to eat and retain the food they prepared.

While Isaac remained in the area he surveyed land and designated building sites. Some of his instructions from an earlier visit had been followed. A few trees had already been felled. Since most of the Indians had never built a cabin they had no idea how to stack logs.

"When I return to my Saint Joseph River mission I'll choose some laborers to come and help you," he told the Chief. "Sam has brought tools and supplies. He will work with you and make more tools for you."

While returning to Carey, a sudden blinding blizzard forced Isaac to spend the night in a small village. Many of the Indians there were in a terrible state of intoxication. He left the next morning, choosing bad weather over the bad situation.

Wildly blowing snow made high drifts. His faithful horse pushed through but both he and horse were cold and near exhaustion when they reached Carey Mission. Fortunately, Daniel Dusenbury saw him ride in and called Calvin who was nearby. They helped Isaac dismount and half carried him home. The horse trotted to the corral.

Christiana was sewing by the fire when Daniel flung the door open. "Oh, my soul," she said as she saw her snow covered husband. "Let's get him out of those clothes and into bed." Isaac slept for several hours. Later, as he was dressing, she realized with a shock how very thin he had become and immediately prepared him a bowl of mush.

In the mail Isaac found waiting was an official letter from Governor Cass which amused him. He read it aloud after evening devotions. "Listen to this, 'The 1824 Legislation Council of the Michigan Territory formally requests that Thursday, November 25th be set aside as a holiday for giving thanks to our Almighty Lord.' Can you imagine?" he asked. "We give thanks every day. Doesn't everyone?" A loud resounding "Amen" echoed throughout the room.

The weather cleared enough by mid-December so that two hired men were able to leave for Chief Noonday's village to help construct buildings at Thomas Station Mission.

Compared to the pork roast of 1822, the January first celebration welcoming 1825 was another small one. Most food had been prepared the last days of December. Early New

Year's morning, Christiana tiptoed to the window. She tried to scrape enough frost away to peer out into the darkness. What she managed to see were large snowflakes filtering down, adding to drifts already on the frozen ground. She sighed and hurriedly placed three logs atop the embers.

As she dressed, she heard Isaac and the children waking. Isaac's cough had kept both of them awake most of the night. She had hoped he would sleep late.

"How's the weather this morning?" he asked as he approached the fireplace.

"Snowy and dreary," she answered. "Looks windy, too, but I guess we better try to get outdoor fires going. Visitors will need them to keep warm. Don't know if we should try to prepare food outside today."

Isaac started to pull on his heavy coat. Moving his arms started another bout of coughing. "Sit down, Isaac! I'll get the cough remedy Singing Bird made. Stay inside. Just tell me what you want done."

He sighed as he took his jacket off. "You have enough to do, my dear."

Christiana frowned. He saw her displeasure. "I'll stay indoors, at least until our neighbors arrive. I'll be writing a brief message for today. Our young ones can stay here out of your way," he told her.

She pulled on a heavy shawl and tied her bonnet. "I'll go get a kettle of corn mush so you can all eat here." When she stepped outdoors she was surprised by the mild temperature. The wet snowflakes were changing to rain. The ground was thawing. After taking food from the kitchen back to her family, she followed the slippery path to the boys' cabin to enlist help.

Four boys worked with her, trying unsuccessfully to build fires. "It's just too miserable," she admitted. "We will cook some in the kitchen and serve in the school building.   It is likely going to be a small turnout."

Johnston and Daniel carried two large kettles containing venison and broth from the kitchen.   Boys brought in more logs.   The girls assigned to cooking chores followed with large bowls of vegetables.   No sooner had they placed the kettles onto the fireplace cranes then the sound of loud voices were heard.

Christiana opened the door and was horrified to see several Indian men rolling and fighting in the muddy yard.   Within minutes a crowd gathered.   "Run and get Reverend McCoy," yelled her brother William.   "These men have been drinking whiskey.   We've got to get them out of here!"

Robert and Johnston joined William and they separated the fighters.   Isaac arrived in time to help escort them into the woods. The mission crowd wandered away. Grace and Fanny joined Christiana who was still standing in the doorway.   The three of them went into the school building.

"That drunken fight is a bad omen," said Grace, shaking her head in disgust.

"Nonsense," replied Christiana.   "The actions of those men are proof that we have work to do here.   They need guidance and forgiveness."

"You are right, sister McCoy," Fanny said.   "Our pupils need to see us doing those two things."

Grace hung her head like a scolded child and silently started setting out soup bowls.   Rain continued to fall, turning the melting snow into a sea of mud.   Eventually neighoring Indians arrived to welcome the new year.   Their muddy footprints added to those of the mission family.   Combined with the spilled food on the rough plank floor and desks, it caused the women to groan at the prospect of cleaning up.

In spite of the weather and crowded conditions, the celebration was a jovial affair. Isaac's message was brief. They listened politely. Late into the afternoon everyone took part in a slow shuffled dance around the room accompanied by the drums Chiefs Chebass and Topinabe supplied.

Robert Simmerwell had been teaching his blacksmith apprentices to make bells in the smithery. They had practiced on small bells for animals to wear. He whispered to one of the boys, "Mark, go bring all the bells we've made. They will add music to the dance." Everyone was given at least two bells and took great delight in ringing them. Fanny smiled at Robert, showing her approval. He winked in response, causing her to blush.

Tired as they were, Christiana and Mary swept and scrubbed the building by candlelight, long after everyone else had retired for the night.

The next morning Isaac exclaimed how pleased he was that their school was being accepted by the neighboring villages. "So many told me how happy they are to have Carey Mission here. They promised to send more children and to attend Sunday services."

Taking advantage of the January thaw, Isaac and Fanny conducted baptisms in the river. On the twelfth, three Indian pupils took part in the ceremony; on the seventeenth, four men. Both occasions included celebrations of prayers and singing around bonfires.

True to their word, neighboring chiefs sent or brought children to be enrolled at the school. By mid-January, Isaac wrote in his diary that ninety persons were fed daily at their table. Sixty- seven of them were pupils.

From the formation of the mission, Christiana had insisted on cleanliness for all members. They received no food until faces and hands were washed and hair was neatly smoothed down. Clothing might be patched and not a perfect fit, but had to be clean. The women were helping the girls make matching dresses from material woven on their looms.

During cold winter months, when food was scarce in the villages, it was not unusual for a young brother or sister of a pupil to appear in a meal line. They were surprised at how quickly they were recognized. If old enough, they sometimes remained as pupils but usually the women cleaned them up, fed them and returned them to their family. Christiana longed to keep them all.

One cold moon-lit February evening after devotions, the McCoys strolled leisurely toward their cabin. "Look at the stars. Aren't they beautiful?" Christiana stood gazing upwards, enjoying a rare quiet time with Isaac. "It seems a shame to go indoors."

Suddenly they heard a man shouting, "Mrs. McCoy! Mrs. McCoy! My wife is in need of assistance." As he got closer, Christiana recognized Squire Thompson. He and his family were living in the blacksmith's cabin until their own cabin was built. Robert had moved to the boy's dormitory to make room.

"Tell Singing Bird to come, and bring birthing things," she told Isaac. Then she quickly followed Squire. As they opened the door, she saw three small children huddled by the fireplace. "Squire, bundle up the young ones and take them over to my cabin. Children, you be sure and look at the sky," she said as she smiled. "Maybe you can count the stars for me."

The children left with their father and she walked swiftly to the bed, talking soothingly to Faith, "Everything's going to be fine. I've delivered lots of babies." She busied herself, straightening bedcovers and emptying the water bucket into the iron kettle in the fireplace. The logs crackled as she tossed another one on the fire.

"I had a doctor for the others," moaned Faith. "They came easier than this one. I think I've been working too strenuous." She screamed in pain.

"That's probably the reason," replied Christiana, wondering where Singing Bird was and beginning to worry as she wiped sweat from both their brows.

After a timid knock on the door, Delilah entered carrying a basket of clean cloths and herbs. "Singing Bird is busy delivering a baby," she whispered to her mother. "She told me what to bring. Should I stay?"

Christiana took a minute to study her sixteen-year old daughter. Realizing that she had been her age when she married Isaac, she said, "Yes, I can use your help. You may as well learn now about childbirthing. First thing is to make some tea with these herbs you brought. Tea will relax Mrs. Thompson and ease her pain. I think the water in the kettle is hot enough."

After she drank the peppermint and rosemary mixture, Faith was calm enough to allow Christiana to massage her stomach and gently reposition the baby. Minutes later, with one last loud scream, Thompson's tiny daughter was born.

Although Delilah was looking pale, she followed all her mother's instructions. She tenderly washed the baby and wrapped her in clean cloths. Christiana took care of Faith's needs.

"You did just fine, Faith. I do believe you have just delivered the first white settler's child in this part of Michigan Territory." Delilah brought the baby to the bed. "She is perfect," Christiana said, handing the baby to her mother.

"Delilah, you were very good help! Go tell the Thompson family they can come home now. I'll stay here till morning."

Christiana sat by the fireplace long after the family arrived and went to bed. She thought about her own baby, due in a couple of months, and wondered whose baby Singing Bird had just delivered. It was a quiet time for thinking.

At daybreak she built up the fire and cooked corn meal for the Thompsons' breakfast. Shortly after cleaning up she returned to her own family and repeated the routine. Later, when she entered the cooking cabin to help prepare the noon meal she was startled to hear a baby crying. As she approached the fireplace she saw a new cradle board hanging from a hook. On further inspection she discovered a tiny Indian baby wrapped inside. "Singing Bird, whose child is this?" Then, looking at her friend, she knew. "Oh my! Singing Bird, you are a mother!"

Singing Bird gazed at the floor but murmured quietly, "Yes, I have a son."

"Last evening Delilah said you were delivering a baby. I never dreamed it was your own. This is wonderful! In a short time I will also have a new one. They can grow up together," Christiana said happily. "Singing Bird, you rest today. Others can do this work." Singing Bird ignored her offer.

The supply of flour and salt was nearly exhausted early in March. Calvin was sent to Bertrands with a list of needed articles. He was fascinated with the trading post and always was first to volunteer to make the trip.

He returned waving a stack of envelopes. "Here's a letter from Rice," he called to his father as he pulled his horse to a stop outside the cabin. Isaac took the letters inside as Calvin led the horse to the cooking cabin and unloaded bulging sacks purchased on credit.

"There is a letter here from the Baptist Mission Board. I'd better read it first. I hope it is in answer to our money requests!" He moved closer to the candle, smiling as he read the message. "Oh, it is! It's the long awaited answer to our prayers. Now we can finally pay Bertrand."

"He asked me today if there was some way to make payment on our winter's purchases," commented Calvin who had just come inside.

"He has been our good friend. He has helped us more than anyone. Unfortunately, this check might cause a problem."

Isaac shook his head. "We can't give him the total amount. We need to buy things he doesn't stock. Well, I'll just have to go speak to him about it."

Isaac handed Rice's letter to Christiana and Calvin who were patiently waiting. They took turns reading. "Rice and Josephus are living with a teacher at their college," Christiana told the others in the cabin. "They are earning their room and board by helping this teacher grade papers, chopping wood and other chores."

Isaac began re-reading the Board letter and scowled. "What's wrong?" asked Christiana.

"The Board is allowing us money equal to two-thirds of the cost of the buildings. That is not enough to cover the salary of the hired men. Besides, I itemized every cost for supplies and seed and clothing. This money doesn't begin to cover our expenses." He shook his head in disbelief.

"We should rejoice that some money arrived. We need more, of course, but if our crops are successful we won't be in debt for food. Perhaps we can even sell some," she said, trying to cheer him.

"The last few days I've been writing the winter reports. I've listed items we purchased and made lists of needed supplies. Let's pray when these reports are read by various boards and officials they will recognize our needs and respond."

The winter ended early. By the tenth of March men were able to begin working in the fields. "Come along and enjoy the nice weather, Brother Isaac," Daniel Dusenbury said one morning as he stopped by the cabin.

Isaac longed to go but refused. "I'd best be working on my sermon." Two days later, however, he did ride out and watched them prune trees. He admired the perfect straight rows of trees which had been planted the previous year. "That's a fine orchard forming!" he called to the boys. He loved the smell of new soil and wished he felt healthy enough to work outside. He dismounted his horse and bent to grab a handful of the rich loam, rubbing it in his fingers.

One of the men watched him and understood. "This is good land, Brother McCoy. You chose it well. Still a mite too cold for early plowing and seed planting but fine for pruning trees."

Neighboring Indians were seen returning from their winter hunt. A few chose land near Carey Mission to cultivate. They were given plows, hoes and shovels Robert and his pupils had made in the smithery. The principal chief, Topinabe, had about thirty families from his village improving land. Isaac loaned, or in some cases gave, them livestock from mission flocks and herds. They soon built fences to keep them from wandering. The McCoys were pleased their Indian neighbors were using some of the white men's ways they had been taught.

Not all time was spent in school or completing chores. Busy as she was, Christiana kept informed of all the happenings at the mission. She noticed several developing romances occurring in the mission family. On several occasions she called young girls aside, advising them to discourage a boy's attentions and to spend more time studying. She asked Johnston to speak to the young men. The relationship between Fanny Goodrich and Robert Simmerwell was beyond her control. Instead, their wedding was scheduled for March seventeenth.

16

Delilah and the older girls discussed the approaching wedding event each afternoon as they worked together. Only Delilah had attended a real wedding. She took delight in explaining the ceremony in great detail. "It is customary to give presents," she told them. "It should be something for their home." The Indian girls understood as it was also their custom to give gifts when couples mated.

They decided as a group to make a warm, colorful quilt. Each girl was to make a six inch square. Delilah told her mother of their plan. "Mrs. Dusenbury and Mrs. Polke will assist you with the finishing process," Christiana told them.

In order to have a variety of material, Christiana allowed them to bring all the charity boxes down from the loft. "While you look through the boxes, search for bits of lace. I am going to help Miss Goodrich make her best dress a little fancier." As she looked at the pretty young girls, Christiana got an inspiration. "See if you can find nice outfits or trinkets for yourselves in the boxes. Let's make this a festive occasion. The dreariness of winter is over!"

The quilt could only be worked on after other chores were finished and when Fanny, their teacher, was not around. Bright pieces of material were quickly tucked away whenever she appeared. Three girls took turns weaving a rug from leftover cloth lengths. The gifts were to be a surprise.

Meanwhile, boys had secrets also. They were building two chairs and a table, hiding them from the blacksmith but not from the girls. The Thompsons' home was nearing completion and they had moved their furniture from the blacksmith's cabin. The newlyweds would live there.

Women and girls always spent Saturday mornings doing domestic chores. Since the McCoys did not allow work on Sundays, extra baking and food preparation was done on Saturdays. Cabins and dormitories were cleaned and bedding aired.

During cold or rainy weather school books and materials were put away so Sunday services could be held in the school. In nice weather they moved benches outdoors.

The wedding day occurred on a Saturday, causing an unusual amount of activity. Even the boys got involved by helping little girls move furniture, clean sooty windows, inside and out, shoveling ashes from fireplaces, sweeping floors and placing extra candles around to overcome a dark rainy day.

Delilah, remembering the wedding decorations she'd seen when living with the Wrights, had Calvin help her cut pine boughs. They spread them around the stand their father would use to hold his Bible and marriage papers.

While they were in the woods she found tiny white flowers peeking from under leaves. She gently picked them and later laid them in a wooden bowl. The bowl was placed on the long table at the back of the room.

"Doesn't it look and smell wonderful?" she asked her brother. His answer was a shrug of shoulders.

"Let's move the teacher's desk to the back corner and put the gifts on it," suggested one of the girls.

"Oh, let's cover it with the quilt. It is so beautiful!"

"Should we tell the boys to bring their chairs in?"

"We also have a table," replied Mark, who overheard the conversation. "We made some burl bowls for them too."

"Go get the things you made. We can lay the rug on your table. Isn't this exciting?" Delilah said, squealing with delight.

Christiana was astounded when she arrived to check on the preparations. "Oh, they will be so pleased! I am certain they don't expect gifts. You have all worked very hard. It looks so clean and even smells nice."

"Mama, may I make a cake layer like you other ladies are doing?" asked Delilah. "The work is almost done here."

"Yes, I guess so, if you want to. Why don't you add some nuts to the batter. That would be a nice addition."

The ceremony was scheduled for 1:30 P.M. to be followed by a celebration party. Thanks to Bertrand's help everyone for miles around was invited.

"When may we put on our best dresses?" asked a shy little girl, her cheeks pink with excitement.

"As soon as the work is finished, you dress up. I'm going to need a couple of girls in the kitchen. Some of you boys should help Miss Goodrich carry her belongings to the blacksmith cabin." The women had already scrubbed the cabin and hung new curtains.

All work ceased by noon. After a simple and quick lunch and cleanup, everyone began their personal preparations. The girls helped each other comb and braid hair, giggling as they added bows or bits of jewelry. They abandoned their moccasins and struggled to squeeze their feet into stiff shoes. They laughed as they watched a few older girls, including Delilah, wobble along in high-heeled charity shoes. All dresses had bits of lace or beads added to the collars or cuffs. The boys were neat and clean but except for a few new shirts, unadorned.

Looking very prim and proper, everyone quietly filed into the school. They sat quietly on familiar benches, awaiting the arrival of the bride and groom. Youngest children, unsure of what to expect, begin to fidget. Impressed by the solemn occasion, most sat as quietly as they did during church services. The Dusenburys and Polkes sat between pupils, enforcing good behavior.

Fanny had made friends on her visits to Indian villages. A group of young Indian women, including the Bertrand girls, arrived and sat in the back row. Several curious men peered through windows but didn't come inside. Chiefs Tobinabe and Chebass entered in all their regalia. They were followed by their wives, children and other villagers. William greeted them and ushered the chiefs to rows of chairs in front of school benches. Others stood along the walls. Remaining seats were taken by the Thompson family and the hired men who worked at Carey Mission. Robert was well liked by the men he presented with farm tools.

Two Indian boys played soft bird-like music on wood flutes. Calvin planned to blow his trumpet but Delilah hid it. Johnston entered with Isaac, followed by the bridegroom. Johnston remained at the door as the other men made their way to the altar. Obviously nervous and impatient, Robert's eyes shifted back and forth from his shiny boots to the doorway.

Delilah also kept turning to watch the doorway. Johnston blushed as their eyes met. Isaac opened his marriage book of order, and then watched for the bride. The wind howled through the cracks under the door and around windows. Candles had been lit and were flickering from the drafts. Finally the door opened. Christiana entered, neatly dressed with a white shawl on her shoulders, closely followed by Fanny. They strolled up the aisle followed by Johnston. The bride's dark brown dress, trimmed with lace at the neck and cuffs, fit perfectly. She carried her Bible. A tiny bouquet of the wild flowers Delilah had found were nestled in her bright red hair.

The couple smiled happily at each other as they clasped hands. Johnston and Christiana remained up front as witnesses. Isaac cleared his throat. "Ladies and gentlemen," he began, "we are gathered here in this solemn occasion to join Fanny Goodrich and Robert Simmerwell in matrimony." All wiggling and whispering ceased as the vows were repeated by the couple. When the Reverend McCoy stated, "I now pronounce you man and wife," he smiled, hugged Fanny and shook Robert's hand.

The newlyweds turned to face their friends and students. Everyone stood, clapping their hands, delighted as they watched Robert lean over and kiss Fanny.

Christiana led the way to the back of the room just as Singing Bird entered, carrying the wedding-stack cake. "Oh look, Robert," exclaimed Fanny. "There are five layers! How will we ever cut it?"

"Looking at all these hungry youngsters, I think we will have to find a way," the new groom replied, watching their pupils admire the tall delicacy.

From the corner of her eye, Christiana observed Delilah flirting with Johnston. Disturbed, she strolled toward them. "Perhaps you can help dish up the food," she said, touching her daughter's arm. "Johnston, would you help cut the meat?" The three of them walked to the table and began o fill plates, too busy to talk.

Christiana was proud of the mannerly way the children behaved. "This party is a good experience," she said quietly to Isaac as she handed him a plate. "Once they leave school and get into society they will need to know about weddings and social things."

Isaac looked around the crowded room. "I hope they all get the chance to do just that! This is a fine group of young people with lots of ambition and talents. Yes, I hope they get a chance to use their training and get even more schooling."

"Clean your plates!" called the groom. "We have the cake cut. Come get some." The children wasted no time getting in line for a slice.

"You be sure to save two pieces for you and Robert to enjoy later tonight," whispered Grace. Fanny followed her instruction and put some aside. She blushed as Grace offered a bit of wifely advice. "You must always set aside time each day to spend with your husband. There will be interruptions and obligations but married folks need time alone."

In just minutes, the cake disappeared as all the guests were served. Fanny thanked the women, which included Delilah and Faith Thompson, who had each made a cake layer. "I truly appreciate your use of precious flour and sugar and eggs. Thank you for this special treat!"

"The cake isn't the only surprise for you. Come see what we made for you!" said two little girls, as they pulled their teachers toward the gifts they'd stacked in the corner.

Robert and Fanny were amazed. "We have so few pieces of furniture I didn't know how we would manage. Now I don't have to worry about it," said Fanny as she touched each item. "These things are made so beautifully! Thank you all!"

Several Indian baskets, containers of maple sugar, beaded moccasins, woven mats and carved bowls had been added to the gift collection. Bertrands brought two brightly striped wool blankets from their trading post.

The party continued late into the afternoon, with everyone admiring gifts and singing songs. As guests were leaving, Isaac said "This has been a perfect day!"

Christiana thought so too until she overheard a teenage girl saying, "I wish we could have weddings every Saturday." Delilah had replied, "It would be nice wouldn't it."

Bertrand and his family were the last visitors to depart. As he rode off, he waved his hat. "Newlyweds don't need us hanging around on their weddin' night," he hollered. His loud laughter echoed into the woods and was answered by calls of nearby wolves.

Logs were added to the fire and candles were replaced. "As long as we are all here together, we'll have our nightly devotions," Isaac said. Christiana smiled as she watched the young ones nodding their heads, trying hard to stay awake. Two small boys actually fell over fast asleep and had to be carried to their cabin when worship ended. Older boys and girls helped the Simmerwells carry gifts to their cabin. After all the items were moved, Robert waved and closed the door.

Isaac was surprised but pleased to find Fanny in her usual spot the next morning, welcoming Indian families to Sunday services. The day was dreary. Cold north winds blew dark clouds across the gray sky. "Robert started the fire early to take the chill off the meeting room," she commented.

"I didn't really expect you two to attend this morning," Isaac replied, smiling. "Now I find that you got here before I did and have everything ready. I really appreciate your help, but--."

Fanny interrupted, "We are here to share duties. I wouldn't feel right about staying away! Robert and I plan to spend all our life working together, like you and your wife."

Isaac patted her arm tenderly, then moved on to greet his congregation. Everytime the door swung open a blast of chill air swept into the room. Logs sputtered. Smoke puffed up the chimney but more of it blew into the room causing fits of coughing. By the time the three-hour service ended everyone had sore red eyes from the smoke.

March winds gradually brought warmer days. With loud thundering cracks, the ice broke on the river, opening the waterway for returning Indians. Annual maple syrup events once again took place. Isaac postponed any distant travels but began visiting nearby Indian villages again, often staying overnight.

As always, Christiana remained in charge during his absence but her patience was near the breaking point. There was never a free minute. Caring for sick youngsters, cleaning spring mud from clothes and floors, smoke filled cabins, everything irritated her. By afternoon each day, she was so physically tired it took great effort to place one foot in front of the other.

She was also weary of their monotonous diet of cornmeal, beans and venison. She longed for fresh fruit and vegetables. Most of all she wished for sunshine and an end to her twelfth pregnancy.

"Sit down awhile," Delilah said, seeing her mother's pale face. "I'll help the girls at the loom today. You rest!"

"I can't! I just saw some men ride in. I'll have to see what they want." Christiana pulled a shawl over her shoulders and stepped outside. She hesitated and stepped back as three angry-looking men approached.

"We're United States Government surveyors, here to speak to Reverend Isaac McCoy."

"Please, follow me," she said. "It is much too unhealthy to remain outdoors in this dismal weather." Since classes had not begun, she led the way to the school. "My husband is absent from the mission. I'm Mrs. McCoy, you may speak to me in his place."

The men exchanged doubtful looks. "We are having Indian problems. I certainly do not believe you can solve them!" the youngest man rudely stated. "Isn't there a man in charge during your husband's absence?"

Christiana's blue eyes flashed in anger. "I've solved many school and Indian problems! I am a responsible person, very capable of listening to your problem." She did not want it known that all the men had gone with Isaac to distribute plows and other tools made in the smithery.

"He didn't mean to offend you," interrupted the oldest of the three. "Perhaps we might sit by the fire and talk?"

Christiana nodded and took a seat. The men drew up benches across from her. "I am Samuel Woods," the oldest man said, then introduced the others. "The young man is Robert Small, the other his brother, Thaddeus."

Delilah, checking on her mother, had followed them. She listened with interest. After introducing her, Christiana asked her to bring them some chicory coffee.

"A hot drink would be appreciated ma'am," Sam commented, trying to placate her.

"Are you quite sure there isn't a man we can talk to?" interrupted Robert, apparently still unaware of Christiana's growing wrath.

"Young man, I find your attitude insulting! Perhaps your attitude is the cause of your Indian problem. Indians, like women, can tell when you consider their intelligence less than that of white men."

The other two men squirmed uncomfortably. "Robert, you better wait outside while we have our discussion with Mrs. McCoy," said Thaddeus. "I beg your forgiveness for my brother."

Robert stomped out, almost upsetting Delilah as she arrived carrying a tray of steaming coffee cups. "Would you like me to stay, Mama?" she asked as she gave them their drinks.

"We will only be here a short time," her mother answered, glaring at the men. Delilah left.

The men looked at each other, trying to decide who should speak. Finally, Thaddeus cleared his throat and began. "Our job, Mrs. McCoy, is surveying land for the United States Government. Do you know the work surveyors do?"

"My husband is a surveyor, among his other professions."

"Oh, well then you know it is necessary to do this work before a roadway can be built across this southern Michigan Territory and on into Illinois Territory."

"I am aware of that possibility. My husband receives many official government letters, both from our Governor and from the President of the United States. Carey Mission Station is not isolated from the rest of the country."

The surprised look on Samuel Wood's face pleased her. "So, what is the problem you are having?" she asked.

Samuel took over the conversation. "Each day our men drive stakes with colored ribbons marking the road boundaries. The next morning the stakes are removed or re-positioned. It is like a big game to these Indians."

Christiana bit her tongue to keep from laughing. "You are right. It is a game."

Samuel was irritated by her smile. "I know it sounds humorous but it is a tragedy! Day after day we re-establish our roadway and seldom make any gain."

"We never advance! Our work must be completed by the fifteenth of April and we are stalled in your area," interjected Thaddeus. "We've talked to a few landowners and to Bertrand at his trading post. Everyone says only Reverend McCoy can convince the Potawatomi to stop their mischief."

"They don't seem to understand our talk, even when we use interpreters," Samuel continued. "They know we are laying out a road. They say they don't need one."

"They are right, aren't they?" asked Christiana. "They have used the same established trails for many years. Why do they need a new road?"

"This one will be straighter and wider, making it easier to get wagons and even carriages into the area."

Christiana sat quietly, watching the fire. She understood exactly what the Indians must feel. She wondered why these men couldn't. "Have you, or the government you represent, considered the fact that the road would take more of their land away from them? Can't you understand they don't want wagons and carriages to scare deer and other game and bring more white men to take their land?" Her eyes flashed. "You must see their side of this situation. You are on their land. You are staking claims and taking away what is theirs."

"We are not taking it away! They can use the road. It is to their advantage!" said Samuel. "Do you think if we offered money they would stop fighting the road?"

"I would not suggest that," Christiana replied, shaking her head. "The land is not something they want to sell."

"What would you suggest then, Ma'am? We are at our wits end. The work of cutting out trees and brush, crossing wet lands, working in snow, rain, heat, cold, mosquitoes, snakes---

our men are worn out and growing sickly. We only have three or four weeks left. We are desperate!"

"I can see that. It occurs to me that a solution might be worked out." Christiana watched sputtering logs glowing in the fireplace while she formed her suggestion.

The men watched her, waiting to hear her suggestions. "Perhaps," she said, "you could establish your road by widening the present Indian trails. They usually follow waterways. If you had studied them you'd realize these paths were chosen as easiest and quickest ways through an area. They avoid wettest lands." She stood up and added logs to the fire. After a pause she continued. "You white men have gone to much unnecessary work when the way was already laid out for you. I believe the Indians have always allowed and even expected others to follow their trails. So, you see, gentlemen, there is no need for a different way through the area. You were wrong to lay claim to land and build a roadway." Christiana stopped talking and let her words sink in.

Samuel stood up and paced in front of the fireplace. Thaddeus sat quietly, stunned. After a few minutes Samuel spoke. "I think we've met a wise woman, Thaddeus."

"A very wise lady! I can't believe we overlooked such an obvious thing. We'll have to send letters to our employers and suggest changes. Can we quote you on some of your ideas, Mrs. McCoy?"

"Yes, of course."

"We were told your husband has good understanding of the Indians but you seem to know how they think too."

"I'm not sure it is 'Indian thinking'. When you look at both sides of problems the solution comes from common sense." She smiled. "Tell the chiefs you want to make their paths wider and smoother so they can travel easier. You can get the names and locations of the chiefs from Joseph and Madeline Bertrand at the trading post."

Christiana shook her head, then added, "You are lucky the Potawatomi are a peaceful tribe. They could have done serious harm instead of playing games with your stakes."

The men hung their heads, looking like school boys who had been scolded. "We'll find Robert and return to the trading post. Thanks for your advice."

Christiana wished them success and watched as they rode away. Isaac laughed heartily when told of the visit. "You are so wise, my dear. I couldn't possibly have come up with a better plan for them. I do wish I had been here to listen to you though."

17

Unlike other years, April 1825 arrived warm and dry. Early on April seventh Christiana knotted her shawl around her shoulders and went outdoors to watch the sunrise. Two little girls heading for breakfast joined her. "Hush, I think I hear robins chirping. Let's stop at the log bench. Maybe we will see them," she whispered. Soon several fat birds hopped near their feet, pecking the ground in their search for worms.

Christiana gazed at the pink and blue sky, enjoying the peace of the morning. Suddenly, sharp pain stabbed in her back. She bit her tongue to keep from frightening the girls or the birds.

"Girls, you'd better hurry off to eat. I'm going back home." Another pain hit. When it passed she started walking. She met Johnston on the path and smiled. "Will you tell Singing Bird to come to my cabin? I'll send Delilah to take her place at breakfast."

"Are you all right? I can walk with you," he offered, noticing how pale she looked.

"I think I will be fine. Go along," she said, continuing along the path. When she entered the cabin she found her daughters getting ready to leave for breakfast and school.

"Delilah, fill a kettle with water and put it to heat, then please go help dish up breakfast. Sarah and Anna you run along. Tell Papa I won't be coming to school today."

Delilah looked at her mother with alarm. "Is it the baby? Shouldn't I stay and help?"

"Singing Bird will attend me, but I would appreciate having you care for your sisters. I'll be fine. Don't fret!" Christiana started readying things for her twelfth birthing.

Singing Bird quietly entered the cabin. Her own infant son slept in his cradleboard fastened to her back. She carried a basket of supplies. Her slow methodical movements were soothing. Christiana lay on the bed, relaxed after drinking the herbal concoction her friend prepared.

At noontime Isaac stood nervously gazing at the cabin. Most of his children had been born in his absence. He was unsure as to what he should do. Some of the men joined him briefly and then went on to eat. During the morning Mary and Grace stopped in to check on Christiana and reported back to him. All he could do was wait.

He paced back and forth until, to his amazement, he heard a faint cry. Worried, he approached the cabin and threw open the door. Singing Bird stepped away from the bed. He saw Christiana's tired smile. "Come meet your fourth son," she said.

Singing Bird gathered up things to be washed. Slipping the cradleboard onto her back, she left. Isaac gently brushed Christiana's hair from her forehead, then touched the baby's tiny waving fist. "He is so tiny. I'd forgotten how small they come."

"His name is Isaac. This son will be your namesake." Isaac looked at her determined face and offered no complaint. He gazed at his wife and newborn son wishing, as he often did, that there could be more restful days for his beloved partner. "Tell Delilah she can bring the others in. Then I think little Isaac and I will sleep awhile."

Isaac slowly and quietly, but very happily, left to find Delilah and then returned to school. When he told ten year old Sarah, she looked very disappointed. "I was hoping the baby would be born on the thirteenth," she said.

"What is so important about that day?" he teased her. "Oh, Papa, you know it is my birthday and brother Josephus' too, but that's no matter, we all three have April birthdays."

April, like always, became a rainy month. As each day grew warmer, grass turned green, flowers appeared in meadows and woods. Late in the month, a heavily loaded supply wagon rumbled into the muddy yard and was quickly surrounded by curious children and adults. Christiana hurriedly wrapped up baby Isaac and joined the group. "What's in there? Is it things for the mission or some new settler?" she asked her brother who was helping direct the driver.

"Stand back so he can pull closer to the storage shed," William yelled, then turned to Christiana. "This man is hoping to settle in the area. Only a few of these things are his. The Baptist Board paid him to bring supplies to us. Isn't that amazing? Of course we don't know yet what they chose to send."

Calvin and another boy guided the horses into position so the wagon could be unloaded. The driver jumped down and introduced himself as Benjamin Potter. "I came with Baldwin Jenkins. He moved here last year from Ohio. Might be you remember him. Nathan Young came too. We're going to help clear land and get some planting done. I'm hoping to build. I guess I'd better unload what stays here."

Isaac and two hired men rode in from the fields where they had been mending fences. They watched with Christiana as the wagon was unloaded. She told Isaac the background of the supply wagon as the hired men helped William.

"Let's take off the sacks first, then the crates will come easier," William said, climbing up on the wheel. "Sacks of seed! Now we can for certain get our planting done. Seed potatoes in this one, wheat, corn, this is wonderful!"

"Ladies," said Benjamin, "Here is a crate marked clothing or is it cloth? There are two barrels of flour and one of sugar and some salt. Here's a crate of books, that's for sure not mine," Benjamin said laughing. "Let's see, what else?"

"What is that putrid smell?" asked some little girls, holding their noses.

Just then Calvin pulled out a large slatted crate. A loud squawking startled him. He nearly dropped it. "Chickens! Half of them must be dead, way it smells."

"Carry it to the pigs' pen to open it," Christiana said, holding her nose. "After the live ones scoot out, bury the rest. Nancy, get a pan of water for the poor things. We'll give them some dried corn meal later."

"I sure hope we can save them. Eggs would be a blessing!" the women agreed as they watched children chase chickens into the pen.

By the time Benjamin drove his wagon out everything was stored in place. "Praise the Lord for all these beneficial gifts! They arrived at just the perfect time but better than that I believe the Board members finally understand our needs," said Isaac.

"And praise be, are finally willing to fill them," added Christiana solemnly.

By mid-May young apple and peach trees began blossoming. Their sweet fragrance filled the air. As Christiana regained her strength she strolled around the orchard picking a few branches to take home..

Isaac joined her as she stood watching new lambs jumping alongside their mothers. "Spring is a beautiful time isn't it?" she said looking around. "How soon can the fields be planted?"

"They are hoping to plant wheat yet this week. You know, I've been thinking lately that what we need most here is a way to grind our wheat into flour. Getting it from Fort Wayne or Ohio is too expensive and risky."

"Yes, we've lost many barrels in the transporting."

"If our wheat prospers like I hope it does, we will have to take it far away to be milled." Isaac said. "Our primitive hand mill requires too much strength and time. Those grinding stones we have are too heavy to turn. We need to figure out a better way."

"That might be something to challenge the thinking of the older boys."

Isaac looked at his wife in amazement. "Why didn't I think of that? Their young creative minds can probably solve this dilemma. I'll speak to their teachers and encourage them to challenge their pupils."

By the end of May, after much experimenting and discussion, the boys designed and built a grinding method. The new mill would use horse power. Two horses in collars were strapped to long wooden arms. The arms were fastened across an old wagon wheel. As the horses walked they moved the grinding stones in a circle. In just a few hours, grain or corn between the stones was finely ground. Cornmeal and flour would no longer be a scarcity. The procedure was amazing to watch. Children sometimes climbed on horses' backs, riding round and round until dizzy. Sometimes they fell off laughing.

More visitors rode or walked in to Carey Mission all spring. Seeing the evidence of excellent farmland, and learning of the possibility of acquiring assistance and tools from the mission, made men want to settle nearby.

"I don't mind helping them but the barrels of whiskey they bring alarms me," Isaac told the other missionaries. "They are too eager about giving or selling it in exchange for tools and food. I'm afraid the Indians are going to neglect their fields if they continue to drink the abominable substance."

Taking two young men with him one afternoon, they rode to Topinabe's new village. There they found the inhabitants engaged in horrid bacchanalian revels. After searching among them awhile Isaac found a full whiskey keg. He tried to empty it but a drunken man caught him. Isaac was kicked and hit violently. His companions managed to rescue him. When Isaac's wounds were bandaged and he recovered, they rode on. They passed three drunken Indians lying asleep in the woods. Many others wandered intoxicated along the trail. "I can't describe how discouraged I feel," Isaac said.

Isaac emphasized over and over in his sermons and talks to his family and pupils, "The best therapy for discouragement is hard work!" The McCoys made sure everyone in their charge had a mixture of work, worship and play each and every day. Food was plentiful and wholesome during spring and summer months. Everyone's health improved. Women and girls were constantly sewing garments, trying to keep up with the children's growth and normal wear and tear.

Toward the end of June an Indian canoe was spotted by children as they played along the river. As it approached they recognized one of trader Burnett's sons. "I came to visit Abraham and to give a message to Reverend McCoy," he said as he paddled his canoe to shore.

The children pointed to the fields where boys were hoeing. The young man walked in that direction and finally located his brother. Abraham was happy to see him. Together they found Isaac so Abraham could help interpret his brother's message. "A schooner arrived on Lake Michigan with supplies for my father's trading post. When crates were brought to shore some had your name on them," Abraham said. "Many crates were unloaded. My father sent my brother to tell you."

Isaac looked puzzled. "Do you have any idea what is in the cargo or who sent the crates?"

"The captain told my father, 'The goods were sent by persons in different parts of the United States.' That is all I know."

"Abraham, tell your brother we will ready our pirogues and go collect the boxes. You go along. You can visit your family."

When Isaac and Christiana talked later, he expressed his hope for medical supplies and more tools and books.

"Yes, but it could just be more impractical clothes and shoes."

As it turned out they were both correct. Crates of clothing were sorted and stored in the loft. The rest of the benevolent gifts were put to immediate and good use. "I recognize some of these names as people I spoke to in various churches and meetings two years ago on my Eastern journey," Isaac said as he read notes tucked in boxes. "I didn't get much response at the time but my message must have touched their hearts."

Christiana wiped her tears, truly moved by people's generosity. "I wonder if I would be so generous to folks with so many needs in a faraway place. We get a bit angry at the clothes they send but since they don't really know how we live we should be more tolerant. The other things and money are always useful."

We need to thank the Lord for working through these people and for all gifts we receive," Isaac agreed.

On a hot July day, better for being outdoors in the shade, Isaac sat at his desk writing reports. The air in the cabin was stifling. Flies trapped indoors with him were very annoying. Pushing back his chair, he went to stand in the doorway.

Several girls sat under the trees snapping green beans into baskets. Singing Bird's son and little Isaac slept on a blanket beside their mothers. Men and older boys were coming in from the fields.

As he watched the boys, Isaac's thoughts returned to letters he'd been writing. He was still trying to arrange advanced schooling for their pupils. Seven young men had surpassed all expectations by learning every subject presented to them. They deserved the challenge a college could offer.

After many discussions and prayers with other mission workers, Isaac still was unsure about the best way to get the boys enrolled. Lack of money continued to block his goal, and caused him to delay action.

Suddenly, an inspiration hit. He knew how to handle the problems. Scurrying back to his desk, he picked up a new pen and again began composing letters. He added additional pages to all his reports, requesting money for the boys' higher education. These new pages would include information about each boy by listing all their completed subjects, test scores and teachers' comments. Men in official positions would surely be impressed enough to influence colleges. Letters could also be forwarded to colleges.

Isaac began humming his favorite hymns as he compiled the letters. Just as darkness settled over the mission, he finished. For the first time in ages he happily joined the others for evening prayers.

The next morning Isaac had Calvin saddle his horse while he packed saddlebags with letters and reports. He rode to Bertrands. "When you hear of anyone going to Detroit or Fort Wayne, please have them take these to be mailed," he begged his friend.

While he was at the trading post he was astonished to see several tools that had been made at the mission and given to the Indian neighbors. "How did these get here?" he asked.

"I took them in trade from white settlers. They got them from Indians in exchange for whiskey. It is sad thing," Bertrand replied. "I don't trade whiskey! I now have all kinds of Indian tools and cooking pots and clothing. All were traded for evil drink."

Isaac believed his friend but felt very sad and angry." Whiskey makes men do strange things. We thought they would be using these tools to help them live better."

"They don't live good. Everyday I hear about murders and fighting. They can't control themselves when they swallow this evil drink."

"I wish I knew how to stop the supply coming into our territory," Isaac muttered as he headed home.

The busy summer routine kept Isaac occupied at Carey Mission and left no time to dwell on outside problems. Late in August Isaac was invited to a Potawatomi religious festival. Not knowing what to expect, he went alone.

Aged Chief Topinabe led the ceremonies. He delivered a speech of considerable length without rising from his seat. Isaac understood many parts of the speech by observing gestures. Long periods of sitting and singsong voices made him drowsy. A sudden loud shout from the edge of the circle abruptly aroused everyone. The Chief jumped to his feet. All eyes turned in the direction of the shout. No one was visible. Isaac smiled to himself thinking someone had cleverly managed to break the long sit.

Topinabe droned on, complaining that hunting and fishing were both disappearing. Isaac hoped he wasn't claiming that white men had taken away their livelihood. Isaac began to wonder if he was in danger. He began to fidget, studying the faces of others in the circle. Seeing a few friendly reactions, he relaxed.

A movement at the edge of the woods caught his eye. He watched as two white traders approached and sat behind the invited guests. Isaac didn't recognize them. He was curious but switched his attention back to Topinabe. Minutes later he noticed the men had moved closer into the circle. They seemed to be talking to Indians sitting beside them. As Isaac watched, he saw small bottles being passed, then realized what was happening.

He groaned silently, trying to think of a way to stop the liquor distribution without interrupting the Chief. Just then a bottle was passed to Isaac. Without thinking, he tossed it into the fire. It broke. Flames shot up from the alcohol, startling everyone. Several men chuckled. Soon everyone was laughing and tossing bottles. Chief Topinabe jumped up. Raising his decorated stick he nodded to the drummers. Instantly, everyone stood. They formed a snakelike line of dancing, weaving around the sputtering fire.

Isaac stepped out of the dance. He looked for the traders, but they found him first. "Don't know who you are mister, but you sure wasted lots of whiskey," one of them snarled angrily.

"You must be crazy!" growled the other.

"I'm Reverend Isaac McCoy."

"Oh yeah, we've heard of you. You're the one doesn't want Indians to have good times."

"I'm the one who doesn't think whiskey makes a good time," replied Isaac.

"Well, selling it makes us rich and we are having good times. That's two things you aren't going to change!"

The Indians were whooping and gesturing, acting out stories as they danced. The traders glared at Isaac, then nodded towards the swirling line of dancers. "They're acting like wild men. Let's go back to our camp."

"You'll be hearing from us later, McCoy. You should be ashamed, wasting all that good whiskey."

Isaac considered leaving when a frantic dancer suddenly yelled and lifted a deer head from a cooking kettle. Hot steamy broth dripped down on the dusty ground as he held it by the antlers, presenting it first upwards then towards the startled people. After tossing it back into the kettle he licked his hands, then picked up bowls offering them to others.

Chief Chebass had been watching Isaac. He moved quietly beside him. "Don't offend them. We must share his food," he said softly. "Come with me. Let us eat in friendship." Isaac had a difficult time swallowing but managed to remain calmly with Chebass.

Chief Topinabe finished eating and sat down. Then with eyes closed he began another speech. Soon an elderly man picked up a stick, strolled to the drums, and began drumming. Another rattled a gourd. Women formed a circle, shuffling in slow quiet steps around the circle of men. The sun set. As everyone grew sleepy, they disappeared into their huts and teepees. Isaac pulled his blanket from his horse and slept by the fire, heading back to the mission before sun up.

Routines at Carey Mission rarely changed. Busy with mission obligations, Christiana had no time for relaxation. Her favorite quiet time occurred mornings before the heat of the day as she sat milking cows. Watching the sunrise and listening to bird songs filled her with a calming peace.

Each morning, Calvin faithfully came to help carry milk pails to the cooking cabin. There, milk was strained through cloth by domestic helpers. Some was churned into butter or made into cheese but the children drank most of it. Evening milking was done by girls or other women.

Garden vegetables were equally eaten and preserved. Summer vanished quickly into fall harvest time. Over 300 bushels of wheat was harvested. For the first time since they arrived at Carey Mission there was more than enough for their needs.

18

Without consulting anyone, Isaac decided to make a trip to Ft. Wayne before snow fell. "I'll be taking some surplus vegetables and grain," he told everyone who had gathered to hear his plans. "I'll be taking sacks of wheat to sell. You men can grind our flour from the rest." He smiled. "Who feels the need to get away from here the most and can go with me?" For a brief moment, Christiana wished she could travel with her husband but reality overcame longing. Strangely, all the missionaries seemed to have a reason to remain at the mission.

"Maybe one or two of the older boys should go," Johnston suggested. "The experience would be good for them."

Isaac agreed. He took Mark and Luke, two of the oldest pupils. They found most of the Indian villages deserted as they traveled along the way. "They have already left for winter trapping and hunting, I guess," the boys decided. Occasionally they met a few Indian women and children gathering nuts which they happily traded for Isaac's turnips and squash.

Evenings, as the boys prepared their meal, Isaac wrote letters or in his diary. After eating they sat around campfires chatting. "Seems like an early winter is coming. Notice the heavy dark clouds?" asked Luke.

"Yes, could be snow clouds," Mark concluded.

"Remember two winters ago when we nearly starved? Our farm work has certainly saved us from that. Crops produce more each year!" they cheerfully agreed.

"Your school work will produce good results, too," Isaac commented, using this opportunity to talk to the boys. "I know you young men can do well in college. Then you will be able to get jobs as teachers or ministers or doctors."

They spent the last evening before reaching Ft. Wayne taking baths and washing clothes in a cold stream, hanging them on bushes to dry. "It is important to look presentable," Isaac smiled at his shivering companions. "One of the first things we are going to do is have a hot meal at the stagecoach inn. I have enough money for that," he promised.

They drove the wagon behind the trading post. Isaac walked to the inn. The boys were to join him after the horses were fed and watered.

Several men recognized Isaac and greeted him warmly. Following the usual exchange of family news, he told them the purpose of his visit. "This time I am hoping to sell wheat instead of buying it."

Isaac sat at a small table and read the menu. Suddenly a commotion occurred at the doorway. "No Indians allowed in here!" the innkeeper yelled, pushing Mark and Luke outside.

Isaac jumped to his feet and stepped in front of the man. "These boys are with me!"

"Well then, you'd better stay with them. You leave too!"

"Why can't they come in here and eat?" asked Isaac, becoming very angry. "They are pupils in my school, not savages."

"No Indians allowed! They can't hold their liquor, they fight, they are dirty. They have no manners. My white customers won't come eat if Indians are here."

"These boys are clean. They don't drink! They have fine manners, maybe even better than some of your white customers. Don't worry! We will leave. Somehow I don't think I could swallow your food!"

Isaac's outburst surprised other men eating there. They remembered him as a mild mannered person. When Isaac left, slamming the door, they felt embarrassed but didn't interfere.

"Come on boys, we'll go into the trading post and buy something to cook tonight. Probably even sell our wheat and vegetables there." He led the way, talking and calming his feelings as they walked. "I have some other business to conduct and I need to mail letters. I'm hoping there are letters to take back. We will talk about this episode later when my anger cools."

The boys trudged solemnly behind. Nothing like this had ever happened to them before. They hesitated at the trading post door. "Maybe we should wait at the wagon," said Mark.

Isaac shook his head, stepping inside he motioned for them to enter. "You won't be treated badly here. Believe me, from now on I'll do my best to keep you from being humiliated."

Later all of the items Isaac and the boys unloaded and carried in were purchased or exchanged for the salt, sugar and coffee they needed. There was more than enough cash to purchase candle molds and sewing supplies Christiana had requested. Isaac bought gun powder, traps and items for the smithery. "Before winter sets in, it's best to purchase necessities."

He watched with disgust as two customers rolled kegs of whiskey to the doorway. "Where are you headed?" he asked.

"Taking the trail to Saint Joseph River territory. You ever been on it?"

Isaac's fingers tightened into fists but his voice remained calm. "Yes, I've traveled it since it was just an Indian path," he replied wearily. "Are you traders or settlers?"

"Haven't decided yet. You goin' that way? We're lookin' for someone to get us into Injun camps."

"Want to do some tradin'. What we got here," one of the men said, patting the kegs, "is something them Injuns really love."

"You are wrong about that," said Isaac raising his voice. "Your whiskey is not welcome in that territory. I live there but I won't be showing you the way!" He turned abruptly and walked to the door, but not before he heard the men's comments.

"Not too friendly is he? Must be an Injun lover judging from the two with him."

"That's Reverend McCoy. He and his wife are missionaries. They love everyone," the trading post clerk told the men.

Loud laughter followed as Isaac stormed out. The boys were shocked to see tears running down his face. "Let's move our wagon to the edge of the woods. I don't think I have the strength to mingle with any more folks," he said, wiping his eyes. "I never was so disappointed at my fellow man as I am right now. If violence was the answer I'd fight every one we've met today."

The boys hopped into the wagon beside him. "You taught us that fighting does not solve problems."

"I regret to say I came very close twice today. This has been a very frustrating day! Let's eat our meal, then we need to reflect back on the good things that occurred, like selling our surplus and buying our supplies. The day hasn't been totally horrible. We need to thank the Lord for that!"

Early the next morning Isaac walked back to Ft. Wayne while the boys waited and repacked the wagon. He talked with several men he knew at the fort. He picked up two bundles of letters, one for Carey Mission and one designated for Bertrand's for new settlers to claim. The boys watched as Isaac slipped the mail under the wagon seat and picked up the reins. "We're heading home, boys!" he told them.

"Aren't you going to read your letters?" asked Luke.

"I want to, desperately, but I don't think we should linger here. When we stop for a meal I'll open the packet."

When they stopped at noon the boys built a small cooking fire. Isaac searched through the mail. When he did not find any letters from his sons or from colleges where he'd requested information, he repacked them under the seat. "This has been one of the worst journeys I have ever made," he told the boys sadly. "I want to get home as quickly as possible!"

It was several days after their return before Isaac told Christiana how rudely the boys had been treated. "All the years we lived there and in all the visits since, I have never seen such actions." Tears gathered in his eyes as he recalled the sad events.

Christiana tenderly patted his arm. "There must be a reason," she said. "Perhaps Indians there have been drinking whiskey and causing problems, just like our neighbors. So far we have avoided it here at the mission. Maybe it is just because we keep everyone so busy."

The end of October chores included picking apples, making candles and soap, pulling the last turnips, drying pumpkins, squash and apples for winter use. Boys chopped and stacked wood outside every building and slung new bedding straw into animal sheds. Whenever Christiana sat down, she spun wool into yarn or helped the girls knit. Isaac helped butcher hogs and salt meat to preserve it. Their Indian domestics dried fish and meat strips on long sticks placed between poles.

The days grew shorter. Winds increased and the weather changed. "It will be a hard winter, lots of nuts, thick coats on animals," Singing Bird predicted.

"This year I hope we have enough food and medicine to keep everyone healthy," Grace Dusenbury commented to other women as they sat shelling corn. "So far the babies and youngsters are strong."

"It seems we have made plenty of warm clothes and stockings. Singing Bird has taught girls to line moccasins with rabbit fur but truly the boys need sturdy boots when they hunt or do chores," Christiana said. "I wish we had a cobbler nearby. Indian women working here know how to tan leather, it is too bad we can't use it for shoes."

"We'll have to inquire of all the new settlers," Fanny said. "Seems like one of them is bound to know the trade."

On a snowy cold November afternoon when they least expected visitors, two missionaries, Jotham Meeker and W. M. Crosby arrived at the mission. Christiana was not happy to have two additional mouths to feed. "It would have been better to receive additional helpers in the summer months," she complained to Isaac.

He was startled by her remark. "Remember, my dear, they will lighten some of your workload. We must always be grateful for willing workers." He missed seeing her glare at him.

Five days after their arrival, Jotham presented Isaac a packet of letters. "These were in the bottom of my satchel. I forgot all about them. They were given me in Detroit."

The angry look on Isaac's face surprised him. "Brother Meeker, we seldom receive mail and long for it with a terrible desire. Distributing it is a first priority!

Jotham felt his face redden as he realized he had been scolded. "I do thank you for bringing it," continued Isaac. "I'll sort it, then you can take letters to their rightful owners. It will be a good way for you to get familiar with other workers here."

After Jotham left, Isaac sat at his desk. His hands shook slightly as he tore open an official looking letter from Hamilton College. Christiana glanced at him as she sat mending. His face seemed to glow. She watched him read and waited for an explanation.

He slowly removed his glasses, then smiled. He stood and walked to her. "Good news. No, wonderful news! My dear, our seven advanced students have been accepted! I finally received an answer to the July letters I sent to colleges." He gave her the letter and began to pace the floor. "Unfortunately, we still have the tuition problem. They made no mention of scholarships, but the Lord will provide somehow. There is still the Mission Board and friends willing to spend for education."

Christiana didn't know how to respond. She was as excited as Isaac but talk of money always overwhelmed her. "Our Lord will provide, Isaac, but we always need other help too."

At prayer time that evening, the McCoys shared the news with the entire mission. All the pupils were surprised and delighted, although the adults mirrored Christiana's state of mind.

Later the young men eligible for college expressed concerns. "We better not set our hopes too high. Without money we won't be able to go," one of the seven told his classmates.

One young man reminded the others about Rice and Josephus. "They are earning their room and board by working for college instructors. We could do that too."

Mark and Luke looked at each other, remembering their visit to Ft. Wayne. "How will we be treated in a city and in a white man's school?" asked Luke.

"Reverend McCoy will expect us to do our best. We will become examples for others to follow," said Mark.

"We have been taught to help each other. This will be no different. We will go together and work hard," another boy stated.

Luke sighed, "Yes, we can be friends to each other even if no one else likes us."

"One thing for certain, we all know how to work," they agreed, laughing but serious.

19

During the final days of December, weather cleared enough men could go deer hunting. They were reminded to invite everyone they met to the New Year celebration at Carey Mission.

The day before the party was spent butchering venison and skinning rabbits to roast outdoors. Oldest boys dug burning pits and laid logs in preparation for lighting very early the next morning. Women and girls baked bread and prepared vegetables for soup.

Christiana didn't sleep well and realized she was shivering and cold. Before daylight she got out of bed, added a log to the fire, then went to the window. It was coated with ice. She tried to scrape it off, gave up and went to the door. Hard as she pulled, she couldn't open it. It was frozen shut.

"Isaac," she whispered, as she crawled back into bed, "we have had an ice storm. I thought I heard it raining but it must have been freezing rain."

He got up and dressed. When he could not budge the door either they tried to think of solutions. "We could pour hot water around the opening but then it might freeze again."

"If we held a burning log there it might set the door on fire."

"I wonder if all the buildings are iced," Isaac worried aloud. "Maybe it is only north facing sides. Our door is facing that direction. Oh, but our window is on the west."

"We are going to have to get out and rescue others. Everyone will be waking up and hungry very soon," Christiana said.

A few minutes later they heard her brother William pounding on their door, "Everything is covered with ice out here! We have big problems. Can I come in?"

"We can't open the door!" Isaac and Christiana shouted. The baby woke up screaming. Their little girls were now up and raced around the table, adding to the confusion.

"I'll be back with help," William shouted, after he failed to open the door.

Christiana calmed her children, then dressed herself and them warmly. "I have some cornmeal here. Sarah, you and Anna stir some into the kettle of hot water, then you may all eat."

Soon they heard men's voices and scraping noises, followed by a loud thunk! The door swung open and the men came inside. The whole family hurried over to peer out. Everything was coated with ice. Branches broken from maple trees cluttered the yard. Everything glistened. Curious, a few children ventured outside trying to walk. They laughed as they fell time and again on slippery paths.

"We'll go make sure all the cabin doors open so folks can get out," William said.

"Then we need to help the animals. They are wearing ice coats and bawling 'cause they can't move. Some of them are frozen to the ground. It is awful!" Robert told them.

"I helped Fanny and Grace walk over to start cooking but the kitchen wood supply is low. Woodpiles are covered with thick ice. When the boys get the logs pried loose they may not burn," William said, shaking his head in frustration.

"We have some hot water here. We can use it to help thaw some animals, but how are we going to get water to them?" asked Isaac, alarmed with the growing need.

"We'll have to drag buckets and slide our way to the corrals. The water won't be hot by the time we get it there," Robert replied.

Women worked for hours trying to keep fires going so water could be heated. Men carried it to the animals. Boys brushed horses. Children rubbed the sheep and cows with rough sacks. Pigs and horses had been somewhat sheltered by shed roofs and mostly needed feeding. Chickens lay silently on the ground frozen to death.

Logs sputtered in fireplaces as ice turned to water, threatening to put out flames. They ate food which had been prepared ahead for their New Year gathering. "No one can come join us today," said Fanny as she dished up lukewarm soup.

Most animals had revived and fires were burning again by evening. Everyone, young and old, fell exhausted into their beds.

Up to the sixteenth of January no word had arrived from the Baptist Board about financial assistance for the boy's college costs. "Christiana, I've sent Sarah to fetch Johnston and William. I want you to join us," Isaac said one cold blustery morning.

She sighed deeply, fearful of what she was about to hear. She knew her husband's restless tossing and turning night after night was the result of an unsolved problem. She had been waiting for just such a meeting to occur. Now she quietly arranged four chairs close to the hearth.

Isaac halted his impatient pacing and sat beside her. "I wonder what's taking them so long," he muttered. A few minutes later they heard voices and stamping of feet as the men tried to remove snow from their boots. The door swung open. Cold air rushed into the cabin. The men hung their coats on pegs and joined the McCoys.

"January thaw hasn't started yet," Johnston said, trying to sound cheerful.

"Well, I am hoping it holds off awhile," Isaac stated, looking very serious. "I feel the necessity of a trip East. Frozen rivers are usually easier to cross."

Christiana's heart sank. It was what she had feared. She dreaded every trip he made but winters were the worst. She recalled their journey to establish the mission with all its frightening hardships. "Must you go right now?"

With only a quick glance, Isaac could tell her thoughts but ignored her question. "The month is half gone. We haven't received any letters from the Board." He shook his head sadly. "We have to get these older boys into college!"

"Are we destitute of funds?" asked Johnston. "I thought we had set aside some money for them."

"We do have a small amount but most of our money is allotted for other necessities."

"If my government salary had arrived from Detroit, I would gladly give it to the cause," Robert said.

Isaac started his pacing again then stopped, saying, "Educating these children is our most important goal. We have seven boys ready for college." He stood thinking, then said, "I am determined to get them enrolled! They should have been enrolled the first week of January."

A coughing spell forced him to grab a chair for support. After a few minutes he continued, "I decided in the night that the boys and I must leave yet this week. With the Lord's help we will find a way. Christiana always says that and I believe her. I need your help to get ready and to take care of things here while I am gone."

"Isaac, the boys don't even have proper clothing," Christiana said, thinking of all the things they would need.

Johnston shook his head, agreeing with her. "Besides that, they will need books and supplies."

"It all comes down to money," Robert commented sadly.

"Yes," Isaac said. "Lack of money. Actually, that is our only problem. We may have homemade clothes, but they are warm. We have blankets to sleep in at night. We have food to eat along the way. We have good horses to ride."

He smiled slightly. "In all my journeys I have found good Christian folks willing to help me. I believe it will happen this time too."

Christiana wished her faith was as firm as his, but she joined the men in promising Isaac that Carey Mission would be kept in good order during his journey. Charity boxes were once again brought down so she and the girls could search for boys' outfits or garments to rip up and make into shirts and underwear.

The youngest girls spent afternoons knitting stockings, mittens, hats and scarves. Older girls sewed shirts. Women remade discarded trousers.

Excitement increased as their departure day drew nearer. In spite of herself, Christiana found herself caught up in the preparation fun. She was very pleased that Isaac also acquired a new frock coat and shirt for the journey.

The February morning they left was clear and cold. When packing the previous day they had decided to ride three horses and load a wagon pulled by two horses instead of taking eight horses. Bedding, shovels and basic tools, food, cooking utensils, and boxes containing clothes and school records along with five boys filled the wagon totally.

All gaiety ended as the travelers looked back to wave to their silent mission family. Christiana wiped tears from her eyes, swallowed hard, then returned to her cabin. Moving furniture, sloshing hot soapy water while she scrubbed the rough floor boards always lifted her depression.

Later, in a much improved mood, Christiana pulled her shawl back on and walked to school. Baby Isaac was being cared for each day by women in the kitchen. All her other children were in school.

Shaking snow clumps from her skirt bottom, she scraped her shoes on the doorsill. When she entered the building, morning devotions had just ended. "Classes are late in starting today," she said, standing in front of all the pupils. "Watching our college bound men leave took a half hour away. Now we must work extra hard." She looked at all the serious young faces and smiled. "Soon you will all be leaving here to go to college."

While the pupils started their lessons, Christiana moved to the window. She was thinking again of the seven boys wondering if they would ever return. She turned and watched Fanny working with the older girls and hoped Isaac would find a way to get them into higher education too.

Christiana, like everyone else, worked diligently performing all the duties of the mission. Winter days were long and dreary. Coughs and sickness brought on by cold weather added to the usual concerns and care. At night, alone in bed, Christiana always thought of Isaac and wondered how he and the boys were enduring.

Extremely cold weather kept streams and rivers frozen, making travel easier and faster for Isaac and the boys. Only three times did they have to shovel and push the wagon along snow covered trails. Roadways around more populated areas in Indiana were packed from constant use.

Isaac was pleased to reach J.R. John's home in Troy, Ohio, in just nine days. They slept in their barn but were well fed in their home. While Isaac went to the small cemetery to locate his daughter Maria's grave, Mrs. John packed travel food for them. Isaac left letters with the Johns to be sent back to Carey Mission. The Johns promised to solicit friends and churches for college funds. It was six below zero as they moved toward Dayton.

When they arrived there, Isaac planned to visit the Phillips' home. First he helped the boys take shelter in an abandoned three-sided cattle shed at the edge of town. They pulled the wagon across the opening and fastened up a canvas cover to

.

block the wind. They had trouble making their cold stiff fingers work. "I can't even feel my toes," one of the boys said.

Isaac left and the boys sat huddled together and eventually felt warmer. Tears ran down their cheeks as their frozen eyelids thawed. "Now, my hands and feet are itching. Oh, it is awful!" Mark exclaimed.

"Mine too," echoed the others.

"These wool stockings and mittens have worn thin. There is no warmth in them."

"I have new ones in my box of clothes but I am saving them to wear at school."

"That's stupid! We may freeze to death and not get to college."

"Don' call me stupid. I'm as smart as you."

Suddenly a fight broke out. The horses stomped their feet and whinnied as three boys rolled around under the wagon, scattering dusty straw. The fight ended just as fast as it had started and the boys sat down grinning. "Well, I guess that got us warmed up," Luke remarked. "Let's see if we can scrape together a meal. I'm hungry!"

While they ate meager rations they made plans for the next days. "Lets use some of the boards in here and make rabbit traps or a fire."

" We don't know how long Reverend McCoy will be, so we better gather firewood and take care of ourselves."

" We can go out two at a time. Let's double up on coats. The ones in here will stay warm enough until we get a fire going."

Years before when he and his family had been in desperate need Isaac had been treated kindly by Horatio Phillips, a leading merchant in Dayton. They had met only a few times since but had corresponded often. Much as he disliked asking for money, Horatio seemed a good prospect.

Although Isaac appeared unannounced at the Phillips home he was greeted and admitted with kindness. The generosity of his friend, both in money and food, overwhelmed Isaac. He was given the guest room for the night. Isaac marveled at all the comforts. He felt guilty thinking of the boys and all the primitive conditions at Carey Mission.

Mrs. Phillips mended his torn jacket. She insisted he take two heavy coats and boots her husband no longer wore. "I hope you will stay long enough so I can sort through drawers and closets. I know there are shirts and trousers our sons have outgrown or don't need. Your college boys might as well have them."

Two days later, Horatio hitched his horse to a sleigh loaded with clothing and food and followed Isaac back to the boys. He had given Isaac an additional saddled horse. Mrs. Phillips had prepared a warm wholesome meal and wrapped it in blankets which they were to keep also. "Best of wishes to you, young men," Horatio said as he shook their hands. "Travel safely!"

After repacking boxes and supplies, they started out the next morning for Wheeling, West Virginia. The weather cleared somewhat but anxiety, fatigue and exposure made Isaac so sick he was unable to sit on his horse. He moved to the wagon and four boys rode horses.

Following the Cumberland Road, which curved like a stream across the countryside, they reached the city on the twenty-second of February. They went to the general store where Isaac sent a letter to Christiana with a birthday message for Nancy, their seven-year old daughter. There were two letters waiting for him.

"Listen to this," he said to the boys, "Word has been received from Choctaw Academy in Kentucky that they will accept Indian males for training at their school."

The boys looked at each other with surprise. "Weren't we close to there when we were in Dayton?" asked Mark. "Are we going back?"

"What type of training would we get there? Is it one of the schools you wrote to?" asked Luke.

"I'm not familiar with that college or its programs, so we are not going back!" Isaac replied emphatically.

As they continued their journey east, they stopped at mail stations along the way. More letters instructed them to go to Kentucky, but they kept going east until they reached Cumberland, Maryland. Isaac found lodging for the boys. He went on to Washington where he joyfully visited Rice and Josephus at Columbian College.

"I am so pleased to find you both healthy and succeeding in your studies. Your mother will be happy to know you are well fed and clothed," he said as he looked them over. "Everyone at home sends their regards. By the way you have a new brother," he added, smiling.

"We know that. I received my January birthday letter from Mama," Rice replied happily. "It is heartwarming to see you, Papa!"

Both boys hugged their father, then sat on their bed facing him. He sat at the table in the tiny attic room they shared.

"We already wrote and told about the chores we do in exchange for room and board. Evenings we study. Sundays we go to church. There is little time for leisure but we have made friends here," Josephus told him.

"I wish your mother could see how you both look!" Isaac said, repeating himself. "I'll be walking with you to your school tomorrow. I plan to visit your college president and see if he will accept seven more boys into the school."

"I don't know what the reasons are but there are no Indians enrolled here, Papa," Rice said sadly.

Isaac brushed and cleaned his clothes before crawling into bed with his sons. The next day he visited the college. After hearing his request, the president invited him to attend the board meeting to present his appeal. He listened politely as the board insisted that being Indian presented no problem in attending their school. Lack of tuition money was a barrier.

Rice and Josephus borrowed horses and rode with their father back to Cumberland to visit the boys. Isaac tried not to show how discouraged he felt as he spoke to all of them. After much discussion, the boys offered a solution. "We are not without tuition money," said Luke. "We already talked it over and decided that one or two of us will use the money and attend here. The rest of us will go back to Carey Mission until more money is available. You choose who stays, Reverend McCoy."

Isaac swallowed hard, blinking to keep from crying. "I can't believe it must come to this. Let me go talk to the president of the college again. He needs to know how honorable you boys are, that you will sacrifice so even a few can attend."

Isaac rode back with Rice and Josephus and once again visited the college. He was informed at that meeting that there wasn't room for them after all. Discouraged beyond belief, he went to his sons' boarding house and spent the afternoon alone and in prayer. Rice and Josephus bid him farewell the next morning.

As he rode back to Cumberland an idea developed in his mind. The boys were eagerly awaiting him. He didn't tell them what had happened but they listened carefully to his new plan. "We are continuing our journey," he told them. "The Lord has made it very clear to me that we must go on together! You have all completed your courses. You are fine young men. You deserve to continue your education! Any college should be proud to have you. We are going to New York. There are fine colleges there."

Along the way they occasionally met families headed for the new Erie Canal to board canal boats and journey toward Lake Erie. According to them it would save time and was not too expensive. "We need to go look at this great canal. I don't guess we could afford the fees," Isaac said, laughing at the thought. "I just can't imagine how such a system for lowering and raising boats would be engineered. We should see it."

"Maybe we could get employment there. It is all hand dug isn't it?" asked Mark. "We aren't afraid of hard labor. I read in the Cumberland newspaper you brought us that they pay seventy- five cents a day."

"Money is useful, but don't let the desire for it rob you of your education. Remember you are here to study. When you finish your training then you can earn money in your chosen career," Isaac told the boys, always consistent in his teacher role.

In a few days they reached Clinton, New York. Much to everyone's relief, all were welcomed into Hamilton College, a fine liberal arts college for men. It had been founded by a missionary to the Iroquois and offered many fields of study.

Finding housing for them took several days. Isaac located the Baptist church in town and met with several of their deacons to present his dilemma. "I am a Baptist minister and missionary. I have seven well educated and work disciplined young men in my care. We have traveled from Michigan Territory in severe winter conditions. We arrived here without funds for food and shelter. They have been enrolled in Hamilton College. They will need housing and meals for the school year." He looked at their kind faces and continued. "They are familiar with chores and are willing to work. Can you suggest any possible solution?"

The men looked at each other and smiled. "You have no idea how many times we have heard this request," one man responded. "Most of the students lack money and this church does what it can to assist them."

"I am one of the founders of the seminary," said Samuel Payne. "My wife will no doubt scold me, but we have a small farm and could use about four young men to help with the planting. They could do chores for room and board. I'll pay wages for farm work."

Isaac swallowed hard, trying not to show his emotions. "They won't disappoint you. They have experience with planting right through to harvest."

"Well," said another, "I could pay a young man to work in my general store. I could put a cot in the back room. He could sleep there and buy his meals at the college."

"My wife and I have a spare room. It would be good to have a young man around. Since our daughter married we've been alone. Frankly, the house is too quiet. Actually we'd have room for two. They could carry in our water and split wood, and probably do some other chores," an elderly man said.

The next few days were spent moving the boys and their meager belongings into their various homes, arranging classes and borrowing text books and supplies. When the time came for Isaac to leave he felt his first sense of achievement in many months.

Before they parted company, Isaac took the boys with him to Utica. They spent several days watching mules pulling boats on the new canal. Irishmen working along the muddy banks were rough and loud. "I don't think you fellows would fit in well here," he said on their final evening, as they avoided the drinking parties. "Life in Clinton is much more what I'd prefer for you."

The boys looked at each other and smiled. "We won't be disappointing you!" Luke assured him.

Isaac sold the wagon and all but one horse. Keeping a few coins for himself, he gave each boy a few coins for emergency use. He packed his belongings into two saddlebags, carefully wrapping a fancy teapot Mrs. Phillips wanted Christiana to have. He had used money from his own meager cash to buy her a packet of tea.

On his journey back to Michigan Territory, Isaac visited several colleges, hoping to find openings for more pupils. He spoke at many churches, telling people about Carey Mission, its needs and goals. He also brought the subject of advanced schooling for females to the attention of several educators whose acquaintances he'd made. This new idea was not favored.

Warm spring days followed him as he crossed the states. He stopped at farms and watched crops being planted, often sleeping in barns. He was fascinated with the way farmers pruned fruit trees and was anxious to reach home so he could teach the boys.

On little Isaac's first birthday his father arrived home. The entire missionary family gathered to greet him, delighted to have him back. Everyone was especially eager to hear about the college boys. Tired as he was, Isaac spent the evening relating their many experiences. He told them over and over about the generous gifts they had received. "Tomorrow I want you to tell me all the things that have been happening here. Tonight I am looking forward to sleeping under my own roof."

Christiana had spent many tearful nights missing Isaac. Daytime hours she maintained her example of strength. Now she could once again enjoy sharing responsibilities.

His first morning home, Isaac presented her gifts as they sat talking. She seldom received presents and fondled the teapot over and over. "As soon as water heats we will have a cup of tea," she laughed. "Doesn't that sound fancy? Imagine that!

We will sip tea and talk, just like rich folks. I'll have to find a safe place for the teapot so young hands can't reach it."

"I am very pleased I could bring you something so nice," Isaac said smiling lovingly. "I have good things to tell you besides. Rice and Josephus are advancing in their studies and act extremely mature. I know it is a hardship for you to have our family separated but truly it is the right thing to do." He patted her hand. "We need to think about sending Sarah and young Christiana away to school."

As a mother, Christiana had a difficult time dealing with that thought, especially since Delilah had disliked her time away so much. "They are too young, Isaac."

"I know what you are thinking, but they can go together. That will be easier than Delilah had it. We agreed earlier."

"I would like to keep them here awhile longer. I know the time will come when they must leave, but not just yet," she said as she put her tea things away. She walked to the window and watched the children playing, wishing their lives could always be so carefree.

Later, Christiana saddled a horse and joined Isaac on his ride around newly plowed fields. When they reached the peach and apple orchards they decided to walk and tied the horses to a tulip tree. "Smell those blossoms, aren't they sweet?"

"Look out for the bees, they think so too," Isaac warned. "I'm worried that it may be too late to prune but I guess we'd better. Some of the trees need shaping," he said as they walked through the orchard.

"Do you know how to do it?"

"On my way home, I stayed at fruit farms a few times. They were trimming before the flowers opened. Pruning encourages better fruit growth. Tomorrow I'll come out and teach the others."

"What a pleasant day to be working outdoors," Isaac said the next day, gazing at the blue sky. The warmth of the sun felt good on his back. He carefully lifted a branch and nipped its end with his knife. "See how that opens up the center of the tree? Now the sun can reach the fruit." All the hired men and boys watching nodded in agreement. "Let's go two by two down the rows to trim. I'll let you know when to stop for the day."

A couple of hours later he checked his pocket watch and began a final inspection in each row. As he caught up with workers he broke off a piece of yellow yarn and tied it to the tree. "Start here tomorrow," he said, then watched as they happily raced back for supper.

He walked back with men from the last row. "Before we finish I'd like a count of the trees. Seems we have a fine orchard."

"We'll need to bring the wagon to load up all the branches or are we going to stack them to burn here?" asked Robert.

"Big branches could be cut and used in fireplaces but I guess the twigs could be burned here. We'll have to sort them," Isaac said.

"Can't let anything go to waste, can we?" said Robert smiling.

"That's what our teachers keep telling us," one of the boys commented. The others nodded in agreement.

Following the evening meal, Isaac read from the Bible. "Tonight the text will be familiar to many of us," he said looking around. He winked at some of the boys and began reading, 'I am the true vine and my Father is the husbandman. Every branch in me that beareth not fruit, he taketh away; and every branch that beareth fruit he purgeth it, that it may bring forth more fruit'." He paused to look again at the boys. Wide-eyed stares met his as he went on to relate biblical meaning to their afternoon's work.

When the session ended everyone left to prepare for bed. Isaac and Christiana went to their cabin to sit before their own fireplace in quiet conversation. Isaac stretched and yawned. "This was a perfect day! The boys learned many lessons today. Besides physical exercise, they used their arithmetic to measure. Pruning required close working together, then our Bible lesson added to the meaningful activities."

Christiana smiled understandingly. "Wouldn't it be nice if it happened that way more often? But, even so, we must rejoice for each good day."

A week or so later, as Isaac stood talking to some visiting land prospectors, he was surprised to see Chief Pokagon with a group of his young warriors ride in. He called Abraham to join them. After a few minutes of friendly greetings the Chief stated his reason for the visit. Although Abraham helped interpret, Isaac now knew many Potawatomi words. Pokagon had learned many English words. "Our council has met. We want permanent log buildings like yours. Will you come to our village and teach us how to build?" Pokagon asked.

"You are good neighbors. It will give us great pleasure to teach you to build sturdy buildings. Then you will live more comfortably all year around," Isaac replied.

"That is what we want. Some of our people no longer want to migrate north for cold weather. They do not want to follow trap lines any longer. They want to live in warm houses here. We will fence our land and become farmers."

The land prospectors appeared bored and wandered away. From the corner of his eye, Isaac noticed them mount their horses and ride off into the woods.

Isaac and Pokagon walked around looking at log cabins. Later they shook hands. Isaac agreed to ride to the Indian village the next week to select trees to be felled.

Isaac watched, puzzled, as he saw the prospectors re-appear and follow Pokagon's group into the woods. Two days later they returned, laughing and waving a paper in the air. "We beat you to it," they said. "This is a contract, signed by the injun chief, giving us the job of putting up their log cabins."

Isaac shook his head, confused. He wondered what terms had been negotiated and why Pokagon done it.

May was a demanding month. The men finished shearing the large sheep herd. Both women and girls were kept extra busy carding and spinning new wool. Many newborn lambs required bottle feeding which the children loved doing. Seeds were planted in the gardens. Women washed clothes, soiled from the long winter's use. Bedding was aired by spreading blankets and quilts on tree branches and bushes. Mattresses were refilled with new prairie grass. Huge kettles of melting fat smoked as they were stirred over outdoor fires. Lye was carefully added to some to make soap. Some kettles had beeswax added and candles were dipped or molded.

Boys and hired men planted corn and grain. Always there were animals to take care of. Sheds were cleaned. Some were enlarged. Fences and buildings were repaired. Fallen trees were dragged to the yard, cut and split.

Busy as it was, there was no particular work needing Isaac's attention. Christiana was too harried to object when Isaac told her he was taking Abraham and Johnston with him to Thomas Station, leaving the other men to supervise.

After visiting Abraham's family at their trading post, they followed the trail along the coast of Lake Michigan. "There is very little white man's invasion here," Isaac said. "Things are certainly peaceful," Johnston agreed. They stopped briefly in Indian villages along the way, enjoying fish and berries presented them.

Chief Noonday proudly welcomed the visitors to Thomas Mission. Abraham again interpreted. "Two buildings are ready for a teacher. We have pupils now. We teach them Indian skills. We also want them to learn white man's ways."

"Governor Cass, our territory leader, has promised to send you teachers." Isaac told the Ottawa leaders and villagers. "While we are here we will teach some letters and arithmetic numbers as we speak to the children."

Johnston volunteered to ride the road to Detroit to meet with the Governor. Isaac agreed, sending a letter and list of needed supplies. Johnston returned two weeks later with good news. "A teacher has already been hired. He will arrive within the month." Johnston brought Isaac a packet of mail which included a letter for Isaac. "The governor received this from Robert and sent it on to you."

Isaac read it aloud to the group surrounding him. "Our white neighbors deal out whiskey to the Indians plentifully, with which they purchase anything the Indians will part with. Even clothing of the Indians, farming and cooking utensils, are exchanged liquor. Articles manufactured for Indians in our smithery have been seen in trading posts and owned by whiskey sellers."

Isaac looked at Chief Noonday. "We did not see evidence of this as we rode north along the trail nor do we see it in your village. I pray you have the strength to keep whiskey away from your people." The chief nodded in agreement.

On their return ride back to Carey, Isaac and Johnston had long conversations. "I'm encouraged by the growth at Thomas Station but I still have misgivings about our own situation," said Johnston sadly.

"I feel the same way. Carey Mission is progressing well but our work with the neighboring villages worries me. I don't know yet how we can stop the growing distribution of whiskey."

The final hours of their journey Isaac tried to keep conversation on more pleasant topics. "It is beautiful in these cool woods. Actually I feel quite rested. I wish my wife could get a much needed respite!"

A week-long rain began the day after they returned. When the water and muddy conditions subsided everyone spent afternoons hoeing. Weeds had sprung up beside new little plants. Mosquitoes were vicious. Red welts covered all exposed flesh. Singing Bird set out pots of salve made from various plants. Everyone spread it on their itching sores.

Although it was still spring the sun grew hot. Isaac worked beside the men and boys in the fields. Once he stopped work to wipe his forehead on his shirt sleeve. "We are getting visitors," he said, looking toward the woods.

"Isn't that Chief Topinabe?" asked Calvin who was hoeing the next row.

"Hey! Stop! You're trampling our plants!" yelled William Polke, as he ran toward approaching Indian ponies.

At first Isaac couldn't believe the men's careless disregard of their garden vegetables. Then he realized how intoxicated they were. He quickly joined William as he tried to chase them out.

"We want drinks," one of the Indians mumbled. "We are thirsty."

"All we have is water. You are welcome to have some," William replied calmly. The group laughed as they swayed and slipped from their ponies.

Chief Topinabe had difficulty sitting upright. "Thirsty, drink, trading post lost. Village gone away," he said in a slurred and garbled English.

"You need to return to your village and sleep. This hot sun is bad for you," Isaac told him in Potawatomi words.

"We trade you this for whiskey," the chief said, holding a fancy beaded shirt over his head.

Isaac and William shook their heads and watched in despair as ponies and staggering men smashed squash and corn plants underfoot.

"What a waste," said Isaac as they left. "Disaster for Indians and vegetables."

Christiana had not been working close enough to see the situation. Isaac told her about it as they walked home that evening. While they were talking a young Indian boy, his face painted in black stripes, rode in calling, "Father McCoy!"

Isaac felt his stomach lurch anticipating a problem. "Here I am," he called. "What do you need me for?"

The boy looked frightened. "Our Chief is dead. Chief Topinabe is dead."

"What happened?" Isaac asked, suspecting the worse.

"His horse threw him off. His head hit rocks. His spirit left. You come to burial. Many people are gathering."

"I'll need to pack a few things." said Isaac. He sent Christiana to find Abraham in case he needed an interpreter. He grabbed his black coat from its peg, picked up his Bible and hurried to mount the horse he had Calvin saddle.

The miserable conditions he came upon in the village depressed and frightened him. Most of the mourners were drunk. Their clothing was filthy and ragged, as was the main building where mourners sat around weeping and wailing. Occasionally, a few men would leap into a dance-like frenzy, screaming and chanting around the burial byre. Isaac tried to console the chief's wives and children. He spoke to them of the danger and evil of liquor. He read to them from his Bible but they mostly ignored him or fell asleep. Only a few promised to change their habits. After two days of wretched situations he went home.

Summer came early. During the heat of the day, classes were held each morning but afternoons were more relaxed. Some days the stifling heat made field work unbearable. As soon as farm and kitchen work were completed the reward was playtime in the cool refreshing river.

The McCoys moved a log bench to the water's edge. They often sat there watching children splash, swim or fish. One particularly hot afternoon, Christiana removed her shoes and dangled her feet in cool muddy water. Seeing how much she liked it, Isaac did the same. Soon all the adults enjoyed wading afternoons.

Weeks after Chief Topinabe's burial the distant beating of drums still persisted. "How long will that ceremony last?" asked Christiana. "I'm tired of hearing the sound of drums!"

Isaac shook his head. "I think it will end when a new chief is selected."

"I thought his son would become chief."

"Maybe they are celebrating their new leader, not mourning the old. There are still many rituals we don't know about, aren't there?"

"I guess someone from here should ride to their village again, but to be honest, I fear we will find the same drunken disorder. I prefer not to witness it!" Isaac sighed. Turning his eyes to the opposite river bank, he was startled to see a white man leading his horse toward the water.

"Reverend McCoy, is that you?" called the man. "Remember me? I'm the government agent. Judge John Leib. Governor Cass sent me."

"Come across!" they called. Christiana hastily dried her feet with her skirt and pulled on her shoes. Isaac used some long dry grass and finished drying just before the agent joined them.

He greeted everyone warmly, even remembering names. The men walked toward the buildings. Two young boys led Mr. Leib's horse to the corral. The agent remained for several days, inspecting as before every aspect of the mission, its buildings, fences, crops, animals as well as the school programs, students and teachers.

20

One day Isaac accompanied Judge Leib to several nearby villages. "The governor always wants to know how you are getting along with your neighbors."

"We help them all we can. Recently we started to give them animals. Then we had to teach them to erect fences to keep them from destroying their crops."

Topinabe's village had quieted down by the time they reached there. "We have a serious problem with the newly arriving land seekers. They trade whiskey for just about anything the Indians have. If this continues it will destroy these people."

Judge Leib listened to Isaac's concerns but offered no solution. "Why do they drink the rotten stuff?"

"I can't answer that yet. I have a theory but don't know yet if it is true. I also don't know how to stop the problem!" said Isaac.

Christiana was surprised to find the judge sitting with the young girls one morning. He was carefully dipping a pen into ink and forming circles with the rest of the penmanship class. The next afternoon she saw him hoeing corn with the boys. Another day he made everyone laugh as he helped capture a run away pig.

"He is such a cheerful man, we will be sorry to have him leave," Christiana mentioned to Fanny as they walked to classes.

"Yes, he just mingles with everyone. He acts like a judge though, asking lots of questions," she said, laughing. "He is checking every detail. From what I've heard, I think he is satisfied with the teachings in our school."

"I have heard him giving many compliments too."

The morning he left he told the McCoys, "My report to the governor will be very favorable. I'm extremely impressed with your many improvements. I feel like I'm visiting friends when I come here. God willing, I hope to visit again. I'm going to Thomas Mission Station next."

Christiana made sure he had food for his journey. Isaac handed him two letters to take back to Detroit, one for Governor Cass and one for the Baptist Mission Board. The children waved fondly as he departed.

During the last week of July, 1826, a violent thunderstorm kept everyone confined indoors. From time to time Christiana ventured to her window to watch. As a flash of bright lightning lit up the dark sky, she saw a teenage Indian boy she didn't recognize running toward the cabin. She rushed to open the door.

"Follow me! Something to see!" he shouted.

Isaac joined Christiana at the door. When they saw the terror on the boy's face, they quickly grabbed raingear from their pegs. Isaac held up his hand, stopping his wife. "I'll go alone. If I need help I'll come back and get you."

He followed the boy, barely able to keep up his pace. After about a mile and a half, the boy stopped and pointed to a woman's horribly mutilated body. Isaac gagged, then swallowed hard, trying not to be sick. The woman's head laid some distance away. He recognized her as a poor destitute woman who had resided at Carey Mission several months. Her son was a pupil at the school.

Man sized moccasin prints were visible in the deep mud around her body. From the evidence the murder appeared to have been done by a Potawatomi man or men.

"Grab that piece of wood and help me dig a grave," Isaac told the boy. "I don't want anyone else to see this. Do you know who did this?" he asked, as he dug into the soft ground with a large pointed stone he'd found.

No answer was given. Isaac found he had been left alone to finish the gruesome task. He caught a glimpse of movement in the brush and realized the boy was running away. After a brief prayer over the shallow grave Isaac wiped his hands on damp leaves and walked slowly back home. Circumstances of the murder were too shocking to relate. He prayed he could find a gentle way to tell her son of her death. Rain soaked, he trudged into the cabin.

One look at his face and Christiana prepared herself for bad news. "What happened?"

"Poor little Running Deer is now an orphan," Isaac said sadly. "I refuse to tell the details. I must go talk to him."

"Perhaps you should bring him to our cabin. He could become a member of our family. Girls, think of a Bible name we can give him," she said to their young daughters playing on the bed. Delilah was mending. The McCoys had previously adopted orphans despite the fact their own family was large.

By the time Isaac returned with the boy, a name had been chosen with Delilah's help. She smiled at him as she removed his rain soaked shirt, dried him off and pulled a blue striped one over his head. "Welcome to the McCoy family, Joseph," she said very formally. "This is your brightly dyed garment, just like the story we heard last night of Joseph and his special coat."

A slight smile crossed his tear stained face. Christiana hugged the little boy, then lead him to her rocking chair. "I always sit here when I am sad. You can do that too."

After a few minutes of rocking, Joseph joined little Isaac on the floor playing with a deerskin ball. Eleanor picked up a tiny birchbark canoe and handed it to Joseph. "I got this today for my fifth birthday. I want you to have it." Isaac and Christiana looked at each other with pride.

"I play with it. It still be yours," Joseph said, which pleased everyone.

Thunder and lightning continued all night. Water leaked through roofs. When the rainstorm ended, fallen limbs were gathered. Wet clothes and damp quilts were hung to dry. Late August, when the ground finally dried, summer harvest began.

Summer changed to fall with all its usual duties keeping everyone busy. While the women and girls dried and preserved food and seeds, men and boys cut grain and corn for animal feed. Corn shucks were stacked to dry for bedding. Flour and meal were ground, then stored in barrels in the kitchen loft. Stacks of cheese and strings of dried apples and beans hung from the log rafters.

Geese were heard honking overhead as they migrated south. Wood was piled, ready to split for fireplaces. Soap bars were stacked. Candles were dipped and hung in the lofts, handy for use in the dark winter days. Children spent many wet fall days mixing mud, leaves and horse hair and then filling gaps and chinking logs in all the buildings. Badly split wooden shingles were replaced by hired men. The McCoys were well satisfied with the winter preparations.

"With so much to do in October, I probably shouldn't go away but I truly feel my presence is needed at a treaty making council Bertrand told me about when I was last there," Isaac said as he sat at breakfast with Christiana and Johnston.

"I knew the Indians were gathering again like they did last fall. Where is the council meeting? There must be close to two hundred Indians camped along the Saint Joseph. Is it going to be held somewhere else?" Johnston asked.

"They are heading far south of here on the Wabash River. I expect twice as many souls will attend as are already here." Isaac paced back and forth trying to decide if he should go. "Bertrand said the chiefs want me to accompany them so I can interpret other white men's bargaining messages. If I go I'll need to take an interpreter to assist my understanding."

"I think you need to go," said Christiana, although she dreaded the separation. "Perhaps you should take a few of our older pupils. It would be quite an experience for them to watch their tribesmen make property decisions."

"You are right, after all, the choices made there will effect their future," agreed Johnston.

"That settles it then, I'll go. I can take five or six pupils along."

"Be sure to include some girls," Christiana reminded him.

Within the week three boys and two girls were selected. Warm clothing and food was packed. The day before they were to leave Isaac rode along the river to tell the leaders he would be joining them. "Close to five hundred people have gathered," he told Christiana when he returned.

Because of the large numbers of people their movement south was slow. Unfortunately, within the first three day's journey their most expert hunters, close to fifty men and boys, had not managed kill any game. When the procession halted for the night Isaac's group heard many complaints of hunger. The food Isaac and his pupils brought was nearly depleted. All around them children were crying. People became ill.

Chief Saugana, as leader of the group, spoke to his followers on the fourth morning. "I had a dream last night which explained our poor luck in hunting. It is the fault of Chief Chebass. He probably failed to make a sacrificial feast before we began our journey. Now our gods have not provided us with food. Chebass acted as a white man, offering no prayers or sacrifices. Now, the Great Spirit is punishing us all."

Isaac tried to intervene and correct Chief Saugana's theory. "White men do offer prayers before they begin journeys. Our God helps us but we must also help ourselves. Perhaps the hunters must go farther away from the noise the people are making. The noise could be frightening game away." The Chief and his council wouldn't listen to Isaac. He was tempted to return home but instead kept himself and his pupils near the end of the line of travelers.

Chebass was forced to remain where he was and fast for a day. Everyone else continued their travel. Twelve men with blackened faces, showing hunger and want, proceeded with their hunting. Six men went on each side of the trail. They were told to return by noon with four deer Chief Saugana had seen in a dream.

Isaac was astounded when it actually occurred. A general halt was called when the hunters laid four deer at Chief Saugana's feet. "What is going to happen now?" Isaac asked his pupils who were acting as interpreters.

"We are stopping while a feast is prepared." Isaac and the pupils remained in the background as deer parts were boiled, even heads, legs and feet. Everyone feasted except Chebass.

"The feast is considered his. For that reason it is necessary for him to continue his fast until sun down," explained Isaac's companions. After the meal, several speeches were made. The march resumed. Watching and listening to the ceremony made Isaac realize how firmly Indians held to their superstitions. The next day five deer and a bear were killed. During the three remaining days of the journey they had plenty of food. Isaac's group shared in the meals.

Back at the Carey Mission, Christiana gazed at the bright falling leaves. "What a beautiful day! Look at that blue sky, not a cloud in sight!" she said to the group of youngsters standing in line for the noon meal. "It's perfect for a walk in the woods. I love the sound and feel of dry leaves crunching under foot."

"Let's take the girls on a search for nuts this afternoon," Delilah said when she heard her mother.

Fanny joined them and agreed to the outing. "We could collect pretty leaves too. We can press them and learn to identify the different shapes." She laughed. "There are always lessons to learn."

"Let's invite all the women and children to join us. We may not have many more days like this. We all deserve an afternoon with no chores." Christiana told them. "You come too, Singing Bird. We can cut some sassafras roots for tea and maybe find some grapes to press for juice." "We also need gourds for dying wool into bright colors," Singing Bird commented.

They started out in orderly fashion but soon were running to catch swirling leaves or dashing from tree to tree scooping nuts into baskets. Delilah and Fanny sat down to sort and discard empty shells squirrels had nibbled. Fanny said "The children can crack nuts and we'll add them to cakes someday soon."

After about an hour the children were called to a peaceful oak opening. Christiana suggested they sit quietly and listen, trying to identify birds and their songs. Almost as a reward, a V shaped flock of geese flew over, honking loudly. Everyone laughed and watched in awe.

Christiana removed her long blue apron and tied the corners together to make a tote. "Let's fill this with pine cones as we head home. They make good fire starters. Two boys carried the apron. The children made a game of tossing cones into it.

Suddenly, four people on horseback blocked their way. Christiana stepped ahead of the others. She recognized the two Indian guides but the white people were strangers. "I'm Mrs. McCoy from Carey Mission. Perhaps you were looking for me? We just spent a wonderful afternoon enjoying God's gifts."

"We are the Slaters. I am Leonard," he said in his eastern accent. "This is my wife Abigail. We're newly arrived from Worchester, Massachusetts. We have been appointed to work here with you."

Christiana gasped, totally surprised, unsure what to say. She could see their weariness. She invited the young couple to her home. "We must get you off those horses and let you rest. Follow me. We can talk later." Fanny and Delilah led the children back. Calvin motioned for the Indian guides to follow him to the corral.

Delilah kept all the children outside. Christiana promised the Slaters uninterrupted use of her cabin for several hours. "We'll come get you for the evening meal. By then we'll have a cabin ready for you."

During the remainder of the afternoon mission women cleaned and readied a small cabin which had been used for storage. Strings of pumpkin, squash and beans were drying across the corners. Baskets of turnips and potatoes filled much of the floor space. "Where can we put these things?" they asked over and over.

"Wouldn't it be handy if we could have a storage hole in the ground or a cave so we could keep things cold in summer and keep things from freezing in winter? That's what we had back home," said Fanny. "Until something better is built, there is room in our loft for some of these things."

"We will have to ask the men to help. These things must be carried away. We also have to locate furnishings," Grace said.

"There are a couple of chairs and an old table here but everything needs scrubbing. That bed in the corner needs new rope and a mattress," Christiana said looking around the room. "I'll go talk to the men."

"The girls and I will get some candles from the school. I'll tell Calvin to get some boys and bring in some firewood,"

Delilah offered. "They'll be able to carry water so we can clean the place."

"Surely they have blankets and towels with them. I wonder what else they will need? I wonder how long they have been traveling?" Grace Dusenbury asked, as she swept the floor a second time.

That evening, all the adults met in the school. They were introduced to Abigail and Leonard and enjoyed hearing the fascinating details of the Slater's journey. "We took a small carriage from our home to Albany, New York, where we boarded a freight boat on the Erie Canal. We traveled night and day, except Sundays, until we reached Buffalo, New York, nine days later."

Christiana and Johnston glanced at each other, remembering Isaac's comments about the canal and how expensive the costs were.

"From there we went to Erie, Pennsylvania where we took passage on a steamboat to Detroit which took two days. We had been told to go to the Francis Browning home when we reached the city. They received us cordially and had us wait there until our Indian guides arrived with saddle horses so we could start out for your mission," Leonard told them.

Abigail sighed. "We waited two weeks! Although the Brownings were most gracious, I think they were glad to see us leave. Some of our furniture was put aboard ship in New York. We were led to believe it will reach Lake Michigan port before winter."

"It took us nine days to reach Carey Mission. It was cold and wet most nights as we spread our blankets on the ground. One night we stayed in a pretty village beside the Kalamazoo River. A French trader named Numaiville let us sleep in his cabin. Someday I'd like to go back there." He sighed as he recalled the place. "For now however, we are happy to be here. We have much to learn but we plan to work hard," Leonard concluded.

"In spite of our afternoon rest, right now we are looking forward to unpacking our belongings and settling down for the night. I'm sure you folks are too," Abigail said yawning. "Thank you for preparing a place for us so quickly!"

Two weeks after the Slaters arrived, Isaac and his pupils returned from the Wabash treaty council. Isaac was pleased to meet the newcomers. "Looks like you have settled right into the routine." He smiled. "Leonard, I hear you have been leading nightly devotions and Abigail, you are instructing fine needlework. Bless you both!"

Isaac read the treaty disbursements to the entire mission family the second morning they were back. "Fifty-eight Indian scholars at Carey Mission were each given a quarter acre of land. $500 worth of goods, which means clothing, food, blankets, were also allotted to our pupils. I'll prepare a list of pupils receiving allotments. You should look for your name on the list. Clothing and food will be sent directly here since this is where you live." He dismissed the boys and girls and spoke to the adults. "These contributions will be useful because as usual the payment from the Mission Board has been delayed," he explained. "Money for salaries hasn't come either."

Later in the week Isaac spoke to the pupils about the importance of their land grants and distributed the papers. To his great disappointment, some boys made a secret trip to Bertrands trying to trade their land parcels for fancy boots and rifles. Another boy told Isaac and he confronted them upon their return. They told Isaac and Christiana, "We have no use for land here. We do not need land here! When we are older, we will leave for college or look for employment. We will live somewhere else," they insisted. The McCoys had no rebuttal. They were pleased to learn later that Bertrand had refused to take or trade the boy's land grants.

21

Mid October activities centered on Johnston's upcoming journey to Thomas Station which had to be completed before rivers froze.

"Is there space for more things?" asked Christiana.

"Depends on what you want to add. It can't be anything tall or heavy enough to break the farming tools that it will be sitting on."

"Just clothing and shoes," she replied, hoping to get rid of charity surplus. "We also have some seeds they'll be needing for spring planting."

"Everything will be repacked and secured when I get to the river mouth," Johnston said. "Crates need to be nailed tight before we load everything on another boat."

"That's right! Turbulent waters can bounce things around, even split them open," said Isaac. "Of course you may find calm northern waters, we've had such a dry season."

The large pirogue the boys had built from rough boards and pine pitch was packed to overflowing. There was just room for two men among crates of apples, squash and other vegetables being sent to help feed people over the winter.

On the twentieth of October, Johnston and a newly hired Frenchman left Carey. Although everyone was in a joyful mood as they waved farewell, Christiana thought she saw Delilah wipe tears from her eyes.

The plan was to sail up the St. Joe river to its mouth, then put the pirogue and supplies on a Lake Michigan schooner headed for the Grand River. From there they would again use the pirogue to reach Thomas Station. The men would remain there to help finish construction of buildings before winter set in.

In early November a young Ottawa Indian arrived on horseback with a letter from Johnston. Isaac read it aloud after evening devotions. "On October twenty-eighth, the schooner anchored about a mile from shore. Our pirogue was lowered into white-capped waves and was towed ashore by a long-boat. Our garments were soaked. We were near freezing as the cold water splashed and tossed us about. I feared for my life!"

As they listened, Christiana became alarmed as Delilah gasped and grew pale. She moved closer and put her arm around her daughter as Isaac continued.

"Waves ran so high as to threaten to turn all into the lake. In spite of stormy weather all cargo arrived safely and is being used. Thanks be to God!"

Delilah relaxed and regained her composure, much to her mother's relief. It was now obvious Delilah had a strong attachment to her teacher. Christiana wondered where it would lead.

November's gray sky forecasted winter. Winds switched from the north bringing in a swirl of snowflakes. Chief Pokagon came riding through the snow toward McCoy's cabin.

Isaac had been working all morning at his desk, writing letters and reports. Weary and feeling discouraged he stared out of the window. When he saw Pokagon, his mood changed. He smiled. Then he remembered their broken agreement in the spring. As he opened the door, he wondered what prompted this visit.

"Father McCoy, come see our village!" Pokagon called. He didn't dismount and showed no sign of friendship.

Isaac grabbed his coat and hat and pulled them on. Pokagon's gruff attitude confused him. As he walked toward the horse shed he passed Delilah. "Tell your mother not to expect me until nightfall. I'm going to Pokagon's village.

"Did I do something to make you angry?" Isaac asked as they rode side by side through an open meadow.

Pokagon turned his stoic face toward Isaac and shrugged. "You will see."

The snow stopped falling but after more miles of silence, Isaac felt chilled inside and out. They rode across a shallow part of the river. Isaac's eyes searched the horizon for new buildings. He pulled his horse to a halt. "What happened?" he asked when he couldn't see any.

"Your white friends took our furs to buy materials. They did not return to build houses," Pokagon told him sadly. "We cut down trees. We cleared land like they told us. They did not do what they said. Now snow is falling. We have no warm houses for the winter."

"Chief Pokagon, why do you say they are my friends? I did not know them. They came to the mission to ask about land for sale. I don't even remember their names."

"I saw them at your mission listening to our talk. Later that day they told us you sent them to build for us. I thought those white men were like you and I could trust them. I signed their paper. I wondered why you did not come with them. Now, once again my village people do not trust white men."

Isaac, fighting back tears, shook his head. "I am very sorry those men flayed you. I am disappointed for you. I thought you did not want me to build cabins and that you chose them instead. Let's ride to the village," he said, praying he could come up with a solution as they rode. "Show me the cleared areas and trees you cut."

Pokagon pointed to stacks of fallen trees. Some were cut into twelve-foot lengths, others still had branches attached. Teepees stood in a circle outside the cleared land. Shivering people stood huddled around a crackling bonfire. Some turned their backs as the riders approached.

As the men dismounted and walked toward the fire, Indians moved away. A few went into teepees. "You will not walk from my presence!" Pokagon shouted. "Father McCoy has come to speak. You will listen to him!"

The villagers shuffled back within hearing distance. No one looked at Isaac as he spoke. "Once again you have been tricked by evil white men. They are like crows around a carcass, picking on people who can't help themselves." Isaac saw a few smiles and continued. "They are not my friends or your friends. I am angry that they cheated you! I do not want you to think all white men are alike."

He took a deep breath and stood as straight as he could. "I will see that justice is done. The trees you cut will be used to build three log cabins before snow gets deep. I will come back with good white men and tools. Tomorrow work will begin. You will not be cheated again!"

Pokagon walked with him to the horses. "I will be glad to be your friend again," he said. "Tomorrow when you return I will have men ready to learn this building skill."

"That will be good," Isaac replied. "Working together can make us friends."

He stopped at Thompson's cabin on his way back to Carey Mission, offering to hire him and any other neighbor willing to help with the building and fencing he'd promised Pokagon. Since the first snow had already fallen, Isaac worried about finishing the buildings before severe weather arrived.

Squire Thompson, still struggling to make a productive farm, accepted a barter of vegetables and flour for his labor. To Isaac's relief, snow held off. With the help of other neighbors, many mission workers and Indians, not only were the buildings erected in two weeks but rail fences were set in place around some cleared areas.

At the invitation of Pokagon's village, the entire mission family rode in wagons or on horses to join in celebration when all work was completed. As a final act of friendship Pokagon was presented with some stock hogs and a cow, hoping to encourage the Indians to raise animals.

"In the spring I will send men to plow land for planting. The fences we put up are to keep animals from eating your crops. The hogs need to be confined in a strong pen so they don't wander. It would be good to build shelters to protect them and the cow from winter weather," Isaac told Pokagon. "Next summer we will give you some sheep."

The day after the celebration, the Slaters visited the McCoys voicing a concern. "We haven't noticed any preparations for a Thanksgiving celebration."

Isaac and Christiana exchanged glances. "We have never held one," Christiana said. "We received a letter from Governor Cass proclaiming a day to be set aside for giving thanks. Since we do that everyday, we felt we were doing our duty."

"In Massachusetts it is a day of feasting with friends and family. Everyone brings food to share. It is held in November after the harvest. We give prayers of thanks and sing hymns of praise. It is a truly joyful time," Leonard told them.

"Perhaps we should honor Thanksgiving day," Christiana said, as she thought about it.

"It seems to be quite like our New Year's celebration. All of our neighbors come to visit us on that day. We supply the food," Isaac explained to the newcomers. "I like the idea of sharing our harvest bounty. Let's begin a new tradition. I'll be going to Bertrands' soon. He can put out the invitation."

Near the end of each month it had become customary for someone from the mission to take outgoing mail to the trading post. There were usually letters there awaiting pickup. Sometimes the missionaries left produce or things they'd made to barter, in hopes other settlers would buy or trade them.

Bertrand kept an account and subtracted sales from the mission purchases.

Christiana usually took one or two older girls with her when she made the monthly purchases and exchanges but this time Isaac decided to go. Of all the young women enrolled in the school, one in particular impressed Christiana with her keen ability to select and bargain. Little Fawn, nicknamed 'Miss Purchase', was chosen to accompany Isaac and two boys who needed to be measured for boots.

Isaac took a wagon packed with tools made in the blacksmith shop, baskets of squash and turnips, loom-woven rugs and shirt yardage, boxes of candles and soap the girls had made.

One of the boys and Miss Purchase rode horses. When her horse bucked and reared, she pressed her knees into his sides having a difficult time hanging on. The other horse galloped faster, his rider yelling in boyish delight. After a few minutes of racing, they got the horses back in control and returned to the wagon.

"Well done," Isaac called. "I guess our horses need to be ridden more often. If they act up again we'll tie them to the wagon and you will ride with us."

They crossed the river and left its clearing behind, heading into the woods. Snow hung heavy on the tree branches from an earlier storm. In the distance they could see the chimney smoke of the trading post. "You may ride on ahead, Miss Purchase," Isaac called as he watched her carefully maneuver her horse.

Bertrand gathered Isaac in a friendly bear hug as he entered the trading post. "What you bring?"

"The boys will unload," answered Isaac. "Go ahead with your list, Miss Purchase. I'll take care of the mail."

"Miss Purchase. That's a funny name," Bertrand said, laughing in his jolly booming voice. "She's one that's purchasing. That's funny! Miss Purchase, Ho Ho!"

While she located things on the list, Isaac told Bertrand about the Thanksgiving celebration and invited him to bring his family and tell other nearby settlers.

As the stack of items grew the boys carried in the things to be used as barter. They laughed as Bertrand had them stand on boards and traced around their feet with a charred stick. "I give pictures to cobbler when he come for supplies. Next month they be boots."

"Bertrand, can you tell me postage rates for sending many pages?" asked Isaac.

"Oh, sure, somewhere I have written it down," he said, shuffling papers and looking through scraps of paper hanging from a nail.

Faith Thompson and two traders watched impatiently. "Maybe I could find it while you take care of these other folks," offered Isaac.

"You look, that's all right," Bertrand agreed.

Isaac saw how restless his three young companions were getting and suggested they start back to Carey. "You boys can ride double. I'll drive the wagon back."

A strong north wind had developed. Snow swirled, nearly blinding the horses as they rode under trees. Miss Purchase tried to hold her spirited horse back but when a clump of snow fell on his nose, he spooked. Instantly, he reared up on his hind legs, then charged swiftly ahead.

She hung on tightly, bending low in the saddle but she failed to see a low hanging limb. It knocked her off the horse's back. She fell screaming into a bush of pointed branches. The horse raced on. The boys heard her scream and forced their horse to turn back. They found her crumpled on the ground, pale and still, but breathing. A long red slash marked her forehead.

"Should we move her?" asked one of the boys.

"I don't think so. I'll stay here. Go, get Reverend McCoy. I'll cover her with my coat. Give me your coat too. Now go!"

Isaac had just finished loading the wagon when he saw a horse racing toward him. "Reverend McCoy! Come fast, Miss Purchase is hurt!"

Isaac ran back inside the trading post. "Can I borrow a horse? One of my pupils is hurt."

"Not Miss Purchase, is it?" asked Bertrand. "Take my pinto. I'll follow with your wagon."

"Yes, it's the girl," Isaac said as he mounted and rode off.

Bertrand grabbed medicine and blankets. Tossing them into the wagon he climbed in. Whipping the horses into reckless speed he arrived shortly after Isaac. The little girl had recovered enough to open her eyes when she heard Bertrand exclaiming, "Poor little Miss Purchase. Poor little girl."

"What happened?" she asked weakly.

"You narrowly escaped serious injury. A tree limb knocked you off the horse," Isaac told her.

Bertrand gently spread medicine on her wounds. "Sit up slow. You have big headache. You lucky fell on bush. Broke fall. Could be worse. Bush saved your life."

"Gently now, let's lift her into the wagon," Isaac said. "No more wild horseback rides today. You boys tie your horse on behind. Thank you, Bertrand! Once more you have proven to be our good friend. If my wild horse shows up at your place, sell it!"

Betrand climbed on his pinto and headed home. As Isaac drove toward Carey Mission, they could hear him singing for a long time. After they crossed the river Isaac noticed a fresh track on their trail. He wondered who had bypassed the trading post and headed directly for Carey Mission.

Miss Purchase moaned occasionally as they bounced along. Isaac stopped twice to make sure she was warmly covered. The boys watched as he padded her head with a blanket. "Don't let her move her head, she could injure herself badly."

When they pulled into the yard they saw people standing around a horse. "Mr. Lykins is back!" one of the boys said happily.

Isaac jumped down. "Welcome back Johnston! Folks, we need some help here!" he called. "Miss Purchase is injured, we need to move her into our cabin."

Two men carried her inside. Christiana settled her on the trundle bed. Singing Bird entered the cabin with her medicine pouch. After she washed the wound, she made an herb compress. "I will care for her. You go," she told the others.

The wagon was quickly unpacked and the boys drove it over to the small barn. After they turned the horses into the corral, they went to school. All the pupils had gone back to their classes after greeting their returning teacher.

"Show me what you have in your lap, Delilah," whispered her sister, Sarah, who sat beside her.

Delilah blushed. Slowly she opened a beaded deerskin bag and pulled out a tiny carved deer. "Johnston gave these to me for my birthday."

Sarah smiled. "He must really like you. I don't remember him giving presents before."

"We are just friends," Delilah said quietly. "You better get back to your penmanship."

The first Thanksgiving at the Carey Mission Station was held on the last Thursday in November, 1826. At first Abigail and Leonard had insisted that a pilgrim menu should be followed. Unfortunately the boys returned after a long hunt with only one scrawny wild turkey. A very small handful of dried cranberries was all that remained from those bartered earlier at Bertrand's. This further discouraged Abigail. They settled for venison, squash and dried corn, with pumpkin pie for dessert.

Neighbors arrived early, dressed in their finest outfits, very pleased at the chance to socialize with each other. Many of them brought baskets with bowls of food they had prepared. It was a happy occasion until Isaac noticed Squire Thompson sharing a whiskey bottle with some men including Indian chiefs. "Please put that evil substance away!" he said glaring at his neighbor. "Surely you must know it is not allowed here!"

Squire laughed and put the cap back on the bottle. "We are just having a friendly drink. It warms the innards on a cold day like this."

"Put it away! Keep it put away, if you want to stay here! I hope and pray you are not one who is selling liquor. It ruins lives. All you men know that. Don't drink it!" Isaac said, looking sternly at each one of the men. He walked away disgusted and discouraged, wondering if he could ever forgive his neighbor.

Later, when he gave his Thanksgiving message, he looked at Squire and said, "We are thankful for trustworthy friends. When we work together, we can improve the lives of others."

When Isaac turned his attention elsewhere, Squire sauntered away. Johnston watched him enter the smithery. Curious, he walked close enough to the building to overhear Squire talking to Robert.

"Do you want a drink of this fire water?" he asked, laughing. "Or are you as narrow minded as the Reverend?"

"Whiskey is harmful. It ruins health and makes people do horrible things," Robert replied. "We don't want it here!"

Squire laughed again, "What I'm selling won't hurt anyone. I always add water to what I buy. If Indians complain it hasn't got any kick I go mix in a little tobacco, then they're satisfied and pay more."

"Neighbor, I think you better leave! I'm about to hit you and I don't want to do that. Get out of here!" Robert shouted, using all his will power to keep his fists still.

Johnston joined the two of them. Squire left to locate his family. Soon their wagon rumbled down the trail. Robert told Isaac about Thompson's departure. The men agreed it had been a very discouraging Thanksgiving day.

December arrived in a blizzard. Snow continued to fall, keeping Carey Mission isolated from all outsiders until a mid-January thaw. The traditional open house celebration on New Year's day became a day of prayer and hymn singing for only pupils and mission adults.

Isaac spent days sitting at his desk. He found the only way to deal with his thoughts about liquor and its affects on Indians was to write them down. He had kept journals for years and now decided to write a book. As he wrote he prayed, trying to find solutions to problems that constantly baffled him. The cabin was dark. Candles flickered as wind draughts blew through cracks around the window and door and down the chimney. His eyes were red and sore. He stopped often to rub them. Even when the family was home, Isaac sat at his desk, his back to everyone, concentrating on his work. He barely heard them.

Schoolwork, chores and worship left little time for anything else in Christiana's days. She made sure the children had time for play. They took turns wearing warm coats and boots so they could toss snowballs and play games in the snow. She enjoyed hearing their happy voices as she worked indoors.

Near the end of January, Lt. David Hunter rode in carrying mail from Ft. Wayne. Although visitors were not unusual, he got everyone's attention immediately. It was a strange sight to see a man guarded by two soldiers with muskets. The guards walked on foot beside the horse. "A new mail route has been established between Chicago and Fort Wayne," the lieutenant told the McCoys. "Yours is the first white settlement between them. From now on your mail won't be delivered to Bertrand's trading post." All the adults were pleased, especially Isaac.

The three men were tired and cold and welcomed the invitation to remain a few days. They slept in Polke's loft and took their meals with the adults. While they remained, Isaac hurriedly gathered his manuscript pages and prepared them for sending to a publisher. Others at the mission took the opportunity to write far-away friends and relatives. Christiana wrote to Rice and Josephus including birthday greetings to Rice. Isaac sent letters to the Baptist Board and several colleges.

As mid-February approached, Christiana was amazed at how swiftly the winter was passing. "This has been our healthiest winter ever," she said one afternoon. She and the other women and girls sat by the fireplace sewing and knitting. "Probably it's because we have a more proper diet, thanks to all your work in the garden and preserving."

"Our clothing is sturdier too," commented Grace, smoothing her long wool skirt. "I guess our bodies have adjusted to this climate."

"Well, whatever it is, I'm glad the usual harsh coughing hasn't interrupted our sleep every night," Mary added.

"Still, it will be nice to have the sunshine melt away our snow. Oh how I long to open doors to get rid of the smoke smell and burning eyes," Fanny said, sighing.

22

Several men and boys were busily working one afternoon. Under Robert's direction they were building wagon wheels in the blacksmith shop. Two Indians from the Ottawa tribe appeared unexpectedly. They spoke rapidly and gestured excitedly. Robert motioned for Abraham to come interpret.

The men leaped, pointed, swinging their arms. Then they covered their ears as if to ward off loud sounds. It was almost a dance. Abraham watched and listened, and eventually translated their actions.

"A week ago, on a cold dark night, a white shooting star swept across the sky right over Thomas Mission Station," Abraham said. "A loud sound followed the light. It frightened everyone. All the people at Thomas Mission saw it because they were sitting outside around a campfire to keep warm."

Isaac had just returned from Pokagon's village and joined them. Abraham turned to Isaac. "They were sent here by their leader to find out if it is a bad omen. They ask, 'Is our God unhappy that trees are being cut down and used for buildings?'" Isaac drew his Bible from his shoulder bag and held it up. "Tell them God loves everyone. He wants us all to live in comfortable places. Trees are meant to be used for churches, schools, houses, boats and fires. The light in the sky was not a sign from God. It was a thing of nature, something beautiful to be admired, not feared. God was not showing anger, he was showing something beautiful to enjoy."

Isaac's answer, followed by the interpretation, took so long it had a soothing effect and calmed everyone. "Tell the visitors to eat with us and spend the night. Abraham, I want you to help me write a quick message they can take back to Chief Noonday."

Isaac hoped he'd reassured the men but when he saw them leave right after they ate their bowls of stew, he wasn't sure. "I don't think I convinced them."

Robert shook his head. "They'll no doubt make stops at other villages along their way and tell their tale. They'll probably neglect to relate what you said."

Isaac shrugged his shoulders in despair. "I sent a message to their chief, telling him to continue building living quarters for the Slaters. They'll be leaving us as soon as weather permits. Once they are living at Thomas Station they can answer these religious questions as they arise."

Snow began to melt. "Soon visitors will again appear at Carey Mission. Look, the wind has blown the clouds away," Delilah said cheerfully as she walked beside Johnston on their way to school.

"It is a beautiful sky, isn't it? Now if it would just dry up the mud, I'd be pleased," he commented. "I'm leading the Slaters to Thomas Mission Station as soon as trails are passable."

Delilah looked surprised. "How long will you be away?"

"I hope to come back immediately. There is always so much farm work to do here in the spring. Will you miss me?" he asked, teasing.

She blushed and swallowed hard before answering. "You are the best teacher I have. Of course I will miss you!"

Sarah and Anna caught up with them. Much to Delilah's relief, the conversation changed back to weather. "I'm not going to wear my shawl. It's too hot!" said Sarah. "Do you ever remember another March like this?"

"Papa just went into the school," Anna said, pointing. "We'd better hurry." Busy as he was, Isaac seldom came into school unless something important had occurred.

When all pupils were in their seats, Isaac stood by the fireplace. Everyone sat quietly waiting for him to speak. "Yesterday's mail delivery brought good news I wish to share. A school in Vermont has room for two of our boys. As soon as they are selected, some adult will travel with them to get them enrolled."

Instead of signs of happiness he'd expected, the room grew very quiet. The boys looked at each other, wondering who would be selected. The teachers felt the burden of choosing the most qualified pupils. The girls wondered if they would be selected to get advanced education. Isaac's thoughts were on the burden of paying for pupils to be better educated. So far the cost amounted to $1350, way beyond available means.

When the selection was completed, the Simmerwells asked if they might accompany the two boys. Robert was familiar with the school, having grown up in the east. Fanny had never met his family. Isaac agreed it seemed like the perfect opportunity. "I'm certain my family will pay our return passage on the new canal," said Robert. "We will be back here before farm work commences," he promised.

After much discussion the McCoys agreed the timing was right for Calvin to join his brothers. He could travel east with the Simmerwells. Calvin could then earn his room and board the same as Rice and Josephus. They prayed financial assistance for all the boys.

Christiana had to resume teaching in the Simmerwell's absence. The following week, Leonard, Abigail and Johnston began spending afternoons packing for their move to Thomas Station in mid-March.

Isaac spent many evening hours at his desk, trying to budget the little money they had. He told Christiana, "Expenses are exceedingly heavy. Besides supporting our seventy Indian children we have had to try to meet expenses of Thomas Station. It will be easier when the Slaters manage affairs there."

Christiana worried and fretted over what Isaac had told her. After several sleepless nights, she became ill. "I'm really tired and feeling sickly," Christiana told Delilah as they walked to Sunday services. She held her daughter's arm for support and walked slowly.

"I think you should return home. Papa will understand."

"There is too much to do, child. Someone has to oversee the food preparation. We have extra people here today to take part in the baptisms. They will be hungry."

"Mrs. Dusenbury and Aunt Mary will help, so can the girls and I. Slaters are helping Papa, so we can manage."

"I'll sit near the back and leave if I feel worse," Christiana whispered as they found seats.

Kettles of rabbit stew were bubbling over several outdoor bonfires. The smell wafted into the building. Church service ended and the crowd headed outside. The women and girls Delilah had contacted hurried to ladle soup into bowls. Christiana tried to swallow some broth but gave up after a fit of coughing. Sarah led her back home and helped her into bed.

During the afternoon Christiana felt somewhat better. She stood in the doorway to listen as hymns were sung down by the river where the baptisms were taking place.

As the sun lowered in the sky, neighbors left. Benches were carried back to the school building. All dirty kettles and bowls were scoured clean. Isaac had been too busy to miss Christiana. He was surprised to find her flushed and weak and in bed. He immediately fell to his knees, praying for her recovery. Delilah took charge of her younger brother and sisters.

The following morning the Slaters got help loading their newly built furniture, books and clothing into a wagon. Johnston added a barrel of flour, a freshly butchered hog and a sack of cornmeal.

"My wife has prepared food for your journey," Daniel Dusenbury told them. "Should be all you need along the way."

"I want you to take this extra quilt and these rugs. They might come in handy," Mary Polke told Abigail.

Isaac had everyone clasp hands and form a circle while he gave a final prayer. "Christiana and I wish you the Lord's blessing as you teach and preach in new territory. Travel safely."

Abigail expressed concern. "Do you think we will encounter difficulties traveling?"

"No, I didn't mean to alarm you. The trail is familiar to Johnston."

"I wish Thomas Station was closer. Leonard and I will miss all you people!"

"I hope your cabin is ready. Once you are settled you will like it there," Isaac said. "Some of us will be coming to visit from time to time."

"Once we are situated there, we plan to remain a long time. We will be happy doing the Lord's work," Leonard said.

"You are fine healthy Christian workers. You can accomplish many good things," Isaac added.

"Speaking of health, we will pray for your wife's recovery," Abigail said as she took the reins. Looking around to be sure everything was packed, the men mounted their horses. With a final wave, Abigail drove the wagon out of the clearing.

Delilah stood wistfully watching long after the wagon disappeared, then sighed and went into the cabin to care for her mother and family.

With the Slaters and Simmerwells gone, it put extra work burdens on all the adults. Delilah began to teach the youngest children plus help at home. Sick as she was, Christiana managed to spend some mornings teaching. Afternoons, she supervised sewing or weaving in her cabin.

"The sheep will soon need shearing," she mentioned to Isaac. "They have very thick wool this year. It will make wonderful yarn."

"The boys can do shearing, but are you up to all the work that follows?"

"The girls know how to card and comb wool. They can spin too. We can do the dyeing later, after I'm feeling better."

"Well then, I guess we'll gather sheep this week," Isaac said. "They will have to remain in fenced areas awhile to calm them. I wish Robert was here to sharpen our tools and perhaps make some more."

Robert didn't arrive in time. Johnston, however, returned on the tenth of March, a week before the shearing began. He looked thin and very weary as he dismounted. Isaac invited him into their cabin. Delilah quickly ladled a bowl of broth from the kettle she'd brought over for her mother's lunch.

"Ah, you've given me just what I need," he said, watching Delilah blush. "I'm so glad to be back here." Before he finished eating his eyes shut and his head nodded.

"You need sleep," Christiana commented. "Go up in the loft, no one will bother you there."

"I am very tired, but don't you want to hear about my journey?"

"We can wait. Get some rest!"

"Just let me say things are progressing well at Thomas Station. Buildings are being erected, fences are in place. The Slaters' cabin was ready. They are happy to be there." With that brief summary, he gathered strength and climbed up to rest.

Christiana rested in her rocker while Delilah cleared the table and swept the floor. "Isaac, you and Delilah go on with your teaching. Take the young ones with you. Things will be fine here."

Later, when Johnston climbed down he found Christiana rocking and knitting. They talked about the new mission and his travel experiences. "It isn't the best time of the year to spend three nights in the wilderness," he said. "I did spend one night in a village beside Gun Lake. Indians there told me every spring they heard loud noises exploding over the water. That's why they gave it that name." He laughed, "I think the noise must be caused from ice breaking up."

"After I left that area I traveled alone. Fortunately, although the water was icy cold, I was able to swim the horses across the Grand and Kalamazoo Rivers. Our own Saint Joseph wasn't as much of a problem." Johnston walked to the fireplace and tossed on another log.

"I met a few of our Indian neighbors returning from their winter trapping. Women were in canoes stacked high with fur pelts. They will be arriving soon to start the maple taps, I guess."

"Singing Bird told me syrup won't run good this spring. It takes cold nights and warm days. It is already too warm."

"Ha, that might change. Sometimes we see snow in April." Johnston gathered his belongings and started for the door. "I'll move back into the school loft with the boys but I'm thinking about building myself a small cabin."

Christiana studied his face as she asked, "You planning to live alone then?"

Blushing, he answered, "Not forever. The person I want to share my life with isn't quite ready, but when she is the house will be ready."

Christiana sat thinking about what he had said long after he left.

By April, Christiana's health was much improved. The Simmerwells return eased her responsibility. Teaching became secondary to spring activities. Fruit trees blossomed, lambs and calves were born and frolicked in the pastures. The sheep were sheared. Fields were plowed and early planting was done.

Christiana supervised their garden plantings. She joined Singing Bird in her search for dandelion greens and early medicinal plants. Singing Bird gave birth to a tiny daughter and named her Ruth. "That's my favorite Bible story," she said.

Christiana's own baby, Isaac, had his second birthday. Sarah and Josephus became twelve and nineteen. Occasionally small gifts were given but no celebrations were ever held, partly because Indian pupils never mentioned birth dates.

Rice and Josephus had written to say Calvin had arrived and was living with them. Once again Christiana and Isaac discussed sending their daughters away for advanced education. Since they still had no funds, that goal was again postponed.

In the spring of 1827, visitors were a constant interruption but they were always welcomed. Some were seeking new land to settle, others were looking for employment as teachers or builders or farmers. They were usually put right to work. Wages were meager but food and shelter were more than adequate.

Six men came as a group during the summer, searching for a location which offered good water power. One evening all the adults gathered to listen to their plans to establish a complete settlement including a mill. The men stayed at Carey Mission a few days, then followed the St. Joseph River from one end to the other. Eventually they found just what they desired. It was south of Carey Mission on a creek which emptied into the river below Elkhart in Indiana. When they returned to Carey to tell the McCoys, Isaac agreed to take some boys and survey the land for them. Isaac welcomed the pay. When the survey was completed the men went half way back to Ft. Wayne to the land office and purchased it. The McCoys had mixed feelings about a new development in the area. New settlers were not necessarily good neighbors.

In July a son of Chebass, probably in a drunken fit, brutally murdered the son of an Indian named Owl. Then he set fire to Shakwaushuk's dwelling. One of Shakwaushuk's wives, a daughter of Chebass, came to find Isaac.

"My brother has become very troublesome. The people in my village are about to look for my brother to kill him," she said. "If he comes here, warn him."

A few hours later Chief Chebass arrived and called on Isaac in great distress. "A council will be held tomorrow so the family of the murdered man can demand vengeance on my son. He was drunk and participated in murder. Will you come speak kind words about my son?"

"I will come and tell of evils brought on by drunkenness," Isaac replied. "Will the council listen to the words of a white man?"

"We honor you as a fair man. Your words will be heard. I will take a horse to the council as atonement for the offense. My son and the horse will be placed near each other. The victim's family make their choice, one or the other."

Isaac went to the Potawatomi council and spoke to the group gathered around the huge bonfire. He awaited the decision in an agony of hopes and fears. Toward sundown, he watched with great joy as the horse was chosen. The offender was not executed.

Near the end of July, the son of Chebass rode in and presented Isaac with a small intricately carved horse as his token of thanks. Later on Isaac gave the gift to Eleanor for her sixth birthday, telling her the story of its significance. Her large brown eyes puddled in tears as she listened.

Farming, a full time summer occupation for the hired men, also gave the boys and young men plenty of exercise plus excellent work experience. Both boys and girls still spent mornings in the classrooms, in spite of the heat trapped inside the building.

Gardening and milking cows, then processing milk into cheese or butter, along with daily food preparations kept the girls busy. A few Indian women were hired to do laundry and some of the cooking, cleaning and sewing. Christiana and the older girls had woven yards of cloth. Christiana was thrilled when it was finally possible to sew matching shirts and dresses into uniform outfits like she had always yearned to do. "That's been a goal of mine for several years," she told her women friends. "Gone are the tattered and worn clothes of the past!"

Summer was not just a time of work but a healthy mixture of school, work and play. Actually, when chores were finished on Saturdays everyone was free to spend the day as they wished. That was the day when young romance became obvious as boys and girls spent time together. Christiana and the other women kept watchful but flexible control. Sometimes pupils left to visit their families over the weekend or families came to Carey Mission for church services or meals.

Daily worship always followed evening meals. Isaac preached one or two sermons each Sunday with music and singing in between. Musical instruments were used to play hymns. Indians loved to sing accompanied by flutes. The pupils were allowed to put away school clothes and wear fancy outfits on Sundays. Christiana and other adults were often amused at the creative use of charity box articles.

"We finally have a comfortable and acceptable routine established," Isaac said as he sat on the steps of Johnston's new little cabin.

"Yes, the mission is going well. My own life has areas to improve, but in time I think that will be fine too."

Isaac looked at his colleague and smiled. "Thinking about a wife? Have you met someone we don't know about?"

"I'll talk to you about her later. Right now I'm concentrating on furnishing this cabin!" With that terse statement, Johnston went inside and shut his door.

Isaac decided to walk down and watch the boys fish. As he followed the path along the river he noticed smoke rising from the other side but some distance away. Later he saw canoes down river. He groaned as he realized the Sauk Indians had arrived in the area on their annual journey to Canada for annuities. The British were still giving them payments for war service against the United States in the early 1800's.

Isaac walked swiftly back to the mission to remind and warn everyone of the danger this tribe presented. "They are only passing through our area but they are cannibals! They wear scalps they've collected. They take prisoners or captives. Stay out of their way!" In a few days the tribe was gone and forgotten, but in late August a large body of Sauk returned from Detroit. Once again, Isaac confined the mission group's activities.

A few days later, Pokagon and his wife visited Carey Mission bringing a nearly naked Indian boy about eleven years old. "He won't talk. I think he is a Sioux. The Sauks captured him. They treated him very bad. I traded three horses with bridles and saddles and other property equal to a fourth horse for him," Pokagon told the McCoys.

"I will go find some proper clothes for him," Christiana said. "The poor boy is covered with scars. It is a good thing you removed him from such bad treatment."

While she was away, Isaac showed the boy the scrub basins offering him the chance to wash. He pulled a bucket of water from the well and handed gourds of water to Pokagon and his wife as well as the boy. "You have done a good deed, helping this unfortunate boy. I wonder why he doesn't talk to you?"

Pokagon shook his head. "I have not heard him speak. He is frightened, like a shy rabbit but he has not tried to run away."

When Christiana returned with clothing the boy smiled slightly. "He likes you," Pokagon said. "Thank you for these things." A few minutes later the three left.

Four days later, much to the McCoys' surprise, Pokagon and the boy returned to Carey Mission. Arrangements were then made for the boy to be enrolled in school.

"I do not have sons for you to teach but I want you to show this boy how to read and speak and do things in the white man's way. He will come each day to learn."

True to his word, Pokagon sent the boy on his pony each morning. He walked eagerly into school. Sometimes other children from Pokagons' village came with him. Although they wouldn't enter the building, they sat outside the windows and listened. They ate heartily at the noon meal, then joined in hoeing and weeding in the gardens.

"They earn their meals by all the chores they do," Isaac commented to Johnston as they supervised afternoon activities. "I wish we could get them into classrooms."

"Pokagon's boy came from a hostile tribe. We should be thankful he is adjusting so well to civilized living and continues to come. All these children are learning useful skills," replied Johnston.

"Well, since the purpose of our mission is to improve lives, I guess we are doing our job," said Isaac, smiling. "The Potawatomi Indians are basically intelligent, peaceful folks. We are fortunate to be among them."

Isaac was reminded of his statement when Calvin Britain arrived at Carey to teach. "I saw many fights occurring as I stopped at Indian villages along the way," he told the mission brethren.

"Were they also drinking?" the men asked. "Alcohol makes them do crazy and evil things."

"Yes, I saw liquor bottles tossed around in every village. They were not hostile to me but I didn't linger," Calvin replied.

"There have been large groups of Indians traveling this summer. They talk of past wars and battles as they move across the trails. At night they re-enact stories in their dancing and singing. No doubt the travels stimulate and excite them to fighting," Isaac said. "If they are drinking besides, we'll see more problems arising."

23

The people at Carey Mission had no idea how serious the liquor problem had become. In mid-August, 1827, a startling event took place. Isaac and Christiana walked to school as usual after breakfast. They were surprised to see Chief Saugana with fifteen other chiefs ride in dressed in all their finest regalia.

They dismounted and strolled toward the McCoys. Abraham also saw them and hurried to the McCoys, ready to interpret.

Saugana spoke, "Winnebagos have invited Potawatomis to join them in a war to exterminate whites. Our brother, we are sorry to hear some Indians have been fighting with white people. This is not good!"

Isaac and Christiana clasped hands, not knowing what to expect.

He continued. "We will not join them. We will remain in peace. We are happy that you have come to live among us. You are our friends. It is certain you will know everything that passes among whites. If anything should occur that we ought to know for our safety, we desire you to inform us and advise us what to do."

The McCoys listened respectfully as Abraham repeated Saugana's speech.

"We will understand all that occurs among Indians. If we hear anything of danger to you we will inform you. Finally, I can say no more then. You take care of us. We will take care of you."

When Saugana finished speaking the chiefs turned and mounted their horses, leaving as quickly and quietly as they had come. Isaac and Christiana looked at Abraham in astonishment.

"No Potawatomi approved the idea of a war against whites. He was reassuring you," Abraham told them, then turned and proudly walked back to school.

As Isaac and the other missionaries discussed the visits from the chiefs, it became very obvious that feelings of unrest were developing. Indian leaders were concerned as white settlers encroached on their lands, especially since they usually brought supplies of alcohol.

Isaac spent several hours pacing the floor before composing a letter to Governor Cass outlining his concerns. He requested a meeting to discuss enforcing boundaries for the protection or safety of Indian villages and for Carey Mission.

Early in September a reply letter came announcing the Governor's upcoming arrival on the fourteenth. The Governor requested that preparations be made for a meeting of area chiefs to be held at Carey Mission. Isaac sent runners to each village. Within days, Indians began appearing in all their brightest finery.

Mission women were heard sputtering about the visitors. "This morning two young mothers walked right into our cabin. They helped themselves to all the white bread I made yesterday," complained Grace.

Fanny smiled and said, "They are used to sharing, I guess. What one person has, everyone should enjoy."

"Their little ones run naked. Are we going to have to clothe them all?" asked Mary Polke. The women shared a good laugh as they listened to each other. "As always, we'll do what we can with what we have," Christiana proclaimed.

Classes were interrupted by children and their pet dogs running into the school. Everyone became upset. The final straw occurred when hired men stormed into Isaac's cabin reporting that all the peach trees had been stripped of fruit.

To keep peace, Isaac decided to talk with the chiefs to try to set rules. "We encourage your curiosity. We would like to have your children sit quietly in our school. They will be taught to read and write and learn many things there. We will show your men our farming and blacksmith methods. Your girls and women can come afternoons and learn to weave and knit. We will supply you with tools but your people must not take things without permission. That is not the white man's way!"

"We have witnessed white men exchange things," acknowledged Saugana, spokesman for the chiefs. "If we eat your food we will give you fish we catch in river."

Isaac wished he was better able to converse and understand the Indian language and ways. Discouraged, he returned home. Christiana was busily sweeping the floor. "I Just finished threading the loom," she said. "The girls can begin weaving this afternoon."

Little Isaac was picking up stands of thread caught on the rough floorboards. His father lifted him to his shoulders after hugging him close. "You are a good helper," he said, "I'm going to take you outside to play while I write some letters. Stay close to the cabin."

Isaac quietly watched as his son picked up acorns and brightly colored leaves. After awhile he turned to speak to Christiana who was standing in the doorway. "I wonder what the Governor will accomplish when he talks to the Indians here. I hope he arrives early. More problems are turning up every day."

Christiana planned to help prepare the noon meal but as she walked she caught a glimpse of two boys teasing little and darting around trees to hide from her. She called to them. They approached shyly and stood, eyes lowered. She realized the boys were not pupils. "Follow me," she motioned and led them to the well. "Wash your faces and hands and smooth your unruly hair." Their garments were skimpy and ill fitting so she led them back inside her cabin to find new outfits. She pulled shirts and trousers from a shelf and left while the boys changed. Next, they all went to school where Fanny took charge.

Christiana was constantly on the move. As more Indians arrived for the Governor's meeting, meal preparations became more demanding. Her kitchen gardens were becoming depleted. She was grateful that the winter supply was now drying in lofts. She hoped they would not need to take any from those reserves. Indians were catching fish and occasionally shared their catch along with rabbits and deer they hunted.

On September thirteenth Governor Cass, accompanied by government advisors, arrived just before sunset. Canvas tents were set up near the river. Johnston vacated his newly built cabin and offered its use to the governor, who gratefully accepted. The weary men barely spoke to anyone. "All we need is sleep!" they said and retired for the night.

The next morning, as Isaac walked into Johnston's cabin he found the governor and two other officers surrounded by survey maps. "Good morning, friend! Last night's sleep was the best I've had in months," said the governor. "For months, Indian problems have kept me on the move all across the territory and in all kinds of weather and sleeping conditions. I appreciate a safe cabin and bed! What a luxury!"

"Glad we can accommodate you," Isaac said, smiling. "My eldest daughters will bring breakfast for you and your men."

"We will be content to get in line with the rest of your mission family. We are certainly tired of pemmican or whatever else we could find."

Isaac laughed heartily. "Traveling rations get hard to swallow, especially in rainy or winter storms. I am forced to be away for long periods too, so I know what you mean."

Delilah and Sarah entered with baskets of johnnycake and fried pork strips along with cups of hot chicory coffee for the men. The governor thanked them and after helping himself sent the girls outside to serve the rest of his men.

"Did you see how pretty Johnston's cabin is?" Delilah asked her sister. "That's the first time I've seen it. It is just the kind of place I'd love to live in, small and clean and new."

"I like our cabin just fine. Why would you want to move?" Sarah asked. "Anyway I didn't see anything but the men and they scared me. I'm only glad I didn't spill anything on them!"

Isaac waited while the meal was eaten. "My wife and I will welcome the chance to show you around Carey Mission when you wish."

"Because of all the reports, both yours and my inspectors, I feel well acquainted with Carey. I must say I support and admire what you are doing here."

Isaac beamed at his comments, then cleared his throat before saying, "Some problems have arisen since we were last in touch. In July a mother of one of our pupils was brutally murdered. We witnessed the scene." His eyes showed signs of tears. "Liquor bottles were strewn all around her body. We see lots of signs of drunkenness. We have to find a way to halt the supply of whiskey to this area!"

"There isn't any fur trading in summer. What do they exchange for whiskey?"

"That's another problem," Isaac replied. "Some tools manufactured here at Carey Mission and given to Indians have turned up in trading posts."

The governor shook his head in dismay as Isaac continued.

"Clothing, shoes, guns, whatever these traders see value in, are bought but the farming tools disappoint me most. Those tools were meant for Indians to use so they can support themselves and establish a new way of living. They are pushing that aside. Every time we venture off our property we find idle, drunken Indians, men and women. They are neglecting themselves, their children and their village duties."

"I have seen these pitiful conditions too," Governor Cass stated. "Actually, that's one of the main reasons I am here. Many villages in my territory are deserted. Some are in such depressed states they need to be burned down. The Indians must be relocated to villages that have wiser and stronger leadership."

"How can you enforce their moving?" asked Isaac. Other mission workers and the governor's advisors had now joined the discussion. All eyes were on the governor, waiting to hear his answer.

"There will be a treaty offered. The United States government is willing to pay for the abandoned land which will then be available for sale to white settlers eager to homestead. They will put land to good use. Indians will receive money in exchange for the ceded land."

"Money to be used for whiskey," replied Johnston. "That is making a vicious circle! They will end up in the same way, neglecting the fields, their children and themselves in the new villages."

"Yes, that is true. What next, Governor Cass? Are you going to buy more land and move them again?" asked William Polke, with an angry look.

"I don't believe that will happen," replied the governor. "I know there are powerful Indian leaders in area villages. They are here at Carey Mission now. I will urge them to take in these displaced people. Those receiving money can, and I believe will, purchase tools, horses, household goods and make homes again. I expect them to work and live like their role models, like they do here at your mission."

When they heard him praise Carey Mission as a good example the men became subdued. Further discussion was ended when all but Isaac, Governor Cass and his men left the meeting to perform their daily chores.

The governor and his men continued to meet, discussing and preparing details for the treaty. Except for meals, they worked without interruption. Isaac occasionally joined the group.

It was obvious to Isaac that Governor Cass had read and pondered the letter he'd sent him telling about Potawatomi's problems. "I appreciate your observations, Reverend McCoy. It truly disappoints me that unprincipled white traders are taking advantage of the natives. The sale of whiskey concerns me, especially when it is exchanged for tools and furs and food supplies, all part of their livelihood." His face showed his displeasure.

"Yes," agreed Isaac. "Alcohol causes them to lose control. They crave more and more until they are willing to sell everything they own. Some of them turn violent when they drink. As I said before, we have seen serious results."

"Whatever makes the Indians start drinking to the point of no control? I know lots of white men who drink alcohol but they don't lose control of their senses."

"Well, I'm not certain when they first started drinking. Probably they were exposed to liquor when they fought in early American wars alongside white men. Actually, I think there are two reasons why it affects them more than their white brothers," Isaac replied.

"Really? What are they?"

"First, I fear there is something in their body system that causes a different reaction. Some get violent, some fall asleep, some act very silly and others are very complacent, easy going. All these changes are detrimental to health, work habits and of course family or tribe stability."

"You didn't answer the question of why they drink."

"I think that has to do with their religious beliefs. They believe it is necessary to have visions or dreams to show them or guide them to future actions. They have discovered that when they drink whiskey, they sleep and dream quicker. They are willing to risk everything to get into this dream state," Isaac said sadly.

"That's an interesting theory," Governor Cass replied, rubbing his chin. "What is the solution?"

Isaac quietly stared off into the distance. He finally replied, "I wish I knew. I am convinced, however, that Indians need protection or isolation from greedy white men. I'm afraid white men's greed can't be stopped! I don't believe I can, or should, change all Indian religious beliefs. All I can do is pray about it everyday!"

"Do you think the treaty I propose holds the possibility of success?" Governor Cass asked quietly.

Isaac sighed but didn't answer. The treaty discussions continued. Each day Issac began by offering a prayer for guidance. Ideas were shared, plans were offered. Finally, after many compromises, an agreement was reached. Shortly after breakfast on the seventeenth the weary men emerged and approached the waiting chiefs. An assembly was called.

Following two days discussion with tribal leaders, Governor Cass presented his written treaty document for signatures. A number of small reservations were ceded to the United States in order to consolidate some of the dispersed bands of the Potawatomi tribe in Michigan territory. This treaty was to keep white settlements, as far as practical, from the marked trail leading from Detroit to Chicago. Some reservations ceded were on land north along the St. Joseph River near Burnett's trading post. Indians from that ceded area indicated they would remain in the vicinity of Carey Mission.

Isaac cringed when the Indians were given $500 in goods and paid $2,500 in money. The peace pipe was passed around the circle of leaders. Women and children watched respectfully. Adding to the solemn occasion, Isaac thanked Governor Cass and his aides for their work and the treaty. He offered a prayer that all Potawatomi would benefit from the agreement.

Campfires were extinguished. As smoke filled the air, the Indians began gathering their children and possessions. The following morning, after thanking the McCoys, the governor and his men left. Only a few Indians remained.

Christiana had supervised the school while men teachers worked on the treaty. She was relieved to have Isaac take over her duties. "This afternoon we will all work to clean the debris left from our visitors," Isaac announced at breakfast.

Christiana and Isaac worked side by side, raking scattered items into large piles to be burned. They failed to notice three young white men approaching on horseback. As the horses drew up in front of them they gasped in unison. Their three oldest sons were home.

Tears of joy poured from their eyes as they rushed to greet the boys they'd missed so much. "Welcome home!" Isaac shouted as their weary sons slid from their equally tired horses.

"We didn't expect you," said their mother, "but what a sight for sore eyes!"

The boys hugged their parents and smiled at others gathering around them. "We wanted to get home in time to celebrate John Calvin's sixteenth birthday," Rice said as he smiled at his blushing brother.

"That's right, we wanted to be here so you could see that he has turned into a man," said Josephus.

All their sisters happily hugged them. Little Isaac cried and tugged on his mother's skirt, confused by all the excitement. Rice picked him up and carried him to the cabin. Later when Josephus rocked him in their mother's chair they both fell asleep.

Christiana looked around the crowded cabin and smiled contentedly. Isaac rose from his chair, patted her on the shoulder and walked to his desk. He took his journal down, stating aloud as he wrote, "Feeling it to be a duty we owed to our children to send them, a portion of the time, to school in white settlements and without a settled home ourselves, my wife and I had been much deprived of their society. This evening, September 21st, 1827, our three sons arrived on a visit from Lexington, Kentucky, where they are now pursuing their studies. It has been years since I and my poor wife have had all our living children present. For this great favor, after years of anxious separation, we record our gratitude to God, our heavenly father."

The next afternoon, Isaac, accompanied by his sons, rode around the fields of the mission compound. "Your mother and I were certainly surprised to learn you transferred to a different college." Isaac said when they stopped to rest.

"We sent letters telling you," Rice stated. "Obviously, they got lost. We wondered why you didn't acknowledge our graduation from Columbian College."

Josephus laughed. "We're taking advanced classes now in Kentucky. Can you believe I'm going to be a doctor like Rice?"

Isaac was amazed and pleased that they had completed so much of their education so quickly. "Your mother and teachers will be as happy as I to learn of your achievements.

"The excellent education we had in your schools gave us a very good background, Papa," Josephus said. Rice nodded in agreement.

The next morning the four of them headed for the trading post to talk with Bertrand and purchase supplies. At the edge of the woods they came upon four sleeping Indians surrounded by broken and scattered whiskey bottles.

The closer they got to Bertrand's the more intoxicated men and women they encountered. Isaac's heart sank as he recognized them. "These Indians were just at Carey for treaty talks," he told the boys. "Twenty-four hours and all their money seems to be spent."

"Surely they aren't getting liquor at Bertand's are they?" asked Rice.

"No! He won't sell whiskey. They get it from white settlers in the area. They make a large profit from sales."

"Before the treaty money was given them, how did they get money anyway?" asked Josephus.

"They don't need money. These traders take anything of value in exchange," Isaac explained, wiping tears from his cheeks. "I told the governor all about the situation. He and his aides were convinced after his talks to them they would use the gifts and money he paid for the land to build better lives."

"Why did the governor gave them money? Didn't he know Indians don't understand money?" Rice asked.

"I wish you could have sat in on the long discussions, son," Isaac replied. "Governor Cass has negotiated many land treaties. He was convincing when he told us that there is no other substance available for paying. If the government was trading items, like animals or wagons, the values would depend on things like size or age. Deciding things worth would vary. There isn't any fair way to barter unless the government set different prices according to size or age or color or whatever makes people choose one over the other. Money in hand gives the chance to make choices."

"Well, I guess I can understand that," Rice said. "What does the governor expect Indians to do with their treaty money?"

"He talked to the village leaders about combining the money of everyone in each village. That would allow them to purchase things the village needs like tools, seeds and farm animals."

"They could help pay the way for their children to attend school," Josephus said smiling.

"There are many wise leaders in the villages. They will make good decisions," Isaac said. "Unfortunately, not everyone will give their money to their chief. Some may choose to spend theirs instantly, not thinking of the future. They are the ones we see now. They're victims of their own weakness. My heart breaks for them!"

In spite of a cheerful visit with Bertrand, they rode silently home. Isaac felt especially sad, thinking he had somehow failed to help his Indian neighbors.

One morning a week before the boys were to return to college they came to talk to their parents. They had been involved in daily chores and activities with little chance for family conversations. "Mama, Papa, we have a suggestion we'd like to discuss," Rice began. As they sat around the table, Isaac and Christiana listened.

"You'll be pleased to know Josephus and I still earn room and board doing odd jobs. We attend the Baptist Church in Lexington. We live in members' homes near the college," said Rice.

"We have told many folks about our family and Carey Mission. They are always interested," Josephus interjected.

Rice looked at his mother and father before he continued. "Three different families have offered room and board, plus some housework, for our sisters to come to school in Kentucky."

Isaac heard Christiana gasp. "Well, well, God has been listening to our prayers," he said.

Christiana smiled, knowing no amount of discussion would change Isaac's belief. "I guess they must be good Christian families to offer this opportunity."

"Sarah and little Christiana could live together in one home. Josephus and I will be close by," Rice stated, knowing that should make his mother happy. "Nancy could come too if you wish."

"They can travel back with us," Josephus added.

Christiana gasped again. "Nancy is much too young! She's barely started school. She certainly isn't ready for any advanced classes." She sighed. "Their clothes, my goodness, we'll have to hustle to get them ready. Oh, Isaac, are we doing right? Should we ask the girls or tell them?"

Isaac smiled. "It is right for them to go. We will tell them tonight. If we get no strong objections, it is decided!" he stated firmly.

The girls reacted happily, eager to travel with their brothers. They rushed to tell everyone their good news. Calvin had decided not to go with them. Money was scarce, as was his enthusiasm for attending school. "I'll study Rice's old books for now," he told his parents. He secretly wanted somehow to become owner of a trading post just like Bertrand. Christiana was very happy to have him back home. The cabin had quickly become unusually quiet.

Isaac seemed depressed after the children left for Kentucky. Christiana watched helplessly as he sat quietly at his desk, sometimes with head in hands, often writing letters or in his journal. Finally he admitted the reason for his despair. "I have been agonizing over problems brought on by the recent treaty."

On the twelfth of October his mood suddenly changed. He surprised her by saying, "My dear, I'm making a journey east. I have written to officials in many capacities, including the President of the United States, asking for advice and help with our Indian neighbors."

Christiana gasped. "The President? Isaac, I know you are concerned but what do you hope to accomplish? Aren't you frightened at the thought of meeting those important men?"

"I've spent days and nights praying. I feel called to present the Indian problems to people who are in a position to solve them. I must overcome my own fears for the good of the cause. I hate putting a burden on you and my fellow missionaries but I must go." He reached over and took her hand. "I will need your help with preparations."

Two days later Christiana stood at the window with little Isaac in her arms watching her husband saddle his horse. Her tears splashed her dress front and her son. He began crying. "Oh my, everything will be all right," she said wiping both their faces with her apron. Sighing, she walked to the door and called, "Are you ready for the food packet?"

Isaac came toward the cabin smiling. "That's the final item. Looks like I'll eat well judging by the size of this package," he said, taking it from her.

"Many is the time when we didn't have much to send with you. Still, with money so scarce maybe this will reduce your spending needs." Looking at his scruffy travel clothes she sadly shook her head. "I can't help wishing you had better clothes! Going to large cities and meeting with important men, you should have more than one suit."

"Now, now, my dear, don't fret so! I'm not going to put on airs. The important thing is to exchange ideas on Indian problems, not to compare fashionable suits. You'd be surprised how little regard these men give to appearances. Anyway, the supply of handsome shirts you packed will look fine enough."

He noticed she had prepared a plate of buttered bread and a cup of chicory coffee. He sat down to enjoy it. "I'll take part of this in hand to eat on the trail. Walk me to the horse. I must leave now."

Glancing briefly at Christiana's stomach, he said, "You must take special care of yourself. Let Meeker and Lykins take charge of the school and mission." Jothan Meeker, sent by the Baptist board to assist in financial areas earlier in the year, had proved a very capable assistant. "I know you will work alongside the men like always, but give them the big problems that arise!"

Several adults were waiting outside to wish him a safe journey. Calvin, Nancy and Eleanor lined up to hug their father. Delilah came running from school to add her farewells. He turned once more to Christiana, "I'll be missing your fortieth birthday, my dear, but I will say special prayers for your good health and happiness on November eighteenth," he told her as he held her tightly.

"Don't forget little Anna has the same birthday. Oh, by the way, she wants to be called Christiana now," she reminded him.

Isaac smiled. "No, I won't forget to keep her in my prayers, along with all our children." He looked around. "All of you be good!"

"Return as soon as possible," Christiana said. "May God grant you a safe and healthy journey!"

Within a few minutes he was out of sight. The children ran off to school. Christiana returned to the cabin and placed the baby in his highchair with a toy. She grabbed her scrub brush and fixed a pail of soapy water. By the time she had her puncheon floor clean, her feelings of loneliness were under control. "Work makes me feel better," she told little Isaac as she turned him loose.

24

Except for daily observations of drunken, ill-clothed Indians sleeping or staggering among the trees, Isaac's days on the trail were uneventful. Blue skies overhead and bright colored falling leaves mingled to give him quiet thinking time. Evenings he wrote in his diary or made notes by the light of small campfires in preparation for his upcoming meetings. Occasionally he met traders whose horses were packed with whiskey bottles. It was all he could do to keep from attacking them. One evening he shared a meal with homesteaders heading toward Carey Mission. Several of their children were ill. He gave the mother some quinine, praying he would not need the medicine for his own maladies.

Most of the way to Detroit he followed surveyor marked trees. As he approached cities he rode on actual cleared roadways. Recent rainfall turned dirt city streets into mud but mostly he traveled much faster than he had previous times. He arrived in Pennsylvania before the end of October. Nights were chilly. He often slept on frosty ground.

In Philadelphia he located the Baptist Mission Board office. Following a day of long meetings there, one executive invited him home. The man's wife greeted him kindly, but not before Isaac saw a look of distaste cross her face. "I must look very disreputable. I have been traveling two weeks without much chance to neaten up." As he said it, he thought of his conversation with Christiana before he left.

"I am sorry if I appeared unkind. You will welcome a bath and hot meal before you spend the night. Our maid can launder and mend your things."

He ate lavishly prepared meals on fine china. His thoughts returned to the primitive lifestyle at Carey Mission. Although he was not envious for himself, he wished there were finer things for his family.

He headed for New York. His first stop was at Hamilton College where he visited the Indian pupils he'd enrolled two years earlier. "I'm delighted at excellent reports I have received from your instructors," he told them. Isaac beamed as he observed the well dressed, well adjusted young men sitting in the lounge with him. "How are you managing your finances?"

"Two of us are living at the Baptist minister's home. We're doing it in exchange for cleaning the church and grounds. We eat two meals a day there or sometimes carry a lunch to school," one of the boys told him. "Mostly, the work can be done on Saturdays. We have plenty of time to study"

"The rest of us get room and board for chores in various businesses or homes. The town people accept us kindly. We earn extra money for books or clothes by helping farmers."

"We like being here," another young man responded, "although being in a city is very different."

"We can never thank you enough for helping us, Reverend McCoy. You gave us the right education to fit into this school." They took turns giving examples of things they remembered from Carey Mission.

"I'll never forget our winter arrival here and how you wouldn't let us give up."

"I remember Mrs. McCoy going through charity boxes and sewing shirts and pants for us, and the girls knitting all those stockings and mittens."

"Mr. Lykins always made us rewrite our lessons until we got them right. Everything had to be spelled correctly and neat."

The mood changed when one of the boys told Isaac about their classmate who had run away. "He just couldn't stand being so confined. He missed hunting in the woods and all his Indian ways."

"Well, college isn't for everyone. Fortunately for us all, some people like to farm or work with their hands and not so much with their minds. We are all different. I'm pleased things are going well here for the rest of you. When you graduate you will do well in the jobs you are training for," Isaac assured them.

When Isaac had stopped in Philadelphia to talk with city leaders he had received many promises of financial aid for his pupils. He hadn't counted on their help but had been very pleased when an envelope of cash was slipped into his hand. He now presented it to the boys and was humbled when they refused it.

"We don't need it! We are able to take care of ourselves. Keep it for others to use," they insisted.

Isaac wiped tears he couldn't control. The endorsement the boys gave his work and beliefs and goals, plus their generosity, overwhelmed him. His departure was as difficult as it had been when bidding his family farewell a month earlier.

His next destination was Washington. As he rode he reflected on the presentation he was about to make. Its importance was re-affirmed by visits he'd been making. Christiana and he had dedicated their lives to the betterment of the lives of their Indian pupils and neighbors. Isaac prayed that he would be able to portray problems and needs in order to convince these dignitaries. He hoped they would suggest solutions. "I can certainly offer many examples," he thought.

Weather in mid-November was certainly not pleasant but it had its advantages. Since no one wanted to be outdoors on wet and chilly days, Isaac had no problems getting appointments.

Isaac's interview with President Adams was a total surprise. Originally frightened by the President's gruff exterior, he later recognized him as a man of vision and easy to like. Although the two men were seventeen years apart in age. their children were about the same ages. Another similarity shared, both men kept diaries recording history in the making.

Isaac was invited to the White House for tea. Once again he was aware of differences in living conditions. He felt guilty knowing how few advantages he gave his own children. It gave him uncomfortable feelings. Meeting the Adams family made him homesick. He did, however, enjoy the President's sons who were home on school vacations. They were obviously used to their expensive surroundings, servants and parties but also felt obligations toward poorer, less fortunate people.

"What kind of classes are taught in your mission school for Indians?" the oldest son asked.

Isaac answered all their questions. They insisted he stay longer and he relaxed by listening to musical selections the boys played throughout the evening.

"I have two sons studying to be doctors, although one may change his mind," he told them. "They were home for a visit just before I left. You remind me of them."

During discussions the next two days in the President's office, Isaac revealed his concerns about white men's encroachment on Indian lands, culture and livelihood. "They cheat when trading furs and items Indian women make. They take land and even personal belongings in exchange for liquor. Whiskey is causing terrible disaster."

The President's committee listened attentively to Isaac's concerns and his examples of the terrible occurrences.

It became obvious that President Adams wanted governmental control of land and national protection of Indian tribes. As other leaders participated in the discussions, however, Isaac concluded they didn't want the government involved.

"If Indians could be isolated from white men until they can be educated in our ways, I believe the two cultures could be blended," Isaac stated one afternoon. Aware of the mixed feelings, he hoped for a compromise.

Isaac wanted Indians to govern themselves but he also wanted their land protected from ruthless land grabbers. He also wanted to stop the killing of wildlife just for the fur or worse, for sport. "The Indians depend on animals for food. They use the skins for clothing and for shelters. They even use the tiniest bones for needles. They do not waste any part of an animal!"

The committee's debates seemed endless. Finally John Quincy Adams had heard enough and dismissed them all. He once again invited Isaac to the White House.

Back in the house where he was staying, Isaac carefully brushed and smoothed his frock coat, dressing for the visit. He was treated as a friend. No mention was made of the committee's work until Isaac was ready to leave.

"I am particularly impressed with your work with Indians. You are not only schooling their children, you are educating the adults by teaching them to build homes, put up fencing, farm. It is very impressive! I will write you my final decision on the matters we discussed," said President Adams, as he shook his hand in farewell. "I have truly enjoyed meeting you!"

Mrs. Adams presented Isaac with a beautiful shawl to take home to Christiana. "You have told us so many instances of her faithful and productive works, I just know I would like her. This gift is an expression of my admiration."

Isaac remained in the city several more days. Letters arrived from Christiana telling about their Thanksgiving celebration. Johnston and Jothan Meeker wrote about school happenings and the usual Indian concerns. Governor Cass wrote to wish him success in his meetings.

Isaac spent evenings writing letters to his family and to various officials he thought might be sympathetic to Indian problems. He visited many government offices. He spoke to everyone who would listen. As he walked the city streets he read nameplates on all the doors and copied names and addresses of organizations he could contact later. Some were charitable or religious and some business.

When he finally was satisfied that he had accomplished all he could, Isaac devoted time to personal endeavors. His first stop was on Tenth Street at the publishing house where he had mailed his manuscript.

"Look at these stacks. Our readers can't keep up with the volumes that arrive each month. What is the name you gave your book?" one of the publishers asked. "Maybe if I can find it I can move it closer to the top of the pile."

Isaac felt sick with disappointment. "The book is a history of Baptist Indians. It portrays the former and current conditions of their settlement and future prospects." The man was not impressed when Isaac said, "I just spent many days with President Adams discussing Indian problems, working with him to find solutions. It is an important book! It will shed light on the situation to anyone who reads it."

While Isaac spoke, several readers at nearby desks set aside manuscripts they were reading and listened. "I would like to read your book," one of them said. "Find it in the pile and I will look at it next."

Isaac smiled at the young man. "Thank you! I appreciate your offer. I guess I should wait my turn but it is filled with remarks truly important to the governing of our country. It needs to be published so it can be read by many people."

"Reverend McCoy, understand, just because it gets read doesn't mean it will get published. It probably will require some rewriting. At best it could take years. We only publish a few books each year," the publisher said. He watched Isaac's sad face grow pale. "I'm sorry if you didn't know that."

Isaac swallowed hard. "I'm not a patient man. It will be difficult to wait but I have faith. I believe it will eventually be published. Thank you for your assistance," he said, "also your honesty." He left the office in need of fresh air.

He was staying at the home of a Baptist minister and became well liked by the congregation. He had spoken to missionary societies in several area churches, describing Carey Mission and answering many questions about Indians. The majority of people were astounded to learn Indians were not hostile savages and could be educated.

Following his talks there was often an outpouring of contributions, sometimes money but usually books or clothing. Occasionally food items and furniture were offered. Isaac used any money to purchase barrels of flour, sugar and blacksmith supplies. He made arrangements for large items to be shipped in the spring.

By the middle of December Isaac was ready to leave Washington, although the weather was poor for traveling. As he tried to tie bundles on his horse it became apparent that he could not carry everything he had accumulated. Seeing his predicament, a church member gave him a pack horse and two sacks of oats for feed. Other folks added blankets and a tent to make his journey home more comfortable. "We'll send clothing and things to your mission from time to time," they promised.

Isaac smiled, recalling the odd assortment charity boxes contained. "We are grateful for assistance. My wife always manages to put everything to good use. Thank you for your generosity," he said with convincing sincerity.

He followed the snow-covered roadway but it soon disappeared into a narrow trail. One morning, when he peered from his tent, every bush and tree branch was glittering, encased in ice. Slipping and sliding, he made his way to the sheltering pine where the horses were tied. With aching fingers, he managed to pry open saddlebags. He leaned on the tree trunk to keep from falling. He took out a small food packet for himself, untied a bag of oats and scooped out handfuls for the horses, before carefully returning to his tent.

He nibbled at his frozen food and spent his time writing in his journal until his cold hands became too numb. The next day he repeated the activities. The third morning he awoke to the sound of water dripping and he knew the temperature had warmed. He was pleased to get a small cooking fire built. While his small pot of coffee heated he fed the horses and wiped them dry with a blanket he'd slept on. He shook the wet tent, rolled it and added it to his pack.

The rising sun warmed his aching body. He walked between the lethargic horses until their gait improved. Isaac sang hymns, which improved his own spirits. By noon he mounted his horse and rode until dusk.

On his sixth day of travel the woods seemed unusually quiet. Isaac, deep in thought, was startled when he heard what sounded like a distant call for help. As he listened he reached for his rifle. Hearing it again, he changed directions. Riding toward it, the voice grew louder. "Hello, hello! I'm coming!" he called out.

Suddenly, straight ahead, he saw and heard a large wolf snarling as it circled a tree. Looking upwards, Isaac spotted a very frightened young man straddling a limb. The wolf turned and charged the horses with bared teeth. Isaac took quick aim. With one shot, he killed the animal just as it leaped.

The man dropped to the ground, shaking so badly he could hardly stand. "Yesterday my horse ran away with all my belongings. While I was searching for him that huge wolf treed me. I've been up there all night," he said pointing.

"You must be really cold and tired, " Isaac said. "Ride my horse. I'll walk awhile."

"I'll walk too, my arms and legs are so stiff I can hardly feel them. Am I far off the trail?"

"The trail is close. Good thing, or I wouldn't have heard you. Which way are you headed?" asked Isaac.

"Going east, back to New York. I'm homesteading in Ohio but going back to get my family. Wish I could skin that wolf and show folks," he said glancing down at the animal.

Isaac laughed. "Might scare your family to know how big and mean they can get. Better not show them in advance of their move." Isaac shared his jerky and cornbread. When the young man still kept looking at the wolf, Isaac offered to skin it.

"I could use the skin as a blanket if I can't find my horse and equipment," he said. "Wolves don't always attack humans do they?" he asked as he watched Isaac work with his knife.

"They have to be awfully hungry to get that mean," Isaac told him. "At my place we have them hanging around sheep and chickens and have to scare them off."

Carrying the bloody skin over his shoulder, the young man walked alongside Isaac's horses until they parted at the trail. Isaac gave him food, a cooking pan and a blanket. "Good luck in finding your horse. I could help you more if you were going my direction. I'd enjoy having someone to talk to."

Isaac had his heart and mind set on reaching Carey Mission before the new year of 1828 began. He traveled as many daylight hours as he and the horses could tolerate. If no recent travelers had followed the trails it was difficult to discern which way to go. He watched for blazed surveyor marks on trees or twisted branches the Indians sometimes used.

In spite of his knowledge as a surveyor and the use of his compass, he wandered hopelessly lost one whole day in blowing snow. As darkness fell he crawled under a low hanging pine branch to spend the night. The horses whinnied toward morning.

Isaac woke with a start. He heard men talking. Following the sound, he came upon two French trappers eating rabbits they were roasting. They reached for their guns as he approached. When they saw he was unarmed, they relaxed. "I am lost, can you show me the trail?" Isaac asked.

They handed him a cup of steaming coffee and pointed to the meat. Although they didn't speak much English, when Isaac drew a map in the snow they pointed him in the right direction.

His own food supply was dwindling. He was grateful for the hot breakfast. Memory of it remained with him all day. He had developed a deep cough and the medicine he carried wasn't helping. He longed to be home.

At that moment Isaac decided to return home by way of Ft. Wayne so trails would be more familiar. To do that he had to back track a distance. It was near the end of January before he arrived at their old mission school. The Garards, who had replaced them as administrators, still lived there although the school had closed. They invited him to remain with them. The McCoys had often stayed with them during recent visits to Ft. Wayne. Isaac felt welcome there. Mrs. Garard's medicines helped rid him of his sore throat.

The next day when Isaac visited the Fort's postal office, he was surprised to find a letter from Christiana waiting for him. He read a few lines, then sat down. Her list of problems overwhelmed him.

"Is something wrong, Isaac?" asked Samuel Garard who was with him.

"This is a letter from Christiana written the second of January. She says I am much needed at home. Here I sit. Just about everyone there is ill or has been. The doctor was there when she wrote."

"I remember your son coming to get him. Calvin asked if we could come to help take charge of Carey Mission for a time. We couldn't. We were not healthy enough to risk traveling through the floods at the time."

"Oh, my! Her letter says the rivers were too high to get help, Samuel. I must get on the trail immediately!"

"You need rest first. Anyway, that was nearly a month ago. By now things have changed. Everyone is no doubt recovered. These were probably the usual winter ills."

Isaac shook his head sadly. "You don't know Christiana. She isn't one to complain. Things must be really bad! Besides, a new baby is expected about now. I must go."

"My wife and I could go with you if you wait a day or two."

"I would appreciate your company. I know your wife's presence would be good for Christiana," Isaac sighed. "I guess it would be foolish to leave without gathering some needed supplies from here. It would save someone else from having to make the journey."

Their four horses picked their way over the rough and often slippery trail. Creek and river crossings required extreme caution. Open water often had chunks of sharp ice floating. If they bumped the travelers or the horses they left bloody marks. Still, open water was safer to cross than weak ice.

As they entered Michigan Territory they stopped in Indian villages. The Indians usually recognized Isaac and welcomed them around their campfire and often provided shelter for the night. Isaac read to them from his Bible and tried to remind them of God's teachings but as soon as he rolled out his blankets they began sharing whiskey bottles. Often before the night passed, Isaac and the Garards were the only sober persons.

Small outbreaks of violence usually occurred as whiskey bottles emptied. It was difficult to sleep soundly. They always left before daybreak. Indians were still sleeping off the effects of a night of drinking.

One morning, after a fitful night of coughing, Isaac was too sick to travel. An Indian woman brought him an herbal concoction to drink. She rubbed a salve of animal fat on his chest. He was too weak to object. He began to sweat. Women brought more medicine. He slept peacefully all night and awoke completely cured, never knowing for sure what he had been given. The Garards had been very worried but were amazed and thankful for the care they all received.

After nine days on the trail Isaac happily recognized the stand of trees marking the edge of Carey Mission. Even his horse seemed to know it was home and galloped faster. Familiar faces appeared in doorways as they rode in. "I'm home!" Isaac called out as he searched through the faces, looking for Christiana.

25

When Christiana didn't appear, Isaac quickly pushed his way through the greeters. As he entered the cabin he heard a tiny baby crying. Christiana, startled, looked up from her rocker. "Isaac!" she exclaimed as she jumped up. "I didn't hear you arrive. Your new son was making too much noise."

In one long stride, Isaac rushed to take them both into his arms. "Are you all right?" he asked. "When was he born? I tried to get here sooner. I got your letter in Fort Wayne and came right away. Oh, and the Garards came with me."

"The baby came six days ago, on February second. He is still without a name, waiting for you. Where are the Garards? You must bring them in."

Isaac held the baby a minute, then handed him back to his mother. "I'll go find the Garards and talk to the brethren who are waiting outside. Has everyone recovered from the illnesses you wrote about?"

"Yes, thanks to our generous Lord, we are mostly well. "I will tell you all about it later."

It took several hours for Isaac to greet each and every adult and child. He listened to the many mission problems they had solved. Then he inspected the property. By the time he returned home to spend time with his own family, he was exhausted.

The Garards had moved their belongings into Johnston's cabin and went immediately to bed after saying, "We'll help teach tomorrow and take over the care of the baby, Christiana, so you and Isaac can have time alone."

In spite of all his good intentions, Isaac was not able to stay asleep. In the middle of the night, he awoke and went to his desk. He lit a candle and began reading reports and letters stacked there. His sudden groan awoke Christiana. She jumped from bed to rush to his side. "What is wrong?"

"I can't believe this!" he exclaimed. "I have to leave immediately for Washington. President Adams has called a meeting on Indian Affairs. I am to be the chairman."

"But Isaac, you just got here. We haven't even named the baby. You don't have any clean clothes. You haven't even heard all the things I have to tell you." Christiana burst into tears and sank to the floor beside his chair. "Please, can't someone else go?"

"I am sorry!" he said as he sat beside her. "If I had not gotten sick or gone to Fort Wayne, I would have been home sooner. I wish we could have more time, but yes, I have to go. I'll stay a day or two. Then I must leave." He helped her to her feet, led her to bed. He sat there, rubbing her back, until she tearfully fell asleep.

The next two days were spent washing and mending Isaac's clothes so he could pack them into saddlebags with his books and papers and food. All the time they packed, he and Christiana talked. Among other things, they decided to name their new son Charles. His name was the thirteenth child added to the list in the family Bible.

On the morning of his departure, Christiana donned the new shawl Mrs. Adams had sent. It was her gesture of acceptance. She vowed to remain stoic. Watching Isaac mount his horse and ride off again required all her fortitude. The other women watched her, shaking their heads but admiring her courage.

The Garards took over many duties of supervising school and farm chores. "You capable folks are a blessing to us all!" William told them. The other missionaries, still recovering from various sickness, agreed.

 Christiana felt stronger each day and soon resumed afternoon knitting classes. The doctor had warned her not to get chilled, so she didn't spend much time outdoors. Rather than walking the muddy paths formed by the melting snow, she held her new son up to the window. "Charles, one of these days when we look out there I hope to see your father returning."

Evenings were spent quietly. Several older girls joined Delilah around the table where they sewed by candlelight. Under Fanny's supervision, the mission boxes had been searched for suitable outfits. The girls enjoyed ripping off lace and removing buttons and fancy trims they could add to other garments. As they worked they dreamed or joked about their future weddings. When they dressed in their Sunday outfits, the sight of a bright ribbon or flower on otherwise plain garments brought a smile from the older women.

One evening Christiana was busily finishing a new dress for Nancy's approaching ninth birthday. She and Delilah were alone. "I miss Sarah and Christiana," Delilah said with a sigh, "but I wouldn't cut short my sisters chance for schooling for anything."

"I've been thinking about them too. I hope their Papa gets a chance to visit Kentucky and see them and their brothers this time. You will have to write them, just in case he didn't. Anyway, we have John Calvin, Nancy and Eleanor here and little Isaac and the baby."

"Mostly, we need Papa to be here," Delilah said with a sigh.

Suddenly Christiana gasped. She clutched her stomach. "Oh! I'm bleeding again," she whispered as she slid from her chair in a faint.

Delilah ran to open the door and screamed. "Help! I need help!"

Singing Bird dropped the pail she had just filled at the well and ran toward McCoy's cabin. Grace and Daniel Dusenberry, just returning from an evening stroll, also heard and ran to help. Nancy awoke and scooted down the peg steps from the loft to rush to her sister, not even seeing her mother on the floor.

"Mama is sick. Go get Calvin and Johnston! Hurry Nancy!"

Delilah stepped back, letting Singing Bird and the Dusenberrys enter the cabin. She pointed. Christiana was lying in a pool of blood.

"Get a wet cloth, Delilah," Grace told her. "Daniel, lift her legs onto the chair seat. She's fainted, we have to revive her!"

"I'll get medicine and clean rags," Singing Bird said and headed to the cooking cabin.

As Delilah gently washed her mother's face and hands, Christiana opened her eyes. "Mama, lie still. Help is here. Just rest quietly."

Singing Bird returned and began mixing herbs from her deerskin pouch. "Stir these into cup of hot water," she instructed Grace, "make her drink."

Singing Bird began packing clean rags between Christiana's legs. Delilah located her mother's night gown. She and Grace put it on her, after removing her soiled clothes.

Calvin and Johnston followed Nancy into the cabin. They were shocked at what they saw. "You men are just in time to carry her to bed," Grace said, giving them something to do.

Delilah and Nancy took brushes and a pail of water to scrub stains from the puncheon floor. Calvin spoke quietly to Daniel and Johnston. "Should I go get the doctor again?" asked Calvin, "I know the way. I'm not afraid!"

"You are a good son to offer," Daniel told him, touching his shoulder, "but this may just be a slight relapse. By morning she could recover. We'll wait and see."

"Calvin and I will leave now. Everything is under control," Johnston added, smiling at Delilah. "Send someone if you need us again."

Charles had been sleeping peacefully in his cradle. He awoke screaming. Grace picked him up and changed his diaper. The crying continued. "Do we have any nursing mothers at the mission?" she asked Singing Bird. "Christiana is in no condition to nurse this infant."

Delilah and Nancy exchanged horrified looks. "You're not going to take the baby away!" Delilah said emphatically.

"Only to be fed, Delilah. Believe me it is not that uncommon. It would be best for your mother and Charles."

Singing Bird nodded in agreement. "One cooking helper has new babe. I will take this one to her," she said and left with the hungry baby.

Grace took a folded quilt from the bed and spread it on the floor near the fireplace. "I'll rest here tonight."

"Nancy, you and Eleanor take little Isaac to the Girards. Tell them about Mama and then come back home," Delilah told her sisters. She pulled the rocking chair beside their mother's bed. Every time Christiana moaned in her sleep, Delilah jumped up to check her condition.

Before dawn Singing Bird quietly entered to replace Christiana's soiled packings and give her medicine. Grace and Delilah awoke and helped. "I go fix morning foods now," Singing Bird said.

"Where is baby Charles? Is he all right? Mama will miss him!" Delilah asked in a demanding tone. Singing Bird left without answering which irritated her. "When Mama wakes up she'll ask for him. I will have to go find him."

"Don't fret so, Delilah. Let Singing Bird be in charge of that problem," Grace said, trying to soothe things. "Our concern is your mother's health."

Hearing voices, Christiana awoke fully. She tried sitting up but intense pain brought tears. "Delilah, come closer. I need to talk." Delilah put a smile on her face and approached the bed.

"I'm sorry we woke you. Are you feeling better?"

Christiana tried again to sit but was unable. "I'm not sure what happened. This bleeding and all this pain causes me to think I am dying." She hesitated, then whispered, "In your father's absence I must make arrangements for you children."

"Mama! Don't say such a thing!" Delilah scolded. "You are going to recover. We have medicine. We are taking care of you like the doctor showed us before."

Grace stepped beside the bed. She leaned over to gently hold her friend. Christiana sighed and let her tears fall. Weakly, she said, "I need to talk to my brother and Johnston. Please, will you get them?"

Tears swelled in Grace's eyes. She turned to pat Delilah's arm. "Go get the men."

Delilah quickly pulled a shawl from pegs by the door. She went first to Polke's cabin and spoke with her uncle. She found Johnston and Calvin rebuilding a wagon for Garards to use when they returned home. She asked them to come with her.

They gathered around Christiana's bed. They could see she was very ill. Calvin stepped back and motioned to his sister. "Should I go for the doctor?" he asked again. Delilah shrugged her shoulders, not knowing how to answer.

Christiana made an effort to sit up. Delilah propped a pillow under her shoulders. "My spirit is low. I fear my life is ending," Christiana said quietly but firmly.

"Sister McCoy, what would you have us do?" asked Johnston.

With a sad smile, she answered. "Before I die, I would like you to stop calling me sister and become my son."

"What is she saying?" William asked. "She must have a fever making her act strange."

"I have been thinking about it all night as I felt my weakness growing, William. I wish to see at least one of my daughters happily wedded." She sighed. After a few minutes she continued. "Anyone with eyes can tell Delilah and Johnston love each other."

Delilah blushed. Johnston cleared his throat. "I have loved her a long time. I haven't acted on it until Delilah was old enough and ready to be married. Are you ready, dear one?" he asked as he stepped to her side.

Delilah slowly lifted her tear filled eyes to his. "Yes," she whispered, "I love you. I am ready."

The room was quiet, then Christiana spoke. "Please, William, you have been a judge. You can marry Delilah and Johnston. Please conduct the wedding."

Johnston turned and looked at Delilah and smiled.

"It best be done today!" Christiana continued. Her voice strengthened. "Isaac will understand. If he was here he would do as I ask."

The men looked at each other and nodded. "We will do as you wish," they said in unison. Grace and Delilah had tears running down their faces. Calvin gulped to swallow his tears.

Sick as she was, Christiana smiled as Johnston hugged Delilah. In spite of the situation, Delilah felt a rush of happiness and love. "Oh, my. I don't have a dress."

"Go talk to Robert and Fanny about the wedding," Grace told her. "They will know what to do."

Christiana closed her eyes. "I must rest now. I'll leave the details to you."

Later Nancy and Eleanor climbed from the loft and tiptoed to the bed. "Are you feeling better, Mama?" Nancy asked as she rubbed her mother's hand. Christiana opened her eyes briefly and smiled.

"It's time for you girls to leave for breakfast. I know you took little Isaac to the Garards. Bring him home before you go to school." She fell asleep talking. "Where is Charles, Delilah?" Christiana shouted as she suddenly woke.

Delilah rushed to her mother. "Don't fret about the children, Mama. You sleep. Others will take care of things."

When her sisters returned with little Isaac, Delilah led them outside, "Don't look so sad. I have good news for you. Johnston and I have decided to be married tonight. You can tell the others."

"But Mama is sick, shouldn't we wait to have a party?" Nancy asked. "By tonight she will be well," Eleanor predicted. "She likes parties."

Grace stayed with Christiana. "When Singing Bird comes we will make you more comfortable but you must sleep now."

"I will sleep awhile, then I intend to help," she sighed. "I want a nice wedding for Delilah."

Fanny and Robert were surprised and concerned to hear about Christiana's unexpected illness. They were even more surprised at her sudden request for a wedding. Fanny, however, immediately went to her trunk and pulled out her wedding dress. "With some quick altering, you may wear this. You will look beautiful!" she told Delilah. Delilah sat down, exhausted. "I'm so worried about Mama!"

"Having this wedding may very well improve your mother's health, said Fanny. "Anyway, we must follow her instructions." "Christiana remains in charge here, you know," Robert said, smiling. "She is quite a woman! She's going to recover, Delilah. She has to!"

Word of Christiana's illness and the approaching wedding spread quickly. Classes were held as usual in the morning. During the afternoon the adults fulfilled their usual duties except for Fanny who supervised wedding preparations. The Garards decided to pack their belongings and move into McCoys' loft for a few nights to be more helpful. "Besides, Johnston's house has to be vacated," Mrs. Garard smiled.

Under Mary's supervision, the older girls scrubbed Johnston's cabin. Calvin and a few boys helped Delilah carry her belongings to her future home. Furniture was rearranged. Mary hung fresh curtains at the windows. The boys who had been sleeping in Johnston's loft moved their mats and belongings to the Jothan Meekers' or Polke's cabins.

Younger children busily filled water buckets and wood boxes. School benches and desks were rearranged for the evening festivities. Burned short candles were replaced. When the floor was swept and everything was dusted, everyone left in a party mood to dress in their fanciest outfits.

Most pupils remembered the Simmerwell's wedding. They told newcomers what to expect. Excitement grew as evening approached. The wedding time was scheduled for six o'clock. The evening meal would be eaten afterwards.

Christiana, using her stoic determination and with Grace's help, managed to sit up and be dressed. She insisted that she and everyone else at the mission would attend. "Even if I have to be carried and be propped in a chair, I will be there!" Later she demanded, "Whoever has baby Charles must bring him to me! All my family will sit together to honor Delilah."

When the time came to leave for the school, Christiana was bundled warmly. Jothan Meeker and her brother moved her rocking chair to a waiting wagon, then returned to carry Christiana. She sat beside Calvin who drove them the short distance. After her chair was in place, she was carried inside and situated beside her children. Baby Charles was laid in her lap. She was pale and weak but smiled and greeted everyone.

A warming fire burned brightly, adding to the candles' glow. To add to the quiet dignity of the event, an opening prayer was offered. Delilah's uncle William solemnly opened the official book of the wedding ceremony.

"Come forth, Delilah McCoy and Johnston Lykins. Let us follow the procedure as presented in this book," William began in his best judicial voice.

Both Delilah, who looked beautiful in Fanny's dress, and Johnston, in his best clothes, appeared nervous. When it was their turn to speak, however, the vows were repeated with confidence and commitment. Everyone smiled as he placed a gold band, purchased in Detroit months before, on her finger.

Delilah gazed lovingly at her new husband. When he bent to kiss her the children giggled. The newlyweds turned and walked down the aisle to Christiana. They each tenderly kissed her cheek. "Bless you both," she whispered, wiping an escaping tear.

Hungry and restless, the children were happy to see bowls and plates of food being carried in by kitchen workers. While the eating line formed, some of the older boys took out flutes and violins and played background music.

Unlike the Simmerwell wedding, only a few gifts were stacked on a table. Most of the women told Delilah they still had to add some finishing touches and would bring her presents later. "I'll be making you a chair," Calvin said.

By the time everyone had eaten it was far beyond usual bedtime. The young ones were sent off. Christiana was extremely weary and weak. Catching her brother's eye, she motioned to him. "Are you ready to leave?" asked William. When she nodded, Mary took Charles and searched for Singing Bird.

"I'd like to thank everyone, especially Robert and Fanny for making this such a fine event," Christiana told William. "See if you can bring them over here." The older boys and girls began sweeping the floor and carrying food scraps to the pigs.

All the adults joined Christiana in complimenting the Simmerwells. After everyone expressed hope for Christiana's swift recovery, they watched the newlyweds walk hand in hand toward their new home.   Calvin helped prepare his mother for her ride home. The men carried her back to the wagon.   Fanny and Robert banked the fire, extinguished candles and left.

Mary and Grace walked to the McCoy cabin. After the men carried Christiana inside, the women got her settled for the night. "Your fortitude is amazing but you must get back to your warm bed," Grace told her.

"The Garards will be in the loft with the children. They'll help if I need them. You can go home and rest," Mary told Grace.

"She seems much stronger, but I wonder if it's true," Grace whispered. "I'll go if you promise to send one of the children if you need me."

Mary added a log to the fire and sat in the rocking chair, tired from the active day. Just as she was nodding off to sleep, Christiana softly called. "Mary, please bring me the family Bible!"

Shocked and thinking the worse, Mary jumped up. She grabbed the heavy book and took it to her. Christiana gritted her teeth and raised herself to a sitting position. She opened the Bible to the center pages. "See if you can find ink and a pen on Isaac's desk. I must record Delilah's marriage."

Mary breathed a sigh of relief. After she handed her the pen and ink, she held the book while Christiana wrote the names and dates. When the task was completed they both relaxed and settled down to sleep.

The following morning Christiana awoke feeling much stronger. Her health continued to improve and three days later Charles was returned to her care. Delilah joined the other women in taking turns caring for her mother and household chores. By mid-March Christiana had recovered enough to resume most of her duties.

"I give full credit to our Lord for answering all the prayers offered for me, and for the medicine and care I have received," she stated during evening prayer services.

One afternoon as she napped with her small sons she thought she heard Isaac's voice. She sat up, listening, but all was quiet. That happened twice more. Then she got up and opened the door. No one was around. The boys were sleeping. She grabbed her shawl and wrapped it around her. Leaving her sons inside she walked around the cabin. She stopped abruptly as she caught sight of a horse galloping across the frozen fields.

Its rider waved his arms, calling her name. "Isaac!" she shouted. "I knew you were coming," as he jumped to the ground beside her. "I heard your voice in a dream and I knew."

He hugged her briefly, then stepped back. "You are so thin and pale. Have you been sick?"

His arrival had not gone unnoticed. Several men joined them. "You must be very tired and cold. Go inside with your wife, she has things to tell you," Jothan said. "We can talk to you later."

"Welcome back," several called from a distance.

Isaac was astounded to hear of Christiana's near death. He accepted news of Delilah's wedding with mixed feelings. Although he wished he'd performed the wedding, he was happy to have Johnston as his son-in-law. That evening he gave the couple his blessings.

When asked about his visit to Washington he brushed aside their questions. "I'll reveal my conversations and meetings later. Right now I just want to be with my family while I concentrate on the mission and assist you hard workers."

Each day the ice on the river cracked and weakened. Winter's heavy snow melted, adding to the rising water. As the March days warmed, flooded areas returned to normal and the thick mud eventually dried. The Garards bid farewell, returning to Ft. Wayne to await a new mission assignment.

Neighboring Indians began their spring return to the villages. Although the women went right to work tapping maple trees men began hanging around the mission. The hard winter had left all of them thin and malnourished. Their clothing was ragged. They begged for food, especially bread, offering even their moccasins in exchange.

Isaac and some men rode to villages taking seeds and tools ready to help with planting. They knew food would continue to be scarce but planting would help keep villagers busy. Pelts from the winter traps had been exchanged for whiskey at Thompson's new store or taken to new trading posts in the area. Villages were desolate.

26

"Mama, we saw two robins," seven year old Eleanor said one May morning as she led little Isaac indoors. Christiana laughed as her son held up two fingers. The children had just returned with their teachers from taking part in the annual maple sugar ceremonies. Warm days and cold nights had made this year's sap flow abundant. Nancy held a birch bark container of syrup. "Many Moons told me to give this to you, Mama," she said. "I have sugar candy for Papa. Where is he?"

"Put it on his desk. He is helping trim fruit trees."

"Does he always have to work? We hardly ever get to see him," Nancy whined.

Christiana's earlier pleasant mood vanished. Her eyes flashed and her voice grew loud. "We all have work to do! That is why we are put on earth! Speaking of that, it is time for you and Eleanor to help me. Wash your sticky hands. You can card and spin this new wool."

Piles of newly shorn sheep's wool filled baskets which were stacked in every corner. Now that Delilah was married with her own home to care for, Christiana felt overburdened with household chores. While baby Charles slept she taught little Isaac to sweep the floor, emphasizing to her daughters how no one escapes work.

With farm work well under way, Isaac and Johnston had again visited Indian villages hoping to find improvements in their way of living. Instead, what they saw in many places were half dressed intoxicated men and women and neglected children.

Very often Indian women came to the mission followed by dirty, hungry children. Mary and Grace cleaned them up and fed them. They were allowed to attend school. To Isaac's great disappointment these children, especially older ones, often ran away or were reclaimed by parents when sober.

Carey Mission's success, in both school achievements and agriculture crops, was repeatedly overshadowed by the discouraging circumstances in the Indian villages.

Isaac continued writing letters to Governor Cass seeking his advice or assistance. He wrote to the Baptist Missionary Board and to President John Quincy Adams. Isaac met with all the adults at Carey Mission reviewing his earlier visit with President Adams and his advisors. He ended the discussions by reading the letters he was about to mail.

His letters all stated, "Our prospects of usefulness in this area are completely blighted. The Indians around us daily grow more indifferent to everything which would improve their lives or minds. From intemperance and other evils resulting from the proximity of white settlements, they are rapidly wasting away." The group listened quietly, with tears in their eyes, nodded in agreement and left.

By early June, government advisors had responded with a variety of suggestions and ideas. Isaac carefully and prayerfully studied their replies. He then formulated a plan of action.

With John Calvin's help, half of the McCoy's cabin loft was turned into an office. They built a large shelf-like table where Isaac spread out stacks of papers and letters. Maps of the territory, United States maps and Lewis and Clark surveys were fastened over the log walls. Isaac sat there every spare hour, studying and praying. Nancy and Eleanor fell asleep many nights listening to the shuffling of papers in the other end of the loft.

One hot June afternoon when Christiana returned from hoeing their garden, Isaac called down from his hideaway. "I am requesting your presence, my dear. Please come up."

His voice sounded so cheerful and young, she was astonished. Gathering her skirts in one hand she started to climb the pegs. "Here, let me help," he said, reaching for her arm and helping her step into his loft office.

Christiana shook her head as she saw all the papers covering the table, shelves and stacked on the floor. "How can you find anything?"

"I know it is chaos! However, from all these papers, with hours of work and God's help, I believe a solution for the Indian problems has appeared. Sit down. I'll tell you." Isaac's smile brightened the loft. "Oh, my dear, I feel like a fifty pound weight has been lifted from my shoulders. I believe it can work!"

Looking at his face she could see a change in her husband. Clearing a spot on the narrow bench, she sat waiting for him to continue.

"I don't know where to begin, since most of this information will be new to your ears," Isaac said. He paced back and forth. "During our entire marriage we have discussed things and made plans together." Christiana nodded in agreement, growing uneasy as he hesitated.

Taking a deep breath, he sat beside her and took her hand. "All of these letters and reports," he said pointing to the stacks, "are in response to our concerns for the welfare of our Indian neighbors. Because of my letters and visits and talks, Baptist officials, Michigan's Governor and even the President of our United States are now aware of the discouraging situations we face every day." He stopped a minute to collect his thoughts. "These leaders have listened to our growing concerns about the ruination alcohol creates. You will be sad to learn the problem is wide spread across our nation."

Christiana looked surprised. "I know it grows worse here daily, but I didn't think other tribes were effected."

"That's right!" he interrupted. "Now, brace yourself. I'll tell you the rest. Different changes or rules have been suggested for us to try. Some of them we have already seen fail," Isaac took his wife's hand. "The solution I offered the President when I visited there was to isolate Indians in an area and to refuse outsiders entrance. Something like the religious Utopia we saw years ago in southern Indiana."

Christiana sighed, remembering the peaceful and productive community they'd visited, then realized Isaac wasn't done talking.

"The President and his advisors have enlarged on my idea. They want all Indians moved beyond the Mississippi River." Christiana's eyes opened wide in surprise.

"The new frontier is unsettled. It is their belief that no white man would want to go there, so alcohol's influence will end."

"What do you think?" asked Christiana. "Will Indians agree to move? Will all the Indian tribes want to live together? They all have their own leaders, don't they? Would they want to change leaders and rules?"

"I don't have all the answers, my dear, but it sounds like a possible solution. In my estimation, it depends on the land itself. If each tribe could be relocated to land similar to land they now have and not be crowded together, they could live in peace. They would want rivers to fish and wooded areas to hunt and land to farm."

"Is there such a place? Who has been there, across the Mississippi, to locate these areas?" she asked. Then looking at Isaac, she suddenly knew. "You are going to see, aren't you?" Isaac nodded in agreement. Her eyes filled with tears.

"When? If you go look at the land and find it satisfactory, will you agree with the President and his advisors? Didn't we have land like that here? Now white men have found it and ruined it!"

Deflated, Isaac watched Christiana's falling tears. "I am afraid our time here is ending. We can't be useful to people who are exposed to alcohol and the dismal conditions it brings."

"You mean we are all leaving? Are we giving up?" Christiana straightened her shoulders and dried her tears, "Or, are we taking our mission school somewhere else?"

"That's not decided," Isaac replied. "I am volunteering to be in the survey group looking for suitable land, especially for our Potawatomi and Ottawa people."

"Who else will be going and for how long?"

"My idea is to have Indian leaders go with me. I'd also like to have Johnston along to help survey. He understands the situation. I respect his ability and advice."

"Isaac! He is newlywed. You don't want to do that to Delilah, do you?"

"It has to be his decision, my dear. If we move with the Indians I would hope they would choose to go with us."

"How soon will you leave?"

"Looking at the growing problems, I think it must be soon. It could take several months, maybe even a year. There is suitable staff here now to carry out mission duties. Our family life will suffer but the cause will be worth it!"

"Isaac, what will happen to our missionary family and all the property and buildings if we leave?"

"You certainly come up with a list of questions! The land, of course, belongs to the Michigan Territory. I hope to convince Governor Cass to make a cash payment for buildings and the orchards and improvements on the land. The money could be sent to the Baptist Missionary Board. I pray they would fund new buildings and equipment for the new location."

By the time they climbed down from the loft after two hours of discussion, Christiana had become resigned to Isaac's plan. Isaac was more subdued. He agreed to postpone telling the Carey Mission people.

Many times during the next few days, Isaac and Christiana expressed mixed feelings about the future. Finally, after spending several restless nights, Christiana said, "We must tell our brother and sister missionaries about the President's order."

A meeting was held. A stunned silence filled the school as Isaac spoke. "Christiana and I know this comes as a surprise. No one knows the deplorable situation better than you. We have succeeded in educating and training youngsters in our school. Farm crops and animals are doing well. We are not giving up! We are making changes."

Christiana stood up to speak, "I believe in my heart that if the Indians move, God will require us to go also. Our determination to improve the lives of Indian people remains constant."

When she sat down, a murmur of agreement was heard among the missionaries. One by one they stood up. Soon everyone was holding hands. Isaac offered a lengthy prayer of gratitude for their commitment and support.

Two days later, with a clear conscience, Isaac left for Thomas Station. He took Calvin with him. They drove a wagon packed with newly forged hoes and rakes. At Burnett's trading post they added two crates of charity clothing that had arrived on a ship from the east. The Slaters and Chief Noonday welcomed their visit. They too were astounded by his message from the President.

While there, Isaac hoped to enlist two or three Ottawa leaders to join his survey group. He spoke directly to his friend Chief Noonday. "You are the one who had the vision to move our Fort Wayne school to the Michigan Territory. You saw the need for educating your young people into the white men's ways. You helped choose the best locations for Carey and Thomas Missions. I would appreciate your wisdom in selecting new land for the Ottawa and Potawatomi."

The Chief stared into the distance for several minutes. Eventually, he turned back to Isaac. "I will help you help my people!"

Isaac was extremely pleased to have Chief Noonday as one of the men willing to participate. Two other men were chosen. The three men agreed to be at Carey Mission by July first, the departure date.

Back at Carey Mission, Isaac issued an invitation to their Potawatomi neighbors to come for a council. The leaders expressed concerns when Isaac spoke. "I fear for your future if you continue present conditions," he told them. After much discussion three Potawatomi leaders were selected to go with him. "We will survey lands across the Mississippi River. We will look for suitable locations offering hunting and fishing like this area."

During the council, a letter arrived from Governor Cass telling Isaac to invite Potawatomi leaders to a treaty making council at Carey the middle of September, 1828. Lewis Cass had long been familiar to them in his role as Indian Agent. They agreed to return, but Isaac saw the confusion and sadness on their faces. His own heart felt heavy. He hoped they would not be required to surrender more land in exchange for monies and eventually liquor.

After his council ended, Isaac gave several young men lessons in surveying. They measured Carey Mission farm fields and each orchard, plus all the buildings, so accurate information could be presented to the Governor.

Knowing he would be not available for the Governor's council, Isaac spent considerable time preparing data. The value of the mission property needed to be determined. Robert Simmerwell and Jothan Meeker were appointed to be in charge in Isaac's absence. They agreed to work with Governor Cass in setting a dollar exchange for improvements made to the land.

Summer farming was in full swing. Fruit and vegetables were so abundant that surplus was shipped in canoes and pirogues to Burnetts' trading post. Isaac had, in anticipation of large crops, made these arrangements when he stopped on his last journey to Thomas Station. From Burnett's, crates and barrels were to be transported to Lake Michigan. There they could be loaded and put on ships to be carried to ports around the Great Lakes. Burnett kept ledgers of his dealings with

Carey Mission. Money received for supplies was to be exchanged at a later date.

Christiana insisted they preserve food for their winter's needs in the same manner they always had. "We may or may not be moving the mission this year, either way we will need food!"

Before the end of June, Isaac received final orders from President Adams. He read them to Christiana. "You are instructed to repair to regions west. Report the conditions of the country suitable for an Indian mission."

A letter from Governor Cass commissioned him to select a new place for Michigan Indians and to consider choosing a suitable site for themselves. Isaac and Christiana were elated to learn that a mission like Carey was in the plan.

Johnston and Delilah thought long and hard about his accompanying the survey group. In the end, he gave in to his desire and agreed to go. Preparations and packing were efficiently completed.

By sunset on July first, 1828, all survey groups had arrived. The following morning Isaac strapped bulging saddlebags on his horse. He returned to his cabin.

"I've packed travel food," Christiana said, handing him a large tote. "I know you will hunt and fish, but this is for times you can't." Isaac tried to visualize where it would fit, as he smiled and thanked her.

She continued to bustle around the cabin, checking to make sure he hadn't missed anything. "Come sit with me," he said. "We are both dreading my leave taking but let's enjoy a few minutes." She dutifully sat across from him, trying to hold back tears. She glanced out of the window. "Looks like pleasant weather to start out. Have the others eaten and finished packing?"

"I didn't see our son-in-law but the others are ready."

Christiana sighed, "Poor Delilah, so newly wedded and now having her husband leave for heaven only knows how long. It will be hard on her if he is gone when her baby is born. Do you think that will happen?"

"That puts us into winter," Isaac replied, hesitating. "I'd like to say we'll be back, but we can't tell how difficult it will be to find suitable land. Once we finally locate what we are searching for, it has to be surveyed. Then arrangements must be made to legally obtain it. Getting mail to and from the President will be time consuming, I fear. Traveling back here will take time too. I believe it will take months, my dear."

He held her hand and smiled. "Delilah has her mother nearby. You were never so fortunate. She's surrounded by friends."

Christiana nodded. "You are right. Our own selfish needs are not as important as the problems facing you."

Isaac detected a sharpness in her voice. Avoiding the possibility of an argument, he pushed back his chair and reached for the tote he'd set by his feet. "I'm ready to summon everyone for morning prayer around our pack horses. Then we must depart!"

Biting her lip, Christiana stood bravely beside Delilah, as the men disappeared into the woods. Delilah's eyes were red. Her face was swollen. "I will be all right, Mama," she said. "Johnston and I agree this is an important venture. I am willing to do my part here and there too, when it is time to move."

"We need to keep busy. I need to scrub my floor. You can go teach some classes," Christiana said. As they walked the well-worn path, they made plans. "Do you want to move back home?"

"I am comfortable in my own home, Mama, but it will be lonesome. Could Nancy or Eleanor come stay?"

"Your sisters help care for their little brothers, but I guess Nancy could manage that alone." As an early birthday surprise, Eleanor was allowed to move in with her sister. Delilah found her seven-year-old sister to be a perfect companion.

Summer rains brought swarms of mosquitoes. Breezes during the day kept them on the move. Outdoor smudge fires were lighted at night to help keep them away from cabins and make sleeping easier.

August was very hot. Men and boys changed their schedules so that field work was done in the mornings. Picking fuzzy peaches and cutting hay under the blazing sun made them particularly itchy and uncomfortable.

Afternoon classes were held in the shade of buildings or under trees. Girls met in the school in the mornings. They sewed or prepared meals outdoors. Time was allotted late each afternoon for river activities. They swam, fished or played, all means for cooling off.

During one of the hottest spells, Fanny presented Robert with a beautiful red-haired daughter. Singing Bird, who delivered her, delighted in calling her Redbird. Her parents named her Faith.

Visitors still appeared often at Carey Mission. It was not uncommon for men to leave their families there while they searched for land to homestead. Women and children took advantage of meals and shelter, enjoying fellowship and schooling. Fortunately, food was plentiful in the summer. Christiana and the mission women often discussed how disappointing it was to meet folks who seemed kind and pleasant, but later change to cheaters or sellers of whiskey.

Knowing the winter could be harsh, Christiana put all girls and women to work drying and stringing squash, apple slices and beans to be hung in the lofts. Singing Bird taught them to dry fish and strips of venison when men took time to hunt. "If we must make our move this winter, we will have food," Christiana told the women.

Robert Simmerwell had many problems. One morning, while making his usual walk around the mission, he found two white traders sleeping on the river bank. The canoe they had arrived in held crates of liquor. Robert woke them and ordered them off the property. They pulled out guns but fortunately the sudden appearance of a group of children as witnesses made them change their minds. They jumped into their canoes and paddled down river. "I should have dumped their cargo in the river," Robert said, disappointed in himself.

Later in the day two young Indian boys came up missing. All available men took part in the search for them. When the boys were discovered at the traders' camp drinking, several enraged mission workers entered the camp with rifles pointed. The drunken pupils were quickly grabbed and led to waiting horses. Jothan Meeker, in a fit of anger, began smashing all bottles in sight. With guns still aimed at them the frightened traders ran for the river and rapidly paddled their canoes south. The boys later admitted they had followed the men and had not been kidnapped as believed.

"With this episode I'm completely convinced our mission is in jeopardy. When even our young men, who know the evils of liquor, are tempted to try it I fear we are losing control!" Robert told the others at a meeting that evening. Fanny, who sat in the audience holding their new baby, shivered as she heard and saw her husband's discouragement.

By late August wheat and oats were cut and gathered onto wagons. The old mill wheels nosily ground grain into flour as horses slowly plodded round and round the circle. Jothan rode back from Bertrand's one afternoon with exciting news. "A young fellow has built a mill downstream. We should send someone to find out the charges."

"With this year's bountiful harvest our horses will be wore out, that's for sure!" William said, shaking his head.

"We can't afford to lose horses or spend cash," Jothan replied. "Do you think we could barter with him?"

"I'll ride down tomorrow, if you want," offered William.

"Take a sack of wheat grain with you and see how fine the mill grinds," suggested Jothan. "We can afford at least one sack of flour if you have to pay."

William returned with good news and finely milled flour, which Christiana immediately used to make delicious bread. "He'll be willing to grind for us, William told Jothan. "He'll keep one sack for every six he grinds. Sounds more than fair to me."

Everyone agreed but there was a sadness in Robert's next comment. "Too bad we're now getting good crops and easier work, just when we have to leave."

Several teachers told Robert they planned to leave the mission. He could understand their frustration, feeling depressed himself. Enrollment was decreasing. He could not justify encouraging them to remain. Some were returning to their home states, others were planning to homestead in the area. Timothy Smith and Calvin Britain who had come from New York in 1827 had helped with the farming in addition to their teaching.

"We are going to miss your smiling faces," Jothan told them, "also your strong backs!"

Christiana hugged the men saying, "You've become like family. It is hard to bid farewell!"

"Don't worry about that," Calvin replied. "We're not going far. We saw some land near the mouth of the river up by Lake Michigan where we're going to settle. Whenever you Carey folks journey our way, plan to stay at our places!"

Indian problems were creeping more and more into everyday life of the mission. Horses, livestock and personal belongings, like blankets and saddles, were being stolen over night or, worse, in broad daylight.

Toward the middle of September, chiefs and leaders from many Indian villages began to appear on the mission property in response to the Governor's treaty call. On the twentieth the Carey Mission Treaty Council began. Col. Pierre Menard, on behalf of the United States, and Governor Cass discussed the purchase of Indian land between the St. Joseph River and Lake Michigan. Bertrand's and Burnett's plots of land were reserved.

Governor Cass always endeavored to deal fairly with Indians. The council was a congenial time. Indian women prepared large quantities of corn and squash, mixed with whatever game or fish the men brought to them. Tobacco-filled pipes were passed among the circles of men. Dancing and story telling occurred around nightly campfires.

Chief Pokagon and young Chief Topinabe made their village requests when it was their time to speak. "We wish to keep small reservations for each family. If our neighbor, Carey Mission, moves away we will need cattle and farming tools from the government. Maybe we will need to be taught how to use more tools."

When final talks were ended, it was stipulated in usual treaty form that the tribe was to receive certain annuities, goods and cash in consideration of ceded lands. They were also to receive annually a quantity of iron and tobacco. A sum of one hundred dollars per annum was to be paid to young Chief Topinabe to pay for a permanent blacksmith for his village. The government also agreed to pay for three laborers to work for the tribe four months a year for ten years.

The treaty was signed by Col. Menard, Governor Cass, Topinabe, Pokagon and sixty seven other Potawatomi chiefs and leaders. Land from the Indiana state border to north of the St. Joseph River in Michigan Territory was ceded.

Robert Simmerwell presented the documents left by Isaac to Governor Cass. "I agree. Payment for the Carey Mission improvements in buildings, fields and orchards will be sent to the Baptist Missionary Board in Boston whenever the missionaries should remove from said land," he stated.

Staying on a few days after the treaty council, Governor Cass walked the farm fields with Robert, Jothan and William. One cool afternoon he joined the men and boys picking apples. "This is an amazing crop. Good too," he said after biting into the juicy red fruit.

"I know you must hate the idea of leaving this place," he commented to Christiana as they ate together one evening.

"It will be hard to leave," she admitted, "but we can't allow our Indian friends to live in such squalor. Isaac believes we must lead them to a place where they can live more productive lives." She sighed, then added, "Horrible things are happening here. Just last week a man slit the throat of his wife. The Indians have become completely demoralized"

"I am aware of that. I have seen terrible conditions in all my recent travels," he said. "It is heart breaking. I don't know the answer to these problems. I hope your husband will find it. I feel guilty leaving here to return to our magnificent new Capitol building with all its rooms and elaborate furnishings knowing the conditions I've seen."

In October Jothan received a letter from the Governor stating the cash amount he would allot for Carey Mission. He read it to Christiana before sharing it with other missionaries. "The amount payable, whenever the missionaries should remove, will be $5,721.50, to be paid to the Baptist Mission Board in Boston. $641.50 is for the crops and the rest, $5080. for improvements in fields and orchards and buildings. The monies are to be set aside by the Baptist Board for use by Isaac McCoy and his followers to establish a mission school in new territory. Signed, Governor Cass."

"I don't know if that is a goodly amount," Christiana remarked as the letter was discussed. Some of the missionaries seemed to scoff as they heard the figures.

Displeased, she took it upon herself to make a silencing statement. "We must remember--God will provide what we need. He always has. He always will! We may want more but that does not mean we need it." No one had the courage to challenge her remarks.

Fall tasks kept everyone hustling. Wood was chopped into length and stacked close to each building. Animal shelters were stocked with bedding straw. Feed sacks were piled in shelters. Drying fruit and vegetables hung in the lofts. Crates of squash and apples and potatoes were covered in a lean-to beside the cooking cabin. Even the youngest girls spent every spare moment knitting stockings, mittens and hats.

Very few Indian families were seen heading north for winter trapping. Since they had secure cabins and had begun farming and storing food supplies, more villages were occupied during winters.

Snow fell early, starting in October, and by mid-November all the trails were blotted out. The river remained open but ice built up along the shore. "We're about isolated for the winter," the men commented as they cleaned hunting guns and readied traps.

No mail arrived from Isaac or Johnston. Delilah and Christiana had many conversations as they wondered and worried about the welfare of their husbands. Delilah began sewing and knitting for her expected baby. "With all the babies at the mission, we don't think you need to make clothes." Fanny and the other women told her teasingly. "I have some I'll give you," each offered.

"I just want to keep busy," Delilah said. "I guess I should be spending my time knitting mittens instead."

"No, no, dear, don't feel guilty. You work hard enough," her mother said as she rescued Charles from crawling too near the fireplace.

December storms froze the river. Young trees popped as they froze. Later, branches weighed down with heavy snow broke and crashed to the ground. One fell on Meeker's roof, but fortunately only minor repairs were needed.

Even during harsh weather conditions an occasional Indian family made their way to the mission begging for help. Wearing skimpy clothing or wrapped in thin blankets because they had traded everything else for liquor, they were cold, hungry and ill. The mission workers took care of needs if they could, then sent them home.

Much to everyone's surprise a man on horseback, accompanied by two men on foot and carrying muskets, came onto the property one late December afternoon. Christiana had them come inside her cabin. She made them hot herb tea. Their faces and hands were so nearly frozen it took awhile before they could talk or drink.

"What are you doing out in weather like this?"

"We are delivering mail, Mrs. McCoy. I am Lt. David Hunter, don't you remember me? I carry mail from Chicago to Fort Wayne. These two soldiers are guarding the mail and me."

"Oh, my gracious! I didn't recognize you under all your ice covering. Do you have mail for us? "

"I have a packet for Carey Mission Station."

She smiled as she watched him dig a large packet from his saddle bag. When he handed it to her she peered inside. She recognized Isaac's handwriting. "Nancy, she said, "go find Robert and Delilah." The mail carriers returned to Bertrand's for the night. Christiana gave them dry mittens and johnnycake to eat along the trail.

27

When the men left Christiana sat in her rocker, waiting, almost afraid to open the packet. Robert, the first to come, gently took the letters and sorted them. "There are two here for you, one for Delilah. The rest are for us teachers and Jothan. I'll take these and leave you alone to enjoy your mail."

Christiana broke the seal on a letter written back in August. Tears flooded her eyes as she read, "I received a letter from Rice containing very satisfactory intelligence that Sarah, at age thirteen, has lately been baptized. She is our first child to make a public profession of religion. My prayers have increased in fervor for my dear children. The Lord has been very merciful to us in relation to our children. The necessity of having them scattered, not among relatives or particular friends, but as I may say, among strangers has given us both much uneasiness. It is good to learn they benefit from their schooling."

Delilah entered the cabin to find her mother weeping. "I miss my dear husband and my absent children. I know in my heart that the Lord is working in all our lives, but I long to have them all back home."

Delilah knelt by the rocking chair. "Do you think we will ever be all together again, Mama? Even if we all become missionaries, our paths may lead us separate ways."

A stubborn look came over Christiana's face. She wiped her eyes. Before she handed Delilah her letter she said, "I will insist that all my children go with their father and I when we leave this mission!"

Delilah held her letter lovingly. "This is the first letter I ever received from my husband," she said sighing. "Do you mind if I take it home to read it?"

"I think you should. Tonight I'll let you girls and John Calvin read your father's letters after we return from prayers. I'm sure Robert will tell us what his mail held."

Christiana called to Delilah as she headed for the door. "The young man who brought the mail will be staying at Bertrands for two nights. If we hurry we can write letters. Someone from here can ride to the trading post to give them to him."

Christiana had her youngest daughters and John Calvin write short remarks in her letter to Isaac. Delilah's letter to Johnston took her all evening to compose but was ready for Robert to take in the morning. He also planned to ride to the new mercantile in the little settlement beyond Bertrands to purchase school supplies. Christiana's list included a large family Bible which she intended to present to Delilah. Delilah requested thread and flannel material be added to Robert's list. Christiana sent butter and cheese to use as barter.

Near the end of December, Robert talked to Christiana and Fanny. "It doesn't really seem necessary to hold a New Year's Day celebration since we are already feeding village groups each day." Neither of the women agreed, so in the established tradition everyone spending the winter in the surrounding villages was invited.

As always the Chiefs and leaders came dressed in their most regal finery. This year some brought deer meat and dried fish to add to stew kettles. William and Robert both offered prayers for the new year of 1829. Although the weather was mild for January, the wholesome, nourishing meal was eaten while standing around large warming campfires.

Christiana was astounded to overhear Indian leaders say, "We can live in peace, like we used to, if we leave this land. The whites want this land. They will not follow us." She kept those words in her mind, hoping they didn't mean Indians didn't want white missionaries to move with them.

Later, she spoke to the men about her concerns. "Since we don't know what Isaac is accomplishing, I guess we just need to wait," William said.

"It seems we are waiting for many things," Christiana commented with a sigh. Then one condition changed. Delilah woke with sharp cramping pains the second week of January. Eleanor ran frantically to get her mother and Fanny. By nightfall a tiny cry marked the arrival of the McCoy's first grandchild.

Calvin carried the cradle Charles had outgrown over to his sister's. Soon, other visitors arrived, bringing newly knitted sweaters, blankets or used items from their babies. Delilah named her son William and happily entered his birth in her new Bible.

Christiana worried about Delilah living alone. As a solution, she moved her family to Lykin's cabin every night for two weeks. Delilah was young and strong. It soon became obvious she wished to manage her own household. "You have cared for many children at a time, Mama, surely I can care for one infant!"

Winter activities were soon replaced by usual demands of early spring. As the snow and ice melted into muddy trails, visitors once again appeared. Lt. Hunter, still escorted by foot soldiers, returned bringing welcome mail. "These letters come from Missouri and Kansas. That is far away! No wonder mail took so long."

Christiana was pleased when she read that Isaac had received their letters from Carey Mission. After all letters were read, Robert shared good news from his mail following evening prayers.

"Reverend McCoy has located land for our Indian tribes." Robert waited a few minutes for the murmurs to quiet. He smiled. "He says it is even more beautiful than here. It is along the Missouri River in Lousiana Purchase Territory." He pointed to the approximate area on a large map he had nailed to the wall.

"He has written to our new President, Andrew Jackson, describing the surveyed area and recommending its claim. We won't know until later mail if it will be approved and if we are going there. Right now we are thankful Brothers Isaac and Johnston are well and safe!"

Christiana gathered her children at bedtime. "We received mail today. Your father wrote he must go back to Washington before he can come home. I fear it will be summer before we see him," she told them.

As Indians wandered through the mission, Robert and others told them about the new land in the west. Their replies varied. Some wanted to leave immediately, others had little desire to move. Pokagon refused to discuss it. "I will never leave!" he said and walked away. Most of the remaining missionaries planned to follow and assist the McCoys wherever they went.

In March, just before spring pruning, plowing and planting were scheduled to start, Johnston returned. "I'm home! Hello, Hello everybody!" he shouted, causing everyone to drop whatever they were doing. Delilah recognized his voice and quickly grabbed her son. She ran as fast as she could toward the approaching horse.

Christiana clutched her chest as she stood watching. Frightened, she wondered why Johnston was alone. Johnston swooped Delilah into the saddle. They rode until they reached her. "Isaac is all right. No need to worry," he said to reassure her. "I came on ahead. He went to Washington."

As Johnston and Delilah dismounted at her feet, Christiana breathed a sigh of relief, smiled and hugged Johnston. Johnston beamed as he took his small son in his arms. "So this is little Will. He is perfect, Delilah, just like his Mama."

The day after his arrival a severe snow storm blanketed the land. All work stopped. Johnston had everyone come to the school. He told them of the expedition and answered questions. "Isaac took letters to Washington from the Ottawa and Potawatomi leaders who accompanied us. They are pleased with the land we saw. They want to make new homes there. They are asking that we missionaries go with them."

"Will our Baptist leaders and the Governor agree?" asked Jothan. Several others had questions.

"Isaac is meeting with Honorable John Eaton in Washington to ask permission to fill any vacancy that occurs in an Indian agency. This would allow us all to move as a group. He will have an answer before he leaves there."

"When will that be?"

"Is he coming soon?"

"He is very tired, as am I, but he is hoping to attend the graduation of his sons in Lexington the end of April. He plans to take Sarah and young Christiana with him. He has asked me to bring the rest of the family to Ohio for a rest and time together in May. He has only spent seventeen days with them in the last ten months." Christiana felt a warm glow of hope and happiness at the idea of having all their children together. She knew God was answering her prayers.

"Should we be plowing and planting, or closing the school?" asked Robert.

"I think we should go ahead with the farm work. If we should get instructions to move we will harvest what we can and leave the rest for those not going. The school enrollment will be reduced when the tribe begins to move. Until then we should live as usual."

Christiana's health and spirits improved as she began preparations to join Isaac. Moving the family would take time. Things had to be sorted and packed. New wagons had to be built, crates had to be filled.

Since only she and her children were going in May, many things would remain to be used in their absence. Excitement over their reunion mixed with sadness over leaving friends behind. The dread of an unknown future kept Christiana's thoughts in constant turmoil.

Singing Bird, her best Indian friend, was undecided about moving to the new land. The Dusenburys were eager to move to the new land to continue their work as missionaries. Many Indian pupils would journey with them when the time came to move. Christiana's brother William and his family decided to return east where he'd once again serve as a judge. Jothan Meeker delayed his decision. Fanny and Robert agreed to stay on at Carey Mission keeping the school open until all details, money and legal, were fulfilled. Jothan would assist them.

In May, leaving all but her family behind, Christiana stood inside her cabin and took one last look around. All the familiar furniture and memories swirled around her as she grabbed the door handle and firmly latched it.

With one sad, backward glance she turned to the group of well wishers. As she climbed into her wagon beside John Calvin, Johnston and Delilah waved from theirs.

"Our whole family will soon be all together again," she told her children. With a big smile on her face, she once again picked up the reins to begin a new journey. Isaac was waiting!

EPILOGUE

After their brief family reunion and respite in 1830, the McCoys made one last visit to Carey Mission and Thomas Station. Isaac officially resigned his position as superintendent. They led a group of Indians into Missouri to begin a new settlement. Isaac and Christiana sold their "retirement" property in Ohio to raise the money for this migration. The Dusenburys accompanied them.

Things did not go well. During the first two years, illness and death claimed four sons: Drs. Josephus and Rice, two and a half year old Charles, and a new-born infant. In 1833 two daughters left in marriage. John Calvin opened a general store in Westport, Missouri. (He later became "father of Kansas City.") Despite these changes and set-backs, Christiana with her remarkable stoic efficiency continued to work beside Isaac.

In August 1833 the Simmerwells closed Carey Mission and joined their missionary brethren in Missouri. From there, along with 17 Indian leaders, they gathered at Shawnee Mission House in Kansas to organize a church and continued their work as missionaries and teachers.

In 1836 the Slaters closed Thomas Mission Station and moved to Berrien County, Michigan, founded a mission school for Ottawa Indians and continued their work.

Isaac continued to travel and act as consultant to presidents. He published books of his thoughts and observations on needed Indian reforms and assistance and corresponded with many influential leaders. He devised a plan whereby all Indians would be resettled on individual plantations and become beneficiaries of civilization and missionary teachings. Unfortunately, his plan was modified and absorbed into the much resented government program for forced removal of all Indians to specially designated land beyond the Mississippi River. President Jackson offered Isaac an appointment as Commissioner of Indian Affairs. Isaac declined.

In 1842 the McCoys severed ties with the Baptist Board of Missions and Isaac became the first Corresponding Secretary/General Agent of the American Indian Mission Association in Louisville, Kentucky.

Isaac died in 1846 from exposure in a storm. Isaac's last words to Christiana were "Tell the brethren to never let the Indian mission decline." Isaac and Christiana had been married 43 years.

Christiana died in 1851. Of their 14 children, only three survived them. Eleven had died during their parent's time as missionaries.

Isaac's extensive collection of letters, journals and other papers were presented to the Kansas State Historical Society on July 9, 1879, by John Calvin McCoy, their only surviving son.

ISBN 141202142-1

Printed in Great Britain
by Amazon.co.uk, Ltd.,
Marston Gate.